1976

FEN DAYS

is kept o

"HIS MAJESTY REPLIED, I MUST BE SEARCHED BY TWO OF HIS
OFFICERS."—Page 29.

GULLIVER'S TRAVELS

INTO

SEVERAL REMOTE NATIONS OF THE WORLD.

By JONATHAN SWIFT, D.D.,

DEAN OF ST. PATRICK'S, DUBLIN.

ILLUSTRATED BY GORDON BROWNE AND C. E. BROCK.

A. L. BURT COMPANY, PUBLISHERS,
52-58 DUANE STREET, NEW YORK

PREFACE.

THIS edition of GULLIVER'S TRAVELS is practically a reprint of the original edition, the only alterations being the omission of certain coarse passages which would offend modern taste.

Footnotes are given, chiefly explanatory of obsolete words and obscure expressions, or elucidative of various matters in regard to which many readers may desire information.

CONTENTS.

CHAPTER III.

CHAPTER IV.

CHAPTER V.

CHAPTER VI.

CHAPTER VII.

CHAPTER VIII.

PART II.

A VOYAGE TO BROBDINGNAG.

CHAPTER I.

CHAPTER II.

CHAPTER III.

CHAPTER IV.

CHAPTER V.

CHAPTER VI.

CHAPTER VII.

CHAPTER VIII.

PART III.

A VOYAGE TO LAPUTA, BALNIBARBI, LUGG-NAGG, GLUBBDUBDRIBB, AND JAPAN.

CHAPTER I.

CHAPTER II.

CHAPTER III.

CHAPTER IV.

CHAPTER V.

CHAPTER VI.

CHAPTER VII.

CHAPTER VIII.

CHAPTER IX.

CHAPTER X.

CHAPTER XI.

Part IV.

A VOYAGE TO THE COUNTRY OF THE HOUYHNHNMS.

CHAPTER I.

CHAPTER II.

CHAPTER III.

CHAPTER IV.

CHAPTER V.

CHAPTER VI.

CHAPTER VII.

CHAPTER VIII.

CHAPTER IX.

CHAPTER X.

CHAPTER XI.

CHAPTER XII.

INTRODUCTION.

THE author of GULLIVER'S TRAVELS and of other notable writings was Jonathan Swift, D.D., latterly and for many years Dean of St. Patrick's, Dublin, and one of the greatest wits and satirists our country has produced. He was born in Dublin, November 30, 1667, of English parents; his father, also called Jonathan, being a cousin of the poet Dryden, his mother a lady belonging to Leicestershire. His father, who was connected with the legal profession, died seven months before the birth of the future dean, whose mother was left in poor circumstances, and had to depend on the bounty of relatives. When the child was a year old, his nurse carried him off with her to Whitehaven, whither she was called by the illness of a relative, and here he

remained till about his sixth year, his mother thinking it better for his health to let him stay than to
take him home.   By the assistance of an uncle he
was sent to school at Kilkenny, and when fourteen
years old to Trinity College, Dublin.   Swift, though
a great reader, was by no means a diligent or well-
behaved student, and he left the university in some
disgrace, having only obtained his degree of
Bachelor of Arts " by special favor."

He now (1688) went to his mother's in Leicestershire, and she, being a relative of the wife of the
eminent statesman, Sir William Temple, advised
him to see what this powerful personage could do
for him.   Having applied to Sir William, the latter
took him into his own house as a sort of secretary,
and in this situation he continued for several years.
While here he was introduced to William III., who
often visited Temple privately ; and the king is
said to have offered to make him a captain in a
cavalry regiment.   In 1692 he obtained the degree
of Master of Arts from the University of Oxford,
the influence of his patron being probably exerted
in his favor.   He still continued to reside with Sir
William Temple, but a coldness arose between them,
and in 1694 Swift went over to Ireland and entered
the church.   He did not long remain, however, for
Sir William, who was now getting old and infirm,

soon wished him back again, and Swift returned to stay with him till he died.

In 1699 Swift was appointed to the living of Laracor, about twenty miles from Dublin, and this living he held in conjunction with others till he was appointed to the deanery of St. Patrick's in 1713. At Laracor he took up his residence in 1700, and entered energetically upon the duties of a country clergyman, reading prayers twice a week, and preaching regularly every Sunday. It is said that upon one of the Wednesday services he found nobody present but his parish clerk, Roger Coxe, whereupon he changed the "dearly beloved brethren" of the Book of Common Prayer into "dearly beloved Roger." Laracor was his regular place of residence for the next ten years, though his visits to London were frequent.

Soon after his settlement here he began his career as an author by publishing in 1701 a "Discourse of the Dissensions between the Nobles and Commons in Athens and Rome," which, though professedly treating of ancient times, was really directed against the dissensions existing among English politicians of the day. This was followed a few years afterward by his celebrated "Tale of a Tub," and "Battle of the Books." The former was a satire, in a kind of allegorical form, on the Roman Catholics and Dissenters, and a vindication of the Church of England. It secured him the highest reputation as a wit, but did him no small injury as a divine from its frequent coarseness and irreverence. The "Battle of the Books" had to do with the respective merits of the ancient and the modern authors.

In 1710 he came to London on a mission to procure the abolition of certain duties which the Irish clergy had to pay to the crown. He remained in the metropolis three years; and, while hitherto he had been connected more or less with the Whig party, he now openly joined the Tories, and wrote political tracts on their behalf, which were of immense service to them. He was eager to obtain a bishopric in England; but Queen Anne is said to have had doubts as to his orthodoxy (mainly on account of the "Tale of a Tub"), and the highest dignity he could obtain was the deanery of St. Patrick's.

He accordingly returned to Dublin, and for the rest of his life had to submit to an unwilling residence in the country of his birth, and in a society that was not congenial to his tastes. But, though he had no liking for Ireland, he could not shut his eyes to the injustice under which her people suffered; and roused by the law forbidding woollen goods to be exported to any country but England, he proposed that the Irish should rely entirely on their own manufactures, and wear nothing whatever of English make. This made him highly popular in Ireland, and his popularity was greatly increased by the publication of a series of letters with the signature, "M. B. Drapier," denouncing the contract which a person named Wood had obtained for supplying Ireland with copper coinage, and scourging the abuses of government generally. In 1726 appeared GULLIVER'S TRAVELS, the most widely read of all his works. Of it we shall speak more particularly below.

About two years after this a severe blow fell upon Swift, in the death of the lady known as Stella, whose relations toward him were of a singular nature, and have not even yet been altogether cleared of mystery. Stella was a pet name bestowed upon her by Swift, her real name being Esther Johnson. When Swift became acquainted with her she was living in the house of Sir William Temple, her mother also being a member of the household in the capacity of companion to Sir William's sister. She was then a mere girl, and received lessons from Swift; and soon between teacher and pupil a warm attachment grew up. When Swift went to live at Laracor, Miss Johnson, accompanied by a Mrs. Dingley, at his suggestion took up her residence in the same neighborhood, and on the occasions of Swift's absence the two ladies occupied the parsonage house, as they did afterward the deanery. In the years 1710–1713, when Swift was in England, he kept a minute account in the form of a journal of all his doings and experiences, and this he transmitted from time to time to Stella. In it grave matters are mingled with playfulness, nonsense, and expressions of endearment; Swift usually writes of himself under the name of Presto (*presto* being Italian for quick or swift). It is believed by some that the two were privately married in 1716, but this is doubtful; and altogether Swift's conduct in the matter is difficult to be accounted for. Stella seems to have had very considerable personal attractions, besides being a person of great good sense and of much vivacity, if not even wit.

The fate of another lady was also closely connected with Swift's life. This was Miss Esther Vanhomrigh, with whom he got acquainted in London in 1712, she being then eighteen or twenty years old, and he about forty-five. Notwithstanding this disparity the young lady conceived a violent passion for him, and Swift was evidently not altogether insensible to her attractions. In his poem of "Cadenus and Vanessa" she gets the latter poetical appellation, the dean himself being Cadenus (L. *decanus*, a dean). She went over to Ireland to be near him, but finding that her passion was utterly hopeless she died of a broken heart.

From the death of Stella, Swift became more morose and gloomy, and his life more retired. For several years he continued to write both in prose and verse, but by 1736 his memory was nearly gone. In a few years more he sank into hopeless lunacy, the fate which he had feared overtook him, and on the 19th of October, 1745, he was released by death. He left the greater part of his fortune to an asylum for lunatics.

The character of Swift is not altogether a pleasing one. His best qualities were his constancy in friendship where his friends were really worthy (such as Pope, Gay, and Arbuthnot), his integrity and truthfulness, his zeal for religion, his hatred of oppression, his patriotic ardor on behalf of the country of his birth. On the other hand, he was proud, domineering, careless of the feelings of others, irritable, and altogether misanthropic; but these more repulsive characteristics may have been partly due to the ill health from which he suffered so much. As to his personal appearance, he is said to have been "tall, strong, and well made, of a dark complexion, but with blue eyes, black and bushy eyebrows, nose somewhat aquiline, and features which remarkably express the stern, haughty, and dauntless turn of his mind." In genius and originality he was perhaps unequaled by any English writer of the eighteenth century. Although he wrote a good many poetical pieces he can hardly be considered as a real poet; and this his kinsman Dryden plainly told him, much to Swift's chagrin. His strength lies in wit, humor, satire, ridicule, and especially in a kind of grave irony, in which the most extraordinary assertions and suggestions are put forward with a superficial appearance of simplicity and good faith.

GULLIVER'S TRAVELS was published in 1726 in two volumes, the original title being "Travels into Several Remote Nations of the World. In Four Parts. By Lemuel Gulliver, first a Surgeon, and then a Captain of Several Ships." Though Swift's intimate friends knew who the author was, the world at large was much puzzled. Its popularity was great and immediate, and has been as lasting as it was great. So strong an air of truthfulness did the narrative possess, and so little were some parts of the world then known, that persons were not wanting who believed they were reading a genuine account of travels. One old salt is reported to have said that he knew Captain Gulliver very well, only he lived at Wapping not at Rotherhithe.

The four parts of which the work consists are each very distinct in subject. The first, the voyage to Lilliput, is generally considered the most pleasing of the four. In it we are shown creatures of the most diminutive size, made in all respects after the model of mankind, and we are thus led to consider whether the passions, aims, and ambitions by which we are actuated are not really as petty and insignificant as we cannot help thinking those are by which the Lilliputians are inspired. In this part of the work there are supposed to be numerous allusions to the court and politics of England; thus Flimnap, the treasurer, is said to stand for Sir Robert Walpole, the High-heels and the Low-heels for the Tories and the Whigs, the Big-endians and the Little-endians for the Roman Catholics and Protestants, Blefuscu for France, and so on.

In the voyage to Brobdingnag the telescope is turned, as it were, and everything is on a scale quite the reverse of what prevails in Lilliput. We are now confronted with creatures of enormous size, and human actions and sentiments are shown as they might appear to beings equally rational with ourselves and of a bulk and strength immensely greater. Thus the aim in both these fictions is the same, only it is attained by opposite methods.

The voyage to Laputa is on the whole less interesting, though the marvels which it contains are sufficiently striking. Here Swift directs his satire chiefly against pretenders to science and projectors of schemes that could never lead to anything practical, and merely intended to dupe the unwary.

The last part of GULLIVER'S TRAVELS is a savage satire against humanity at large, and in many places can only inspire pain and disgust. The incidents and particulars of the story, too, are so glaringly impossible that our imagination is never held captive as in the other three narratives. It is here that Swift best succeeds in what he himself said was the aim of the whole work—"to vex the world rather than to divert it." "Yet," as Sir Walter Scott remarks, "the picture of the Yahoos, utterly odious and hateful as it is, presents to the reader a moral use," representing mankind in the state "to which our species is degraded by the willful subservience of mental qualities to animal instincts, of man, such as he may be found in the degraded ranks of every society, when brutalized by ignorance and gross vice."

PART I.
A VOYAGE TO LILLIPUT.

GULLIVER'S TRAVELS.

PART I.

A VOYAGE TO LILLIPUT.

CHAPTER I.

The Author gives some Account of Himself and Family—His
First Inducements to Travel—He is Shipwrecked, and
Swims for his Life—Gets safe on Shore in the Country
of Lilliput—Is made a Prisoner, and carried up the
Country.

My father had a small estate in Nottinghamshire;
I was the third of five sons. He sent me to
Emanuel College in Cambridge, at fourteen years old,

where I resided three years, and applied myself close to my studies; but the charge of maintaining me, although I had a very scanty allowance, being too great for a narrow fortune, I was bound apprentice to Mr. James Bates, an eminent surgeon in London, with whom I continued four years; and my father now and then sending me small sums of money, I laid them out in learning navigation, and other parts of the mathematics useful to those who intend to travel, as I always believed it would be, some time or other, my fortune to do. When I left Mr. Bates I went down to my father, where, by the assistance of him and my uncle John, and some other relations, I got forty pounds, and a promise of thirty pounds a-year, to maintain me at Leyden.* There I studied physic two years and seven months, knowing it would be useful in long voyages.

Soon after my return from Leyden, I was recommended by my good master, Mr. Bates, to be surgeon to the Swallow, Captain Abraham Pannell, commander; with whom I continued three years and a half, making a voyage or two into the Levant,† and some other parts. When I came back

* The university of Leyden has long been celebrated; and in the seventeenth and eighteenth centuries many persons went from England to study medicine there.

† The eastern portion of the Mediterranean and its coasts.

I resolved to settle in London; to which Mr. Bates, my master, encouraged me; and by him I was recommended to several patients. I took part of a small house in the Old Jewry; and, being advised to alter my condition, I married Mrs.* Mary Burton, second daughter to Mr. Edmund Burton, hosier, in Newgate Street, with whom I received four hundred pounds for a portion.

But my good master Bates dying in two years after, and I having few friends, my business began to fail; for my conscience would not suffer me to imitate the bad practice of too many among my brethren.† Having, therefore, consulted with my wife and some of my acquaintance, I determined to go again to sea. I was surgeon successively in two ships, and made several voyages, for six years, to the East and West Indies, by which I got some addition to my fortune. My hours of leisure I spent in reading the best authors, ancient and modern, being always provided with a good number of books; and when I was ashore, in observing the manners and dispositions of the people, as well as learning their language; wherein I had a great facility, by the strength of my memory.

---

* " Mrs." was formerly applied to unmarried ladies.

† He would not play the quack, or use low methods of getting patients.

The last of these voyages not proving very fortunate, I grew weary of the sea, and intended to stay
at home with my wife and family. I removed from
the Old Jewry to Fetter Lane, and from thence to
Wapping, hoping to get business among the sailors;
but it would not turn to account.* After three
years' expectation that things would mend, I accepted an advantageous offer from Captain William
Prichard, master of the Antelope, who was making
a voyage to the South Sea.† We set sail from
Bristol, May 4, 1699, and our voyage at first was
very prosperous.

It would not be proper, for some reasons, to
trouble the reader with the particulars of our adventures in those seas; let it suffice to inform him, that,
in our passage from thence to the East Indies, we
were driven by a violent storm to the northwest of
Van Diemen's Land.‡ By an observation we found
ourselves in the latitude of 30 degrees 2 minutes
south. Twelve of our crew were dead by im-

---

* It would not "pay."

† This was formerly the usual name of the Pacific Ocean,
or of the southern portion of it.

‡ The geography of this part of the globe was not very well
known in Swift's time. A place northwest from Van Diemen's Land (Tasmania), and in latitude 30° 2′ S., would be in
Australia, or off its west coast.

moderate labor and ill food : the rest were in a very weak condition. On the 5th of November, which was the beginning of summer in those parts, the weather being very hazy, the seamen spied a rock within half a cable's length of the ship; but the wind was so strong that we were driven directly upon it, and immediately split. Six of the crew, of whom I was one, having let down the boat into the sea, made a shift to get clear of the ship and the rock. We rowed, by my computation, about three leagues, till we were able to work no longer, being already spent with labor while we were in the ship. We, therefore, trusted ourselves to the mercy of the waves; and in about half an hour the boat was overset by a sudden flurry* from the north. What became of my companions in the boat, as well as of those who escaped on the rock, or were left in the vessel, I cannot tell, but conclude they were all lost. For my own part, I swam as Fortune directed me, and was pushed forward by wind and tide. I often let my legs drop, and could feel no bottom; but when I was almost gone, and able to struggle no longer, I found myself within my depth : and by this time the storm was much abated. The declivity was so small, that I walked near a mile before I got to the

---

* Squall or gust of wind.

shore, which I conjectured was about eight o'clock
in the evening. I then advanced forward near half
a mile, but could not discover any sign of houses or
inhabitants; at least I was in so weak a condition
that I did not observe them. I was extremely
tired; and with that, and the heat of the weather,
and about half a pint of brandy that I drank as I
left the ship, I found myself much inclined to sleep.
I lay down on the grass, which was very short and
soft, where I slept sounder than ever I remember to
have done in my life, and, as I reckoned, above nine
hours; for when I awaked it was just daylight. I
attempted to rise, but was not able to stir; for as I
happened to lie on my back, I found my arms and
legs were strongly fastened on each side to the
ground, and my hair, which was long and thick,
tied down in the same manner. I likewise felt
several slender ligatures across my body, from my
armpits to my thighs. I could only look upward;
the sun began to grow hot, and the light offended
mine eyes. I heard a confused noise about me, but,
in the posture I lay, could see nothing except the
sky. In a little time I felt something alive moving
on my left leg, which, advancing gently forward
over my breast, came almost up to my chin; when,
bending mine eyes downward as much as I could, I
perceived it to be a human creature not six inches

high, with a bow and arrow in his hands, and a quiver at his back. In the meantime, I felt at least forty more of the same kind (as I conjectured) following the first. I was in the utmost astonishment, and roared so loud that they all ran back in a fright; and some of them, as I was afterward told, were hurt with the falls they got by leaping from my sides upon the ground. However, they soon returned; and one of them, who ventured so far as to get a full sight of my face, lifting up his hands and eyes by way of admiration, cried out, in a shrill but distinct voice, *Hekinah degul:* the others repeated the same words several times; but I then knew not what they meant. I lay all this while, as the reader may believe, in great uneasiness. At length, struggling to get loose, I had the fortune to break the strings and wrench out the pegs that fastened my left arm to the ground; for, by lifting it up to my face, I discovered the methods they had taken to bind me, and, at the same time, with a violent pull, which gave me excessive pain, I a little loosened the strings that tied down my hair on the left side, so that I was just able to turn my head about two inches. But the creatures ran off a second time, before I could seize them; whereupon there was a great shout, in a very shrill accent, and, after it ceased, I heard one of them cry aloud,

Tolgo phonac; when, in an instant, I felt above an
hundred arrows discharged on my left hand, which
pricked me like so many needles; and, besides, they
shot another flight into the air, as we do bombs in
Europe, whereof many, I suppose, fell on my body
(though I felt them not), and some on my face,
which I immediately covered with my left hand.
When this shower of arrows was over, I fell a-
groaning with grief and pain; and then, striving
again to get loose, they discharged another volley,
larger than the first, and some of them attempted,
with spears, to stick me in the sides; but, by good
luck, I had on me a buff jerkin,* which they could
not pierce. I thought it the most prudent method
to lie still; and my design was to continue so till
night, when, my left hand being already loose, I
could easily free myself: and as for the inhabitants,
I had reason to believe I might be a match for the
greatest armies they could bring against me, if
they were all of the same size with him that I saw.
But fortune disposed otherwise of me. When the
people observed I was quiet, they discharged no
more arrows; but, by the noise I heard, I knew
their numbers increased: and about four yards from
me, over against my right ear, I heard a knocking

---

* Close jacket or waistcoat of leather.

for above an hour, like that of people at work; when, turning my head that way, as well as the pegs and strings would permit me, I saw a stage erected about a foot and a half from the ground, capable of holding four of the inhabitants, with two or three ladders to mount it; from whence one of them, who seemed to be a person of quality, made me a long speech, whereof I understood not one syllable. But I should have mentioned, that, before the principal person began his oration, he cried out three times, *Langro dehul san* (these words and the former were afterward repeated and explained to me); whereupon, immediately, about fifty of the inhabitants came and cut the strings that fastened the left side of my head, which gave me the liberty of turning it to the right, and of observing the person and gesture of him that was to speak. He appeared to be of a middle age, and taller than any of the other three who attended him; whereof one was a page, that held up his train, and seemed to be somewhat longer than my middle finger; the other two stood one on each side to support him. He acted every part of an orator; and I could observe many periods of threatenings, and others of promises, pity, and kindness. I answered in a few words, but in the most submissive manner, lifting up my left hand and both mine eyes to the sun, as calling him

for a witness: and being almost famished with
hunger, having not eaten a morsel for some hours
before I left the ship, I found the demands of
nature so strong upon me that I could not forbear
showing my impatience (perhaps against the strict
rules of decency) by putting my finger frequently
on my mouth, to signify that I wanted food. The
hurgo (for so they call a great lord, as I afterward
learned) understood me very well. He descended
from the stage, and commanded that several ladders
should be applied to my sides, on which above an
hundred of the inhabitants mounted, and walked
toward my mouth, laden with baskets full of meat,
which had been provided and sent thither by the
king's orders, upon the first intelligence he received
of me. I observed there was the flesh of several
animals, but could not distinguish them by the
taste. There were shoulders, legs, and loins, shaped
like those of mutton, and very well dressed, but
smaller than the wings of a lark. I eat them by
two or three at a mouthful, and took three loaves
at a time, about the bigness of musket-bullets. They
supplied me as fast as they could, showing a thousand
marks of wonder and astonishment at my bulk and
appetite. I then made another sign, that I wanted
drink. They found by my eating that a small
quantity would not suffice me; and, being a most

ingenious people, they slung up, with great dexterity, one of their largest hogsheads, then rolled it toward my hand, and beat out the top. I drank it off at a draught, which I might well do, for it did not hold half a pint, and tasted like a small* wine of Burgundy, but much more delicious. They brought me a second hogshead, which I drank in the same manner, and made signs for more; but they had none to give me. When I had performed these wonders, they shouted for joy, and danced upon my breast, repeating several times, as they did at first, *Hekinah degul.* They made me a sign that I should throw down the two hogsheads, but first warning the people below to stand out of the way, crying aloud, *Borach mivolah;* and when they saw the vessels in the air there was an universal shout of *Hekinah degul.* I confess I was often tempted, while they were passing backward and forward on my body, to seize forty or fifty of the first that came in my reach, and dash them against the ground. But the remembrance of what I had felt, which probably might not be the worst they could do, and the promise of honor I made them—for so I interpreted my submissive behavior—soon drove out these imaginations. Besides, I now considered my-

* Not strong; not going to one's head.

self as bound by the laws of hospitality to a people who had treated me with so much expense and magnificence. However, in my thoughts I could not sufficiently wonder at the intrepidity of these diminutive mortals, who durst venture to mount and walk upon my body, while one of my hands was at liberty, without trembling at the very sight of so prodigious a creature as I must appear to them. After some time, when they observed that I made no more demands for meat, there appeared before me a person of high rank from his imperial majesty. His excellency, having mounted on the small of my right leg, advanced forward up to my face, with about a dozen of his retinue; and producing his credentials, under the signet-royal, which he applied close to mine eyes, spoke about ten minutes without any signs of anger, but with a kind of determinate resolution; often pointing forward; which, as I afterward found, was toward the capital city, about half a mile distant, whither it was agreed by his majesty in council that I must be conveyed. I answered in few words, but to no purpose, and made a sign with my hand that was loose, putting it to the other (but over his excellency's head, for fear of hurting him or his train), and then to my own head and body, to signify that I desired my liberty. It appeared that he understood me well enough, for he shook his head by way of disapprobation, and held his hand in a posture to show that I must be carried as a prisoner. However, he made other signs, to let me understand that I should have meat and drink enough, and very good treatment. Whereupon, I once more thought of attempting to break my bonds; but again, when I felt the smart of their arrows upon my face and hands, which were all in blisters, and many of the darts still sticking in them, and observing likewise that the number of my enemies increased, I gave tokens to let them know that they might do with me what they pleased. Upon this, the *hurgo* and his train withdrew, with much civility and cheerful countenances. Soon after, I heard a general shout, with frequent repetitions of the words *Peplom selan;* and I felt great numbers of the people on my left side, relaxing the cords to such a degree that I was able to turn upon my right. But before this they had daubed my face and both my hands with a sort of ointment, very pleasant to the smell, which, in a few minutes, removed all the smart of their arrows. These circumstances, added to the refreshment I had received by their victuals and drink, which were very nourishing, disposed me to sleep. I slept about eight hours, as I was afterward assured; and it was no wonder, for the physicians, by the emper or's order has mingled a sleepy potion in the hogs-heads of wine.

It seems that upon the first moment I was discovered sleeping on the ground, after my landing, the emperor had early notice of it by an express,* and determined in council that I should be tied in the manner I have related (which was done in the night, while I slept), that plenty of meat and drink should be sent to me, and a machine prepared to carry me to the capital city.

This resolution, perhaps, may appear very bold and dangerous, and I am confident would not be imitated by any prince in Europe, on the like occasion. However, in my opinion, it was extremely prudent, as well as generous; for supposing these people had endeavored to kill me with their spears and arrows while I was asleep, I should certainly have awaked with the first sense of smart, which might so far have roused my rage and strength as to have enabled me to break the strings wherewith I was tied; after which, as they were not able to make resistance, so they could expect no mercy.

These people are most excellent mathematicians, and arrived to a great perfection in mechanics,† by

---

* A special messenger.

† The art of constructing machinery of all kinds.

the countenance and encouragement of the emperor, who is a renowned patron of learning. This prince has several machines fixed on wheels, for the carriage of trees and other great weights. He often builds his largest men-of-war, whereof some are nine feet long, in the woods where the timber grows, and has them carried on these engines, three or four hundred yards, to the sea. Five hundred carpenters and engineers were immediately set at work to prepare the greatest engine they had. It was a frame of wood raised three inches from the ground, about seven foot long, and four wide, moving upon twenty-two wheels. The shout I heard was upon the arrival of this engine, which, it seems, set out in four hours after my landing. It was brought parallel to me as I lay. But the principal difficulty was to raise and place me in this vehicle. Eighty poles, each of one foot high, were erected for this purpose, and very strong cords, of the bigness of pack-thread, were fastened by hooks to many bandages, which the workmen had girt round my neck, my hands, my body, and my legs. Nine hundred of the strongest men were employed to draw up these cords, by many pulleys fastened on the poles; and thus, in less than three hours, I was raised and slung into the engine, and there tied fast. All this I was told; for, while the whole operation was performing, I lay in a profound sleep, by the force of that soporiferous medicine infused into my liquor. Fifteen hundred of the emperor's largest horses, each about four inches and a half high, were employed to draw me toward the metropolis, which, as I said, was half a mile distant.

About four hours after we began our journey, I awaked by a very ridiculous accident; for the carriage being stopped awhile to adjust something that was out of order, two or three of the young natives had the curiosity to see how I looked when I was asleep; they climbed up into the engine, and advancing very softly to my face, one of them, an officer in the guards, put the sharp end of his half-pike a good way up into my left nostril, which tickled my nose like a straw, and made me sneeze violently; whereupon they stole off unperceived, and it was three weeks before I knew the cause of my awaking so suddenly. We made a long march the remaining part of that day, and rested at night with five hundred guards on each side of me, half with torches, and half with bows and arrows, ready to shoot me if I should offer to stir. The next morning at sunrise we continued our march, and arrived within two hundred yards of the city gates about noon. The emperor, and all his court, came out to meet us, but his great officers would by no means suffer his majesty to endanger his person by mounting on my body.

At the place where the carriage stopped there stood an ancient temple, esteemed to be the largest in the whole kingdom ; which, having been polluted some years before by an unnatural murder, was, according to the zeal of those people, looked on as profane, and therefore had been applied to common use, and all the ornaments and furniture carried away. In this edifice it was determined I should lodge. The great gate fronting to the north was about four foot high, and almost two foot wide, through which I could easily creep. On each side of the gate was a small window, not above six inches from the ground : into that on the left side the king's smiths conveyed fourscore and eleven chains, like those that hang to a lady's watch in Europe, and almost as large, which were locked to my left leg with thirty-six padlocks. Over against this temple, on t'other side of the great highway, at twenty foot distance, there was a turret at least five foot high. Here the emperor ascended, with many principal lords of his court, to have an opportunity of viewing me, as I was told, for I could not see them. It was reckoned that above an hundred thousand inhabitants came out of the town upon the same errand ; and, in spite of my guards, I believe there could not be fewer than ten thousand at several times, who mounted upon my body by the help of ladders. But a proclamation was soon issued to forbid it upon pain of death. When the workmen found it was impossible for me to break loose they cut all the strings that bound me; whereupon I rose up, with as melancholy a disposition as ever I had in my life. But the noise and astonishment of the people, at seeing me rise and walk, are not to be expressed. The chains that held my left leg were about two yards long, and gave me not only the liberty of walking backward and forward in a semicircle, but, being fixed within four inches of the gate, allowed me to creep in and lie at my full length in the temple.

CHAPTER II.

The Emperor of Lilliput, attended by Several of the Nobility, comes to see the Author in his Confinement—The Emperor's Person and Habit described — Learned men appointed to teach the Author their Language—He gains favor by his mild Disposition—His Pockets are searched, and his Sword and Pistols taken from him.

WHEN I found myself on my feet I looked about me, and must confess I never beheld a more entertaining prospect. The country round appeared like a continued garden, and the enclosed fields, which were generally forty foot square, resembled so many beds of flowers. These fields were intermingled with woods of half a stang,* and the tallest trees, as I could judge, appeared to be seven foot high. I viewed the town on my left hand, which looked like the painted scene of a city in a theater.

The emperor was already descended from the tower, and advancing on horseback toward me, which had like to have cost him dear, for the beast,

---

* An old name for a pole or perch (16 1-2 feet); also for a rood of ground.

though very well trained, yet wholly unused to such a sight, which appeared as if a mountain moved before him, reared up on his hinder feet; but that prince, who is an excellent horseman, kept his seat till his attendants ran in and held the bridle while his majesty had time to dismount. When he alighted he surveyed me round with great admiration, but kept beyond the length of my chain. He ordered his cooks and butlers, who were already prepared, to give me victuals and drink, which they pushed forward in sorts of vehicle upon wheels till I could reach them. I took these vehicles, and soon emptied them all; twenty of them were filled with meat, and ten with liquor; each of the former afforded me two or three good mouthfuls, and I emptied the liquor of ten vessels, which was contained in earthen vials, into one vehicle, drinking it off at a draught, and so I did with the rest. The empress and young princes of the blood, of both sexes, attended by many ladies, sat at some distance in their chairs,* but upon the accident that happened to the emperor's horse they alighted and came near his person, which I am now going to describe. He is taller, by almost the breadth of

---

* That is sedans or sedan-chairs, such as were formerly common, a kind of box for one person, borne by two men by means of poles, and serving the purpose of a cab.

my nail, than any of his court, which alone is
enough to strike an awe into the beholders. His
features are strong and masculine, with an Austrian
lip and arched nose; his complexion olive, his
countenance erect, his body and limbs well propor-
tioned, all his motions graceful, and his deportment
majestic. He was then past his prime, being
twenty-eight years and three-quarters old,* of which
he had reigned about seven in great felicity, and
generally victorious. For the better convenience
of beholding him I lay on my side, so that my face
was parallel to his, and he stood but three yards
off; however, I have had him since many times
in my hand, and therefore cannot be deceived in
the description. His dress was very plain and
simple, and the fashion of it between the Asiatic
and the European; but he had on his head a light
helmet of gold, adorned with jewels, and a plume
on the crest. He held his sword drawn in his hand
to defend himself if I should happen to break loose;
it was almost three inches long, the hilt and scabbard were gold enriched with diamonds. His voice
was shrill, but very clear and articulate, and I could
distinctly hear it when I stood up. The ladies and

---

* The lives of the Lilliputians were considerably shorter than
ours, it must be understood.

courtiers were all most magnificently clad, so that the spot they stood upon seemed to resemble a petticoat spread on the ground embroidered with figures of gold and silver. His imperial majesty spoke often to me, and I returned answers, but neither of us could understand a syllable. There were several of his priests and lawyers present (as I conjectured by their habits), who were commanded to address themselves to me, and I spoke to them in as many languages as I had the least smattering of, which were High and Low Dutch,* Latin, French, Spanish, Italian, and Lingua Franca,† but all to no purpose. After about two hours the court retired, and I was left with a strong guard to prevent the impertinence and probably the malice of the rabble, who were very impatient to crowd about me as near as they durst, and some of them had the impudence to shoot their arrows at me as I sate on the ground by the door of my house, whereof one very narrowly missed my left eye. But the colonel ordered six of the ringleaders to be seized, and thought no punishment so proper as to deliver them

---

* Or, as we should say, German and Dutch.

† A mixed dialect used in some parts of the Mediterranean coasts as a means of communication between persons of different nationality, and largely consisting of corrupted Italian words.

bound into my hands, which some of his soldiers accordingly did, pushing them forward with the butt-ends of their pikes into my reach. I took them all in my right hand, put five of them into my coat pocket, and as to the sixth, I made a countenance as if I would eat him alive. The poor man squalled terribly, and the colonel and his officers were in much pain, especially when they saw me take out my penknife, but I soon put them out of fear, for looking mildly, and immediately cutting the strings he was bound with, I set him gently on the ground, and away he ran. I treated the rest in the same manner, taking them one by one out of my pocket, and I observed both the soldiers and people were highly delighted at this mark of my clemency, which was represented very much to my advantage at court.

Toward night I got with some difficulty into my house, where I lay on the ground, and continued to do so about a fortnight, during which time the emperor gave orders to have a bed prepared for me. Six hundred beds of the common measure were brought in carriages, and worked up in my house; an hundred and fifty of their beds sewn together made up the breadth and length, and these were four double, which, however, kept me but very indifferently from the hardness of the floor, that was of smooth stone. By the same computation they provided me with sheets, blankets, and coverlets, tolerable enough for one who had been so long inured to hardships as I.

As the news of my arrival spread through the kingdom, it brought prodigious numbers of rich, idle, and curious people to see me; so that the villages were almost emptied; and great neglect of tillage and household affairs must have ensued, if his imperial majesty had not provided, by several proclamations and orders of state, against this inconveniency. He directed that those who had already beheld me should return home, and not presume to come within fifty yards of my house without license from court; whereby the secretaries of state got considerable fees.

In the meantime the emperor held frequent councils, to debate what course should be taken with me; and I was afterward assured by a particular friend, a person of great quality,* who was looked upon to be as much in the secret as any, that the court was under many difficulties concerning me. They apprehended my breaking loose; that my diet would be very expensive, and might cause a famine. Sometimes they determined to starve me, or at least

---

* Of high rank.

to shoot me in the face and hands with poisoned arrows, which would soon despatch me; but again they considered that the stench of so large a carcass might produce a plague in the metropolis, and probably spread through the whole kingdom. In the midst of these consultations, several officers of the army went to the door of the great council-chamber, and two of them being admitted, gave an account of my behavior to the six criminals above mentioned, which made so favorable an impression in the breast of his majesty and the whole board in my behalf, that an imperial commission was issued out obliging all the villages nine hundred yards round the city to deliver in every morning six beeves,* forty sheep, and other victuals for my sustenance; together with a proportionable quantity of bread, and wine, and other liquors; for the due payment of which his majesty gave assignments† upon his treasury— for this prince lives chiefly upon his own demesnes; ‡ seldom, except upon great occasions, raising any subsidies upon his subjects, who are bound to attend him in his wars at their own expense. An establishment was also made of six hundred persons to be my domestics, who had board wages allowed for

---

* Cattle; oxen.   † Orders or drafts for money.

‡ Domains; lands.

their maintenance, and tents built for them, very conveniently on each side of my door. It was likewise ordered that three hundred tailors should make me a suit of clothes, after the fashion of the country; that six of his majesty's greatest scholars should be employed to instruct me in their language; and, lastly, that the emperor's horses, and those of the nobility, and troops of guard, should be frequently exercised in my sight, to accustom themselves to me. All these orders were duly put in execution; and in about three weeks I made a great progress in learning their language; during which time the emperor frequently honored me with his visits, and was pleased to assist my masters in teaching me. We began already to converse together in some sort: and the first words I learned were to express my desire that he would please to give me my liberty; which I every day repeated on my knees. His answer, as I could apprehend it, was, that this must be a work of time, not to be thought on without the advice of his council, and that first I must *lumos kelmin pesso desmar lon emposo;* that is, swear a peace with him and his kingdom. However, that I should be used with all kindness. And he advised me to acquire, by my patience and discreet behavior, the good opinion of himself and his subjects. He desired I would not take it ill, if he gave orders to certain proper officers to search me; for probably I might carry about me several weapons, which must needs be dangerous things, if they answered the bulk of so prodigious a person. I said his majesty should be satisfied; for I was ready to strip myself, and turn up my pockets before him. This I delivered, part in words and part in signs. He replied, that by the laws of the kingdom, I must be searched by two of his officers; that he knew this could not be done without my consent and assistance: that he had so good an opinion of my generosity and justice as to trust their persons in my hands; that whatever they took from me should be returned when I left the country, or paid for at the rate which I would set upon them. I took up the two officers in my hands, put them first into my coat pockets, and then into every other pocket about me, except my two fobs,* and another secret pocket I had no mind should be searched, wherein I had some little necessaries that were of no consequence to any but myself. In one of my fobs there was a silver watch, and in the other a small quantity of gold in a purse. These gentlemen, having pen, ink, and paper about them, made an exact inventory of everything they saw; and when they had done

---

* Small, deep pockets in the front of a person's trousers.

desired I would set them down, that they might
deliver it to the emperor. This inventory I afterward translated into English, and is word for word
as follows:

" *Imprimis*,* In the right coat-pocket of the great
man-mountain (for so I interpret the words *quinbus
flestrin*), after the strictest search, we found only
one great piece of coarse cloth, large enough to be
a footcloth for your majesty's chief room of state.
In the left pocket we saw a huge silver chest, with
a cover of the same metal, which we, the searchers,
were not able to lift. We desired it should be
opened, and one of us, stepping into it, found himself up to the mid-leg in a sort of dust, some part
whereof, flying up to our faces, set us both a-sneez-
ing for several times together. In his right waistcoat pocket we found a prodigious bundle of white,
thin substances, folded one over another, about the
bigness of three men, tied with a strong cable, and
marked with black figures, which we humbly conceive to be writings, every letter almost half as
large as the palm of our hands. In the left there
was a sort of engine, from the back of which were
extended twenty long poles, resembling the palisa-
does before your majesty's court; wherewith we

---

* In the first place ; firstly.   [Pron. im-pri'mis.]

conjecture the man-mountain combs his head; for
we did not always trouble him with questions, because we found it a great difficulty to make him
understand us. In the large pocket, on the right
side of his middle cover (so I translate the word
ranfu-lo, by which they meant my breeches), we
saw a hollow pillar of iron, about the length of a
man, fastened to a strong piece of timber larger
than the pillar; and upon one side of the pillar were
huge pieces of iron sticking out, cut into strange
figures, which we know not what to make of. In
the left pocket, another engine of the same kind.
In the smaller pocket, on the right side, were several
round, flat pieces of white and red metal, of different bulk; some of the white, which seemed to be
silver, were so large and heavy that my comrade
and I could hardly lift them. In the left pocket
were two black pillars irregularly shaped; we could
not, without difficulty, reach the top of them, as we
stood at the bottom of his pocket. One of them
was covered and seemed all of a piece; but at the
upper end of the other there appeared a white,
round substance, about twice the bigness of our
heads. Within each of these was enclosed a prodigious plate of steel; which, by our orders, we
obliged him to show us, because we apprehended
they might be dangerous engines. He took them

out of their cases, and told us that, in his own country, his practice was to shave his beard with one of these, and to cut his meat with the other. There were two pockets which we could not enter;

" We saw certain strange figures circularly drawn."

these he called his fobs; they were two large slits cut into the top of his middle cover, but squeezed close by the pressure of his belly. Out of the right fob hung a great silver chain, with a wonderful kind of engine at the bottom. We directed him to draw out whatever was at the end of that chain, which appeared to be a globe, half silver, and half of some transparent metal; for, on the transparent side, we saw certain strange figures circularly drawn, and thought we could touch them, till we found our fingers stopped by that lucid* substance. He put this engine to our ears, which made an incessant noise like that of a water-mill: and we conjecture it is either some unknown animal, or the god that he worships; but we are more inclined to the latter opinion, because he assured us (if we understood him right, for he expressed himself very imperfectly), that he seldom did anything without consulting it. He called it his oracle, and said it pointed out the time for every action of his life. From the left fob he took out a net, almost large enough for a fisherman, but contrived to open and shut like a purse, and served him for the same use: we found therein several massy pieces of yellow metal, which, if they be real gold, must be of immense value.

"Having thus, in obedience to your majesty's commands, diligently searched all his pockets, we observed a girdle about his waist, made of the hide of some prodigious animal, from which, on the left side, hung a sword of the length of five men; and

---

* Shining; transparent.

on the right, a bag or pouch divided into two cells, each cell capable of holding three of your majesty's subjects. In one of these cells were several globes or balls, of a most ponderous metal, about the big-ness of our heads, and required a strong hand to lift them; the other cell contained a heap of certain black grains, but of no great bulk or weight, for we could hold above fifty of them in the palms of our hands.

"This is an exact inventory of what we found about the body of the man-mountain, who used us with great civility, and due respect to your majesty's commission. Signed and sealed on the fourth day of the eighty-ninth moon of your majesty's auspi-cious reign.

"CLEFREN FRELOCK,   MARSI FRELOCK."

When this inventory was read over to the emperor he directed me, although in very gentle terms, to deliver up the several particulars. He first called for my scimitar,* which I took out, scabbard and all. In the meantime he ordered three thousand of his choicest troops (who then attended him) to sur-round me at a distance, with their bows and arrows just ready to discharge; but I did not observe it,

---

* A scimitar is properly a curved sword such as is worn by the Turks and other Orientals.

for mine eyes were wholly fixed upon his majesty. He then desired me to draw my scimitar, which, although it had got some rust by the sea-water, was in most parts exceeding bright. I did so, and immediately all the troops gave a shout between terror and surprise: for the sun shone clear, and the reflection dazzled their eyes, as I waved the scimitar to and fro in my hand. His majesty, who is a most magnanimous prince, was less daunted than I could expect: he ordered me to return it into the scabbard, and cast it on the ground as gently as I could, about six foot from the end of my chain. The next thing he demanded was one of the hollow iron pillars: by which he meant my pocket-pistols. I drew it out, and at his desire, as well as I could, expressed to him the use of it; and charging it only with powder, which, by the closeness of my pouch, happened to escape wetting in the sea (an inconvenience against which all prudent mariners take special care to provide), I first cautioned the emperor not to be afraid, and then I let it off in the air. The astonishment here was much greater than at the sight of my scimitar. Hundreds fell down as if they had been struck dead; and even the emperor, although he stood his ground, could not recover himself in some time. I delivered up both my pistols in the same manner as I had done my scimitar, and then

my pouch of powder and bullets; begging him that
the former might be kept from the fire, for it would
kindle with the smallest spark, and blow up his imperial palace into the air. I likewise delivered up
my watch, which the emperor was very curious to
see, and commanded two of his tallest yeomen of
the guards* to bear it on a pole upon their shoulders,
as draymen in England do a barrel of ale. He was
amazed at the continual noise it made, and the
motion of the minute-hand, which he could easily
discern; for their sight is much more acute than
ours: and asked the opinions of his learned men
about him, which were various and remote, as the
reader may well imagine without my repeating;
although, indeed, I could not very perfectly understand them. I then gave up my silver and copper
money, my purse with nine large pieces of gold and
some smaller ones; my knife and razor, my comb
and silver snuff-box, my handkerchief, and journal-
book. My scimitar, pistols, and pouch were conveyed in carriages to his majesty's stores; but the
rest of my goods were returned me.

I had, as I before observed, one private pocket,
which escaped their search, wherein there was a
pair of spectacles (which I sometimes use for the

---

* The yeomen of the guard in England are the body-guard
of the sovereign.

weakness of mine eyes), a pocket perspective,* and several other little conveniences; which, being of no consequence to the emperor, I did not think myself bound in honor to discover,† and I apprehended they might be lost or spoiled if I ventured them out of my possession.

---

* An old name for a telescope.

† Show: find out is now the common meaning.

CHAPTER III.

The Author diverts the Emperor, and his Nobility of both
sexes, in a very uncommon manner—The diversions of
the Court of Lilliput described—The Author has his
Liberty granted him upon certain conditions.

My gentleness and good behavior had gained so
far on the emperor and his court, and indeed upon
the army and people in general, that I began to
conceive hopes of getting my liberty in a short time.
I took all possible methods to cultivate this favorable disposition. The natives came, by degrees, to
be less apprehensive of any danger from me. I
would sometimes lie down, and let five or six of
them dance on my hand; and at last the boys and
girls would venture to come and play at hide-and-
seek in my hair. I had now made a good progress
in understanding and speaking their language. The
emperor had a mind one day to entertain me with
several of the country shows, wherein they exceed
all nations I have known, both for dexterity and
magnificence. I was diverted with none so much
as that of the rope-dancers, performed upon a
slender white thread, extended about two foot and

twelve inches from the ground. Upon which I shall desire liberty, with the reader's patience, to enlarge a little.

This diverson is only practised by those persons who are candidates for great employments and high favor at court. They are trained in this art from their youth, and are not always of noble birth or liberal education. When a great office is vacant, either by death or disgrace (which often happens), five or six of those candidates petition the emperor to entertain his majesty and the court with a dance on the rope; and whoever jumps the highest without falling, succeeds in the office. Very often the chief ministers themselves are commanded to show their skill, and to convince the emperor that they have not lost their faculty. Flimnap, the treasurer, is allowed to cut a caper on the straight rope, at least an inch higher than any other lord in the whole empire. I have seen him do the summerset several times together, upon a trencher * fixed on the rope, which is no thicker than a common pack-thread in England. My friend Reldresal, principal secretary for private affairs, is, in my opinion, if I am not partial, the second after the treasurer; the rest of the great officers are much upon a par.

---

* A sort of wooden plate or flat dish.

These diversions are often attended with fatal accidents, whereof great numbers are on record. I myself have seen two or three candidates break a limb. But the danger is much greater when the ministers themselves are commanded to show their dexterity; for, by contending to excel themselves and their fellows, they strain so far that there is hardly one of them who hath not received a fall, and some of them two or three. I was assured that, a year or two before my arrival, Flimnap would have infallibly broke his neck if one of the king's cushions, that accidentally lay on the ground, had not weakened the force of his fall.

There is likewise another diversion, which is only shown before the emperor and empress, and first minister, upon particular occasions. The emperor lays on a table three fine silken threads of six inches long; one is blue, the other red, and the third green. These threads are proposed as prizes for those persons whom the emperor hath a mind to distinguish by a peculiar mark of his favor. The ceremony is performed in his majesty's great chamber of state, where the candidates are to undergo a trial of dexterity, very different from the former, and such as I have not observed the least resemblance of in any other country of the old or the new world. The emperor holds a stick in his hands,

both ends parallel to the horizon, while the **candidates** advancing, one by one, sometimes leap **over**
the stick, sometimes creep under it, backward and
forward, **several** times, according as the stick is

"**Whoever performs** his part with most agility is rewarded with the blue
colored silk."

advanced or depressed. Sometimes the emperor
holds one end of the stick, and his first minister the
other; sometimes the minister has it entirely to
himself. Whoever performs his part with most
agility, and holds out the longest in leaping and

creeping, is rewarded with the blue colored silk ; and red is given to the next, and the green to the third, which they all wear girt twice round about the middle ; and you see few great persons about this court who are not adorned with one of these girdles.

The horses of the army, and those of the royal stables, having been daily led before me, were no longer shy, but would come up to my very feet without starting. The riders would leap them over my hand, as I held it on the ground; and one of the emperor's huntsmen, upon a large courser, took my foot, shoe and all, which was indeed a prodigious leap. I had the good fortune to divert the emperor one day after a very extraordinary manner. I desired he would order several sticks of two foot high, and the thickness of an ordinary cane, to be brought me ; whereupon his majesty commanded the master of his woods to give directions accordingly ; and the next morning six woodmen arrived with as many carriages, drawn by eight horses to each. I took nine of these sticks, and fixing them firmly in the ground in a quadrangular figure, two foot and a half square, I took four other sticks, and tied them parallel at each corner, about two foot from the ground ; then I fastened my handkerchief to the nine sticks that stood erect, and extended it on all sides, till it was as tight as the top of a drum; and the four parallel sticks, rising about five inches higher than the handkerchief, served as ledges on each side. When I had finished my work, I desired the emperor to let a troop of his best horse, twenty-four in number, come and exercise upon this plain. His majesty approved of the proposal, and I took them up, one by one, in my hands, ready mounted and armed, with the proper officers to exercise them. As soon as they got into order they divided into two parties, performed mock skirmishes, discharged blunt arrows, drew their swords, fled and pursued, attacked and retired, and, in short, discovered the best military discipline I ever beheld. The parallel sticks secured them and their horses from falling over the stage; and the emperor was so much delighted that he ordered this entertainment to be repeated several days, and once was pleased to be lifted up and give the word of command; and with great difficulty persuaded even the empress herself to let me hold her in her close chair within two yards of the stage, from whence she was able to take a full view of the whole performance. It was my good fortune that no ill accident happened in these entertainments; only once a fiery horse, that belonged to one of the captains, pawing with his hoof, struck a hole in my handkerchief, and his foot slipping, he overthrew his rider and himself; but I immediately relieved them both, and covering the hole with one hand, I set down the troop with the other, in the same manner as I took them up. The horse that fell was strained in the left shoulder, but the rider got no hurt; and I repaired my hand kerchief as well as I could: however, I would not trust to the strength of it any more in such dangerous enterprises.

About two or three days before I was set at liberty, as I was entertaining the court with these kind of feats, there arrived an express to inform his majesty that some of his subjects, riding near the place where I was first taken up, had seen a great black substance lying on the ground, very oddly shaped, extending its edges round, as wide as his majesty's bedchamber, and rising up in the middle as high as a man; that it was no living creature, as they at first apprehended, for it lay on the grass without motion, and some of them had walked round it several times; that, by mounting upon each other's shoulders, they had got to the top, which was flat and even, and stamping upon it, they found it was hollow within; that they humbly conceived it might be something belonging to the man-mountain; and, if his majesty pleased, they would undertake to bring it with only five horses.

I presently knew what they meant, and was glad at heart to receive this intelligence. It seems, upon my first reaching the shore after our shipwreck I was in such confusion that, before I came to the place where I went to sleep, my hat, which I had fastened with a string to my head while I was rowing, and had stuck on all the time I was swimming, fell off after I came to land; the string, as I conjecture, breaking by some accident which I never observed, but thought my hat had been lost at sea. I entreated his imperial majesty to give orders it might be brought to me as soon as possible, describing to him the use and the nature of it : and the next day the wagoners arrived with it, but not in a very good condition ; they had bored two holes in the brim, within an inch and a half of the edge, and fastened two hooks in the holes ; these hooks were tied by a long cord to the harness, and thus my hat was dragged along for above half an English mile ; but the ground in that country being extremely smooth and level, it received less damage than I expected.

Two days after this adventure, the emperor, having ordered that part of his army which quarters in and about his metropolis to be in readiness, took a fancy of diverting himself in a very singular manner. He desired I would stand like a Colossus,* with my legs as far asunder as I conveniently could. He then commanded his general (who was an old experienced leader, and a great patron of mine) to draw up the troops in close order and march them under me; the foot by twenty-four in abreast,† and the horse by sixteen, with drums beating, colors flying, and pikes advanced. This body consisted of three thousand foot and a thousand horse.

I had sent so many memorials and petitions for my liberty, that his majesty at length mentioned the matter, first in the cabinet, and then in a full council; where it was opposed by none except Skyresh Bolgolam, who was pleased, without any provocation, to be my mortal enemy. But it was carried against him by the whole board, and confirmed by the emperor. That minister was *galbet*, or admiral of the realm, very much in his master's confidence, and a person well versed in affairs, but of a morose and sour complexion.‡ However, he was at length persuaded to comply; but prevailed

---

* The celebrated Colossus of antiquity was a brass statue over 100 feet high at the entrance of the harbor of Rhodes, popularity, but incorrectly, said to have stood with the legs apart so that ships sailed through between.

† In ranks of twenty-four men abreast, or side by side.

‡ Disposition; character.

that the articles and conditions upon which I should
be set free, and to which I must swear, should be
drawn up by himself. These articles were brought
to me by Skyresh Bolgolam in person, attended by
two under-secretaries and several persons of distinction. After they were read, I was demanded to
swear to the performance of them; first in the
manner of my own country, and afterward in the
method prescribed by their laws; which was, to
hold my right foot in my left hand, to place the
middle finger of my right hand on the crown of my
head, and my thumb on the tip of my right ear.
But because the reader may perhaps be curious to
have some idea of the style and manner of expression
peculiar to that people, as well as to know the
articles upon which I recovered my liberty, I have
made a translation of the whole instrument, word
for word, as near as I was able, which I here offer
to the public:

"Golbasto Momarem Evlame Gurdilo Shefin
Mully Ully Gue, most mighty Emperor of Lilliput,
delight and terror of the universe, whose dominions
extend five thousands *blustrugs* (about twelve miles
in circumference) to the extremities of the globe;
monarch of all monarchs, taller than the sons of
men; whose feet press down to the center, and
whose head strikes against the sun, at whose nod
the princes of the earth shake their knees; pleasant
as the spring, comfortable as the summer, fruitful

as autumn, dreadful as winter. His most sublime majesty proposes to the man-mountain, lately arrived at our celestial dominions, the following, articles, which, by a solemn oath, he shall be obliged to perform:

"1st. The man-mountain shall not depart from our dominions without our license under our great seal.

"2d. He shall not presume to come into our metropolis without our express order; at which time the inhabitants shall have two hours' warning to keep within their doors.

"3d. The said man-mountain shall confine his walks to our principal highroads, and not offer to walk, or lie down, in a meadow or field of corn.

"4th. As he walks the said roads he shall take the utmost care not to trample upon the bodies of any of our loving subjects, their horses, or carriages, nor take any of our said subjects into his hands without their own consent.

"5th. If an express* requires extraordinary dispatch, the man-mountain shall be obliged to carry in his pocket the messenger and horse a six days' journey, once in every moon, and return the said messenger back (if so required) safe to our imperial presence.

"6th. He shall be our ally against our enemies in the island of Blefuscu, and do his utmost to destroy their fleet, which is now preparing to invade us.

"7th. That the said man-mountain shall, at his times of leisure, be aiding and assisting to our workmen, in helping to raise certain great stones, toward covering the wall of the principal park, and other our royal buildings.

"8th. That the said man-mountain shall, in two moons' time, deliver in an exact survey of the cir-

---

* A special or pressing message.

cumference of our dominions, by a computation of his own paces round the coast.

"Lastly. That, upon his solemn oath to observe all the above articles, the said man-mountain shall have a daily allowance of **meat and drink sufficient** for the support of 1,728 of our subjects, with free access to our royal person, and other marks of our favor. Given at our palace at Belfaborac, the twelfth day of the ninety-first moon of our reign."

I swore and subscribed to these articles with great cheerfulness and content, although some of them were not so honorable as I could have wished; which proceeded wholly from the malice of Skyresh Bolgolam, the high-admiral; whereupon my chains were immediately unlocked, and I was at full liberty. The

"I stepped over the great western gate and passed very gently."

emperor himself in person, did me the honor to be by at the whole ceremony. I made my acknowledgments by prostrating myself at his majesty's feet : but he commanded me to rise ; and after many gracious expressions, which, to avoid the censure of vanity I shall not repeat, he added, that he hoped I should prove a useful servant, and well deserve all the favors he had already conferred upon me, or might do for the future.

The reader may please to observe, that, in the last article for the recovery of my liberty, the emperor stimulates to allow me a quantity of meat and drink sufficient for the support of 1,728 Lilliputians. Some time after, asking a friend at court how they came to fix on that determinate number, he told me that his majesty's mathematicians, having taken the height of my body by the help of a quadrant,* and finding it to exceed theirs in the proportion of twelve to one, they concluded, from the similiarity of their bodies, that mine must contain at least 1,728 of theirs, and consequently would require as much food as was necessary to support that number of Lilliputians. By which the reader may conceive an idea of the ingenuity of that people, as well as the prudent and exact economy of so great a prince.

---

* A mathematical instrument formerly used in astronomy and navigation, and now replaced by the sextant.

CHAPTER IV.

Mildendo, the metropolis of Lilliput, described, together with
the Emperor's Palace—A conversation between the Author
and a Principal Secretary, concerning the affairs of that
Empire—The Author's offers to serve the Emperor in his
wars.

THE first request I made, after I had obtained my
liberty, was, that I might have license to see Mildendo, the metropolis; which the emperor easily
granted me, but with a special charge to do no hurt
either to the inhabitants or their houses. The
people had notice, by proclamation, of my design to
visit the town. The wall, which encompassed it, is
two foot and a half high, and at least eleven inches
broad, so that a coach and horses may be driven
very safely round it; and it is flanked with strong
towers at ten foot distance. I stepped over the
great western gate, and passed very gently and
sideling through the two principal streets, only in
my short waistcoat, for fear of damaging the roofs
and eaves of the houses with the skirts of my coat.
I walked with the utmost circumspection, to avoid

treading on any stragglers that might remain in the streets; although the orders were very strict that all people should keep in their houses, at their own peril. The garret windows and tops of houses were so crowded with spectators that I thought in all my travels I had not seen a more populous place. The city is an exact square, each side of the wall being five hundred foot long. The two great streets, which run cross and divide it into four quarters, are five foot wide. The lanes and alleys which I could not enter, but only viewed them as I passed, are from twelve to eighteen inches. The town is capable of holding five hundred thousand souls: the houses are from three to five stories: the shops and markets well provided.

The emperor's palace is in the center of the city, where the two great streets meet. It is enclosed by a wall of two foot high, and twenty foot distant from the buildings. I had his majesty's permission to step over this wall; and the space being so wide between that and the palace, I could easily view it on every side. The outward court is a square of forty foot, and includes two other courts: in the inmost are the royal apartments, which I was very desirous to see, but found it extremely difficult; for the great gates from one square into another were but eighteen inches high and seven inches wide.

Now the buildings of the outer court were at least five foot high, and it was impossible for me to stride over them without infinite damage to the pile, though the walls were strongly built of hewn stone, and four inches thick. At the same time, the emperor had a great desire that I should see the magnificence of his palace; but this I was not able to do till three days after, which I spent in cutting down with my knife some of the largest trees in the royal park, about a hundred yards distant from the city. Of these trees I made two stools, each about three foot high, and strong enough to bear my weight. The people, having received notice a second time, I went again through the city to the palace with my two stools in my hands. When I came to the side of the outer court, I stood upon one stool, and took the other in my hand; this I lifted over the roof, and gently set it down on the space between the first and second court, which was eight foot wide. I then stepped over the buildings very conveniently from one stool to the other, and drew up the first after me with a hooked stick. By this contrivance I got into the inmost court; and, lying down upon my side, I applied my face to the windows of the middle stories, which were left open on purpose, and discovered the most splendid apartments that can be imagined. There I saw the empress and the young princes, in their several lodgings, with their chief attendants about them. Her imperial majesty was pleased to smile very graciously upon me, and gave me out of the window her hand to kiss.

But I shall not anticipate the reader with further descriptions of this kind, because I reserve them for a greater work, v ich is now almost ready for the press; containing a general description of this empire, from its first erection, through a long series of princes, with a particular account of their wars and politics, laws, learning and religion; their plants and animals, their peculiar manners and customs, with other matters very curious and useful; my chief design at present being only to relate such events and transactions as happened to the public or to myself during a residence of about nine months in that empire.

One morning, about a fortnight after I had obtained my liberty, Reldresal, principal secretary (as they style him) of private affairs, came to my house, attended only by one servant. He ordered his coach to wait at a distance, and desired I would give him an hour's audience; which I readily consented to, on account of his quality and personal merits, as well as of the many good offices he had done me during my solicitations at court. I offered to lie down, that he might the more conveniently reach my ear; but he chose rather to let me hold him in my hand during our conversation. He began with compliments on my liberty; said he might pretend to some merit in it; but, however, added, that if it had not been for the present situation of things at court perhaps I might not have obtained it so soon. " For," said he, " as flourishing a condition as we may appear to be in to foreigners, we labor under two mighty evils ; a violent faction at home, and the danger of an invasion by a most potent enemy from abroad. As to the first, you are to understand that for above seventy moons past there have been two struggling parties in this empire, under the names *Tramecksan* and *Slameck-san*, from the high and low heels of their shoes, by which they distinguish themselves. It is alleged, indeed, that the high heels are most agreeable to our ancient constitution ; but, however this be, his majesty hath determined to make use of only low heels in the administration of the government, and all offices in the gift of the crown, as you cannot but observe; and particularly that his majesty's imperial heels are lower, at least by a *drurr*, than any of his court (*drurr* is a measure about the four-teenth part of an inch.) The animosities between these two parties run so high that they will neither

eat nor drink, nor talk with each other. We compute the *Tramecksan*, or high heels, to exceed us in
number; but the power is wholly on our side. We
apprehend his imperial highness, the heir to the
crown, to have some tendency toward the high
heels; at least we can plainly discover one of his
heels higher than the other, which gives him a
hobble in his gait. Now, in the midst of these intestine disquiets, we are threatened with an invasion
from the island of Blefuscu, which is the other
great empire of the universe, almost as large and
powerful as this of his majesty. For, as to what
we have heard you affirm, that there are other
kingdoms and states, in the world, inhabited by
human creatures as large as yourself, our philosophers are in much doubt, and would rather conjecture that you dropped from the moon or one of
the stars; because it is certain that an hundred
mortals of your bulk would in a short time destroy
all the fruits and cattle of his majesty's dominions;
besides, our histories of six thousand moons make
no mention of any other regions than the two great
empires of Lilliput and Blefuscu; which two mighty
powers have, as I was going to tell you, been engaged in a most obstinate war for thirty-six moons
past. It began upon the following occasion: It is
allowed on all hands that the primitive way of

breaking eggs, before we eat them, was upon the larger end ; but his present majesty's grandfather, while he was a boy, going to eat an egg, and breaking it according to the ancient practice, happened to cut one of his fingers ; whereupon, the emperor his father published an edict, commanding all his subjects, upon great penalties, to break the smaller end of their eggs. The people so highly resented this law that our histories tell us there have been six rebellions raised on that account; wherein one emperor lost his life, and another his crown. These civil commotions were constantly fomented by the monarchs of Blefuscu ; and when they were quelled the exiles always fled for refuge to that empire. It is computed that eleven thousand persons have at several times suffered death rather than submit to break their eggs at the smaller end. Many hundred large volumes have been published upon this controversy ; but the books of the Big-endians have been long forbidden, and the whole party rendered incapable by law of holding employments. During the course of those troubles, the emperors of Blefuscu did frequently expostulate by their ambassadors, accusing us of making a schism in religion by offending against a fundamental doctrine of our great prophet Lustrog, in the fifty-fourth chapter of the blundecral (which is their Alcoran). * This,

---

* The Koran or Bible of the Mohammedans.

however, is thought to be a mere strain upon the text; for the words are these: that all true believers shall break their eggs at the convenient end. And which is the convenient end seems, in my humble opinion, to be left to every man's conscience, or at least in the power of the chief magistrate to determine. Now, the Big-endian exiles have found so much credit in the Emperor of Blefuscu's court, and so much private assistance and encouragement from their party here at home, that a bloody war hath been carried on between the two empires for thirty-six moons with various success; during which time we have lost forty capital ships, and a much greater number of smaller vessels, together with thirty thousand of our best seamen and soldiers; and the damage received by the enemy is reckoned to be somewhat greater than ours. However, they have now equipped a numerous fleet, and are just preparing to make a descent upon us; and his imperial majesty, placing great confidence in your valor and strength, hath commanded me to lay this account of his affairs before you."

I desired the secretary to present my humble duty to the emperor; and to let him know that I thought it would not become me, who was a foreigner, to interfere with parties; but I was ready, with the hazard of my life, to defend his person and state against all invaders.

CHAPTER V.

The Author, by an extraordinary stratagem, prevents an Invasion — A high Title is conferred upon him — Ambassadors arrive from the Emperor of Blefuscu, and sue for Peace.

THE empire of Blefuscu is an island, situated to the northeast of Lilliput, from which it is parted only by a channel of eight hundred yards wide. I had not yet seen it, and upon this notice of an intended invasion I avoided appearing on that side of the coast, for fear of being discovered by some of the enemy's ships, who had received no intelligence of me; all intercourse between the two empires having been strictly forbidden during the war, upon pain of death, and an embargo* laid by our emperor upon all vessels whatsoever. I communicated to his majesty a project I had formed, of seizing the enemy's whole fleet; which, as our scouts assured us, lay at anchor in the harbor, ready to sail with the first fair wind. I consulted the most experi-

* A command or order preventing them from leaving the seaports.

enced seamen upon the depth of the channel, which
they had often plumbed; who told me that in the
middle, at high-water, it was seventy *glumgluffs*
deep, which is about six foot of European measure;
and the rest of it fifty *glumgluffs* at most. I walked
toward the northeast coast, over against Blefuscu,
and, lying down behind a hillock, took out my small
pocket perspective glass, and viewed the enemy's
fleet at anchor, consisting of about fifty men-of-war,
and a great number of transports: I then came
back to my house, and gave order (for which I had
a warrant) for a great quantity of the strongest
cable and bars of iron. The cable was about as
thick as packthread, and the bars of the length and
size of a knitting-needle. I trebled the cable to
make it stronger, and for the same reason I twisted
three of the iron bars together, bending the extremities into a hook. Having thus fixed fifty hooks to
as many cables, I went back to the northeast coast,
and, putting off my coat, shoes, and stockings,
walked into the sea, in my leathern jerkin, about
half an hour before high-water. I waded with
what haste I could, and swam in the middle about
thirty yards, till I felt ground. I arrived at the
fleet in less than half an hour. The enemy was so
frighted when they saw me that they leaped out of
their ships, and swam to shore, where there could

not be fewer than thirty thousand souls : I then took my tackling, and, fastening a hook to the hole at the prow of each, I tied all the cords together at the end. While I was thus employed the enemy discharged several thousand arrows, many of which stuck in my hands and face; and, besides the excessive smart, gave me much disturbance in my work. My greatest apprehension was for mine eyes, which I should have infallibly lost, if I had not suddenly thought of an expedient. I kept, among other little necessaries, a pair of spectacles in a private pocket, which, as I observed before, had escaped the emperor's searchers. These I took out, and fastened as strongly as I could upon my nose, and, thus armed, went on boldly with my work, in spite of the enemy's arrows, many of which struck against the glasses of my spectacles, but without any other effect further than a little to discompose* them. I had now fastened all the hooks, and, taking the knot in my hand, began to pull; but not a ship would stir, for they were all too fast held by their anchors, so that the bold part of my enterprise remained. I therefore let go the cord, and, leaving the hooks fixed to the ships, I resolutely cut with my knife the cables that fastened the anchors, receiving about

---

* Drive out of the proper position.

two hundred shots in my face and hands; then I took up the knotted end of the cables, to which my hooks were tied, and with great ease drew fifty of the enemy's largest men-of war after me.

The Blefuscudians, who had not the least imag. ination of what I intended, were at first confounded with astonishment. They had seen me cut the cables, and thought my design was only to let the ships run adrift, or fall foul on each other; but when they perceived the whole fleet moving in order, and saw me pulling at the end, they set up such a scream of grief and despair that it is almost impossible to describe or conceive. When I had got out of danger I stopped a while to pick out the arrows that stuck in my hands and face; and rubbed on some of the same ointment that was given me at my first arrival, as I have formerly mentioned. I then took off my spectacles, and, waiting about an hour, till the tide was a little fallen, I waded through the middle with my cargo, and arrived safe at the royal port of Lilliput.

The emperor and his whole court stood on the shore, expecting the issue of this great adventure. They saw the ships move forward in a large half-moon, but could not discern me, who was up to my breast in water. When I advanced to the middle of the channel they were yet more in pain, because

I was under water to my neck. The emperor concluded me to be drowned, and that the enemy's fleet was approaching in a hostile manner: but he was soon eased of his fears; for, the channel growing shallower every step I made, I came in a short time within hearing, and, holding up the end of the cable by which the fleet was fastened, I cried in a loud voice, "Long live the most puissant Emperor of Lilliput!" This great prince received me at my landing with all possible encomiums, and created me a *nardac* upon the spot, which is the highest title of honor among them.

His majesty desired I would take some other opportunity of bringing all the rest of his enemy's ships into his ports. And so unmeasurable is the ambition of princes, that he seemed to think of nothing less than reducing the whole empire of Blefuscu into a province, and governing it by a viceroy; of destroying the Big-endian exiles, and compelling that people to break the smaller end of their eggs, by which he would remain the sole monarch of the whole world. But I endeavored to divert him from this design, by many arguments drawn from the topics of policy as well as justice; and I plainly protested that I would never be an instrument of bringing a free and brave people into slavery.

And, when the matter was debated in council, the wisest part of the ministry were of my opinion.

This open, bold declaration of mine was so opposite to the schemes and politics of his imperial majesty that he could never forgive it. He mentioned it in a very artful manner at council, where I was told that some of the wisest appeared at least by their silence, to be of my opinion; but others, who were my secret enemies, could not forbear some expressions which, by a side-wind, reflected on me. And from this time began an intrigue between his majesty and a junto* of ministers, maliciously bent against me, which broke out in less than two months, and had like to have ended in my utter destruction. Of so little weight are the greatest services to princes when put into the balance with a refusal to gratify their passions.

About three weeks after this exploit there arrived a solemn embassy from Blefuscu, with humble offers of a peace; which was soon concluded, upon conditions very advantageous to our emperor, wherewith I shall not trouble the reader. There were six ambassadors, with a train of about five hundred persons: and their entry was very magnificent, suitable to the grandeur of their master, and the

---

* A party combined for a purpose.

importance of their business. When their treaty
was finished, wherein I did them several good offices
by the credit I now had, or at least appeared to
have, at court, their excellencies, who were privately
told how much I had been their friend, made me a
visit in form. They began with many compliments
upon my valor and generosity, invited me to that
kingdom in the emperor their master's name, and
desired me to show them some proofs of my prodigious strength, of which they had heard so many
wonders ; wherein I readily obliged them, but shall
not trouble the reader with the particulars.

When I had for some time entertained their excellencies to their infinite satisfaction and surprise,
I desired they would do me the honor to present
my most humble respects to the emperor their
master, the renown of whose virtues had so justly
filled the whole world with admiration, and whose
royal person I resolved to attend before I returned to
my own country. Accordingly, the next time I had
the honor to see our emperor, I desired his general
license to wait on the Blefuscudian monarch, which
he was pleased to grant me, as I could plainly perceive, in a very cold manner; but could not guess the
reason, till I had a whisper from a certain person,
that Flimnap and Bolgolam had represented my
intercourse with those ambassadors as a mark of

disaffection; from which I am sure my heart was wholly free. And this was the first time I began to conceive some imperfect idea of courts and ministers.

It is to be observed that these ambassadors spoke to me by an interpreter, the languages of both empires differing as much from each other as any two in Europe, and each nation priding itself upon the antiquity, beauty, and energy of their own tongues, with an avowed contempt for that of their neighbor; yet our emperor, standing upon the advantage he had got by the seizure of their fleet, obliged them to deliver their credentials, and make their speech in the Lilliputian tongue. And it must be confessed, that, from the great intercourse of trade and commerce between both realms, from the continual reception of exiles, which is mutual among them, and from the custom, in each empire, to send their young nobility and richer gentry to the other, in order to polish themselves by seeing the world, and understanding men and manners, there are few persons of distinction, or merchants, or seamen, who dwell in the maritime parts, but what can hold conversation in both tongues; as I found some weeks after, when I went to pay my respects to the Emperor of Blefuscu, which, in the midst of great misfortunes, through the malice of

my enemies, proved a very happy adventure to me,
as I shall relate in its proper place.

The reader may remember, that when I signed
those articles upon which I recovered my liberty,
there were some which I disliked, upon account of
their being too servile; neither could anything but
an extreme necessity have forced me to submit.
But being now a *nardac* of the highest rank in that
empire, such offices were looked upon as below my
dignity, and the emperor (to do him justice) never
once mentioned them to me.

CHAPTER VI.

Of the Inhabitants of Lilliput; their Learning, Laws, and
  Customs; the Manner of Educating their Children---The
  Author's way of living in that Country—His Vindication
  of a great Lady.

ALTHOUGH I intend to leave the description of this
empire to a particular treatise, yet, in the meantime,
I am content to gratify the curious reader with
some general ideas. As the common size of the
natives is somewhat under six inches high, so there
is an exact proportion in all other animals, as well
as plants and trees; for instance, the tallest horses
and oxen are between four and five inches in height,
the sheep an inch and half, more or less; their
geese about the bigness of a sparrow, and so the
several gradations, downward, till you come to the
smallest, which, to my sight, were almost invisible;
but nature hath adapted the eyes of the Lilliputians
to all objects proper for their view; they see with
great exactness, but at no great distance. And to
show the sharpness of their sight toward objects

that are near, I have been much pleased observing a
cook pulling* a lark, which was not so large as a
common fly; and a young girl threading an invisible needle with invisible silk. Their tallest trees
are about seven foot high; I mean some of those in
the great royal park, the tops whereof I could but
just reach with my fist clenched. The other
vegetables are in the same proportion; but this I
leave to the reader's imagination.

I shall say but little at present of their learning,
which for many ages hath flourished in all its
branches among them; but their manner of writing
is very peculiar, being neither from the left to the
right, like the Europeans; nor from the right to the
left, like the Arabians; nor from up to down like
the Chinese; but aslant from one corner of the
paper to the other, like ladies in England.†

They bury their dead with their heads directly
downward, because they hold an opinion, that in
eleven thousand moons they are all to rise again;
in which period the earth (which they conceive to
be flat) will turn upside down, and by this means
they shall at their resurrection be found ready

---

* Plucking the feathers from it.

† This is a hit at the careless way some ladies have of
allowing their writing to run slantwise, instead of straight
across the paper.

standing on their feet. The learned among them confess the absurdity of this doctrine; but the practice still continues, in compliance to the vulgar.

There are some laws and customs in this empire very peculiar; and if they were not so directly contrary to those of my own dear country, I should be tempted to say a little in their justification. It is only to be wished that they were as well executed. The first I shall mention relates to informers. All crimes against the state are punished here with the utmost severity; but if the person accused maketh his innocence plainly to appear upon his trial, the accuser is immediately put to an ignominious death; and out of his goods or lands the innocent person is quadruply recompensed for the loss of his time, for the danger he underwent, for the hardship of his imprisonment, and for all the charges he hath been at in making his defense. Or, if that fund be deficient, it is largely supplied by the crown. The emperor does also confer on him some public mark of his favor, and proclamation is made of his innocence through the whole city.

They look upon fraud as a greater crime than theft, and therefore seldom fail to punish it with death; for they allege that care and vigilance, with a very common understanding, may preserve a man's goods from thieves, but honesty has no fence against superior cunning; and, since it is necessary that there should be a perpetual intercourse of buying and selling, and dealing upon credit, where fraud is permitted or connived at, or hath no law to punish it, the honest dealer is always undone, and the knave gets the advantage. I remember when I was once interceding with the king for a criminal who had wronged his master of a great sum of money, which he had received by order and ran away with; and happening to tell his majesty, by way of extenuation, that it was only a breach of trust, the emperor thought it monstrous in me to offer as a defense the greatest aggravation of the crime; and truly I had little to say in return, further than the common answer, that different nations had different customs; for I confess I was heartily ashamed.

Although we usually call reward and punishment the two hinges upon which all government turns, yet I could never observe this maxim to be put in practice by any nation, except that of Lilliput. Whoever can there bring sufficient proof that he hath strictly observed the laws of his country for seventy-three moons hath a claim to certain privileges, according to his quality and condition of life, with a proportionable sum of money, out of a fund appropriated for that use; he likewise acquires the title of *snilpall*, or legal, which is added to his name, but does not descend to his posterity. And these people thought it a prodigious defect of policy among us when I told them that our laws were enforced only by penalties, without any mention of reward. It is upon this account that the image of Justice, in their courts of judicature, is formed with six eyes, two before, as many behind, and on each side one, to signify circumspection; with a bag of gold open in her right hand, and a sword sheathed in her left, to show she is more disposed to reward than to punish.

In choosing persons for all employments they have more regard to good morals than to great abilities; for, since government is necessary to mankind, they believe that the common size of human understandings is fitted to some station or other; and that Providence never intended to make the management of public affairs a mystery to be comprehended only by a few persons of sublime genius, of which there seldom are three born in an age; but they suppose truth, justice, temperance, and the like, to be in every man's power; the practice of which virtues, assisted by experience and a good intention, would qualify any man for the service of his country, except where a course of study is required. But they thought the want of moral virtues was so far from being supplied by superior endowments of the mind that employments could never be put into such dangerous hands as those of persons so qualified; and at least, that the mistakes committed by ignorance, in a virtuous disposition, would never be of such fatal consequence to the public weal, as the practices of a man whose inclinations led him to be corrupt, and had great abilities to manage, and multiply, and defend, his corruptions.

In like manner the disbelief of a Divine Providence renders a man incapable of holding any public station; for, since kings avow themselves to be the deputies of Providence, the Lilliputians think nothing can be more absurd than for a prince to employ such men as disown the authority under which he acts.

In relating these and the following laws, I would only be understood to mean the original institutions, and not the most scandulous corruptions, into which these people are fallen by the degenerate nature of man. For, as to that infamous practice of acquiring great employments by dancing on the ropes, or badges of favor and distinction by leaping over sticks and creeping under them, the reader is to observe, that they were first introduced by the grandfather of the emperor now reigning, and grew to the present height by the gradual increase of party and faction.

Ingratitude is among them a capital crime, as we read it to have been in some other countries; for they reason thus, that whoever makes ill returns to his benefactor must needs be a common enemy to the rest of mankind, from whom he hath received no obligation, and therefore such a man is not fit to live.

Their notions relating to the duties of parents and children differ extremely from ours. Their opinion is, that parents are the last of all others to be trusted with the education of their own children; and therefore they have in every town public nurseries, where all parents, except cottagers and laborers, are obliged to send their infants of both sexes to be reared and educated, when they come to the age of twenty moons, at which time they are supposed to have some rudiments of docility. These schools are of several kinds, suited to different qualities, and to both sexes. They have certain professors, well skilled in preparing children for such a condition of life as befits the rank of their parents, and their own capacities, as well as inclinations. I shall first say something of the male nurseries, and then of the female.

The nurseries for males of noble or eminent

birth are provided with grave and learned professors, and their several deputies. The clothes and food of the children are plain and simple. They are bred up in the principles of honor, justice, courage, modesty, clemency, religion, and love of their country; they are always employed in some business, except in the times of eating and sleeping, which are very short, and two hours for diversions consisting of bodily exercises. They are dressed by men till four years of age, and then are obliged to dress themselves, although their quality* be ever so great; and the women attendants, who are aged proportionably to ours at fifty, perform only the most menial offices. They are never suffered to converse with servants, but go together in smaller or greater numbers to take their diversions, and always in the presence of a professor, or one of his deputies; whereby they avoid those early bad impressions of folly and vice to which our children are subject. Their parents are suffered to see them only twice a year; the visit is to last but an hour; they are allowed to kiss the child at meeting and parting; but a professor, who always stands by on those occasions, will not suffer them to whisper, or use any fondling expressions, or bring any presents of toys, sweetmeats, and the like.

---

* Rank.

The pension from each family for the education and entertainment of a child, upon failure of due payment, is levied by the emperor's officers.

The nurseries for children of ordinary gentlemen, merchants, traders, and handicrafts, are managed proportionably after the same manner; only those designed for trades are put out apprentices at eleven years old; whereas those of persons of quality continue in their nurseries till fifteen, which answers to twenty-one with us : but the confinement is gradually lessened for the last three years.

In the female nurseries the young girls of quality are educated much like the males, only they are dressed by orderly servants of their own sex; but always in the presence of a professor or deputy, till they come to dress themselves, which is at five years old. And if it be found that these nurses ever presume to entertain the girls with frightful or foolish stories, or the common follies practiced by chambermaids among us, they are publicly whipped thrice about the city, imprisoned for a year, and banished for life to the most desolate part of the country. Thus the young ladies there are as much ashamed of being cowards and fools as the men; and despise all personal ornaments, beyond decency and cleanliness : neither did I perceive any difference in their education, made by their difference of sex, only that the exercises of the females were not altogether so robust; and that some rules were given them relating to domestic life, and a smaller compass of learning was enjoined them: for the maxim is, that among people of quality a wife should be always a reasonable and agreeable companion, because she•cannot always be young. When the girls are twelve years-old, which among them is the marriageable age, their parents or guardians take them home, with great expression of gratitude to the professors, and seldom without tears of the young lady and her companions.

In the nurseries of females of the meaner sort the children are instructed in all kinds of works proper for their sex, and their several degrees: those intended for apprentices are dismissed at seven years old, the rest are kept to eleven.

The meaner families, who have children at these nurseries, are obliged, besides their annual pension, which is as low as possible, to return to the steward of the nursery a small monthly share of their gettings, to be a portion for the child; and therefore all parents are limited in their expenses by the law. For the Lilliputians think nothing can be more unjust than for people to bring children into the world, and leave the burden of supporting them on the public. As to persons of quality, they give security to appropriate a certain sum for each child, suitable to their condition; and these funds are always managed with good husbandry, and the most exact justice.

The cottagers and laborers keep their children at home, their business being only to till and cultivate the earth, and therefore their education is of little consequence to the public: but the old and diseased among them are supported by hospitals; for begging is a trade unknown in this kingdom.

And here it may perhaps divert the curious reader to give some account of my domestic,* and my manner of living in this country, during a residence of nine months and thirteen days. Having a head mechanically turned,† and being likewise forced by necessity, I had made for myself a table and chair con venient enough, out of the largest trees in the royal park. Two hundred sempstresses were employed to make me shirts and linen for my bed and table, all of the strongest and coarsest kind they could get; which, however, they were forced to quilt together in several folds, for the thickest was some degrees finer than lawn. Their linen is usually three inches wide, and three foot make a piece. The sempstresses

---

* Household; domestic affairs.

† Having a turn for mechanics; being naturally clever in contriving and making articles by hand.

took my measure as I lay on the ground, one standing at my neck, and another at my mid-leg, with a
strong cord extended, that each held by the end,
while the third measured the length of the cord
with a rule of an inch long. Then they measured
my right thumb, and desired no more; for, by a
mathematical computation, that twice round the
thumb is once round the wrist, and so on to the
neck and the waist, and by the help of my old shirt,
which I displayed on the ground before them for a
pattern, they fitted me exactly. Three hundred
tailors were employed in the same manner to make
me clothes; but they had another contrivance for
taking my measure. I kneeled down, and they
raised a ladder from the ground to my neck; upon
this ladder one of them mounted, and let fall a
plumb-line from my collar to the floor, which just
answered the length of my coat; but my waist and
arms I measured myself. When my clothes were
finished, which was done in my house (for the
largest of theirs would not have been able to hold
them), they looked like the patchwork made by the
ladies in England, only that mine were all of a
color.

I had three hundred cooks to dress my victuals, in
little convenient huts built about my house, where
they and their families lived, and prepared me two

dishes apiece. I took up twenty waiters in my hand, and placed them on the table; an hundred more attended below on the ground, some with dishes of meat, and some with barrels of wine and other liquors slung on their shoulders; all which the waiters above drew up, as I wanted, in a very ingenious manner, by certain cords, as we draw the bucket up a well in Europe. A dish of their meat was a good mouthful, and a barrel of their liquor a reasonable draught. Their mutton yields to ours, but their beef is excellent. I have had a sirloin so large that I have been forced to make three bites of it: but this is rare. My servants were astonished to see me eat it, bones and all, as in our country we do the leg of a lark. Their geese and turkeys I usually eat at a mouthful, and I must confess they far exceed ours. Of their smaller fowl I could take up twenty or thirty at the end of my knife.

One day his imperial majesty, being informed of my way of living, desired that himself and his royal consort, with the young princes of the blood of both sexes, might have the happiness, as he was pleased to call it, of dining with me. They came accordingly, and I placed them upon chairs of state, upon my table just over against me, with their guards about them. Flimnap, the lord high treasurer, attended there likewise with his white staff; and I

observed he often looked on me with a sour countenance, which I would not seem to regard, but eat
more than usual, in honor to my dear country, as
well as to fill the court with admiration. I have
some private reasons to believe that this visit from
his majesty gave Flimnap an opportunity of doing
me ill offices to his master. That minister had
always been my secret enemy, though he outwardly
caressed me more than was usual to the moroseness
of his nature. He represented to the emperor the
low condition of his treasury ; that he was forced to
take up money at great discount; that exchequer
bills would not circulate under nine per cent. below
par; that, in short, I had cost his majesty above a
million and a half of *sprugs* (their greatest gold
coin, about the bigness of a spangle*); and, upon
the whole, that it would be advisable in the emperor
to take the first fair occasion of dismissing me.

I am here obliged to vindicate the reputation of
a excellent lady, who was an innocent sufferer
upon my account. The treasurer took a fancy to
be jealous of his wife, from the malice of some evil
tongues, who informed him that her grace had taken
a violent affection for my person; and the court

---

* One of the small, round scales of shining metal attached
to some dresses worn by actors on the stage.

scandal ran for some time, that she once came privately to my lodging. This I solemnly declare to be a most infamous falsehood, without any grounds, further than that her grace was pleased to treat me with all innocent marks of freedom and friendship. I own she came often to my house, but always publicly, nor ever without three more in the coach, who were usually her sister and young daughter, and some particular acquaintance: but this was common to many other ladies of the court. And I still appeal to my servants round, whether they at any time saw a coach at my door without knowing what persons were in it. On those occasions, when a servant had given me notice, my custom was to go immediately to the door; and, after paying my respects, to take up the coach and two horses very carefully in my hands (for if there were six horses, the postillion always unharnessed four), and place them on a table, where I had fixed a movable rim quite round, of five inches high, to prevent accidents. And I have often had four coaches and horses at once on my table, full of company, while I sate in my chair, leaning my face toward them; and when I was engaged with one set the coachman would gently drive the others round my table. I have passed many an afternoon very agreeably in these conversations. But I defy the treasurer, or his two informers (I will name them, and let them make their best of it), Clustril and Drunlo, to prove that any person ever came to me *incognito*, except the secretary Reldresal, who was sent by express command of his imperial majesty, as I have before related. I should not have dwelt so long upon this particular if it had not been a point wherein the reputation of a great lady is so nearly concerned, to say nothing of my own; though I had then the honor to be a *nardac*, which the treasurer himself is not; for all the world knows he is only a *glumglum*, a title inferior by one degree, as that of a marquis is to a duke in England; although I allow he preceded me* in right of his post. These false informations, which I afterward came to the knowledge of by an accident not proper to mention, made Flimnap, the treasurer, show his lady for some time an ill countenance, and me a worse; and although he was at last undeceived and reconciled to her, yet I lost all credit with him, and found my interest decline very fast with the emperor himself, who was indeed too much governed by that favorite.

---

* Had the right of going before me on occasions of ceremony.

CHAPTER VII.

The Author, being informed of a Design to accuse him of
High-treason, makes his Escape to Blefuscu—His Reception there.

BEFORE I proceed to give an account of my
leaving this kingdom, it may be proper to inform
the reader of a private intrigue which had been for
two months forming against me.

I had been hitherto, all my life, a stranger to
courts, for which I was unqualified by the meanness
of my condition. I had indeed heard and read
enough of the dispositions of great princes and
ministers; but never expected to have found such
terrible effects of them in so remote a country,
governed, as I thought, by very different maxims
from those in Europe.

When I was just preparing to pay my attendance
on the Emperor of Blefuscu, a considerable person
at court (to whom I had been very serviceable at a
time when he lay under the highest displeasure of
his imperial majesty) came to my house very

privately at night, in a close chair,* and, without
sending his name, desired admittance. The chair-
men were dismissed; I put the chair, with his lord-

" You are to know," said he, " that several committees of council have been
lately called."

ship in it, into my coat-pocket; and giving orders
to a trusty servant to say I was indisposed and gone

---

* See note page 22.

to sleep, I fastened the door of my house, placed the chair on the table, according to my usual custom, and sate down by it. After the common salutations were over, observing his lordship's countenance full of concern, and inquiring into the reason, he desired I would hear him with patience, in a matter that highly concerned my honor and my life. His speech was to the following effect, for I took notes of it as soon as he left me :

" You are to know," said he, " that several committees of council have been lately called, in the most private manner, on your account ; and it is but two days since his majesty came to a full resolution.

" You are very sensible that Skyresh Bolgolam (*galbet*, or high admiral) hath been your mortal enemy almost ever since your arrival. His original reasons I know not; but his hatred is much increased since your great success against Blefusco, by which his glory as admiral is obscured. This lord, in conjunction with Flimnap the high treasurer, whose emnity against you is notorious on account of his lady, Limtoc the general, Lalcon the chamberlain, and Balmuff the grand justiciary have prepared articles of impeachment against you, for treason and other capital crimes."

This preface made me so impatient, being conscious of my own merits and innocence, that I was going to interrupt, when he entreated me to be silent, and thus proceeded :

" Out of gratitude for the favors you have done me, I procured information of the whole proceedings, and a copy of the articles ; wherein I ventured my head for your service.

"*Articles of Impeachment against Quinbus Flestrin, the Man-Mountain.*

" *Article* 1.—That the said Quinbus Flestrin, having brought the imperial fleet of Blefusco into the royal port, and being afterward commanded by his imperial majesty to seize all the other ships of the said empire of Blefusco, and reduce that empire to a province, to be governed by a viceroy from hence, and to destroy and put to death, not only all the Big-endian exiles, but likewise all the people of that empire who would not immediately forsake the Big-endian heresy ; he, the said Flestrin, like a false traitor against his most auspicious, serene, imperial majesty, did petition to be excused from the said service, upon pretense of unwillingness to force the consciences, or destroy the liberties and lives, of an innocent people.

" *Article* 2.—That whereas certain ambassadors arrived from the court of Blefuscu, to sue for peace in his majesty's court ; he, the said Flestrin, did, like a false traitor, aid, abet, comfort, and divert the said ambassadors, although he knew them to be servants to a prince who was lately an open enemy to his imperial majesty, and in open war against his said majesty.

"*Article* 3.—That the said Quimbus Flestrin, contrary to the duty of a faithful subject, is now preparing to make a voyage to the court and empire of Blefuscu, for which he hath received only verbal license from his imperial majesty; and, under color of the said license, doth falsely and traitorously intend to take the said voyage, and thereby to aid, comfort, and abet the Emperor of Blefuscu, so late an enemy, and in open war with his imperial majesty aforesaid.

"There are some other articles; but these are the most important, of which I have read you an abstract.

"In the several debates upon this impeachment, it must be confessed that his majesty gave many marks of his great lenity; often urging the services you had done him, and endeavoring to extenuate your crimes. The treasurer and admiral insisted that you should be put to the most painful and ignominious death, by setting fire to your house at night; and the general was to attend with twenty thousand men, armed with poisoned arrows, to shoot you on the face and hands. Some of your servants were to have private orders to strew a poisonous juice on your shirts, which would soon make you tear your own flesh, and die in the utmost torture. The general came into the same opinion; so that for a long time there was a majority against you; but his majesty resolving, if possible, to spare your life, at last brought off the chamberlain.

" Upon this incident, Reldresal, principal secretary for private affairs, who always approved himself your true friend, was commanded by the emperor to deliver his opinion, which he accordingly did; and therein justified the good thoughts you have of him. He allowed your crimes to be great, but that still there was room for mercy, the most commendable virtue in a prince, and for which his majesty was so justly celebrated. He said, the friendship between you and him was so well known to the world that perhaps the most honorable board might think him partial; however, in obedience to the command he had received, he would freely offer his sentiments. That if his majesty, in consideration of your services, and pursuant to his own merciful disposition, would please to spare your life, and only give order to put out both your eyes, he humbly conceived that, by this expedient, justice might in some measure be satisfied, and all the world would applaud the lenity of the emperor, as well as the fair and generous proceedings of those who had the honor to be his counselors. That the loss of your eyes would be no impediment to your bodily strength, by which you might still be useful to his majesty; that blindness is an addition to courage, by concealing dangers from us; that the fear you had for your eyes was the greatest difficulty in bringing over the enemy's fleet; and it would be sufficient for you to see by the eyes of the ministers, since the greatest princes do no more.

" This proposal was received with the utmost disapprobation by the whole board. Bolgolam, the admiral, could not preserve his temper; but, rising in a fury, said he wondered how the secretary durst presume to give his opinion for preserving the life of a traitor; that the services you had performed were, by all true reasons of state, the great aggravation of your crimes; that the same strength, which enabled you to bring over the enemy's fleet, might serve, upon the first discontent, to carry it back; that he had good reasons to think you were a Big-endian in your heart; and, as treason begins in the heart, before it appears in overt acts, so he accused you as a traitor on that account, and therefore insisted you should be put to death.

" The treasurer was of the same opinion. He

showed to what straits his majesty's revenue was reduced by the charge of maintaining you, which would soon grow insupportable; that the secretary's expedient of putting out your eyes was so far from being a remedy against this evil that it would probably increase it, as is manifest from the common practice of blinding some kind of fowls, after which they fed the faster, and grew sooner fat; that his sacred majesty and the council, who are your judges, were in their own consciences fully convinced of your guilt, which was a sufficient argument to condemn you to death, without the formal proofs required by the strict letter of the law.

"But his imperial majesty, fully determined against capital punishment, was graciously pleased to say, that since the council thought the loss of your eyes too easy a censure,* some other may be inflicted hereafter. And your friend the secretary, humbly desiring to be heard again, in answer to what the treasurer had objected, concerning the great charge his majesty was at in maintaining you, said, that his excellency, who had the sole disposal of the emperor's revenue, might easily provide against that evil, by gradually lessening your estab-

---

* Sentence passed by a court or judge. The word now always means reproof or fault-finding.

lishment; by which, for want of sufficient food, you would grow weak and faint, and lose your appetite, and consequently decay and consume in a few months. Neither would the stench of your carcass be then so dangerous, when it should become more than half-diminished; and immediately upon your death, five or six thousand of his majesty's subjects might, in two or three days, cut your flesh from your bones, take it away by cartloads, and bury it in distant parts, to prevent infection, leaving the skeleton as a monument of admiration to posterity.

" Thus, by the great friendship of the secretary, the whole affair was compromised. It was strictly enjoined that the project of starving you by degrees should be kept a secret; but the sentence of putting out your eyes was entered on the books; none dissenting except Bolgolam, the admiral, who, being a creature of the empress, was perpetually instigated by her majesty to insist upon your death.

"In three days your friend the secretary will be directed to come to your house, and read before you the articles of impeachment; and then to signify the great lenity and favor of his majesty and council, whereby you are only condemned to the loss of your eyes, which his majesty doth not question you will gratefully and humbly submit to; and twenty of his majesty's surgeons will attend, in order to see the operation well performed, by discharging very sharp-pointed arrows into the balls of your eyes, as you lie on the ground.

" I leave to your prudence what measures you will take; and, to avoid suspicion, I must immediately return in as private a manner as I came."

His lordship did so ; and I remained alone, under many doubts and perplexities of mind.

It was a custom introduced by this prince and his ministry—very different, as I have been assured, from the practices of former times—that after the court had decreed any cruel execution, either to gratify the monarch's resentment, or the malice of a favorite, the emperor made a speech to his whole council, expressing his great lenity and tenderness, as qualities known and confessed by all the world. This speech was immediately published through the kingdom; nor did anything terrify the people so much as those encomiums on his majesty's mercy ; because it was observed that the more these praises were enlarged and insisted on, the more inhuman was the punishment, and the sufferer more innocent. And, as to myself, I must confess, having never been designed for a courtier, either by my birth or education, I was so ill a judge of things that I could not discover the lenity and favor of this sentence, but conceived it (perhaps erroneously) rather to be rigorous than gentle. I sometimes thought of standing my trial; for, although I could not deny the facts alleged in the several articles, yet I hoped they would admit of some extenuations. But having in my life perused many state trials, which I ever observed to terminate as the judges thought fit to direct, I durst not rely on so dangerous a decision, in so critical a juncture, and against such powerful enemies. Once I was strongly bent upon resistance; for while I had liberty, the whole strength of that empire could hardly subdue me, and I might easily with stones pelt the metropolis to pieces; but I soon rejected that project with horror, by remembering the oath I had made to the emperor, the favors I received from him, and the high title of *nardac* he conferred upon me. Neither had I so soon learned the gratitude of courtiers, to persuade myself that his majesty's present severities acquitted me of all past obligations.

At last I fixed upon a resolution, for which it is probable I may incur some censure, and not unjustly; for I confess I owe the preserving mine eyes, and consequently my liberty, to my own great rashness and want of experience; because, if I had then known the nature of princes and ministers, which I have since observed in many other courts, and their methods of treating criminals less obnoxious than myself, I should, with great alacrity and readiness, have submitted to so easy a punishment. But, hurried on by the precipitancy of youth, and having his imperial majesty's license to pay my attendance upon the Emperor of Blefuscu, I took this opportunity, before the three days were elapsed, to send a letter to my friend the secretary, signifying my resolution of setting out that morning for Blefuscu, pursuant to the leave I had got; and, without waiting for an answer, I went to that side of the island where our fleet lay. I seized a large man-of-war, tied a cable to the prow, and, lifting up the anchors, I stripped myself, put my clothes (together with my coverlet, which I brought under my arm) into the vessel, and, drawing it after me, between wading and swimming, arrived at the royal port of Blefuscu, where the people had long expected me : they lent me two guides to direct me to the capital city, which is of the same name. I held them in my hands till I came within two hundred yards of the gate, and desired them to signify my arrival to one of the secretaries, and let him know I there waited his majesty's command. I had an answer in about an hour, that his majesty, attended by the royal family, and great officers of the court, was coming out to receive me. I advanced a hundred yards. The emperor and his train alighted from their horses; the empress and ladies from their coaches; and I did not perceive they were in any fright or concern. I lay on the ground to kiss his majesty's and the empress' hand. I told his majesty that I was come, according to my promise, and with the license of the emperor my master, to have the honor of seeing so mighty a monarch, and to offer him any service in my power, consistent with my duty to my own prince; not mentioning a word of my disgrace, because I had hitherto no regular information of it, and might suppose myself wholly ignorant of any such design; neither could I reasonably conceive that the emperor would discover the secret while I was out of his power; wherein, however, it soon appeared I was deceived.

I shall not trouble the reader with the particular account of my reception at this court, which was suitable to the generosity of so great a prince; nor of the difficulties I was in for want of a house and bed, being forced to lie on the ground, wrapped up in my coverlet.

CHAPTER VIII.

The Author, by a lucky accident, finds means to leave Blefusco; and after some difficulties returns safe to his native Country.

THREE days after my arrival, walking out of curiosity to the northeast coast of the island, I observed, about half a league off in the sea, somewhat that looked like a boat overturned. I pulled off my shoes and stockings, and, wading two or three hundred yards, I found the object to approach nearer by force of the tide; and then plainly saw it to be a real boat, which I supposed might by some tempest have been driven from a ship: whereupon I returned immediately toward the city, and desired his imperial majesty to lend me twenty of the tallest vessels he had left, after the loss of his fleet, and three thousand seamen under the command of the vice-admiral. This fleet sailed round, while I went back the shortest way to the coast, where I first discovered the boat. I found the tide had driven it still nearer. The seamen were all provided with cordage, which I had beforehand twisted to a suffi-

cient strength. When the ships came up, I stripped
myself, and waded till I came within an hundred
yards of the boat, after which I was forced to swim
till I got up to it. The seamen threw me the end
of the cord, which I fastened to a hole in the fore-
part of the boat, and the other end to a man-of-war ;
but I found all my labor to little purpose ; for,
being out of my depth, I was not able to work. In
this necessity, I was forced to swim behind, and
push the boat forward, as often as I could, with one
of my hands; and the tide favoring me, I advanced
so far that I could just hold up my chin and feel the
ground. I rested two or three minutes, and then
gave the boat another shove, and so on, till the sea
was no higher than my armpits, and now, the most
laborious part being over, I took out my other
cables, which were stowed in one of the ships, and
fastened them first to the boat, and then to nine of
the vessels which attended me; the wind being
favorable, the seamen towed and I shoved, till we
arrived within forty yards of the shore ; and waiting till the tide was out, I got dry to the boat, and,
by the assistance of two thousand men, with ropes
and engines,* I made a shift to turn it on its
bottom, and found it was but little damaged.

---

* Such as pulleys, capstans, levers, or other mechanical
contrivances.

I shall not trouble the reader with the difficulties I was under, by the help of certain paddles, which cost me ten days making, to get my boat to the royal port of Blefuscu, where a mighty concourse of

'By the assistance of two thousand men I turned the boat on its bottom."

people appeared upon my arrival, full of wonder at the sight of so prodigious a vessel. I told the emperor that my good fortune had thrown this boat in my way to carry me to some place from whence I might return into my native country ; and begged his majesty's orders for getting materials to fit it up, together with his license to depart ; which, after some kind expostulations, he was pleased to grant. I did very much wonder, in all this time, not to have heard of any express* relating to me from our emperor to the court of Blefuscu. But I was afterward given privately to understand that his imperial majesty, never imagining I had the least notice of his designs, believed I was only gone to Blefuscu in performance of my promise, according to the license he had given me, which was well known at our court, and would return in a few days, when that ceremony was ended. But he was at last in pain at my long absence; and, after consulting with the treasurer and the rest of that cabal, † a person of quality was dispatched with the copy of the articles against me. The envoy had instructions to represent to the monarch of Blefuscu the great lenity of his master, who was content to punish me no further than with the loss of mine eyes; that I had fled from justice; and if I did not return in two hours I should be deprived of my title of *nardac*, and declared a traitor. The envoy further added, that, in order to maintain the peace and amity between both empires, his master expected that his

---

* Message or messenger.

† Persons connected with a royal court who engage in some secret scheme or design.

brother of Blefuscu would give orders to have me
sent back to Lilliput, bound hand and foot, to be
punished as a traitor.

The Emperor of Blefuscu, having taken three
days to consult, returned an answer consisting of
many civilities and excuses. He said that, as for
sending me bound, his brother knew it was impossible; that, although I had deprived him of his fleet,
yet he owed great obligations to me for many good
offices I had done him in making the peace. That,
however, both their majesties would soon be made
easy; for I had found a prodigious vessel on the
shore, able to carry me on the sea, which he had
given order to fit up, with my own assistance and
direction; and he hoped, in a few weeks, both empires would be freed from so insupportable an
encumbrance.

With this answer the envoy returned to Lilliput;
and the monarch of Blefuscu related to me all that
had passed; offering me, at the same time (but
under the strictest confidence), his gracious protection, if I would continue in his service: wherein,
although I believed him sincere, yet I resolved never
more to put any confidence in princes or ministers,
where I could possibly avoid it; and, therefore,
with all due acknowledgments for his favorable
intentions, I humbly begged to be excused. I told

him that, since fortune, whether good or evil, had thrown a vessel in my way, I was resolved to venture myself on the ocean, rather than be an occasion of difference between two such mighty monarchs. Neither did I find the emperor at all displeased; and I discovered, by a certain accident, that he was very glad of my resolution, and so were most of his ministers.

These considerations moved me to hasten my departure somewhat sooner than I intended; to which the court, impatient to have me gone, very readily contributed. Five hundred workmen were employed to make two sails to my boat, according to my directions, by quilting thirteen folds of their strongest linen together. I was at the pains of making ropes and cables by twisting ten, twenty or thirty of the thickest and strongest of theirs. A great stone that I happened to find, after a long search, by the seashore, served me for an anchor. I had the tallow of three hundred cows for greasing my boat, and other uses. I was at incredible pains in cutting down some of the largest timber-trees for oars and masts; wherein I was, however, much assisted by his majesty's ship-carpenters, who helped me in smoothing them after I had done the rough work.

In about a month, when all was prepared, I sent

to receive his majesty's commands, and to take my leave. The emperor and royal family came out of the palace: I lay down on my face to kiss his hand, which he very graciously gave me: so did the empress and young princes of the blood. His majesty presented me with fifty purses of two hundred *sprugs* apiece, together with his picture at full length, which I put immediately into one of my gloves, to keep it from being hurt. The ceremonies at my departure were too many to trouble the reader with at this time.

I stored the boat with the carcasses of an hundred oxen and three hundred sheep, with bread and drink proportionable, and as much meat ready dressed as four hundred cooks could provide. I took with me six cows and two bulls alive, with as many ewes and rams, intending to carry them into my own country, and propagate the breed. And, to feed them on board, I had a good bundle of hay and a bag of corn. I would gladly have taken a dozen of the natives, but this was a thing which the emperor would by no means permit; and, besides a diligent search into my pockets, his majesty engaged my honor not to carry away any of his subjects, although with their own consent and desire.

Having thus prepared all things as well as I was able, I set sail on the 24th day of September, 1701, at six in the morning; and when I had gone about four leagues to the northward, the wind being at southeast, at six in the evening I descried a small island, about half a league to the northwest. I advanced forward, and cast anchor on the lee-side* of the island, which seemed to be uninhabited. I then took some refreshment, and went to my rest. I slept well, and I conjecture at least six hours, for I found the day broke in two hours after I awaked. It was a clear night. I eat my breakfast before the sun was up; and, heaving anchor, the wind being favorable, I steered the same course that I had done the day before, wherein I was directed by my pocket-compass. My intention was to reach, if possible, one of those islands which I had reason to believe lay to the northeast of Van Diemen's Land.† I discovered nothing all that day; but upon the next, about three in the afternoon, when I had, by my computation, made twenty-four leagues from Blefuscu, I descried a sail steering to the southeast; my course was due east. I hailed her, but could get no answer; yet I found I gained upon her, for the wind slackened. I made all the sail I could, and in half an hour she spied me, then hung out her

---

* Side sheltered from the wind.

† Australia is a short distance to the north of Tasmania or Van Diemen's Land. There are no islands to the northeast for a long distance.

ancient,* and discharged a gun. It is not easy to express the joy I was in, upon the unexpected hope of once more seeing my beloved country, and the dear pledges I left in it. The ship slackened her sails, and I came up with her between five and six in the evening, September 26th; but my heart leaped within me to see her English colors. I put my cows and sheep into my coat-pockets, and got on board with all my little cargo of provisions. The vessel was an English merchantman, returning from Japan by the North and South Seas; the captain, Mr. John Biddel of Deptford, a very civil man and an excellent sailor. We were now in the latitude of thirty degrees south; there were about fifty men in the ship; and here I met an old comrade of mine, one Peter Williams, who gave me a good character to the captain. This gentleman treated me with kindness, and desired I would let him know what place I came from last, and whither I was bound; which I did in few words, but he thought I was raving, and that the dangers I underwent had disturbed my head; whereupon I took my black cattle and sheep out of my pocket, which, after great astonishment, clearly convinced him of my veracity. I then showed him the gold given me by the Emperor of Blefuscu, together with his majesty's picture

---

* Ensign or flag.

at full length, and some other rarities of that country. I gave him two purses of two hundred *sprugs* each, and promised, when we arrived in Eng land, to make him a present of a cow and a sheep.

I shall not trouble the reader with a particular account of this voyage, which was very prosperous for the most part. We arrived in the Downs on the 13th of April, 1702. I had only one misfortune, that the rats on board carried away one of my sheep; I found her bones in a hole, picked clean from the flesh. The rest of my cattle I got safe on shore, and set them a-grazing in a bowling-green at Green-wich, where the fineness of the grass made them feed very heartily, though I had always feared the contrary; neither could I possibly have preserved them in so long a voyage, if the captain had not allowed me some of his best biscuit, which rubbed to powder, and mingled with water, was their constant food. The short time I continued in England, I made a considerable profit by showing my cattle to many persons of quality and others; and before I began my second voyage, I sold them for six hundred pounds. Since my last return I find the breed is considerably increased, especially the sheep, which I hope will prove much to the advantage of the woollen manufacture, by the fineness of the fleeces.

I stayed but two months with my wife and family; for my insatiable desire of seeing foreign countries would suffer me to continue no longer. I left fifteen hundred pounds with my wife, and fixed her in a good house at Redriff.* My remaining stock I carried with me, part in money and part in goods, in hopes to improve my fortunes. My eldest uncle John had left me an estate in land, near Epping, of about thirty pounds a-year; and I had a long lease of the Black Bull in Fetter Lane, which yielded me as much more; so that I was not in any danger of leaving my family upon the parish. My son Johnny, named so after his uncle, was at the grammar-school, and a towardly child. My daughter Betty (who is now well married, and has children) was then at her needlework. I took leave of my wife and boy and girl, with tears on both sides, and went on board the Adventure, a merchant ship of three hundred tons, bound for Surat,† Captain John Nicholas, of Liverpool, commander. But my account of this voyage must be referred to the second part of my travels.

---

* That is, Rotherhithe, now a part of London, on the south bank of the Thames.

† At one time the chief commercial city in India, about 160 miles north of Bombay.

PART II.

A VOYAGE TO BROBDINGNAG.

PART II.

A VOYAGE TO BROBDINGNAG.

CHAPTER I.

A great Storm; the Long-boat sent to fetch water, the Author goes with it to discover the Country—He is left on shore, is seized by one of the natives, and carried to a Farmer's House—His reception there, with several Accidents that happened there—A Description of the Inhabitants.

HAVING been condemned, by nature and fortune, to an active and restless life, in two months after my return I again left my native country, and took shipping in the Downs, on the 20th day of June, 1702, in the Adventure, Captain John Nicholas, a Cornishman, commander, bound for Surat. We had a very prosperous gale till we arrived at the Cape of

Good Hope, where we landed for fresh water; but discovering a leak, we unshipped our goods and wintered there; for the captain falling sick of an ague, we could not leave the Cape till the end of March. We then set sail, and had a good voyage till we passed the Straits of Madagascar;* but having got northward of that island, and to about five degrees south latitude, the winds, which in those seas are observed to blow a constant equal gale between the north and west, from the beginning of December to the beginning of May, on the 19th of April began to blow with much greater violence, and more westerly than usual, continuing so for twenty days together; during which time we were driven a little to the east of the Molucca Islands,† and about three degrees northward of the line, as our captain found by an observation he took the 2d of May, at which time the wind ceased, and it was a perfect calm, whereat I was not a little rejoiced. But he, being a man well experienced in the navigation of those seas, bid us all prepare against a storm, which accordingly happened the day following; for a

---

* Mozambique Channel.

† How they could get there without encountering Sumatra, Java, Borneo, Celebes, or other islands of those seas, is a mystery. Celebes is a little to the west of the Moluccas; the line (or equator) passes through this group.

southern wind, called the southern monsoon,* began to set in, and soon it was a very fierce storm.

During this storm, which was followed by a strong wind west-southwest, we were carried, by my computation, about five hundred leagues to the east, so that the oldest sailor on board could not tell in what part of the world we were. Our provisions held out well, our ship was staunch, and our crew all in good health ; but we lay in the utmost distress for water. We thought it best to hold on the same course, rather than turn more northerly, which might have brought us to the northwest parts of Great Tartary,† and into the Frozen Sea.

On the 16th day of June, 1703, a boy on the top-mast discovered land.‡ On the 17th we came in full view of a great island, or continent (for we knew not whether), on the south side whereof was a small neck of land jutting out into the sea, and a creek too shallow to hold a ship of above one hundred tons. We cast anchor within a league of this creek, and our captain sent a dozen of his men well armed

* The moonsoons are winds of the Indian Ocean and Eastern seas that blow in the same direction for half the year and in the opposite direction the other half.

† Mongolia, Manchuria, etc.

‡ What and where this land was is explained afterward.

in the long-boat, with vessels for water, if any could be found. I desired his leave to go with them, that I might see the country, and make what discoveries I could. When we came to land we saw no river or spring, nor any sign of inhabitants. Our men therefore wandered on the shore to find out some fresh water near the sea, and I walked alone about a mile on the other side, where I observed the country all barren and rocky. I now began to be weary, and, seeing nothing to entertain my curios-ity, I returned gently down toward the creek; and the sea being full in my view, I saw our men already got into the boat, and rowing for life to the ship. I was going to halloo after them, although it had been to little purpose, when I observed a huge creature walking after them in the sea, as fast as he could; he waded not much deeper than his knees, and took prodigious strides; but our men had got the start of him half a league, and the sea there-abouts being full of sharp pointed rocks, the monster was not able to overtake the boat. This I was afterward told, for I durst not stay to see the issue of that adventure; but ran as fast as I could the way I first went, and then climbed up a steep hill, which gave me some prospect of the country. I found it fully cultivated; but that which first sur-prised me was the length of the grass, which in those grounds that seemed to be kept for hay was above twenty foot high.

I fell into a highroad, for so I took it to be, though it served to the inhabitants only as a foot-path through a field of barley. Here I walked on for some time, but could see little on either side, it being now near harvest, and the corn rising at least forty foot. I was an hour walking to the end of this field, which was fenced in with a hedge of at least one hundred and twenty foot high, and the trees so lofty that I could make no computation of their altitude. There was a stile to pass from this field into the next. It had four steps, and a stone to cross over when you came to the uppermost. It was impossible for me to climb this stile, because every step was six foot high, and the upper stone above twenty. I was endeavoring to find some gap in the hedge, when I discovered one of the inhabit-ants in the next field, advancing toward the stile, of the same size with him whom I saw in the sea pursuing our boat. He appeared as tall as an ordinary spire steeple, and took about ten yards at every stride, as near as I could guess. I was struck with the utmost fear and astonishment, and ran to hide myself in the corn, from whence I saw him at the top of the stile, looking back into the next field on the right hand, and heard him call in a voice many

degrees louder than a speaking-trumpet; but the
noise was so high in the air that at first I certainly
thought it was thunder. Whereupon seven mon-
sters, like himself,* came toward him with reaping
hooks in their hands, each hook about the largeness
of six scythes. These people were not so well clad
as the first, whose servants or laborers they seemed
to be; for, upon some words he spoke, they went to
reap the corn in the field where I lay. I kept from
them at as great a distance as I could, but was
forced to move with extreme difficulty, for the
stalks of the corn were sometimes not above a foot
distant, so that I could hardly squeeze my body betwixt them. However, I made a shift to go forward
till I came to a part of the field where the corn had
been laid by the rain and wind. Here it was impossible for me to advance a step; for the stalks
were so interwoven that I could not creep through,
and the beards of the fallen ears so strong and
pointed that they pierced through my clothes into
my flesh. At the same time I heard the reapers
not above an hundred yards behind me. Being quite
dispirited with toil, and wholly overcome by grief

---

* The Brobdingnagians are represented to be about as much
larger than ordinary human beings as the Lilliputians are
smaller (about twelve times), all their belongings being of a
corresponding magnitude.

and despair, I lay down between two ridges, and heartily wished I might there end my days. I bemoaned my desolate widow and fatherless children. I lamented my own folly and willfulness in attempting a second voyage, against the advice of all my friends and relations. In this terrible agitation of mind I could not forbear thinking of Lilliput, whose inhabitants looked upon me as the greatest prodigy that ever appeared in the world; where I was able to draw an imperial fleet in my hand, and perform those other actions which will be recorded forever in the chronicles of that empire, while posterity shall hardly believe them, although attested by millions. I reflected what a mortification it must prove to me to appear as inconsiderable in this nation as one single Lilliputian would be among us. But this I conceived was to be the least of my misfortunes; for, as human creatures are observed to be more savage and cruel in proportion to their bulk, what could I expect but to be a morsel in the mouth of the first among these enormous barbarians that should happen to seize me? Undoubtedly philosophers are in the right when they tell us that nothing is great or little otherwise than by comparison. It might have pleased fortune to let the Lilliputians find some nation, where the people were as diminutive with respect to them as they were to me. And who knows but that even this prodigious race of mortals might be equally overmatched in some distant part of the world, whereof we have yet no discovery.

Scared and confounded as I was, I could not forbear going on with these reflections, when one of the reapers, approaching within ten yards of the ridge where I lay, made me apprehend that with the next step I should be squashed to death under his foot, or cut in two with his reaping-hook. And therefore when he was again about to move, I screamed as loud as fear could make me; whereupon the huge creature trod short, and, looking round about under him for some time, at last espied me as I lay on the ground. He considered awhile, with the caution of one who endeavors to lay hold on a small dangerous animal in such a manner that it may not be able either to scratch or to bite him, as I myself have sometimes done with a weasel in England. At length he ventured to take me up behind, by the middle, between his forefinger and thumb, and brought me within three yards of his eyes, that he might behold my shape more perfectly. I guessed his meaning, and my good fortune gave me so much presence of mind that I resolved not to struggle in the least as he held me in the air above sixty foot from the ground, although he grievously pinched my sides, for fear I should slip through his fingers. All I ventured was to raise mine eyes toward the sun, and place my hands together in a supplicating posture, and to speak some words in an humble, melancholy tone, suitable to the condition I then was in; for I apprehended every moment that he would dash me against the ground, as we usually do any little hateful animal which we have a mind to destroy. But my good star would have it that he appeared pleased with my voice and gestures, and began to look upon me as a curiosity, much wondering to hear me pronounce articulate words, although he could not understand them. In the meantime I was not able to forbear groaning and shedding tears, and turning my head toward my sides; letting him know as well as I could how cruelly I was hurt by the pressure of his thumb and finger. He seemed to apprehend my meaning; for, lifting up the lappet* of his coat, he put me gently into it, and immediately ran along with me to his master, who was a substantial farmer, and the same person I had first seen in the field.

The farmer having (as I supposed by their talk) received such an account of me as his servant could

---

* Here and also below this word seems to be used as equivalent to skirt.

give him, took a piece of a small straw, about the
size of a walking-staff, and therewith lifted up the

"I pulled off my hat, and made a low bow toward the farmer."

lappets of my coat; which, it seems, he thought to
be some kind of covering that nature had given me.
He blew my hairs aside to take a better view of my

face. He called his hinds about him, and asked them, as I afterward learned, whether they had ever seen in the fields any little creature that resembled me? He then placed me softly on the ground upon all four, but I got immediately up, and walked slowly backward and forward, to let those people see I had no intent to run away. They all sate down in a circle about me, the better to observe my motions. I pulled off my hat, and made a low bow toward the farmer. I fell on my knees, and lifted up my hands and eyes, and spoke several words as loud as I could; I took a purse of gold out of my pocket, and humbly presented it to him. He received it on the palm of his hand, then applied it close to his eye to see what it was, and afterward turned it several times with the point of a pin (which he took out of his sleeve), but could make nothing of it. Whereupon I made a sign that he should place his hand on the ground. I then took the purse, and opening it, poured all the gold into his palm. There were six Spanish pieces of four pistoles* each, besides twenty or thirty smaller coins. I saw him wet the tip of his little finger upon his tongue, and take up one of my largest pieces, and then another; but he seemed to be wholly ignorant what they were. He made me a

---

* A pistole is equivalent to about 16s. sterling.

sign to put them again into my purse, and the purse again into my pocket, which, after offering to him several times, I thought it best to do.

The farmer, by this time, was convinced I must be a rational creature. He spoke often to me; but the sound of his voice pierced my ears like that of a water-mill, yet his words were articulate enough. I answered as loud as I could in several languages, and he often laid his ear within two yards of me; but all in vain, for we were wholly unintelligible to each other. He then sent his servants to their work, and taking his handkerchief out of his pocket, he doubled, and spread it on his left hand, which he placed flat on the ground, with the palm upward, making me a sign to step into it, as I could easily do, for it was not above a foot in thickness. I thought it my part to obey; and for fear of falling laid myself at full length upon the handkerchief, with the remainder of which he lapped me up to the head for further security, and in this manner carried me home to his house. There he called his wife, and showed me to her; but she screamed and ran back, as women in England do at the sight of a toad or a spider. However, when she had awhile seen my behavior, and how well I observed the signs her husband made, she was soon reconciled, and by degrees grew extremely tender of me.

It was about twelve at noon, and a servant brought in dinner. It was only one substantial dish of meat (fit for the plain condition of an husbandman), in a dish of about twenty-four foot diameter. The company were, the farmer and his wife, three children, and an old grandmother. When they were sat down, the farmer placed me at some distance from him on the table, which was thirty foot high from the floor. I was in a terrible fright, and kept as far as I could from the edge, for fear of falling. The wife minced a bit of meat, then crumbled some bread on a trencher, and placed it before me. I made her a low bow, took out my knife and fork, and fell to eat, which gave them exceeding delight. The mistress sent her maid for a small dram-cup, which held about two gallons, and filled it with drink; I took up the vessel with much difficulty in both hands, and in a most respectful manner drank to her ladyship's health, expressing the words as loud as I could in English, which made the company laugh so heartily, that I was almost deafened with the noise. This liquor tasted like a small cider, and was not unpleasant. Then the master made me a sign to come to his trencher side; but as I walked on the table, being in great surprise all the time, as the indulgent reader will easily conceive and excuse, I happened to stumble against a crust, and fell flat on my face, but received no hurt. I got up immediately, and observing the good people to be in much concern, I took my hat (which I held under my arm out of good manners), and waving it over my head, made three huzzas, to show I had got no mischief by my fall. But advancing forward toward my master (as I shall henceforth call him), his youngest son, who sate next him, an arch boy of about ten years old, took me up by the legs, and held me so high in the air that I trembled every limb; but his father snatched me from him, and at the same time gave him such a box on the left ear as would have felled an European troop of horse to the earth, ordering him to be taken from the table. But, being afraid the boy might owe me a spite, and well remembering how mischievous all children among us naturally are to sparrows, rabbits, young kittens, and puppy-dogs, I fell on my knees, and, pointing to the boy, made my master to understand, as well as I could, that I desired his son might be pardoned. The father complied, and the lad took his seat again, whereupon I went to him, and kissed his hand, which my master took, and made him stroke me gently with it.

In the midst of dinner my mistress' favorite cat leaped into her lap. I heard a noise behind me like that of a dozen stocking-weavers at work; and turning my head I found it proceeded from the purring of this animal, who seemed to be three times larger than an ox, as I computed by the view of her head and one of her paws, while her mistress was feeding and stroking her. The fierceness of this creature's countenance altogether discomposed me though I stood at the further end of the table, above fifty foot off; and although my mistress held her fast, for fear she might give a spring, and seize me in her talons. But it happened there was no danger; for the cat took not the least notice of me when my master placed me within three yards of her. And, as I have been always told, and found true by experience in my travels, that flying or discovering* fear before a fierce animal is a certain way to make it pursue or attack you, so I resolved, in this dangerous juncture, to show no manner of concern. I walked with intrepidity five or six times before the very head of the cat, and came within half a yard of her; whereupon she drew herself back, as if she were more afraid of me. I had less apprehension concerning the dogs, whereof three or four came into the room as it is usual in farmers' houses; one of which was a mastiff, equal in bulk to four elephants, and a greyhound, somewhat taller than the mastiff, but not so large.

---

* Showing; letting it be seen.

When dinner was almost done the nurse came in with a child of a year old in her arms, who immediately spied me, and began a squall that you might have heard from London Bridge to Chelsea, after the usual oratory of infants, to get me for a plaything. The mother, out of pure indulgence, took me up, and put me toward the child, who presently seized me by the middle, and got my head in his mouth, where I roared so loud that the urchin was frighted, and let me drop, and I should infallibly have broke my neck, if the mother had not held her apron under me. The nurse, to quiet her babe, made use of a rattle, which was a kind of hollow vessel filled with great stones, and fastened by a cable to the child's waist; but all in vain, so that she was forced to apply the last remedy by giving it suck. I must confess no object ever disgusted me so much as the sight of her monstrous breast, which I cannot tell what to compare with, so as to give the curious reader an idea of its bulk, shape, and color.

This made me reflect upon the fair skins of our English ladies, who appear so beautiful to us, only because they are of our own size, and their defects not to be seen but through a magnifying glass; where we find by experiment that the smoothest and whitest skins look rough, and coarse, and ill-colored.

I remember when I was at Lilliput the complexions of those diminutive people appeared to me the fairest in the world; and talking upon this subject with a person of learning there, who was an intimate friend of mine, he said that my face appeared much fairer and smoother when he looked on me from the ground than it did upon a nearer view, when I took him up in my hand, and brought him close, which he confessed was at first a very shocking sight. He said he could discover great holes in my skin; that the stumps of my beard were ten times stronger than the bristles of a boar, and my complexion made up of several colors altogether disagreeable: although I must beg leave to say for myself that I am as fair as most of my sex and country, and very little sunburnt by all my travels.

On the other side, discoursing of the ladies in that emperor's court, he used to tell me one had freckles, another too wide a mouth, a third too large a nose; nothing of which I was able to distinguish. I confess this reflection was obvious enough; which, however, I could not forbear, lest the reader might think those vast creatures were actually deformed: for I must do them the justice to say they are a comely race of people; and particularly the features of my master's countenance, although he were but a farmer, when I beheld him from the height of sixty foot, appeared very well-proportioned.

When dinner was done my master went out to his laborers, and, as I could discover by his voice and gesture, gave his wife a strict charge to take care of me. I was very much tired, and disposed to sleep, which my mistress perceiving she put me on her own bed, and covered me with a clean white hand-kerchief, but larger and coarser than the mainsail of a man-of-war.

I slept about two hours, and dreamed I was at home with my wife and children, which aggravated my sorrows when I awaked and found myself alone in a vast room, between two and three hundred foot wide, and above two hundred high, lying in a bed twenty yards wide. My mistress was gone about her household affairs, and had locked me in. The bed was eight yards from the floor. I wished to get down, but durst not presume to call; and if I had it would have been in vain, with such a voice as mine, at so great a distance as from the room where I lay to the kitchen where the family kept. While I was under these circumstances two rats crept up the curtains, and ran smelling backward and forward on the bed. One of them came up almost to my face, whereupon I rose in a fright, and drew out my hanger* to defend

---

* A kind of short, broad sword formerly carried.

myself. These horrible animals had the boldness to
attack me on both sides, and one of them held his
forefeet at my collar; but I had the good fortune to
rip up his belly before he could do me any mischief.
He fell down at my feet; and the other, seeing the

"The other made his escape."

fate of his comrade, made his escape, but not without one good wound on the back, which I gave him
as he fled, and made the blood run trickling from
him. After this exploit I walked gently to and fro
on the bed, to recover my breath and loss of spirits.
These creatures were of the size of a large mastiff,
but infinitely more nimble and fierce; so that, if I
had taken off my belt before I went to sleep, I must

have infallibly been torn to pieces and devoured. I measured the tail of the dead rat, and found it to be two yards long, wanting an inch; but it went against my stomach to drag the carcass off the bed, where it lay still bleeding; I observed it had yet some life, but with a strong slash across the neck I thoroughly despatched it.

Soon after my mistress came into the room, who, seeing me all bloody, ran and took me up in her hand. I pointed to the dead rat, smiling, and making other signs to show I was not hurt; whereat she was extremely rejoiced, calling the maid to take up the dead rat with a pair of tongs, and throw it out of the window. Then she set me on a table, where I showed her my hanger all bloody, and wiping it on the lappet of my coat, returned it to the scabbard.

I hope the gentle reader will excuse me for dwelling on these and the like particulars, which, however insignificant they may appear to groveling vulgar minds, yet will certainly help a philosopher to enlarge his thoughts and imagination, and apply them to the benefit of public as well as private life, which was my sole design in presenting this and other accounts of my travels to the world; wherein I have been chiefly studious of truth, without affecting any ornaments of learning or of style.

But the whole scene of this voyage made so strong an impression on my mind, and is so deeply fixed in my memory, that, in committing it to paper, I did not omit one material circumstance: however, upon a strict review, I blotted out several passages of less moment, which were in my first copy, for fear of being censured as tedious and trifling, whereof travelers are often, perhaps not without justice, accused.

CHAPTER II.

A Description of the Farmer's Daughter—The Author carried
to a Market-town, and then to the Metropolis—The Particulars of his Journey.

My mistress had a daughter of nine years old, a
child of towardly parts for her age, very dexterous
at her needle, and skillful in dressing her baby.*
Her mother and she contrived to fit up the baby's
cradle for me against night; the cradle was put into
a small drawer of a cabinet, and the drawer placed
upon a hanging shelf for fear of the rats. This was
my bed all the time I stayed with those people,
though made more convenient by degrees, as I
began to learn their language, and make my wants
known. This young girl was so handy that, after
I had once or twice pulled off my clothes before
her, she was able to dress and undress me, though I
never gave her that trouble when she would let me
do either myself. She made me seven shirts and
some other linen, of as fine cloth as could be got,
which indeed was coarser than sackcloth; and

---

* That is, her doll (an old use of the word).

these she constantly washed for me with her own
hands. She was likewise my schoolmistress, to
teach me the language; when I pointed to anything
she told me the name of it in her own tongue, so
that in a few days I was able to call for whatever
I had a mind to. She was very good-natured, and
not above forty foot high, being little for her age.
She gave me the name of *Grildrig*, which the family
took up, and afterward the whole kingdom. The
word imports what the Latins call *nanunculus*, the
Italians *homunceletino*, and the English *mannikin*.
To her I chiefly owe my preservation in that
country; we never parted while I was there; I
called her my *Glumdalclitch*, or little nurse, and I
should be guilty of great ingratitude if I omitted
this honorable mention of her care and affection toward me, which I heartily wish it lay in my power
to requite as she deserves, instead of being the innocent, but unhappy, instrument of her disgrace, as
I have too much reason to fear.

It now began to be known and talked of in the
neighborhood that my master had found a strange
animal in the field, about the bigness of a *splacnuck*,
but exactly shaped in every part like a human
creature; which it likewise imitated in all its
actions; seemed to speak in a little language of its
own, had already learned several words of theirs, went

erect upon two legs, was tame and gentle, would come when it was called, do whatever it was bid, had the finest limbs in the world, and a complexion fairer than a nobleman's daughter of three years old. Another farmer, who lived hard by, and was a particular friend of my master, came on a visit on purpose to inquire into the truth of this story. I was immediately produced, and placed upon a table, where I walked as I was commanded, drew my hanger, put it up again, made my reverence to my master's guest, asked him in his own language how he did, and told him *he was welcome*, just as my little nurse had instructed me. This man, who was old and dim-sighted, put on his spectacles to behold me better, at which I could not forbear laughing very heartily, for his eyes appeared like the full moon shining into a chamber at two windows. Our people who discovered the cause of my mirth, bore me company in laughing, at which the old fellow was fool enough to be angry and out of countenance. He had the character of a great miser ; and, to my misfortune, he well deserved it, by the cursed advice he gave my master, to show me as a sight upon a market-day in the next town, which was half an hour's riding, about twenty-two miles from our house. I guessed there was some mischief contriving, when I observed my

master and his friend whispering long together,
sometimes pointing at me; and my fears made me
fancy that I overheard and understood some of their
words. But the next morning Glumdalclitch, my
little nurse, told me the whole matter, which she
had cunningly picked out from her mother. The
poor girl laid me on her bosom, and fell a-weeping
with shame and grief. She apprehended some mischief would happen to me from rude, vulgar folks,
who might squeeze me to death, or break one of my
limbs by taking me in their hands. She had also
observed how modest I was in my nature, how
nicely I regarded my honor, and what an indignity
I should conceive it to be exposed for money as a
public spectacle to the meanest of the people. She
said her papa and mamma had promised that Grildrig should be hers; but now she found they meant
to serve her as they did last year, when they pretended to give her a lamb, and yet, as soon as it was
fat, sold it to a butcher. For my own part, I may
truly affirm, that I was less concerned than my
nurse. I had a strong hope, which never left me,
that I should one day recover my liberty; and as
to the ignominy of being carried about for a monster, I considered myself to be a perfect stranger in
the country, and that such a misfortune could never
be charged upon me as a reproach, if ever I should

return to England; since the king of Great Britain himself, in my condition, must have undergone the same distress.

My master, pursuant to the advice of his friend, carried me in a box the next market-day to the neighboring town, and took along with him his little daughter, my nurse, upon a pillion* behind him. The box was close on every side, with a little door for me to go in and out, and a few gimlet holes to let in air. The girl had been so careful as to put the quilt of her baby's bed into it, for me to lie down on. However, I was terribly shaken and discomposed in this journey, though it were but of half an hour: for the horse went about forty foot at every step, and trotted so high that the agitation was equal to the rising and falling of a ship in a great storm, but much more frequent. Our journey was somewhat further than from London to St. Alban's. My master alighted at an inn which he used to frequent; and after consulting awhile with the inn-keeper, and making some necessary preparations, he hired the *grultrud*, or crier, to give notice through the town of a strange creature to be seen at the sign of the Green Eagle, not so big as a *splacnuck* (an animal in that country, very finely

---

* A cushion for a woman to ride behind a man on horseback

shaped, about six foot long), and in every part of the body resembling a human creature; could speak several words, and perform an hundred diverting tricks.

I was placed upon a table in the largest room of the inn, which might be near three hundred foot square. My little nurse stood on a low stool close to the table, to take care of me, and direct what I should do. My master, to avoid a crowd, would suffer only thirty people at a time to see me. I walked about the table as the girl commanded : she asked me questions, as far as she knew my under-standing of the language reached, and I answered them as loud as I could. I turned about several times to the company, paid my humble respects, said *they were welcome*, and used some other speeches I had been taught. I took up a thimble filled with liquor, which Glumdalclitch had given me for a cup, and drank their health. I drew out my hanger, and flourished with it after the manner of fencers in England. My nurse gave me part of a straw, which I exercised as a pike,* having learned the art in my youth. I was that day shown to twelve sets of company, and as often forced to act over

---

* A military weapon formerly used with a long wooden shaft and a steel head.

again the same fopperies,* till I was half-dead with weariness and vexation: for those who had seen me made such wonderful reports that the people were ready to break down the doors to come in. My master, for his own interest, would not suffer any one to touch me except my nurse: and to prevent danger, benches were set round the table, at such a distance as put me out of everybody's reach. However, an unlucky† schoolboy aimed a hazelnut directly at my head, which very narrowly missed me; otherwise it came with so much violence that it would have infallibly knocked out my brains, for it was almost as large as a small pumpion,‡ but I had the satisfaction to see the young rogue well beaten and turned out of the room.

My master gave public notice that he would show me again the next market-day; and in the meantime he prepared a more convenient vehicle for me, which he had reason enough to do; for I was so tired with

---

* Foolish tricks; a meaning in which the word is used by our older writers.

† Mischievous: an obsolete meaning of the word.

‡ A pumpkin or gourd, a fruit allied to the melon and cucumber, which sometimes grows to an enormous size, **weighing 60 or 70 lbs**

my first journey, and with entertaining company
for eight hours together, that I could hardly stand
upon my legs, or speak a word. It was at least
three days before I recovered my strength; and
that I might have no rest at home all the neighboring gentlemen from an hundred miles around, hearing of my fame, came to see me at my master's own
house. There could not be fewer than thirty persons, with their wives and children (for the country
was very populous); and my master demanded the
rate of a full room whenever he showed me at
home, although it were only to a single family : so
that for some time I had but little ease every day of
the week (except Wednesday, which is their Sabbath), although I were not carried to the town.

My master, finding how profitable I was like to
be, resolved to carry me to the most considerable
cities of the kingdom. Having therefore provided
himself with all things necessary for a long journey,
and settled his affairs at home, he took leave of his
wife, and upon the 17th of August, 1703, about two
months after my arrival, we set out for the metropolis, situated near the middle of that empire, and
about three thousand miles distance from our house.
My master made his daughter Glumdalclitch ride
behind him. She carried me on her lap, in a box
tied about her waist. The girl had lined it on all

sides with the softest cloth she could get, well quilted underneath, furnished it with her baby's bed, provided me with linen and other necessaries, and made everything as convenient as she could. We had no other company but a boy of the house, who rode after us with the luggage.

My master's design was to show me in all the towns by the way, and to step out of the road for fifty or an hundred miles, to any village or person of quality's house, where he might expect custom. We made easy journeys, of not above seven or eight score miles a day: for Glumdalclitch, on purpose to spare me, complained she was tired with the trotting of the horse. She often took me out of my box, at my own desire, to give me air, and show me the country, but always held me fast, by a leading string. We passed over five or six rivers, many degrees broader and deeper than the Nile or the Ganges; and there was hardly a rivulet so small as the Thames at London Bridge. We were ten weeks in our journey, and I was shown in eighteen large towns, besides many villages and private families.

On the 26th of October we arrived at the metropolis, called in their language *Lorbrulgrud*, or Pride of the Universe. My master took a lodging in the principal street of the city, not far from the royal palace, and put out bills in the usual form, contain-

ing an exact description of my person and parts.*
He hired a large room between three and four
hundred foot wide. He provided a table sixty foot
in diameter, upon which I was to act my part, and
pallisadoed it round three foot from the edge, and as
many high, to prevent my falling over. I was shown
ten times a day, to the wonder and satisfaction of
all people. I could now speak the language tolerably
well, and perfectly understood every word that was
spoken to me. Besides, I had learned their alphabet, and could make a shift to explain a sentence
here and there; for Glumdalclitch had been my instructor while we were at home, and at leisure
hours during our journey. She carried a little book
in her pocket, not much larger than a Sanson's
Atlas;† it was a common treatise for the use of
young girls, giving a short account of their religion;
out of this she taught me my letters, and interpreted
the words.

---

* Accomplishments.

† A very large atlas formerly in use, by a French geographer.

CHAPTER III.

The Author is sent for to Court—The Queen buys him of his
master, the Farmer, and presents him to the King — He
disputes with his Majesty's great Scholars—An Apartment
at Court provided for the Author—He is in high favor
with the Queen—He stands up for the honor of his own
Country—He quarrels with the Queen's Dwarf.

THE frequent labors I underwent every day made
in a few weeks a very considerable change in my
health ; the more my master got by me the more
insatiable he grew. I had quite lost my stomach,
and was almost reduced to a skeleton. The farmer
observed it, and, concluding that I soon must die,
resolved to make as good a hand of me* as he could.
While he was thus reasoning and resolving with
himself, a *slardral*, or gentleman-usher, came from
court, commanding my master to carry me immediately thither for the diversion of the queen and her
ladies. Some of the latter had already been to see
me, and reported strange things of my beauty, behavior, and good sense. Her majesty, and those

---

* Make as much money out of me.

who attended her, were beyond measure delighted with my demeanor. I fell on my knees, and begged the honor of kissing her imperial foot; but this gracious princess held out her little finger toward me after I was set on a table, which I embraced in both my arms, and put the tip of it with the utmost respect to my lips. She made me some general questions about my country and my travels, which I answered as distinctly, and in as few words as I could. She asked, Whether I would be content to live at court? I bowed down to the board of the table, and humbly answered, That I was my master's slave; but if I were at my own disposal I should be proud to devote my life to her majesty's service. She then asked my master, Whether he were willing to sell me at a good price? He, who apprehended I could not live a month, was ready enough to part with me, and demanded a thousand pieces of gold, which were ordered him on the spot, each piece being about the bigness of eight hundred moidores,* but, allowing for the proportion of all things between that country and Europe, and the high price of gold among them, was hardly so great a sum as a thousand guineas would be in England. I then said to the queen, Since I was now her

---

* A moidore was equivalent to about £1 7s.

majesty's most humble creature and vassal, I must beg the favor that Glumdalclitch, who had always tended me with so much care and kindness, and understood to do it so well, might be admitted into her service, and continue to be my nurse and instructor.

Her majesty agreed to my petition, and easily got the farmer's consent, who was glad enough to have his daughter preferred at court, and the poor girl herself was not able to hide her joy. My late master withdrew, bidding me farewell, and saying he had left me in a good service: to which I replied not a word, only making him a slight bow.

The queen observed my coldness, and when the farmer was gone out of the apartment, asked me the reason. I made bold to tell her majesty that I owed no other obligation to my late master than his not dashing out the brains of a poor harmless creature found by chance in his field; which obligation was amply recompensed by the gain he had made in showing me through half the kingdom, and the price he had now sold me for; that the life I had since led was laborious enough to kill an animal of ten times my strength; that my health was much impaired by the continual drudgery of entertaining the rabble every hour of the day; and that if my master had not thought my life in danger, her majesty would not have got so cheap a bargain. But as I was out of all fear of being ill-treated, under the protection of so great and good an empress, the ornament of nature, the darling of the world, the delight of her subjects, the phœnix of the creation; so, I hoped my late master's apprehensions would appear to be groundless; for I already found my spirits to revive by the influence of her most august presence.

This was the sum of my speech, delivered with great improprieties and hesitation. The latter part was altogether framed in the style peculiar to that people, whereof I learned some phrases from Glumdalclitch while she was carrying me to court.

The queen, giving great allowance for my defectiveness in speaking, was, however, surprised at so much wit and good sense in so diminutive an animal. She took me in her own hands, and carried me to the king, who was then retired to his cabinet.* His majesty, a prince of much gravity and austere countenance, not well observing my shape at first view, asked the queen, after a cold manner, how long it was since she grew fond of a *splacnuck?* for such, it seems, he took me to be, as I lay upon my breast in her majesty's right hand. But this

---

* A private room for writing in, etc.

princess, who hath an infinite deal of wit and humor, set me gently on my feet upon the scrutoire,* and commanded me to give his majesty an account of myself, which I did in a very few words; and Glumdalclitch, who attended at the cabinet door, and could not endure I should be out of her sight, being admitted, confirmed all that had passed from my arrival at her father's house.

The king, although he be as learned a person as any in his dominions, had been educated in the study of philosophy, and particularly mathematics; yet, when he observed my shape exactly, and saw me walk erect, before I began to speak, conceived I might be a piece of clock-work (which is in that country arrived to a very great perfection), con-trived by some ingenious artist. But when he heard my voice, and found what I delivered to be regular and rational, he could not conceal his as-tonishment. He was by no means satisfied with the relation I gave him of the manner I came into his kingdom, but thought it a story concerted be-tween Glumdalclitch and her father, who had taught me a set of words, to make me sell at a higher price. Upon this imagination, he put several other ques-tions to me, and still received rational answers, no

---

* A writing desk.

otherwise defective than by a foreign accent, and an imperfect knowledge in the language, with some rustic phrases which I had learned at the farmer's house, and did not suit the polite style of a court.

His majesty sent for three great scholars, who were then in their weekly waiting,* according to the custom in that country. These gentlemen, after they had awhile examined my shape with much nicety, were of different opinions concerning me. They all agreed that I could not be produced according to the regular laws of nature, because I was not framed with a capacity of preserving my life, either by swiftness, or climbing of trees, or digging holes in the earth. They observed by my teeth, which they viewed with great exactness, that I was a carnivorous animal; yet, most quadrupeds being an overmatch for me, and field-mice, with some others, too nimble, they could not imagine how I should be able to support myself, unless I fed upon snails and other insects, which they offered, by many learned arguments, to evince that I could not possibly do. One of these virtuosi† seemed to think that I might be an embryo, or abortive birth. But this opinion was rejected by the other two, who

---

* Attendance on the king.

† Men skilled in curiosities, artistic works, etc.

observed my limbs to be perfect and finished ; and that I had lived several years, as it was manifest from my beard, the stumps whereof they plainly discovered through a magnifying glass. They would not allow me to be a dwarf, because my littleness was beyond all degrees of comparison ; for the queen's favorite dwarf, the smallest ever known in that kingdom, was near thirty foot high. After much debate, they concluded, unanimously, that I was only *relplum scalcath,* which is interpreted literally *lusus naturæ ;* * a determination exactly agreeable to the modern philosophy of Europe, whose professors, disdaining the old evasion of occult causes, whereby the followers of Aristotle endeavor in vain to disguise their ignorance, have invented this wonderful solution of all difficulties, to the unspeakable advancement of human knowledge.

After this decisive conclusion, I entreated to be heard a word or two. I applied myself to the king, and assured his majesty that I came from a country which abounded with several millions of both sexes, and of my own stature ; where the animals, trees, and houses were all in proportion, and where, by consequence, I might be as able to defend myself,

---

* A sport of nature; a natural curiosity.

and to find sustenance as any of his majesty's subjects could do here; which I took for a full answer to those gentlemen's arguments. To this they only replied with a smile of contempt, saying that the farmer had instructed me very well in my lesson. The king, who had a much better understanding, dismissing his learned men, sent for the farmer, who, by good fortune, was not yet gone out of town. Having, therefore, first examined him privately, and then confronted him with me and the young girl, his majesty began to think that what we told him might possibly be true. He desired the queen to order that a particular care should be taken of me; and was of opinion that Glumdalclitch should still continue in her office of tending me, because he observed we had a great affection for each other. A convenient apartment was provided for her at court: she had a sort of governess appointed to take care of her education, a maid to dress her, and two other servants for menial offices; but the care of me was wholly appropriated to herself. The queen commanded her own cabinet-maker to contrive a box, that might serve me for a bedchamber, after the model that Glumdalclitch and I should agree upon. This man was a most ingenious artist, and according to my directions, in three weeks, finished for me a wooden chamber, of sixteen foot square, and twelve high, with sash-windows, a door, and two closets, like a London bedchamber. The board that made the ceiling was to be lifted up and down by two hinges, to put in a bed, ready furnished by her majesty's upholsterer, which Glumdalclitch took out every day to air, made it with her own hands, and letting it down at night, locked up the roof over me. A nice* workman, who was famous for little curiosities, undertook to make me two chairs, with backs and frames, of a substance not unlike ivory, and two tables, with a cabinet to put my things in. The room was quilted on all sides, as well as the floor and the ceiling, to prevent any accident from the carelessness of those who carried me, and to break the force of a jolt when I went in a coach. I desired a lock for my door, to prevent rats and mice from coming in. The smith, after several attempts, made the smallest that ever was seen among them, for I have known a larger at the gate of a gentleman's house in England. I made a shift to keep the key in a pocket of my own, fearing Glumdalclitch might lose it. The queen likewise ordered the thinnest silks that could be gotten, to make me clothes, not much thicker than an English

---

* Skilled in fine or delicate work.

blanket, very cumbersome till I was accustomed to them. They were after the fashion of the kingdom, partly resembling the Persian, and partly the Chinese, and are a very grave and decent habit.

The queen became so fond of my company, that she could not dine without me. I had a table placed upon the same at which her majesty eat, just at her left elbow, and a chair to sit on. Glumdal-clitch stood upon a stool on the floor near my table, to assist and take care of me. I had an entire set of silver dishes and plates, and other necessaries, which, in proportion to those of the queen, were not much bigger than what I have seen of the same kind in a London toy-shop, for the furniture of a baby-house; these my little nurse kept in her pocket in a silver box, and gave me at meals as I wanted them, always cleaning them herself. No person dined with the queen but the two princesses royal, the elder sixteen years old, and the younger at that time thirteen and a month. Her majesty used to put a bit of meat upon one of my dishes, out of which I carved for myself, and her diversion was to see me eat in minature; for the queen (who had, indeed, but a weak stomach) took up, at one mouthful, as much as a dozen English farmers could eat at a meal; which to me was, for some time, a very nauseous sight. She would craunch the wing of a lark, bones and all, between her teeth, although it were nine times as large as that of a full-grown turkey; and put a bit of bread in her mouth as big as two twelve-penny loaves. She drank out of a golden cup, above a hogshead at a draught. Her knives were twice as large as a scythe, set straight upon the handle. The spoons, forks, and other instruments, were all in the same proportion. I remember when Glumdalclitch carried me, out of curiosity, to see some of the tables at court, where ten or a dozen of those enormous knives and forks were lifted up together, I thought I had never till then beheld so terrible a sight.

It is the custom, that every Wednesday (which, as I have before observed, was their Sabbath) the king and queen, with the royal issue of both sexes, dine together in the apartment of his majesty, to whom I was now become a great favorite; and at these times my little chair and table were placed at his left hand, before one of the salt-cellars. This prince took a pleasure in conversing with me, in-quiring into the manners, religion, laws, govern ment, and learning of Europe; wherein I gave him the best account I was able. His apprehension was so clear, and his judgment so exact, that he made very wise reflections and observations upon all I said. But, I confess, that, after I had been a little too copious in talking of my own beloved country, of our trade, and wars by sea and land, of our schisms in religion, and parties in the state, the prejudices of his education prevailed so far that he could not forbear taking me up in his right hand, and, stroking me gently with the other, after a hearty fit of laughing, asked me, Whether I were a Whig or Tory? Then turning to his first minister, who waited behind him with a white staff, near as tall as the mainmast of the Royal Sovereign, he observed, How contemptible a thing was human grandeur, which could be mimicked by such diminutive insects as I; and yet, said he, I dare engage these creatures have their titles and distinctions of honor; they contrive little nests and burrows, that they call houses and cities; they make a figure in dress and equipage; they love, they fight, they dispute, they cheat, they betray! And thus he continued on, while my color came and went several times, with indignation, to hear our noble country, the mistress of arts and arms, the scourge of France, the arbitress of Europe, the seat of virtue, piety, honor, and truth, the pride and envy of the world, so contemptuously treated.

But as I was not in a condition to resent injuries, so upon mature thoughts I began to doubt whether I was injured or no. For, after having been accus-

tomed several months to the sight and converse of
this people, and observed every object upon which I
cast mine eyes to be of. proportionable magnitude,
the horror I had first conceived from their bulk and
aspect was so far worn off, that, if I had then beheld
a company of English lords and ladies in their finery
and birthday clothes, acting their several parts in the
most courtly manner of strutting, and bowing, and
prating; to say the truth, I should have been strongly
tempted to laugh as much at them as the king and
his grandees did at me. Neither, indeed, could I
forbear smiling at myself, when the queen used to
place me upon her hand toward a looking-glass, by
which both our persons appeared before me in full
view together; and there could be nothing more
ridiculous than the comparison; so that I really
began to imagine myself dwindled many degrees
below my usual size.

Nothing angered and mortified me so much as
the queen's dwarf; who being of the lowest stature
that was ever in that country (for I verily think he
was not full thirty foot high), became so insolent at
seeing a creature so much beneath him, that he
would always affect to swagger and look big as he
passed by me in the queen's antechamber, while ı
was standing on some table, talking with the lords or
ladies of the court, and he seldom failed of a smart

word or two upon my *littleness ;* against which I could only revenge myself by calling him *brother*, challenging him to wrestle, and such repartees as are usual in the mouths of court pages. One day, at dinner, this malicious little cub was so nettled with something I had said to him, that, raising himself upon the frame of her majesty's chair, he took me up by the middle, as I was sitting down, not thinking any harm, and let me drop into a large silver bowl of cream, and then ran away as fast as she could. I fell over head and ears, and, if I had not been a good swimmer, it might have gone very hard with me ; for Glumdalclitch in that instant happened to be at the other end of the room, and the queen was in such a fright that she wanted presence of mind to assist me. But my little nurse ran to my relief, and took me out, after I had swallowed above a quart of cream. I was put to bed : however, I received no other damage than the loss of a suit of clothes, which was utterly spoiled. The dwarf was soundly whipped, and, as a further punishment, forced to drink up the bowl of cream into which he had thrown me ; neither was he ever restored to favor ; for soon after the queen bestowed him on a lady of high quality ; so that I saw him no more, to my very great satisfaction ; for I could not tell to what extremity such a malicious urchin might have carried his resentment.

He had before served me a scurvy trick, which

He had before served me a scurvy trick.

set the queen a-laughing, although at the same time she was heartily vexed, and would have immediately cashiered him if I had not been so generous as to intercede. Her majesty had taken a marrow-bone upon her plate, and, after knocking out the marrow, placed the bone again in the dish erect, as it stood before; the dwarf, watching his opportunity while Glumdalclitch was gone to the sideboard, mounted the stool she stood on to take care of me at meals, took me up in both hands, and, squeezing my legs together, wedged them into the marrow-bone above my waist, where I stuck for some time, and made a very ridiculous figure. I believe it was near a minute before any one knew what was become of me; for I thought it below me to cry out. But, as princes seldom get their meat hot, my legs were not scalded, only my stockings and breeches in a sad condition. The dwarf, at my entreaty, had no other punishment than a sound whipping.

I was frequently rallied by the queen upon account of my fearfulness; and she used to ask me whether the people of my country were as great cowards as myself? The occasion was this: The kingdom is much pestered with flies in summer; and these odious insects, each of them as big as a Dunstable lark* hardly gave me any rest while I sat at dinner, with their continual humming and buzzing about mine ears. They would sometimes alight upon my victuals, and sometimes they would fix upon my nose or forehead, where they stung me to the quick, smelling very offensively; and I could

---

* A common skylark, large numbers of which are caught at Dunstable.

easily trace that viscous matter, which, our naturalists tell us, enables those creatures to walk with
their feet upward upon a ceiling.*   I had much ado
to defend myself against these detestable animals,
and could not forbear starting when they came on
my face.   It was the common practice of the dwarf
to catch a number of these insects in his hand, as
schoolboys do among us, and let them out suddenly
under my nose, on purpose to frighten me and
divert the queen.   My remedy was to cut them in
pieces with my knife, as they flew in the air,
wherein my dexterity was much admired.

I remember, one morning, when Glumdalclitch
had set me in my box upon a window, as she usually
did in fair days, to give me air (for I durst not
venture to let the box be hung on a nail out of the
window, as we do with cages in England), after I
had lifted up one of my sashes, and sat down at my
table to eat a piece of sweet cake for my breakfast,
above twenty wasps, allured by the smell, came flying into the room, humming louder than the drones
of as many bagpipes.   Some of them seized my
cake, and carried it piecemeal away; others flew
about my head and face, confounding me with the
noise, and putting me in the utmost terror of their

---

* It is not yet satisfactorily explained how flies can walk thus.

stings. However, I had the courage to rise and draw my hanger, and attack them in the air. I despatched four of them, but the rest got away, and I presently shut my window. These creatures were as large as partridges; I took out their stings, found them an inch and a half long, and as sharp as needles. I carefully preserved them all; and having since shown them, with some other curiosities, in several parts of Europe, upon my return to England I gave three of them to Gresham College,* and kept the fourth for myself.

---

* An institution in London.

CHAPTER IV.

The Country described—A proposal for correcting modern
Maps—The King's Palace, and some account of the
Metropolis—The Author's way of traveling—The chief
Temple described.

I now intend to give the reader a short description of this country, as far as I traveled in it, which
was not above two thousand miles round Lorbrulgrud the metropolis; for the queen, whom I always
attended, never went further when she accompanied
the king in his progresses, and there stayed till his
majesty returned from viewing his frontiers. The
whole extent of this prince's dominions reacheth
about six thousand miles in length, and from three
to five in breadth: from whence, I cannot but conclude that our geographers of Europe are in a great
error by supposing nothing but sea between Japan
and California; for, it was ever my opinion, that
there must be a balance of earth to counterpoise the
great continent of Tartary; and therefore they
ought to correct their maps and charts, by joining
this vast tract of land to the northwest parts of

America, wherein I shall be ready to lend them my assistance.

The kingdom is a peninsula,* terminated to the northeast by a ridge of mountains thirty miles high, which are altogether impassable, by reason of the volcanoes upon the tops : neither do the most learned know what sort of mortals inhabit beyond those mountains, or whether they be inhabited at all. On the three other sides it is bounded by the ocean. There is not one seaport in the whole kingdom : and those parts of the coasts into which the rivers issue are so full of pointed rocks, and the sea generally so rough, that there is no venturing with the smallest of their boats ; so that these people are wholly excluded from any commerce with the rest of the world. But the large rivers are full of vessels and abound with excellent fish ; for they seldom get any from the sea, because the sea-fish are of the same size with those in Europe, and consequently not worth catching ; whereby it is manifest that nature, in the production of plants and animals of so extraordinary a bulk, is wholly confined to this continent, of which I leave the reasons to be determined by philosophers. However, now and then, they take a

---

* The early editions had a map showing the position and conformation of Brobdingnag.

whale that happens to be dashed against the rocks, which the common people feed on heartily. These whales I have known so large that a man could hardly carry one upon his shoulders; and sometimes, for curiosity, they are brought in hampers to Lorbrulgrud: I saw one of them in a dish at the king's table, which passed for a rarity, but I did not observe he was fond of it; for I think, indeed, the bigness disgusted him, although I have seen one somewhat larger in Greenland.

The country is well inhabited, for it contains fifty-one cities, near an hundred walled towns, and a great number of villages. To satisfy my curious reader, it may be sufficient to describe Lorbrulgrud. This city stands upon almost two equal parts, on each side the river that passes through. It contains above eighty thousand houses, and about six hundred thousand inhabitants. It is in length three *glonglungs* (which make about fifty-four English miles), and two and a half in breadth; as I measured it myself in the royal map, made by the king's order, which was laid on the ground on purpose for me, and extended an hundred feet: I paced the diameter and circumference several times barefoot, and, computing by the scale, measured it pretty exactly.

The king's palace is no regular edifice, but an

heap of buildings, about seven miles round: the
chief rooms are generally two hundred and forty
foot high, and broad and long in proportion. A
coach was allowed to Glumdalclitch and me, wherein her governess frequently took her out to see the
town, or go among the shops; and I was always of
the party, carried in my box; although the girl, at
my own desire, would often take me out and hold
me in her hand, that I might more conveniently
view the houses and the people, as we passed along
the streets. I reckoned our coach to be about the
square of* Westminster Hall, but not altogether so
high; however, I cannot be very exact. One day
the governess ordered our coachman to stop at
several shops, where the beggars, watching their
opportunity, crowded to the sides of the coach, and
gave me the most horrible spectacles that ever an
English eye beheld. There was a woman with a
cancer in her breast, swelled to a monstrous size,
and full of holes. There was a fellow with a wen
in his neck, larger than five woolpacks; and another
with a couple of wooden legs, each about twenty foot
high. But the most hateful sight of all was the
lice crawling on their clothes. I could see distinctly
the limbs of these vermin with my naked eye, much

---

* To occupy as much space as.

better than those of an European louse through a microscope, and their snouts, with which they rooted like swine. They were the first I had ever beheld, and I should have been curious enough to dissect one of them, if I had had proper instruments, which I unluckily left behind me in the ship, although, indeed, the sight was so nauseous that it perfectly turned my stomach.

Beside the large box in which I was usually carried, the queen ordered a smaller one to be made for me, of about twelve foot square, and ten high, for the convenience of traveling : because the other was somewhat too large for Glumdalclitch's lap, and cumbersome in the coach; it was made by the same artist, whom I directed in the whole contrivance. This traveling closet was an exact square with a window in the middle of three of the squares, and each window was latticed with iron wire on the outside, to prevent accidents in long journeys. On the fourth side, which had no window, two strong staples were fixed, through which the person that carried me, when I had a mind to be on horseback, put in a leathern belt, and buckled it about his waist. This was always the office of some grave, trusty servant in whom I could confide, whether I attended the king and queen in their progresses, or were disposed to see the gardens, or pay a visit to some great lady or minister of state in the court, when Glumdalclitch happened to be out of order ;* for I soon began to be known and esteemed among the greatest officers ; I suppose more upon account of their majesties' favor than any merit of my own. In journeys, when I was weary of the coach, a servant on horseback would buckle on my box, and place it upon a cushion before him; and there I had a full prospect of the country on three sides, from my three windows. I had, in this closet, a field-bed and a hammock hung from the ceiling, two chairs and a table, neatly screwed to the floor, to prevent being tossed about by the agitation of the horse or the coach. And having been long used to sea voyages, those motions, although sometimes very violent, did not much discompose me.

Whenever I had a mind to see the town, it was always in my traveling closet; which Glumdalclitch held in her lap in a kind of open sedan, after the fashion of the country, borne by four men, and attended by two others in the queen's livery. The people, who had often heard of me, were very curious to crowd about the sedan, and the girl was complaisant enough to make the bearers stop, and to take me in her hand, that I might be more conveniently seen.

---

* Not in her usual health.

I was very desirious to see the chief temple, and particularly the tower belonging to it, which is reckoned the highest in the kingdom. Accordingly one day my nurse carried me thither, but I may truly say I came back disappointed; for the height is not above three thousand foot, reckoning from the ground to the highest pinnacle top; which, allowing for the difference between the size of those people and us in Europe, is no great matter for admiration, nor at all equal in proportion (if I rightly remember) to Salisbury steeple.* But, not to detract from a nation, to which, during my life, I shall acknowledge myself extremely obliged, it must be allowed, that whatever this famous tower wants in height, is amply made up in beauty and strength. For the walls are near an hundred foot thick, built of hewn stone, whereof each is about forty foot square, and adorned on all sides with statues of gods and emperors, cut in marble larger than the life, placed in their several niches. I measured a little finger which had fallen down from one of these statues, and lay unperceived among

---

* The spire of Salisbury Cathedral is 404 feet high. Objects in Brobdingnag being about twelve times the size of those in Europe the tower here mentioned should have been 4,800 feet high to correspond with the Salisbury spire.

some rubbish, and found it exactly four foot and an inch in length. Glumdalclitch wrapped it up in a handkerchief, and carried it home in her pocket, to keep among other trinkets, of which the girl was very fond, as children at her age usually are.

The king's kitchen is indeed a noble building, vaulted at top, and about six hundred foot high. The great oven is not so wide, by ten paces, as the cupola at St. Paul's :* for I measured the latter on purpose, after my return. But if I should describe the kitchen-grate, the prodigious pots and kettles, the joints of meat turning on the spits, with many other particulars, perhaps I should be hardly believed ; at least a severe critic would be apt to think I enlarged a little, as travelers are often suspected to do. To avoid which censure, I fear I have run too much into the other extreme ; and that, if this treatise should happen to be translated into the language of Brobdingnag (which is the general name of that kingdom), and transmitted thither, the king and his people would have reason to complain that I had done them an injury, by a false and diminutive representation.

His majesty seldom keeps above six hundred horses in his stables ; they are generally from fifty-

---

* The cupola or dome of St. Paul's, London, is 100 feet wide.

four to sixty foot high.   But when he goes abroad
on solemn days, he is attended, for state, by a
militia guard of five hundred horse, which indeed I
thought was the most splendid sight that could be
ever beheld, till I saw part of his army in battalia,
whereof I shall find another occasion to speak.

CHAPTER V.

Several Adventures that happened to the Author—The Execution of a Criminal—The Author shows his skill in Navigation.

I SHOULD have lived happy enough in that country if my littleness had not exposed me to several ridiculous and troublesome accidents; some of which I shall venture to relate. Glumdalclitch often carried me into the gardens of the court in my smaller box, and would sometimes take me out of it, and hold me in her hand, or set me down to walk. I remember, before the dwarf left the queen, he followed us one day into those gardens, and my nurse having set me down, he and I being close together, near some dwarf apple-trees, I must needs show my wit, by a silly allusion between him and the trees, which happens to hold in their language as it does in ours. Whereupon, the malicious rogue, watching his opportunity when I was walking under one of them, shook it directly over r.y head, by which a dozen apples, each of them near as

large as a Bristol barrel, came tumbling about my
ears; one of them hit me on the back as I chanced

"One of the apples hit me on the back."

to stoop, and knocked me down flat on my face;
but I received no other hurt, and the dwarf was
pardoned at my desire, because I had given the
provocation.

Another day Glumdalclitch left me on a smooth grassplot to divert myself, while she walked at some distance with her governess. In the meantime there suddenly fell such a violent shower of hail that I was immediately, by the force of it, struck to the ground; and when I was down the hailstones gave me such cruel bangs all over the body, as if I had been pelted with tennis-balls; however, I made a shift to creep on all four, and shelter myself, by lying flat on my face, on the lee-side of a border of lemon-thyme; but so bruised from head to foot that I could not go abroad in ten days. Neither is this at all to be wondered at, because nature in that country, observing the same proportion through all her operations, a hailstone is near eighteen hundred times as large as one in Europe; which I can assert upon experience, having been so curious to weigh and measure them.

But a more dangerous accident happened to me in the same garden, when my little nurse, believing she had put me in a secure place (which I often entreated her to do, that I might enjoy my own thoughts), and having left my box at home, to avoid the trouble of carrying it, went to another part of the gardens, with her governess and some ladies of her acquaintance. While she was absent, and out of hearing, a small white spaniel, belonging to one of the chief gardeners, having got by accident into the garden, happened to range near the place where I lay; the dog following the scent came directly up, and taking me in his mouth, ran straight to his master, wagging his tail, and set me gently on the ground. By good fortune he had been so well taught that I was carried between his teeth without the least hurt, or even tearing my clothes. But the poor gardener, who knew me well, and had a great kindness for me, was in a terrible fright; he gently took me up in both his hands, and asked me how I did? but I was so amazed and out of breath that I could not speak a word. In a few minutes I came to myself, and he carried me safe to my little nurse, who by this time had returned to the place where she left me, and was in cruel agonies when I did not appear, nor answer when she called. She severely reprimanded the gardener on account of his dog. But the thing was hushed up, and never known at court, for the girl was afraid of the queen's anger; and truly, as to myself, I thought it would not be for my reputation that such a story should go about.

This accident absolutely determined Glumdalclitch never to trust me abroad for the future out of her sight. I had been long afraid of this resolution, and therefore concealed from her some little

unlucky adventures that happened in those times
when I was left by myself. Once a kite hovering
over the garden made a stoop at me, and if I had
not resolutely drawn my hanger, and run under a
thick espalier, he would have certainly carried me
away in his talons. Another time, walking to the
top of a fresh molehill, I fell to my neck in the
hole through which that animal had cast up the
earth, and coined some lie, not worth remembering,
to excuse myself for spoiling my clothes. I likewise broke my right shin against the shell of a snail,
which I happened to stumble over, as I was walking
alone, and thinking on poor England.

I cannot tell whether I were more pleased or
mortified to observe, in those solitary walks, that the
smaller birds did not appear to be at all afraid of me,
but would hop about within a yard distance, looking
for worms and other food, with as much indifference and security as if no creature at all were near
them. I remember, a thrush had the confidence to
snatch out of my hand, with his bill, a piece of cake
that Glumdalclitch had just given me for my breakfast. When I attempted to catch any of these birds
they would boldly turn against me, endeavoring to
peck my fingers, which I durst not venture within
their reach; and then they would turn back uncon-
cerned, to hunt for worms or snails, as they did

before. But one day, I took a thick cudgel, and threw it with all my strength so luckily at a linnet that I knocked him down, and seizing him by the neck with both my hands, ran with him in triumph to my nurse. However, the bird, who had only been stunned, recovering himself, gave me so many boxes with his wings on both sides of my head and body, though I held him at arm's length, and was out of the reach of his claws, that I was twenty times thinking to let him go. But I was soon relieved by one of our servants, who wrung off the bird's neck, and I had him next day for dinner, by the queen's command. This linnet, as near as I can remember, seemed to be somewhat larger than an English swan.

The maids of honor often invited Glumdalclitch to their apartments, and desired she would bring me along with her, on purpose to have the pleasure of seeing and touching me. They would often lay me in their bosoms, wherewith I was much disgusted; because, to say the truth, a very offensive smell came from their skins; which I do not mention, or intend, to the disadvantage of those excellent ladies, for whom I have all manner of respect; but I conceive that my sense was more acute in proportion to my littleness, and that those illustrious persons were no more disagreeable to their lovers, or to each other, than people of the same quality are with us in England. And, after all, I found their natural smell was much more supportable than when they used perfumes, under which I immediately swooned away. I cannot forget that an intimate friend of mine in Lilliput, took the freedom in a warm day, when I had used a good deal of exercise, to complain of a strong smell about me, although I am as little faulty that way as most of my sex : but I suppose his faculty of smelling was as nice with regard to me as mine was to that of this people. Upon this point I cannot forbear doing justice to the queen my mistress, and Glumdalclitch my nurse, whose persons were as sweet as those of any lady in England.

One day, a young gentleman, who was nephew to my nurse's governess, came and pressed them both to see an execution. It was of a man who had murdered one of that gentleman's intimate acquaintance. Glumdalclitch was prevailed on to be of the company, very much against her inclination, for she was naturally tender-hearted: and as for myself, although I abhorred such kind of spectacles, yet my curiosity tempted me to see something that I thought must be extraordinary. The malefactor was fixed in a chair upon a scaffold erected for the purpose, and his head cut off at a blow, with a sword of about **forty foot** long. The veins and arteries spouted up such a prodigious quantity of blood, and so high in the air, that the great *jet-d'eau** at Versailles was not equal for the time it lasted; and the head, when it fell on the scaffold floor, gave such a bounce as made me start, although I were at least half an English mile distant.

The queen, who often used to hear me talk of my sea voyages, and took all occasions to divert me when I was melancholy, asked me whether I understood how to handle a sail or an oar, and whether a little exercise of rowing might not be convenient for my health? I answered that I understood both very well; for although my proper employment had been to be surgeon or doctor to the ship, yet often upon a pinch I was forced to work like a common mariner. But I could not see how this could be done in their country, where the smallest wherry was equal to a first-rate man-of-war among us; and such a boat as I could manage would never live in any of their rivers. Her majesty said, if I would contrive a boat, her own joiner should make it, and she would provide a place for me to sail in. The fellow was an ingenious workman, and by my in-

---

* A jet of water forced high into the air by pressure. There are celebrated artificial fountains at Versailles (11 miles from Paris).

structions, in ten days finished a pleasure-boat, with all its tackling, able conveniently to hold eight Europeans. When it was finished the queen was so delighted that she ran with it in her lap to the king, who ordered it to be put into a cistern full of water, with me in it, by way of trial, where I could not manage my two sculls, or little oars, for want of room. But the queen had before contrived another project. She ordered the joiner to make a wooden trough of three hundred foot long, fifty broad, and eight deep; which, being well pitched, to prevent leaking, was placed on the floor, along the wall, in an outer room of the palace. It had a cock near the bottom to let out the water, when it began to grow stale; and two servants could easily fill it in half an hour. Here I often used to row for my own diversion, as well as that of the queen and her ladies, who thought themselves well entertained with my skill and agility. Sometimes I would put up my sail, and then my business was only to steer, while the ladies gave me a gale with their fans; and, when they were weary, some of their pages would blow my sail foward with their breath, while I showed my art by steering starboard or larboard as I pleased. When I had done, Glumdal-clitch always carried back my boat into her closet, and hung it on a nail to dry.

In this exercise I once met an accident which had like to have cost me my life; for, one of the pages having put my boat into the trough, the governess who attended Glumdalclitch very officiously lifted me up, to place me in the boat; but I happened to slip through her fingers, and should have infallibly fallen down forty foot, upon the floor, if, by the luckiest chance in the world, I had not been stopped by a corking-pin* that stuck in the good gentlewoman's stomacher; the head of the pin passed between my shirt and the waistband of my breeches, and thus I was held by the middle in the air till Glumdalclitch ran to my relief.

Another time, one of the servants, whose office it was to fill my trough every third day with fresh water, was so careless as to let a huge frog (not perceiving it) slip out of his pail. The frog lay concealed till I was put into my boat, but then, seeing a resting-place, climbed up, and made it lean so much on one side that I was forced to balance it with all my weight on the other, to prevent overturning. When the frog was got in it hopped at once half the length of the boat; and then over my head, backward and forward, daubing my face and

---

* A pin of large size formerly used by ladies for various purposes.

clothes with its odious slime. The largeness of its features made it appear the most deformed animal that can be conceived. However, I desired Glumdalclitch to let me deal with it alone. I banged it a good while with one of my sculls, and at last forced it to leap out of the boat.

But the greatest danger I ever underwent in that kingdom was from a monkey, who belonged to one of the clerks of the kitchen. Glumdalclitch had locked me up in her closet, while she went somewhere upon business or a visit. The weather being very warm, the closet window was left open, as well as the windows and the door of my bigger box, in which I usually lived, because of its largeness and conveniency. As I sat quietly meditating at my table I heard something bounce in at the closet window, and skip about from one side to the other: whereat, although I was much alarmed, yet I ventured to look out, but not stirring from my seat; and then I saw this frolicsome animal frisking and leaping up and down, till at last he came to my box, which he seemed to view with great pleasure and curiosity, peeping in at the door and every window. I retreated to the further corner of my room or box; but the monkey, looking in at every side, put me into such a fright that I wanted presence of mind to conceal myself under the bed, as I might

easily have done.   After some time spent in peeping, grinning, and chattering, he at last espied me;
and, reaching one of his paws in at the door, as a

"Reaching one of his paws in at the door, he dragged me out."

cat does when she plays with a mouse, although I
often shifted place to avoid him, he at length caught
hold of the lappet of my coat (which, being made of

that country cloth, was very thick and strong), and dragged me out. He took me up in his right fore-foot, and held me as a nurse does a child she is going to suckle, just as I have seen the same sort of creature do with a kitten in Europe; and when I offered to struggle he squeezed me so hard that I thought it more prudent to submit. I have good rea-son to believe that he took me for a young one of his own species, by his often stroking my face very gently with his other paw. In these diversions he was interrupted by a noise at the closet-door, as if some-body were opening it, whereupon he suddenly leaped up to the window at which he had come in, and thence upon the leads and gutters, walking upon three legs, and holding me in the fourth, till he clambered up to a roof that was next to ours. I heard Glumdalclitch give a shriek at the moment he was carrying me out. The poor girl was almost distracted; that quarter of the palace was all in an uproar; the servants ran for ladders; the monkey was seen by hundreds in the court sitting upon the ridge of a building, holding me like a baby in one of his forepaws, and feeding me with the other, by cramming into my mouth some victuals he had squeezed out of the bag on one side of his chaps,*

---

* Monkeys have cheek-pouches in which they can carry food till they are ready to chew it.

and patting me when I would not eat; whereat the
rabble below could not forbear laughing; neither
do I think they justly ought to be blamed, for without question the sight was ridiculous enough to
everybody but myself. Some of the people threw
up stones, hoping to drive the monkey down; but
this was strictly forbidden, or else, very probably,
my brains had been dashed out.

The ladders were now applied, and mounted by
several men, which the monkey observing, and finding himself almost encompassed, not being able to
make speed enough with his three legs, let me drop
on a ridge tile, and made his escape. Here I sat for
some time, three hundred yards from the ground,
expecting every moment to be blown down by the
wind, or to fall by my own giddiness, and come
tumbling over and over from the ridge to the eaves;
but an honest lad, one of my nurse's footmen,
climbed up, and, putting me into his breeches-
pocket, brought me down safe.

I was almost choked with the filthy stuff the
monkey had crammed down my throat; but my
dear little nurse picked it out of my mouth with a
small needle, and then I fell a-vomiting, which gave
me great relief. Yet I was so weak and bruised in
the sides by the squeezes given me by this odious
animal that I was forced to keep my bed a fort-

night. The king, queen, and all the court, sent every day to inquire after my health; and her majesty made me several visits during my sickness. The monkey was killed, and an order made that no such animal should be kept about the palace.

When I attended the king after my recovery, to return him thanks for his favors, he was pleased to rally me a good deal upon this adventure. He asked me what my thoughts and speculations were while I lay in the monkey's paw; how I liked the victuals he gave me; his manner of feeding; and whether the fresh air on the roof had sharpened my stomach? He desired to know what I would have done upon such an occasion in my own country. I told his majesty that in Europe we had no monkeys, except such as were brought for curiosities from other places, and so small that I could deal with a dozen of them together, if they presumed to attack me. And as for that monstrous animal with whom I was so lately engaged (it was indeed as large as an elephant), if my fears had suffered me to think so far as to make use of my hanger (looking fiercely, and clapping my hand upon the hilt as I spoke), when he poked his paw into my chamber, perhaps I should have given him such a wound as would have made him glad to withdraw it with more haste than he put it in. This I delivered in a firm tone, like a person who was jealous lest his courage should be called in question. However, my speech produced nothing else besides a loud laughter, which all the respect due to his majesty from those about him could not make them contain. This made me reflect how vain an attempt it is for a man to endeavor doing himself honor among those who are out of all degree of equality or comparison with him. And yet I have seen the moral of my own behavior very frequent in England since my return; where a little, contemptible varlet, without the least title to birth, person, wit, or common sense, shall presume to look with importance, and put himself upon a foot with the greatest persons of the kingdom.

CHAPTER VI.

Several contrivances of the Author to please the King and
Queen—He shows his skill in Music—The King inquires
into the state of England, which the Author relates to
him—The King's observations thereon.

I USED to attend the king's levee once or twice a
week, and had often seen him under the barber's
hand, which, indeed, was at first very terrible to
behold; for the razor was almost twice as long as
an ordinary scythe. His majesty, according to the
custom of the country, was only shaved twice a
week. I once prevailed on the barber to give me
some of the suds or lather, out of which I picked
forty or fifty of the strongest stumps of hair. I
then took a piece of fine wood, and cut it like the
back of a comb, making several holes in it at equal
distance with as small a needle as I could get from
Glumdalclitch. I fixed in the stumps so artificially,
scraping and sloping them with my knife toward
the points, that I made a very tolerable comb;
which was a seasonable supply, my own being so
much broken in the teeth that it was almost useless;

neither did I know any artist in that country so
nice and exact as would undertake to make me
another.

And this puts me in mind of an amusement,
wherein I spent many of my leisure hours. I
desired the queen's woman to save for me the combings of her majesty's hair, whereof in time I got a
good quantity; and consulting with my friend the
cabinet maker, who had received general orders to
do little jobs for me, I directed him to make two
chair-frames, no larger than those I had in my box,
and then to bore little holes with a fine awl round
those parts where I designed the backs and seats:
through these holes I wove the strongest hairs I
could pick out, just after the manner of cane chairs
in England. When they were finished I made a
present of them to her majesty, who kept them in
her cabinet, and used to show them for curiosities,
as indeed they were the wonder of every one that
beheld them. The queen would have had me sit
upon one of these chairs, but I absolutely refused to
obey her, protesting I would rather die a thousand
deaths than place a dishonorable part of my body
on those precious hairs that once adorned her
majesty's head. Of these hairs (as I had always a
mechanical genius) I likewise made a neat little
purse, about five foot long, with her majesty's name

deciphered in gold letters, which I gave to Glumdalclitch by the queen's consent. To say the truth, it
was more for show than use, being not of strength
to bear the weight of the larger coins, and therefore
she kept nothing in it but some little toys that girls
are fond of.

The king, who delighted in music, had frequent
concerts at court, to which I was sometimes carried,
and set in my box on a table to hear them : but the
noise was so great that I could hardly distinguish
the tunes. I am confident that all the drums and
trumpets of a royal army, beating and sounding together just at your ears, could not equal it. My
practice was to have my box removed from the
places where the performers sat as far as I could,
then to shut the doors and windows of it, and draw
the window-curtains; after which I found their
music not disagreeable.

I had learned in my youth to play a little upon
the spinet.* Glumdalclitch kept one in her
chamber, and a master attended twice a-week to
teach her : I call it a spinet, because it somewhat
resembled that instrument, and was played upon in
the same manner. A fancy came into my head that
I would entertain the king and queen with an Eng-

---

* An old instrument, a kind of early form of the piano.

lish tune upon this instrument. But this appeared extremely difficult : for the spinet was near sixty foot long, each key being almost a foot wide, so that with my arms extended I could not reach to above five keys, and to press them down required a good smart stroke with my fist, which would be too great a labor, and to no purpose. The method I contrived was this : I prepared two round sticks about the bigness of common cudgels ; they were thicker at one end than the other, and I covered the thicker ends with a piece of a mouse's skin, that by rapping on them I might neither damage the tops of the keys, nor interrupt the sound. Before the spinet a bench was placed, about four feet below the keys, and I was put upon the bench. I ran side-long upon it, that way and this, as fast as I could, banging the proper keys with my two sticks, and made a shift to play a jig, to the great satisfaction of both their majesties ; but it was the most violent exercise I ever underwent ; and yet I could not strike above sixteen keys, nor consequently play the bass and treble together, as other artists do , which was a great disadvantage to my performance.

The king, who, as I before observed, was a prince of excellent understanding, would frequently order that I should be brought in my box, and set upon the table in his closet : he would then command me

to bring one of my chairs out of the box, and sit
down within three yards' distance upon the top of

"In this manner I had several conversations with the king."

the cabinet, which brought me almost to a level
with his face. In this manner I had several conversations with him. I one day took the freedom
to tell his majesty that the contempt he discovered

toward Europe, and the rest of the world, did not
seem answerable to those excellent qualities of
mind that he was master of; that reason did not
extend itself with the bulk of the body: on the
contrary, we observed in our country that the tallest persons were usually least provided with it; that
among other animals, bees and ants had the reputation of more industry, art, and sagacity, than many
of the larger kinds; and that, as inconsiderable as
he took me to be, I hoped I might live to do his
majesty some signal service. The king heard me
with attention, and began to conceive a much better
opinion of me than he had ever before. He desired
I would give him as exact an account of the government of England as I possibly could; because, as
fond as princes commonly are of their own customs
(for so he conjectured of other monarchs by my
former discourses), he should be glad to hear of anything that might deserve imitation.

Imagine with thyself, courteous reader, how often
I then wished for the tongue of Demosthenes or
Cicero, that might have enabled me to celebrate the
praise of my own dear native country in a style
equal to its merits and felicity.

I began my discourse by informing his majesty
that our dominions consisted of two islands, which
composed three mighty kingdoms, under one sove-

reign, besides our plantations * in America. I dwelt long upon the fertility of our soil, and the temperature of our climate. I then spoke at large upon the constitution of an English parliament; partly made up of an illustrious body, called the House of Peers; persons of the noblest blood, and of the most ancient and ample patrimonies. I described that extraordinary care always taken of their education in arts and arms, to qualify them for being counselors both to the king and kingdom; to have a share in the legislature; to be members of the highest court of judicature, from whence there can be no appeal; and to be champions always ready for the defence of their prince and country, by their valor, conduct, and fidelity.† That these were the ornament and bulwark of the kingdom, worthy followers of their most renowned ancestors, whose honor have been the reward of their virtue, from which their posterity were never once known to degenerate. To these were joined several holy persons, as part of that assembly, under the title of bishops; whose peculiar business it is to take care of religion, and of those who instruct the people

---

* Colonies.

† This and most of Gulliver's account of the British institutions is of course meant by Swift to be understood ironically.

therein. These were searched and sought out through the whole nation, by the prince and his wisest counselors, among such of the priesthood as were most deservedly distinguished by the sanctity of their lives and the depth of their erudition; who were indeed the spiritual fathers of the clergy and the people.

That the other part of the parliament consisted of an assembly called the House of Commons, who were all principal gentlemen, freely picked and culled out by the people themselves, for their great abilities and love of their country, to represent the wisdom of the whole nation. And that these two bodies made up the most august assembly in Europe; to whom, in conjunction with the prince, the whole legislature is committed.

I then descended to the courts of justice; over which the judges, those venerable sages and inter-preters of the law, presided, for determining the disputed rights and properties of men, as well as for the punishment of vice and protection of inno-cence. I mentioned the prudent management of our treasury; the valor and achievements of our forces, by sea and land. I computed the number of our people by reckoning how many millions there might be of each religious sect, or political party, among us. I did not omit even our sports and pastimes, or any other particular which I thought might redound to the honor of my country. And I finished all with a brief historical account of affairs and events in England for about an hundred years past.

This conversation was not ended under five audiences, each of several hours; and the king heard the whole with great attention, frequently taking notes of what I spoke, as well as memorandums of all questions he intended to ask me.

When I had put an end to these long discourses, his majesty, in a sixth audience, consulting his notes, proposed many doubts, queries, and objections upon every article. He asked what methods were used to cultivate the minds and bodies of our young nobility, and in what kind of business they commonly spent the first and teachable part of their lives? What course was taken to supply that assembly, when any noble family became extinct? What qualifications were necessary in those who are to be created new lords; whether the humor of the prince, a sum of money to a court lady or a prime minister, or a design of strengthening a party opposite to the public interest, ever happened to be motives in those advancements? What share of knowledge these lords had in the laws of their country, and how they came by it, so as to enable

them to decide the properties of their fellow-sub-
jects in the last resort?   Whether they were always
so free from avarice, partialities, or want, that a
bribe, or some other sinister view, could have no
place among them?   Whether those holy lords 1
spoke of were always promoted to that rank upon
account of their knowledge in religious matters, and
the sanctity of their lives ; had never been com-
pliers with the times, while they were common
priests; or slavish prostitute chaplains to some
nobleman, whose opinions they continued servilely
to follow, after they were admitted into that
assembly ?

He then desired to know what arts were practiced
in electing those whom I called commoners ; whether
a stranger, with a strong purse, might not influence the vulgar voters to choose him before their
own landlord, or the most considerable gentleman
in the neighborhood?   How it came to pass that
people were so violently bent upon getting into this
assembly, which I allowed to be a great trouble and
expense, often to the ruin of their families, without
any salary or pension ; because this appeared such
an exalted strain of virtue and public spirit, that his
majesty seemed to doubt it might possibly not be
always sincere.   And he desired to know whether
such zealous gentlemen could have any views of re-

funding themselves for the charges and trouble they were at, by sacrificing the public good to the designs of a weak and vicious prince, in conjunction with a corrupted ministry. He multiplied his questions, and sifted me thoroughly upon every part of this head, proposing numberless inquiries and objections, which I think it not prudent or convenient to repeat.

Upon what I said in relation to our courts of justice, his majesty desired to be satisfied in several points : and this I was the better able to do, having been formerly almost ruined by a long suit in the Chancery, which was decreed for me,* with costs. He asked what time was usually spent in determining between right and wrong, and what degree of expense? Whether advocates and orators had liberty to plead in causes manifestly known to be unjust, vexatious, or oppressive? Whether party, in religion or politics, were observed to be of any weight in the scale of justice? Whether those pleading orators were persons educated in the general knowledge of equity, or only in provincial, national, and other local customs? Whether they or their judges had any part in penning those laws, which they assumed the liberty of interpreting and

---

* Decided in my favor.

glossing upon* at their pleasure? Whether they had ever, at different times, pleaded for and against the same cause, and cited precedents to prove contrary opinions? Whether they were a rich or a poor corporation? Whether they received any pecuniary reward for pleading or delivering their opinions? And particularly, whether they were ever admitted as members in the lower senate?

He fell next upon the management of our treasury; and said he thóught my memory had failed me, because I computed our taxes at about five or six millions a year, and when I came to mention the issues,† he found they sometimes amounted to more than double; for the notes he had taken were very particular in this point, because he hoped, as he told me, that the knowledge of our conduct might be useful to him, and he could not be deceived in his calculations. But, if what I told him were true, he was still at a loss how a kingdom could run out of its estate, like a private person. He asked me who were our creditors, and where we found money to pay them? He wondered to hear me talk of such chargeable and expensive wars. That certainly we must be a quarrelsome people, or live among very bad neighbors, and that our generals must

* Explaining.

† Payments and acknowledgments of indebtedness.

needs be richer than our kings. He asked what business we had out of our own islands, unless upon the score of trade, or treaty, or to defend the coasts with our fleet? Above all, he was amazed to hear me talk of a mercenary standing army in the midst of peace and among a free people. He said if we were governed by our own consent, in the persons of our representatives, he could not imagine of whom we were afraid, or against whom we were to fight; and would hear my opinion, whether a private man's house might not better be defended by himself, his children and family, than by half a dozen rascals, picked up at a venture in the streets for small wages, who might get an hundred times more by cutting their throats.

He laughed at my odd kind of arithmetic, as he was pleased to call it, in reckoning the numbers of our people, by a computation drawn from the several sects among us in religion and politics. He said he knew no reason why those who entertain opinions prejudicial to the public should be obliged to change, or should not be obliged to conceal them. And, as it was tyranny in any government to require the first, so it was weakness not to enforce the second; for a man may be allowed to keep poisons in his closet, but not to vend them about for cordials.

He observed, that, among the diversions of our

nobility and gentry, I had mentioned gaming: he desired to know at what age this entertainment was usually taken up, and when it was laid down; how much of their time it employed; whether it ever went so high as to affect their fortunes; whether mean, vicious people, by their dexterity in that art, might not arrive at great riches, and sometimes keep our very nobles in dependence, as well as habituate them to vile companions; wholly take them from the improvement of their minds, and force them, by the losses they have received, to learn and practice that infamous dexterity upon others?

He was perfectly astonished with the historical account I gave him of our affairs during the last century; protesting, it was only a heap of conspiracies, rebellions, murders, massacres, revolutions, banishments—the very worst effects that avarice, faction, hypocrisy, perfidiousness, cruelty, rage, madness, hatred, envy, lust, malice, or ambition could produce.

His majesty, in another audience, was at the pains to recapitulate the sum of all I had spoken; compared the questions he made with the answers I had given; then, taking me into his hands, and stroking me gently, delivered himself in these words, which I shall never forget, nor the manner he spoke them in: "My little friend Grildrig, you have made a most admirable panegyric upon your country; you have clearly proved that ignorance, idleness, and vice are the proper ingredients for qualifying a legislator; the laws are best explained, interpreted, and applied, by those whose interests and abilities lie in perverting, confounding, and eluding them. I observe among you some lines of an institution, which, in its original, might have been tolerable, but these half-erased, and the rest wholly blurred and blotted by corruptions. It doth not appear from all you have said how any one perfection is required, toward the procurement of any one station among you; much less, that men are ennobled on account of their virtue; that priests are advanced for their piety or learning; soldiers, for their conduct or valor; judges, for their integrity; senators, for the love of their country; or counselors, for their wisdom. As for yourself," continued the king, " who have spent the greatest part of your life in traveling, I am well disposed to hope you may hitherto have escaped many vices of your country. But, by what I have gathered from your own relation, and the answers I have with much pains wringed and extorted from you, I cannot but conclude the bulk of your natives to be the most pernicious race of little odious vermin that Nature ever suffered to crawl upon the surface of the earth."

CHAPTER VII.

The Author's love of his Country—He makes a proposal of
   much advantage to the King, which is rejected—The
   King's great ignorance in Politics—The Learning of that
   Country very imperfect and confined—Their Laws, and
   Military Affairs, and Parties in the State.

NOTHING but an extreme love of truth could have
hindered me from concealing this part of my story.
It was in vain to discover my resentments, which
were always turned into ridicule; and I was forced
to rest with patience, while my noble and most beloved country was so injuriously treated. I am as
heartily sorry as any of my readers can possibly be
that such an occasion was given; but this prince
happened to be so curious and inquisitive upon
every particular, that it could not consist either
with gratitude or good manners to refuse giving
him what satisfaction I was able. Yet this much I
may be allowed to say in my own vindication, that
I artfully eluded many of his questions, and gave to
every point a more favorable turn, by many
degrees, than the strictness of truth would allow;

for I have always borne that laudable partiality to
my own country which Dionysius Halicarnassensis,*
with so much justice, recommends to an historian:
I would hide the frailties and deformities of my
political mother, and place her virtues and beauties
in the most advantageous light. This was my
sincere endeavor, in those many discourses I had
with that monarch, although it unfortunately failed
of success.

But great allowances should be given to a king,
who lives wholly secluded from the rest of the
world, and must, therefore, be altogether un-
acquainted with the manners and customs that most
prevail in other nations; the want of which knowledge will ever produce many prejudices, and a certain narrowness of thinking, from which we, and
the politer countries of Europe, are wholly exempted; and it would be hard, indeed, if so remote
a prince's notions of virtue and vice were to be
offered as a standard for all mankind.

To confirm what I have now said, and further to
show the miserable effects of a confined education,
I shall here insert a passage that will hardly obtain
belief. In hopes to ingratiate myself further into

---

* Dionysius of Halicarnassus, a Greek historian of the first
century B.C. who wrote on Roman history, rhetoric, etc.

his majesty's favor, I told him of an invention, dis-covered between three and four hundred years ago, to make a certain powder, into an heap of which the smallest spark of fire falling would kindle the whole in a moment, although it were as big as a mountain, and make it all fly up in the air together, with a noise and agitation greater than thunder. That a proper quantity of this powder, rammed into an hollow tube of brass or iron, according to its bigness, would drive a ball of iron or lead with such violence and speed as nothing was able to sustain its force That the largest balls, thus discharged, would not only destroy whole ranks of an army at once, but batter the strongest walls to the ground, sink down ships, with a thousand men in each, to the bottom of the sea; and, when linked together by a chain, would cut through masts and rigging, divide hundreds of bodies in the middle, and lay all waste before them. That we often put this powder into large hollow balls of iron, and discharged them by an engine into some city we were besieging, which would rip up the pavements, tear the houses to pieces, burst and throw splinters on every side, dashing out the brains of all who came near. That I knew the ingredients very well, which were cheap and common; I under-stood the manner of compounding them, and could direct his workmen how to make those tubes, of a size proportionable to all other things in his majesty's kingdom, and the largest need not be above an hundred foot long; twenty or thirty of which tubes, charged with the proper quantity of powder and balls, would batter down the walls of the strongest town in his dominions in a few hours, or destroy the whole metropolis, if ever it should pretend to dispute his absolute commands. This I humbly offered to his majesty, as a small tribute of acknowledgment, in return of so many marks that I had received of his royal favor and protection.

The king was struck with horror at the description I had given of those terrible engines, and the proposal I had made. He was amazed how so impotent and groveling an insect as I (these were his expressions) could entertain such inhuman ideas, and in so familiar a manner as to appear wholly unmoved at all the scenes of blood and desolation which I had painted, as the common effects of those destructive machines: whereof, he said, some evil genius, enemy to mankind, must have been the first contriver. As for himself, he protested, that although few things delighted him so much as new discoveries in art or in nature, yet he would rather lose half his kingdom than be privy to such a secret; which he commanded me, as I valued my life, never to mention any more.

A strange effect of narrow principles and short views! that a prince possessed of every quality which procures veneration, love, and esteem; of strong parts, great wisdom, and profound learning, endued with admirable talents for government, and almost adored by his subjects, should, from a nice, unnecessary scruple, whereof in Europe we can have no conception, let slip an opportunity put into his hands that would have made him absolute master of the lives, the liberties, and the fortunes of his people! Neither do I say this with the least intention to detract from the many virtues of that excellent king, whose character, I am sensible, will, on this account, be very much lessened in the opinion of an English reader: but I take this defect among them to have risen from their ignorance, they not having hitherto reduced politics into a science, as the more acute wits of Europe have done. For, I remember very well, in a discourse one day with the king, when I happened to say, there were several thousand books among us written upon the art of government, it gave him (directly contrary to my intention) a very mean opinion of our under-standings. He professed both to abominate and despise all mystery, refinement, and intrigue, either in a prince or a minister. He could not tell what I meant by secrets of state, where an enemy, or some rival nation, were not in the case. He confined the knowledge of governing within very narrow bounds, to common sense and reason, to justice and lenity, to the speedy determination of civil and criminal causes; with some other obvious topics which are not worth considering. And, he gave it for his opinion, that, whoever could make two ears of corn, or two blades of grass, to grow upon a spot of ground where only one grew before, would deserve better of mankind, and do more essential service to his country, than the whole race of politicians put together.

The learning of this people is very defective; consisting only in morality, history, poetry, and mathematics, wherein they must be allowed to excel. But the last of these is wholly applied to what may be useful in life, to the improvement of agriculture, and all mechanical arts; so that, among us, it would be little esteemed. And, as to ideas, entities, abstractions, and transcendentals, I could never drive the least conception into their heads.

No law of that country must exceed in words the number of letters in their alphabet, which consists only of twenty-two. But, indeed, few of them extend even to that length. They are expressed in the most plain and simple terms, wherein those

people are not mercurial* enough to discover above
one interpretation : and to write a comment upon
any law is a capital crime. As to the decision of
civil causes, or proceedings against criminals, their
precedents† are so few that they have little reason
to boast of any extraordinary skill in either.

They have had the art of printing, as well as the
Chinese, time out of mind : but their libraries are
not very large; for that of the king's, which is
reckoned the biggest, doth not amount to above a
thousand volumes, placed in a gallery of twelve hundred foot long, whence I had liberty to borrow
what books I pleased. The queen's joiner had contrived, in one of Glumdalclitch's rooms, a kind of
wooden machine, twenty-five foot high, formed like
a standing ladder; the steps were each fifty foot
long : it was indeed a movable pair of stairs, the
lowest end placed at ten foot distance from the wall
of the chamber. The book I had a mind to read
was put up leaning against the wall : I first mounted
to the upper step of the ladder, and turning my face
toward the book, began at the top of the page, and
so walking to the right and left about eight or ten
paces according to the length of the lines, till I had
gotten a little below the level of mine eyes, and

---

* Sharp-witted; subtle.   † Cases already settled.

then descending gradually till I came to the bottom; after which I mounted again, and began the other page in the same manner, and so turned over the leaf, which I could easily do with both my hands, for it was as thick and stiff as pasteboard, and in the largest folios not above eighteen or twenty foot long.

Their style is clear, masculine, and smooth, but not florid; for they avoid nothing more than multiplying unnecessary words, or using various expressions. I have perused many of their books, especially those in history and morality. Among the rest, I was much diverted with a little old treatise, which always lay in Glumdalclitch's bedchamber, and belonged to her governess, a grave elderly gentlewoman, who dealt in writings of morality and devotion. The book treats of the weakness of human kind, and is in little esteem, except among the women and the vulgar. However, I was curious to see what an author of that country could say upon such a subject. This writer went through all the usual topics of European moralists, showing, " how diminutive, contemptible, and helpless an animal was man in his own nature; how unable to defend himself from inclemencies of the air, or the fury of wild beasts; how much he was excelled by one creature in strength, by another

in speed, by a third in foresight, by a fourth in
industry." He added, "that nature was degenerated
in these latter declining ages of the world, and could
now produce only small abortive births, in comparison of those in ancient times." He said, "it
was very reasonable to think, not only that the
species of man were originally much larger, but also
that there must have been giants in former ages;
which, as it is asserted by history and tradition, so
it hath been confirmed by huge bones and skulls,
casually dug up in several parts of the kingdom, far
exceeding the common, dwindled race of men* in
our days." He argued, "that the very laws of
nature absolutely required we should have been
made, in the beginning, of a size more large and
robust; not so liable to destruction from every little
accident, of a tile falling from a house, or a stone
cast from the hand of a boy, or of being drowned
in a little brook." From this way of reasoning the
author drew several moral applications, useful in
the conduct of life, but needless here to repeat.
For my own part I could not avoid reflecting how
universally this talent was spread, of drawing
lectures on morality, or indeed rather a matter of
discontent and repining, from the quarrels we raise

---

*This "dwindled race of men," it must be remembered, are
the Brobdingnagians themselves.

with nature. And I believe, upon a strict inquiry, those quarrels might be shown as ill-grounded among us as they are among that people.

As to their military affairs, they boast that the king's army consists of an hundred and seventy-six thousand foot and thirty-two thousand horse: if that may be called an army, which is made up of tradesmen in the several cities, and farmers in the country, whose commanders are only the nobility and gentry, without pay or reward. They are indeed perfect enough in their exercises, and under very good discipline, wherein I saw no great merit; for how should it be otherwise, where every farmer is under the command of his own landlord, and every citizen under that of the principal men in his own city, chosen, after the manner of Venice, by ballot?

I have often seen the militia of Lorbrulgrud drawn out to exercise in a great field near the city, of twenty miles square. They were in all not above twenty-five thousand foot and six thousand horse; but it was impossible for me to compute their number, considering the space of ground they took up. A cavalier, mounted on a large steed, might be about ninety foot high. I have seen this whole body of horse, upon a word of command, draw their swords at once, and brandish them in the air. Imagination can figure nothing so grand, so surprising, and so astonishing! it looked as if ten thousand flashes of lightning were darting at the same time from every quarter of the sky.

I was curious to know how this prince, to whose dominions there is no access from any other country, came to think of armies, or to teach his people the practice of military discipline. But I was soon informed, both by conversation, and reading their histories; for, in the course of many ages, they have been troubled with the same disease to which many other governments are subject; the nobility often contending for power, the people for liberty, and the king for absolute dominion. All which, however, happily tempered by the laws of that kingdom, have been sometimes violated by each of the three parties, and have once or more occasioned civil wars; the last whereof was happily put an end to by this prince's grandfather, by a general composition; and the militia, then settled with common consent, hath been ever since kept in the strictest duty.

CHAPTER VIII.

The King and Queen make a progress to the frontiers—The
Author attends them—The manner in which he leaves
the Country very particularly related—He returns to
England.

I HAD always a strong impulse that I should some
time recover my liberty, though it was impossible
to conjecture by what means, or to form any project
with the least hope of succeeding. The ship in
which I sailed was the first ever known to be driven
within sight of that coast, and the king had given
strict orders that if at any time another appeared it
should be taken ashore, and, with all its crew and
passengers, brought in a tumbrel to Lorbrulgrud. I
was indeed treated with much kindness; I was the
favorite of a great king and queen, and the delight
of the whole court; but it was upon such a foot as
ill became the dignity of human kind. I could never
forget those domestic pledges I had left behind me.
I wanted to be among people with whom I could
converse upon even terms, and walk about the

streets and fields without fear of being trod to death like a frog or a young puppy. But my deliverance came sooner than I expected, and in a manner not very common; the whole story and circumstances of which I shall faithfully relate.

I had now been two years in the country; and about the beginning of the third Glumdalclitch and I attended the king and queen in a progress to the south coast of the kingdom. I was carried, as usual, in my traveling-box, which, as I have already described, was a very convenient closet of twelve foot wide. And I had ordered a hammock to be fixed, by silken ropes, from the four corners at the top, to break the jolts when a servant carried me before him on horseback, as I sometimes desired; and would often sleep in my hammock while we were upon the road. On the roof of my closet, not directly over the middle of the hammock, I ordered the joiner to cut out a hole of a foot square, to give me air in hot weather, as I slept; which hole I shut at pleasure with a board that drew backward and forward through a groove.

When we came to our journey's end, the king thought proper to pass a few days at a palace he hath near Flanflasnic, a city within eighteen English miles of the seaside. Glumdalclitch and I were much fatigued: I had gotten a small cold, but the

poor girl was so ill as to be confined to her chamber.
I longed to see the ocean, which must be the only
scene of my escape, if ever it should happen. I pretended to be worse than I really was, and desired
leave to take the fresh air of the sea, with a page
whom I was very fond of, and who had sometimes
been trusted with me. I shall never forget with
what unwillingness Glumdalclitch consented, nor
the strict charge she gave the page to be careful of
me, bursting at the same time into a flood of tears,
as if she had some foreboding of what was to
happen. The boy took me out in my box, about
half an hour's walk from the palace, toward the
rocks on the seashore. I ordered him to set me
down, and lifting up one of my sashes, cast many a
wistful, melancholy look toward the sea. I found
myself not very well, and told the page that I had
a mind to take a nap in my hammock, which I
hoped would do me good. I got in, and the boy
shut the window close down, to keep out the cold.
I soon fell asleep, and all I can conjecture is, that
while I slept the page, thinking no danger could
happen, went among the rocks to look for birds'
eggs, having before observed him from my window
searching about, and picking up one or two in the
clefts. Be that as it will, I found myself suddenly
awaked with a violent pull upon the ring, which

was fastened at the top of my box for the conveniency of carriage. I felt my box raised very
high in the air, and then borne forward with
prodigious speed. The first jolt had like to have
shaken me out of my hammock, but afterward the
motion was easy enough. I called out several times
as loud as I could raise my voice, but all to no
purpose. I looked toward my windows, and could
see nothing but the clouds and sky. I heard a
noise just over my head, like the clapping of wings,
and then began to perceive the woeful condition I
was in ; that some eagle had got the ring of my box
in his beak, with an intent to let it fall on a rock,
like a tortoise in a shell, and then pick out my body,
and devour it : for the sagacity and smell of this
bird enable him to discover his quarry at a great
distance, though better concealed than I could be
within a two-inch board.

In a little time I observed the noise and flutter
of wings to increase very fast, and my box was
tossed up and down, like a sign* in a windy day. I
heard several bangs or buffets, as I thought, given
to the eagle (for such, I am certain, it must have
been that held the ring of my box in his beak), and
then, all on a sudden, felt myself falling perpen-
dicularly down for above a minute, but with such

---

* That is a *swinging* signboard.

incredible swiftness that I almost lost my breath. My fall was stopped by a terrible squash, that sounded louder to my ears than the cataract of Niagara; after which I was quite in the dark for another minute, and then my box began to rise so high that I could see light from the tops of my windows. I now perceived that I was fallen into the sea. My box, by the weight of my body, the goods that were in it, and the broad plates of iron fixed for strength at the four corners of the top and bottom, floated above five foot deep in water. I did then, and do now, suppose that the eagle, which flew away with my box, was pursued by two or three others, and forced to let me drop, while he was defending himself against the rest, who hoped to share in the prey. The plates of iron fastened at the bottom of the box (for those were the strongest) preserved the balance while it fell, and hindered it from being broken on the surface of the water. Every joint of it was well grooved; and the door did not move on hinges, but up and down like a sash, which kept my closet so tight that very little water came in. I got, with much difficulty out of my hammock, having first ventured to draw back the slip-board on the roof, already mentioned, con- trived on purpose to let in air, for want of which I found myself almost stifled.

How often did I then wish myself with my dear Glumdalclitch, from whom one single hour had so far divided me! And I may say with truth, that, in the midst of my own misfortunes, I could not forbear lamenting my poor nurse, the grief she would suffer for my loss, the displeasure of the queen, and the ruin of her fortune. Perhaps many travelers have not been under greater difficulties and distress than I was at this juncture, expecting every moment to see my box dashed in pieces, or, at least, overset by the first violent blast, or a rising wave. A breach in one single pane of glass would have been immediate death: nor could anything have preserved the windows, but the strong lattice wires, placed on the outside, against accidents in traveling. I saw the water ooze in at several crannies, although the leaks were not considerable, and I endeavored to stop them as well as I could. I was not able to lift up the roof of my closet, which otherwise I certainly should have done, and sat on the top of it; where I might at least preserve myself some hours longer, than by being shut up (as I may call it) in the hold. Or, if I escaped these dangers for a day or two, what could I expect but a miserable death of cold and hunger? I was four hours under these circumstances, expecting, and indeed wishing, every moment to be my last.

I have already told the reader that there were two strong staples fixed upon that side of my box which had no window, and into which the servant, who used to carry me on horseback, would put a leathern belt, and buckle it about his waist. Being in this disconsolate state, I heard, or at least thought I heard, some kind of grating noise on that side of my box where the staples were fixed; and soon after I began to fancy that the box was pulled or towed along in the sea; for I now and then felt a sort of tugging, which made the waves rise near the tops of my windows, leaving me almost in the dark. This gave me some faint hopes of relief, although I was not able to imagine how it could be brought about. I ventured to unscrew one of my chairs, which were always fastened to the floor; and having made a hard shift to screw it down again, directly under the slipping-board that I had lately opened, I mounted on the chair, and, putting my mouth as near as I could to the hole, I called for help in a loud voice, and in all the languages I understood. I then fastened my handkerchief to a stick I usually carried, and, thrusting it up the hole waved it several times in the air, that, if any boat or ship were near, the seamen might conjecture some unhappy mortal to be shut up in this box. I found no effect from all I could do, but plainly perceived my closet to be moved along; and in the space of an hour, or better, that side of the box where the staples were, and had no windows, struck against something that was hard. I apprehended it to be a rock, and found myself tossed more than ever. I plainly heard a noise upon the cover of my closet like that of a cable, and the grating of it as it passed through the ring. I then found myself hoisted up, by degrees, at least three foot higher than I was before. Whereupon I again thrust up my stick and handkerchief, calling for help till I was almost hoarse. In return to which I heard a great shout repeated three times, giving me such trans-ports of joy as are not to be conceived but by those who feel them. I now heard a trampling over my head, and somebody calling through the hole with a loud voice, in the English tongue, if there be any-body below, let them speak. I answered, I was an Englishman, drawn, by ill fortune, into the greatest calamity that ever any creature underwent, and begged, by all that was moving, to be delivered out of the dungeon I was in. The voice replied, I was safe, for my box was fastened to their ship, and the carpenter should immediately come and saw a hole in the cover, large enough to pull me out. I an-swered, that was needless, and would take up too much time; for there was no more to be done, but let one of the crew put his finger into the ring, and take the box out of the sea into the ship, and so into the captain's cabin. Some of them, upon hearing me talk so wildly, thought I was mad; others laughed; for indeed it never came into my head that I was now got among people of my own stature and strength. The carpenter came, and, in a few minutes, sawed a passage about four foot square, then let down a small ladder, upon which I mounted, and from thence was taken into the ship in a very weak condition.

The sailors were all in amazement, and asked me a thousand questions, which I had no inclination to answer. I was equally confounded at the sight of so many pigmies, for such I took them to be, after having so long accustomed mine eyes to the monstrous objects I had left. But the captain, Mr. Thomas Wilcocks, an honest, worthy Shropshireman, observing I was ready to faint, took me into his cabin, gave me a cordial to comfort me, and made me turn in upon his own bed, advising me to take a little rest, of which I had great need. Before I went to sleep I gave him to understand that I had some valuable furniture in my box, too good to be lost; a fine hammock—an handsome field bed —two chairs—a table—and a cabinet. That my closet was hung on all sides, or rather quilted with silk and cotton; that, if he would let one of the crew bring my closet into his cabin, I would open it there before him, and show him my goods. The captain, hearing me utter these absurdities, concluded I was raving; however (I suppose to pacify me), he promised to give order as I desired, and going upon deck, sent some of his men down into my closet, from whence (as I afterward found) they drew up all my goods, and stripped off the quilting; but the chairs, cabinet, and bedstead, being screwed to the floor, were much damaged by the ignorance of the seamen, who tore them up by force. Then they knocked off some of the boards for the use of the ship, and when they had got all they had a mind for, let the hull drop into the sea, which, by reason of many breaches made in the bottom and sides, sunk to rights.* And, indeed, I was glad not to have been a spectator of the havoc they made, because I am confident it would have sensibly touched me, by bringing former passages into my mind, which I had rather forget.

I slept some hours, but perpetually disturbed with dreams of the place I had left, and the dangers I had escaped. However, upon waking, I found myself much recovered. It was now about eight o'clock

---

* Directly, or at once.

at night, and the captain ordered supper **immediately**, thinking I had already fasted too long. **He** entertained me with great kindness, observing **me** not to look wildly, or talk inconsistently; and, **when** we were left alone, desired I would give him **a** relation of my travels, and by what accident I came to be set adrift in that monstrous wooden chest. He said that about twelve o'clock at noon, as he was looking through his glass, he spied it at a distance, and thought it was a sail,* which he had a mind to make,† being not much out of his course, in hopes of buying some biscuit, his own beginning to fall short. That, upon coming nearer, and finding his error, he sent out his long-boat to discover what it was; that his men came back in a fright, swearing that they had seen a swimming house. That he laughed at their folly, and went himself in the boat, ordering his men to take a strong cable along with them. That the weather being calm, he rowed round me several times, observed my windows, and the wire lattices that defended them. That he discovered two staples upon one side, which was all of boards, without any passage for light. He then commanded his men to row up to that side, and fastening a cable to one of the staples, ordered

---

* A ship. † Come close to

them to tow my chest, as they called it, toward the ship. When it was there, he gave directions to fasten another cable to the ring fixed in the cover, and to raise up my chest with pulleys, which all the sailors were not able to do above two or three foot. He said they saw my stick and handkerchief thrust out of the hole, and concluded that some unhappy man must be shut up in the cavity. I asked whether he or the crew had seen any prodigious birds in the air about the time he first discovered me? To which he answered, that discoursing this matter with the sailors while I was asleep, one of them said he had observed three eagles flying toward the north, but remarked nothing of their being larger than the usual size; which, I suppose, must be imputed to the great height they were at; and he could not guess the reason of my question. I then asked the captain how far he reckoned we might be from land? He said, by the best computation he could make, we were, at least, an hundred leagues. I assured him that he must be mistaken by almost half, for I had not left the country from whence I came above two hours before I dropped into the sea. Whereupon, he began again to think that my brain was disturbed, of which he gave me a hint, and advised me to go to bed in a cabin he had provided. I assured him I was well refreshed with his good entertainment and company, and as much in my senses as ever I was in my life. He then grew serious, and desired to ask me freely, whether I were not troubled in mind by the consciousness of some enormous crime, for which I was punished, at the command of some prince, by exposing me in that chest; as great criminals, in other countries, have been forced to sea in a leaky vessel, without provisions; for although he should be sorry to have taken so ill a man into his ship, yet he would engage his word to set me safe on shore at the first port where we arrived. He added that his suspicions were much increased by some very absurd speeches I had delivered at first to the sailors, and afterward to himself, in relation to my closet or chest, as well as by my odd looks and behavior while I was at supper.

I begged his patience to hear me tell my story, which I faithfully did, from the last time I left England to the moment he first discovered me. And as truth always forceth its way into rational minds, so this honest, worthy gentleman, who had some tincture of learning and very good sense, was immediately convinced of my candor and veracity. But, further to confirm all I had said, I entreated him to give order that my cabinet should be brought, of which I had the key in my pocket; for he had already informed me how the seamen disposed of my closet. I opened it in his own presence, and showed him the small collection of rarities I made in the country from whence I had been so strangely delivered. There was the comb I had contrived out of the stumps of the king's beard, and another of the same materials, but fixed into a paring of her majesty's thumb-nail, which served for the back. There was a collection of needles and pins, from a foot to half a yard long; four wasp's stings, like joiner's tacks; some combings of the queen's hair; a gold ring, which one day she made me a present of, in a most obliging manner, taking it from her little finger, and throwing it over my head like a collar. I desired the captain would please to accept this ring in return of his civilities, which he absolutely refused. I showed him a corn that I had cut off, with my own hand, from a maid of honor's toe; it was about the bigness of a Kentish pippin, and grown so hard that, when I returned to England, I got it hollowed into a cup, and set in silver. Lastly, I desired him to see the breeches I had then on, which were made of a mouse's skin.

I could force nothing on him but a footman's tooth, which I observed him to examine with great curiosity, and found he had a fancy for it. He received it with abundance of thanks, more than such a trifle could deserve. It was drawn by an unskill-ful surgeon in a mistake, from one of Glumdal-clitch's men, who was afflicted with the toothache, but it was as sound as any in his head. I got it cleaned, and put it into my cabinet. It was about a foot long and four inches in diameter.

The captain was very well satisfied with this plain relation I had given him, and said he hoped when we returned to England, I would oblige the world by putting it on paper and making it public. My answer was that I thought we were already over-stocked with books of travels; that nothing could now pass which was not extraordinary; wherein I doubted some authors less consulted truth than their own vanity, or interest, or the diversion of ignorant readers; that my story could contain little beside common events, without those ornamental descriptions of strange plants, trees, birds, and other animals; or of the barbarous customs and idolatry of savage people, with which most writers abound. However, I thanked him for his good opinion, and promised to take the matter into my thoughts.

He said he wondered at one thing very much, which was, to hear me speak so loud; asking me whether the king or queen of that country were thick of hearing? I told him it was what I had been used to for above two years past, and that I admired* as much at the voices of him and his men, who seemed to me only to whisper, and yet I could hear them well enough. But when I spoke in that country it was like a man talking in the street to another looking out from the top of a steeple, unless when I was placed on a table, or held in any person's hand. I told him I had likewise observed another thing, that, when I first got into the ship, and the sailors stood all about me, I thought they were the most contemptible little creatures I had ever beheld. For, indeed, while I was in that prince's country I could never endure to look in a glass after mine eyes had been accustomed to such prodigious objects, because the comparison gave me so despicable a conceit of myself. The captain said that while we were at supper he observed me to look at everything with a sort of wonder, and that I often seemed hardly able to contain my laughter, which he knew not well how to take, but imputed it to some disorder in my brain. I answered, it was very true: and I wondered how I could forbear when I saw his dishes of the size of a silver threepence, a leg of pork hardly a mouthful, a cup not so big as a nutshell; and so I went on, describing the rest of his household stuff

---

* Wondered: an old usage of the word, still common in America.

and provisions after the same manner. For, although the queen had ordered a little equipage of all things necessary for me, while I was in her service, yet my ideas were wholly taken up with what I saw on every side of me, and I winked at my own little-ness as people do at their own faults. The captain understood my raillery very well, and merrily replied with the old English proverb, that he doubted mine eyes were bigger than my belly, for he did not observe my stomach so good, although I had fasted all day; and, continuing in his mirth, protested he would have gladly given an hundred pounds to have seen my closet in the eagle's bill, and afterward in its fall from so great a height into the sea; which would certainly have been a most astonishing object worthy to have the description of it transmitted to future ages: and the comparison of Phaëton* was so obvious that he could not forbear applying it, although I did not much admire the conceit.

The captain, having been at Tonquin, was, in his return to England, driven northeastward to the lat-itude of 44 degrees, and longitude of 143. But, meeting a trade-wind two days after I came on board him, we sailed southward a long time, and,

---

* Phaëton, or rather Phaëthon, was a character of Greek mythology, who, driving the horses of the sun, was struck by lightning and fell into the river Po.

coasting New Holland, kept our course west-south-west, and then south-southwest, till we doubled the Cape of Good Hope. Our voyage was very prosperous, but I shall not trouble the reader with a journal of it. The captain called in at one or two ports, and sent in his long-boat for provisions and fresh water; but I never went out of the ship till we came into the Downs, which was on the third day of June, 1706, about nine months after my escape. I offered to leave my goods in security for payment of my freight; but the captain protested he would not receive one farthing. We took kind leave of each other, and I made him promise he would come to see me at my house in Redriff. I hired a horse and guide for five shillings, which I borrowed of the captain.

As I was on the road, observing the littleness of the houses, the trees, the cattle, and the people, I began to think myself in Lilliput. I was afraid of trampling on every traveler I met, and often called aloud to have them stand out of the way, so that I had like to have gotten one or two broken heads for my impertinence.

When I came to my own house, for which I was forced to inquire, one of the servants opening the door, I bent down to go in (like a goose under a gate), for fear of striking my head. My wife ran out to embrace me, but I stooped lower than her knees, thinking she could otherwise never be able to reach my mouth. My daughter kneeled to ask my blessing, but I could not see her till she arose, having been so long used to stand with my head and eyes erect to above sixty foot; and then I went to take her up with one hand by the waist. I looked down upon the servants, and one or two friends who were in the house, as if they had been pigmies and I a giant. I told my wife she had been too thrifty, for I found she had starved herself and her daughter to nothing. In short, I behaved myself so unaccountably that they were all of the captain's opinion when he first saw me, and concluded I had lost my wits. This I mention as an instance of the great power of habit and prejudice.

In a little time I and my family and friends came to a right understanding; but my wife protested I should never go to sea any more; although my evil destiny so ordered that she had not power to hinder me, as the reader may know hereafter. In the meantime I here conclude the second part of my unfortunate voyages.

PART III.

A VOYAGE TO LAPUTA, BALNIBARBI, LUGGNAGG, GLUBBDUBDRIBB, AND JAPAN.

PART III.

A VOYAGE TO LAPUTA, BALNIBARBI, LUGGNAGG, GLUBBDUBDRIBB, AND JAPAN.

CHAPTER I.

The Author sets out on his third Voyage—Is taken by Pirates —The malice of a Dutchman—His arrival at an Island— He is received into Laputa.

I HAD not been at home above ten days when Captain William Robinson, a Cornish man, commander of the Hopewell, a stout ship of three hundred tons, came to my house. I had formerly been surgeon of another ship, where he was master and a fourth-part owner, in a voyage to the Levant. He had always treated me more like a brother than an inferior officer; and, hearing of my arrival, made me a visit, as I apprehended, only out of friendship, for nothing passed more than what is usual after long absences. But, repeating his visits often, expressing his joy to find me in good health, asking, whether I were now settled for life? adding, that he intended a voyage to the East Indies in two months; at last he plainly invited me, though with some apologies, to be surgeon of the ship; that I should have another surgeon under me, besides our two mates; that my salary should be double to the usual pay; and that having experienced my knowledge in sea affairs to be at least equal to his, he would enter into any engagement to follow my advice as much as if I had share in the command.

He said so many other obliging things, and I knew him to be so honest a man, that I could not reject his proposal; the thirst I had of seeing the world, notwithstanding my past misfortunes, continuing as violent as ever. The only difficulty that remained was to persuade my wife, whose consent, however, I at last obtained, by the prospect of advantage she proposed to her children.

We set out the 5th day of August, 1706, and arrived at Fort St. George* the 11th of April, 1707. We stayed there three weeks to refresh our crew, many of whom were sick. From thence we went to Tonquin, where the captain resolved to continue some time, because many of the goods he intended to buy were not ready, nor could he expect to be

* An old name of Madras, the fort or citadel of the town being so named.

despatched in some months. Therefore, in hopes to defray some of the charges he must be at, he bought a sloop, loaded it with several sorts of goods, wherewith the Tonquinese usually trade to the neighboring islands, and putting fourteen men on board, whereof three were of the country, he appointed me master of the sloop, and gave me power to traffic while he transacted his affairs at Tonquin.

We had not sailed above three days, when a great storm arising, we were driven five days to the north-northeast, and then to the east; after which we had fair weather, but still with a pretty strong gale from the west. Upon the tenth day we were chased by two pirates, who soon overtook us; for my sloop was so deep laden that she sailed very slow, neither were we in a condition to defend ourselves.

We were boarded about the same time by both the pirates, who entered furiously at the head of their men; but, finding us all prostrate upon our faces (for so I gave order), they pinioned us with strong ropes, and, setting a guard upon us, went to search the sloop.

I observed among them a Dutchman, who seemed to be of some authority, though he was not commander of either ship. He knew us by our countenances to be Englishmen, and, jabbering to us in his own language, swore we should be tied back to back, and thrown into the sea. I spoke Dutch tolerably well; I told him who we were, and begged him, in consideration of our being Christians and Protestants, of neighboring countries in strict alliance, that he would move the captains to take some pity on us. This inflamed his rage; he repeated his threatenings, and, turning to his companions, spoke with great vehemence in the Japanese language, as I suppose, often using the word *Christianos.*

The largest of the two pirate ships was commanded by a Japanese captain, who spoke a little Dutch, but very imperfectly. He came up to me, and, after several questions, which I answered in great humility, he said we should not die. I made the captain a very low bow, and then, turning to the Dutchman, said I was sorry to find more mercy in a heathen than in a brother Christian. But I had soon reason to repent those foolish words; for that malicious reprobate, having often endeavored in vain to persuade both the captains that I might be thrown into the sea (which they would not yield to, after the promise made me that I should not die), however, prevailed so far as to have a punishment inflicted on me, worse, in all human appearance, than death itself. My men were sent by an equal division into both the pirate ships and my sloop new manned. As to myself, it was determined that I should be set adrift in a small canoe, with paddles and a sail, and four days' provisions; which last the Japanese captain was so kind to double out of his own stores, and would permit no man to search me. I got down into the canoe, while the Dutchman, standing upon the deck, loaded me with all the curses and injurious terms his language could afford.

About an hour before we saw the pirates I had taken an observation, and found we were in the latitude of 46 N. and longitude of 183.* When I was at some distance from the pirates I discovered by my pocket-glass several islands to the southeast. I set up my sail, the wind being fair, with a design to reach the nearest of those islands, which I made a shift to do in about three hours. It was all rocky: however, I got many birds' eggs; and striking fire, I kindled some heath and dry seaweed, by which I roasted my eggs. I eat no other supper, being resolved to spare my provisions as much as I could. I passed the night under the shelter of a rock, strowing some heath under me, and slept pretty well.

The next day I sailed to another island, and thence to a third and fourth, sometimes using my

---

* This would be not very far south of the Aleutian Islands, in the North Pacific.

sail, and sometimes my paddles. But not to trouble
the reader with a particular account of my dis-
tresses, let it suffice that on the fifth day I arrived
at the last island in my sight, which lay south-south-
east to the former.

This island was at a greater distance than I expected, and I did not reach it in less than five hours.
I encompassed it almost round, before I could find
a convenient place to land in; which was a small
creek, about three times the wideness of my canoe.
I found the island to be all rocky, only a little
intermingled with tufts of grass and sweet-smelling
herbs. I took out my small provisions, and, after
having refreshed myself, I secured the remainder in
a cave, whereof there were great numbers; I
gathered plenty of eggs upon the rocks, and got a
quantity of dry seaweed and parched grass, which I
designed to kindle the next day, and roast my eggs
as well as I could; for I had about me my flint,
steel, match, and burning-glass. I lay all night in
the cave where I had lodged my provisions. My
bed was the same dry grass and seaweed which I
intended for fuel. I slept very little, for the disquiets of my mind prevailed over my weariness, and
kept me awake. I considered how impossible it was
to preserve my life in so desolate a place, and how
miserable my end must be. Yet I found myself so

listless and desponding that I had not the heart to
rise ; and, before I could get spirits enough to creep
out of my cave, the day was far advanced. I
walked a while among the rocks : the sky was perfectly clear, and the sun so hot that I was forced
to turn my face from it ; when, all on a sudden, it
became obscure, as I thought, in a manner very different from what happens by the interposition of a
cloud. I turned back, and perceived a vast opaque
body between me and the sun, moving forward
toward the island : it seemed to be about two miles
high, and hid the sun six or seven minutes ; but I
did not observe the air to be much colder, or the
sky more darkened, than if I had stood under the
shade of a mountain. As it approached nearer over
the place where I was, it appeared to be a firm substance, the bottom flat, smooth, and shining very
bright, from the reflection of the sea below. I stood
upon a height about two hundred yards from the
shore, and saw this vast body descending almost to
a parallel with me, at less than an English mile distance. I took out my pocket perspective,* and
could plainly discover numbers of people moving up
and down the sides of it, which appeared to be
sloping : but what those people were doing I was
not able to distinguish.

---

* Telescope.

The natural love of life gave me some inward motions of joy, and I was ready to entertain a hope that this adventure might, some way or other, help to deliver me from the desolate place and condition I was in. But at the same time the reader can hardly conceive my astonishment to behold an island in the air, inhabited by men who were able (as it should seem) to raise or sink, or put it into a progressive motion, as they pleased. But not being at that time in a disposition to philosophize upon this phenomenon, I rather chose to observe what course the island would take, because it seemed for awhile to stand still. Yet, soon after, it advanced nearer, and I could see the sides of it encompassed with several gradations of galleries, and stairs, at certain intervals, to descend from one to the other. In the lowest gallery I beheld some people fishing with long angling rods, and others looking on. I waved my cap (for my hat was long since worn out) and my handkerchief toward the island; and upon its nearer approach I called and shouted with the utmost strength of my voice; and then looking circumspectly, I beheld a crowd gather to that side which was most in my view. I found by their pointing toward me, and to each other, that they plainly discovered me, although they made no return to my shouting. But I could see four or five men running in great haste up the stairs, to the top of the island, who then disappeared. I happened rightly to conjecture that these were sent for orders, to some person in authority, upon this occasion.

The number of people increased, and in less than an hour the island was moved and raised in such a manner that the lowest gallery appeared in a parallel of less than a hundred yards distance from the height where I stood. I then put myself into the most supplicating postures, and spoke in the humblest accent, but received no answer. Those who stood nearest over against me seemed to be persons of distinction, as I supposed by their habit. They conferred earnestly with each other, looking often upon me. At length one of them called out in a clear, polite, smooth dialect, not unlike in sound to the Italian; and, therefore, I returned an answer in that language, hoping at least that the cadence might be more agreeable to his ears. Although neither of us understood the other, yet my meaning was easily known, for the people saw the distress I was in.

They made signs for me to come down from the rock, and go toward the shore, which I accordingly did; and the flying island being raised to a convenient height, the verge directly over me, a chain was let down from the lowest gallery, with a seat fastened to the bottom, to which I fixed myself, and was drawn up by pulleys.

CHAPTER II.

The humors and dispositions of the Laputians described—An account of their Learning—Of the King and his Court—The Author's reception there—The Inhabitants subject to fears and disquietudes—An account of the Women.

AT my alighting I was surrounded by a crowd of people, but those who stood nearest seemed to be of better quality. They beheld me with all the marks and circumstances of wonder; neither, indeed, was I much in their debt, having never till then seen a race of mortals so singular in their shapes, habits, and countenances. Their heads were all inclined either to the right or the left; one of their eyes turned inward, and the other directly up to the zenith. Their outward garments were adorned with the figures of suns, moons, and stars; interwoven with those of fiddles, flutes, harps, trumpets, guitars, harpsichords,* and many more instruments of music unknown to us in Europe. I observed here and there many in the habit of servants, with a blown bladder fastened like a flail to the end of a short

---

* An old form of the piano.

stick, which they carried in their hands. In each bladder was a small quantity of dried peas, or little pebbles, as I was afterward informed. With these bladders they now and then flapped the mouths and ears of those who stood near them, of which practice I could not then conceive the meaning. It seems the minds of these people are so taken up with intense speculations that they neither can speak, nor attend to the discourses of others, without being roused by some external taction* upon the organs of speech and hearing; for which reason those persons who are able to afford it always keep a flapper (the original is *climenole*) in their family as one of their domestics; nor even walk abroad, or make visits, without him. And the business of this officer is, when two or three more persons are in company, gently to strike with his bladder the mouth of him who is to speak, and the right ear of him or them to whom the speaker addresseth himself. This flapper is likewise employed diligently to attend his master in his walks, and upon occasion to give him a soft flap on his eyes; because he is always so wrapped up in cogitation that he is in manifest danger of falling down every precipice, and bouncing his head against every post; and in the streets of jostling others, or being jostled himself, into the kennel.

---

* Touch, contact.

It was necessary to give the reader this information, without which he would be at the same loss
with me to understand the proceedings of these people, as they conducted me up the stairs to the top
of the island, and from thence to the royal palace.
While we were ascending they forgot several times
what they were about, and left me to myself, till
their memories were again roused by their flappers,
for they appeared altogether unmoved by the sight
of my foreign habit and countenance, and by the
shouts of the vulgar, whose thoughts and minds were
more disengaged.

At last we entered the palace, and proceeded into
the chamber of presence, where I saw the king
seated on his throne, attended on each side by persons of prime quality. Before the throne was a
large table filled with globes and spheres and mathematical instruments of all kinds. His majesty took
not the least notice of us, although our entrance was
not without sufficient noise, by the concourse of all
persons belonging to the court. But he was then
deep in a problem; and we attended at least an hour
before he could solve it. There stood by him, on
each side, a young page with flaps in their hands,
and when they saw he was at leisure, one of them
gently struck his mouth, and the other his right
ear; at which he started like one awaked on the

sudden, and looking toward me and the company I was in, recollected the occasion of our coming, whereof he had been informed before. He spoke some words, whereupon immediately a young man with a flap came up to my side and flapped me gently on the right ear; but I made signs, as well as I could, that I had no occasion for such an instrument, which, as I afterward found, gave his majesty and the whole court a very mean opinion of my understanding. The king, as far as I could conjecture, asked me several questions, and I addressed myself to him in all the languages I had. When it was found that I could neither understand nor be understood, I was conducted by the king's order to an apartment in his palace (this prince being distinguished above all his predecessors for his hospitality to strangers), where two servants were appointed to attend me. My dinner was brought, and four persons of quality, whom I remembered to have seen very near the king's person, did me the honor to dine with me. We had two courses of three dishes each. In the first course there was a shoulder of mutton cut into an equilateral triangle, a piece of beef into a rhomboid,* and a pudding into a cycloid.†

---

* A four-sided figure with the opposite sides parallel, one pair longer than the other pair, and the angles not right angles. † A geometrical figure resembling a semicircle with the curve flattened.

The second course was two ducks trussed up into the form of fiddles; sausages and puddings, resembling flutes and hautboys, and a breast of veal in the shape of a harp. The servants cut our bread into cones, cylinders, parallelograms, and several other mathematical figures.

While we were at dinner I made bold to ask the names of several things in their language, and those noble persons, by the assistance of their flappers, delighted to give me answers, hoping to raise my admiration of their great abilities, if I could be brought to converse with them. I was soon able to call for bread and drink, or whatever else I wanted.

After dinner my company withdrew, and a person was sent to me by the king's order, attended by a flapper. He brought with him pen, ink, and paper, and three or four books, giving me to understand by signs that he was sent to teach me the language. We sat together four hours, in which time I wrote down a great number of words in columns, with the translations over against them; I likewise made a shift to learn several short sentences. For my tutor would order one of my servants to fetch something, or turn about, to make a bow, to sit, or stand, or walk, and the like. Then I took down the sentence in writing. He showed me also, in one of his books, the figures of the sun, moon, and stars, the zodiac, the tropic and polar circles, together with the denominations of many figures of planes and solids. He gave me the names and descriptions of all the musical instruments, and the general terms of art in playing on each of them. After he had left me I placed all my words, with their interpretations, in alphabetical order. And thus, in a few days, by the help of a very faithful memory, I got some insight into their language.

The word, which I interpret the flying or floating island, is in the original *Laputa*, whereof I could never learn the true etymology. *Lap*, in the old obsolete language, signifieth high; and *untuh*, a governor; from which, they say, by corruption, was derived *Laputa*, from *Lapuntuh*. But I do not approve of this derivation, which seems to be a little strained. I ventured to offer to the learned among them a conjecture of my own, that Laputa was *quasi* lap outed ;* *lap* signifying properly the dancing of the sunbeams in the sea, and *outed*, a wing, which, however, I shall not obtrude, but submit to the judicious reader.

Those to whom the king had intrusted me, observing how ill I was clad, ordered a tailor to come next morning, and take my measure for a suit of clothes.

---

* A Latin word meaning as if, as it were

This operator did his office after a different manner from those of his trade in Europe. He first took my altitude by a quadrant, and then, with rule and compasses, described the dimensions and outlines of my whole body, all which he entered upon paper; and, in six days, brought my clothes, very ill made, and quite out of shape, by happening to mistake a figure in the calculation. But my comfort was, that I observed such accidents very frequent, and little regarded.

During my confinement, for want of clothes, and by an indisposition that held me some days longer, I much enlarged my dictionary; and when I went next to court, was able to understand many things the king spoke, and to return him some kind of answers. His majesty had given orders that the island should move northeast and by east to the vertical point over Lagado, the metropolis of the whole kingdom below, upon the firm earth. It was about ninety leagues distant, and our voyage lasted four days and a half. I was not in the least sensible of the progressive motion made in the air by the island. On the second morning, about eleven o'clock, the king himself in person, attended by his nobility, courtiers, and officers, having prepared all their musical instruments, played on them for three hours without intermission, so that I was quite stunned with the noise; neither could I possibly guess the meaning, till my tutor informed me. He said that the people of their island had their ears adapted to hear the music of the spheres,* which always played at certain periods, and the court was now prepared to bear their part, in whatever instrument they most excelled.

In our journey toward Lagado, the capital city, his majesty ordered that the island should stop over certain towns and villages, from whence he might receive the petitions of his subjects. And, to this purpose, several packthreads were let down, with small weights at the bottom. On these packthreads the people strung their petitions, which mounted up directly, like the scraps of paper fastened by schoolboys at the end of the string that holds their kite. Sometimes we received wine and victuals from below, which were drawn up by pulleys.

The knowledge I had in mathematics gave me great assistance in acquiring their phraseology, which depended much upon that science and music; and in the latter I was not unskilled. Their ideas are perpetually conversant in lines and figures. If they would, for example, praise the beauty of a

---

* A music, imperceptible to ordinary ears, supposed by the Greek philosopher Pythagoras to be produced by the motions of the heavenly bodies.

woman, or any other animal, they describe it by rhombs,* circles, parallelograms, ellipses, and other geometrical terms, or by words of art drawn from music, needless here to repeat. I observed, in the king's kitchen, all sorts of mathematical and musical instruments, after the figures of which they cut up the joints that were served to his majesty's table.

Their houses are very ill built, the walls bevel, without one right angle in any apartment; and this defect ariseth from the contempt they bear to practical geometry, which they despise as vulgar and mechanic; those instructions they give being too refined for the intellectuals† of their workmen, which occasions perpetual mistakes. And although they are dexterous enough upon a piece of paper, in the management of the rule, the pencil, and the divider,‡ yet, in the common actions and behavior of life, I have not seen a more clumsy, awkward, and unhandy people, nor so slow and perplexed in their conceptions upon all other subjects, except those of mathematics and music. They are very bad reasoners, and vehemently given to opposition, unless when they happen to be of the right opinion, which is seldom their case. Imagination, fancy, and

---

* Figures of a diamond shape.
† Mental powers ; intellects.
‡ Pair of compasses.

invention, they are wholly strangers to, nor have they any words in their language by which those ideas can be expressed ; the whole compass of their thoughts and mind being shut up within the two fore-mentioned sciences.

Most of them, and especially those who deal in the astronomical part, have great faith in judicial astrology,* although they are ashamed to own it publicly. But what I chiefly admired,† and thought altogether unaccountable, was the strong disposition I observed in them toward news and politics, perpetually inquiring into public affairs, giving their judgments in matters of state, and passionately disputing every inch of a party opinion. I have indeed observed the same disposition among most of the mathematicians I have known in Europe, although I could never discover the least analogy between the two sciences; unless those people suppose that because the smallest circle hath as many degrees as the largest,‡ therefore the regulation and management of the world require no more abilities than the handling and turning of a globe ; but I rather

---

* The exploded science or art of foretelling future events from a study of the positions and motions of the sun, moon, and planets.

† Wondered at : an old usage of the word.

‡ Every circle being divisible into 360 degrees.

take this quality to spring from a very common in-firmity of human nature, inclining us to be most curious and conceited in matters where we have least concern, and for which we are least adapted either by study or nature.

These people are under continual disquietudes, never enjoying a minute's peace of mind; and their disturbances proceed from causes which very little affect the rest of mortals. Their apprehensions arise from several changes they dread in the celes-tial bodies. For instance, that the earth, by the continual approaches of the sun toward it, must, in course of time, be absorbed, or swallowed up. That the face of the sun will, by degrees, be encrusted with its own effluvia, and give no more light to the world. That the earth very narrowly escaped a brush from the tail of the last comet, which would have infallibly reduced it to ashes; and that the next, which they have calculated for thirty-one years hence, will probably destroy us. For if, in its perihelion,* it should approach within a certain degree of the sun (as by their calculations they have reason to dread), it will conceive a degree of heat ten thousand times more intense than that of red-hot glowing iron; and, in its absence from the sun,

* That point in the orbit of a planet or comet at which the body is nearest the sun

carry a blazing tail, ten hundred thousand and fourteen miles long; through which, if the earth should
pass at the distance of one hundred thousand miles
from the nucleus, or main body of the comet, it
must in its passage be set on fire, and reduced to
ashes. That the sun, daily spending its rays without
any nutriment to supply them, will at last be wholly
consumed and annihilated; which must be attended
with the destruction of this earth, and of all the
planets that receive their light from it.*

They are so perpetually alarmed with the apprehensions of these and the like impending dangers,
that they can neither sleep quietly in their beds,
nor have any relish for the common pleasures or
amusements of life. When they meet an acquaintance in the morning the first question is about the
sun's health, how he looked at his setting and rising,
and what hopes they have to avoid the stroke of
the approaching comet. This conversation they are

---

* It is held at the present day that the sun is gradually
cooling; but as it is believed that a million of years or so will
make little or no perceptible difference, we need not, like the
Laputians, trouble ourselves about it. As for comets, though
comparatively little is yet known as to their real nature, the
belief is strong among men of science that no danger need be
apprehended from any of them, even if one should come in
contact with the earth.

apt to run into with the same temper that boys discover in delighting to hear terrible stories of spirits
and hobgoblins, which they greedily listen to, and
dare not go to bed for fear.

The women of the island have abundance of
vivacity; they contemn their husbands, and are ex-
ceedingly fond of strangers, whereof there is
always a considerable number, from the continent
below, attending at court, either upon affairs of the
several towns and corporations, or their own particular occasions; but are much despised because they
want the same endowments. Among these the
ladies choose their gallants. The wives and daugh-
ters lament their confinement to the island, although
I think it the most delicious spot of ground in the
world; and although they live here in the greatest
plenty and magnificence, and are allowed to do
whatever they please, they long to see the world,
and take the diversions of the metropolis, which
they are not allowed to do without a particular
license from the king; and this is not easy to be
obtained, because the people of quality have found,
by frequent experience, how hard it is to persuade
their women to return from below.

In about a month's time I had made a tolerable
proficiency in their language, and was able to
answer most of the king's questions, when I had the

honor to attend him. His majesty discovered* not the least curiosity to inquire into the laws, government, history, religion, or manners of the countries where I had been; but confined his questions to the state of mathematics, and received the account I gave him with great contempt and indifference, though often roused by his flapper on each side.

---

* Showed.

CHAPTER III.

A Phenomenon solved by modern Philosophy and Astronomy
—The Laputians' great improvements in the latter—The
King's method of suppressing Insurrections.

I DESIRED leave of this prince to see the curiosities
of the island, which he was graciously pleased to

"The Flying or Floating Island is exactly circular."

grant, and ordered my tutor to attend me. I chiefly
wanted to know to what cause in art or in nature
it owed its several motions, whereof I will now give
a philosophical account to the reader.

The Flying or Floating Island is exactly circular,
its diameter seventy-eight hundred and thirty-seven
yards, or about four miles and a half, and consequently contains ten thousand acres. It is three

hundred yards thick. The bottom, or under surface, which appears to those who view it from below, is one even regular plate of adamant,* shooting up to the height of about two hundred yards. Above it lie the several minerals, in their usual order, and over all is a coat of rich mold, ten or twelve foot deep. The declivity of the upper surface, from the circumference to the center, is the natural cause why all the dews and rains, which fall upon the island, are conveyed in small rivulets toward the middle, where they are emptied into four large basins, each of about half a mile in circuit, and two hundred yards distant from the center. From these basins the water is continually exhaled by the sun in the daytime, which effectually prevents their overflowing. Besides, as it is in the power of the monarch to raise the island above the region of clouds and vapors, he can prevent the falling of dews and rains whenever he pleases. For the highest clouds cannot rise above two miles, as naturalists agree, at least they were never known to do so in that country.†

---

* A term vaguely used to express a metallic or other excessively hard substance. Sometimes it meant the diamond (*diamond* is indeed the same word under another form); sometimes the loadstone or magnet; but Swift evidently does not use it in this latter sense.

† Clouds have been observed as high as five miles.

At the center of the island there is a chasm, about fifty yards in diameter, from whence the astronomers descend into a large dome, which is therefore called *Flandona Gagnole*, or the Astronomer's Cave, situated at the depth of a hundred yards beneath the upper surface of the adamant. In this cave are twenty lamps continually burning, which from the reflection of the adamant cast a strong light into every part. The place is stored with great variety of sextants, quadrants, telescopes, astrolabes,* and other astronomical instruments. But the greatest curiosity, upon which the fate of the island depends, is a loadstone of a prodigious size, in shape resembling a weaver's shuttle. It is in length six yards, and in the thickest part at least three yards over. This magnet is sustained by a very strong axle of adamant passing through its middle, upon which it plays, and is poised so exactly that the weakest hand can turn it. It is hooped round with an hollow cylinder of adamant, four foot deep, as many thick, and twelve yards in diameter, placed horizontally, and supported by eight adamantine feet, each six yards high. In the middle of the concave side there is a groove twelve inches deep, in which the

---

* The astrolabe was an instrument formerly used for the same purposes as the sextant or the quadrant.

extremities of the axle are lodged, and turned round as there is occasion.

The stone cannot be moved from its place by any force, because the hoop and its feet are one continued piece with that body of adamant which constitutes the bottom of the island.

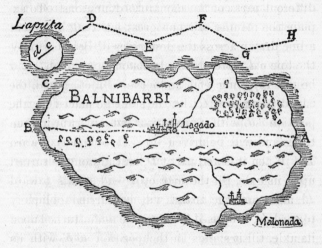

By means of this loadstone the island is made to rise and fall, and move from one place to another. For, with respect to that part of the earth over which the monarch presides, the stone is endued at one of its sides with an attractive power, and at the other with a repulsive. Upon placing the magnet erect, with its attracting end toward the earth, the island descends; but when the repelling extremity points downward, the island mounts directly upward. When the position of the stone is oblique, the motion of the island is so too; for in this magnet the forces always act in lines parallel to its direction.

By this oblique motion the island is conveyed to different parts of the monarch's dominions. To explain the manner of its progress, let A B* represent a line drawn across the dominions of Balnibarbi, let the line c d represent the loadstone, of which let d be the repelling end, and c the attracting end, the island being over C: let the stone be placed in the position c d, with its repelling end downward; then the island will be driven upward obliquely toward D. When it is arrived at D, let the stone be turned upon its axle, till the attracting end points toward E, and then the island will be carried obliquely toward E; where, if the stone be again turned upon its axle, till it stands in the position E F, with its repelling point downward, the island will rise obliquely toward F, where, by directing the attracting end toward G, the island may be carried to G, and from G to H, by turning the stone, so as to make its repelling extremity point directly down-

---

* The cut here given is copied from the illustration contained in the first edition. Balnibarbi is represented as an island, but is afterward spoken of as part of a continent.

ward. And thus, by changing the situation of the stone as often as there is occasion, the island is made to rise and fall by turns in an oblique direction, and by those alternate risings and fallings (the obliquity being not considerable), is conveyed from one part of the dominions to the other.

But it must be observed that this island cannot move beyond the extent of the dominions below, nor can it rise above the height of four miles. For which the astronomers (who have written large systems concerning the stone) assign the following reason : that the magnetic virtue does not extend beyond the distance of four miles, and that the mineral, which acts upon the stone in the bowels of the earth, and in the sea about six leagues distant from the shore, is not diffused through the whole globe, but terminated with the limits of the king's dominions; and it was easy, from the great advantage of such a superior situation, for a prince to bring under his obedience whatever country lay within the attraction of that magnet.

When the stone is put parallel to the plane of the horizon, the island standeth still ; for, in that case, the extremities of it being at equal distance from the earth, act with equal force, the one in drawing downward, the other in pulling upward, and consequently no motion can ensue.

This loadstone, under the care of certain astronomers, who, from time to time, give it such positions
as the monarch directs. They spend the greatest
part of their lives in observing the celestial bodies,
which they do by the assistance of glasses, far
excelling ours in goodness. For although their
largest telescopes do not exceed three feet, they
magnify much more than those of a hundred with us,
and show the stars with greater clearness. This
advantage hath enabled them to extend their discoveries much further than our astronomers in
Europe: for they have made a catalogue of ten
thousand fixed stars, whereas the largest of ours do
not contain above one-third part of that number.*
They have likewise discovered two lesser stars, or
satellites, which revolve about Mars; whereof the
innermost is distant from the center of the primary
planet exactly three of his diameters, and the outer-
most, five; the former revolves in the space of ten
hours, and the latter in twenty-one and a half; so
that the squares of their periodical times are very
near in the same proportion with the cubes of their
distances from the center of Mars; which evidently
shows them to be governed by the same law of

---

* Over 320,000 stars have latterly been catalogued.

gravitation that influences the other heavenly bodies.*

They have observed ninety-three different comets, and settled their periods with great exactness.† If this be true (and they affirm it with great confidence), it is much to be wished that their observations were made public, whereby the theory of comets, which at present is very lame and defective, might be brought to the same perfection with other parts of astronomy.

The king would be the most absolute prince in the universe, if he could but prevail on a ministry to join with him; but those having their estates below on the continent, and considering that the office of a favorite hath a very uncertain tenure, would never consent to the enslaving of their country.

---

* The existence of two satellites or moons revolving about Mars must have been a mere speculation of Swift's own or of some astronomical friend of his. Yet strangely enough it was discovered in 1877 that this planet has two satellites. Their distances and times, however, are somewhat different from those given by Swift. The outer is distant 14,500 miles from the center of Mars, and revolves in 30 hours 14 minutes; the inner is 5,800 miles, and revolves in 7 hours 38 minutes. The diameter of Mars is about 4,400 miles.

† Only the periods of twelve or fifteen comets are as yet known with any exactness; and the true nature of the bodies themselves is uncertain.

If any town should engage in rebellion or mutiny, fall into violent factions, or refuse to pay the usual tribute, the king hath two methods of reducing them to obedience. The first and the mildest course is by keeping the island hovering over such a town, and the lands about it, whereby he can deprive them of the benefit of the sun and the rain, and consequently afflict the inhabitants with dearth and diseases. And if the crime deserve it, they are at the same time pelted from above with great stones, against which they have no defense but by creeping into cellars or caves, while the roofs of their houses are beaten to pieces. But if they still continue obstinate, or offer to raise insurrections, he proceeds to the last remedy, by letting the island drop directly upon their heads, which makes a universal destruction both of houses and men. However, this is an extremity to which the prince is seldom driven, neither indeed is he willing to put it in execution; nor dare his ministers advise him to an action, which as it would render them odious to the people, so it would be a great damage to their own estates, which lie all below; for the island is the king's demesne.

But there is still indeed a more weighty reason why the kings of this country have been always averse from executing so terrible an action, unless upon the utmost necessity. For, if the town intended to be destroyed should have in it any tall rocks, as it generally falls out in the larger cities, a situation probably chosen at first with a view to prevent such a catastrophe; or if it abound in high spires, or pillars of stone, a sudden fall might endanger the bottom or under surface of the island, which, although it consists, as I have said, of one entire adamant two hundred yards thick, might happen to crack by too great a shock, or burst, by approaching too near the fires from the houses below, as the backs both of iron and stone will often do in our chimneys. Of all this the people are well apprised, and understand how far to carry their obstinacy, where their liberty or property is concerned. And the king, when he is highest provoked and most determined to press a city to rubbish, orders the island to descend with great gentleness, out of a pretense of tenderness to his people, but indeed for fear of breaking the adamantine bottom, in which case, it is the opinion of all their philosophers, that the loadstone could no longer hold it up, and the whole mass would fall to the ground.

By a fundamental law of this realm neither the king, nor either of his two elder sons, are permitted to leave the island; nor the queen, till she is past child-bearing.

CHAPTER IV.

The Author leaves Laputa, is conveyed to Balnibarbi, arrives
at the Metropolis—A Description of the Metropolis and
the Country adjoining—The Author hospitably received
by a great Lord—His conversation with that Lord.

ALTHOUGH I cannot say that I was ill treated in
this island, yet I must confess I thought myself too
much neglected, not without some degree of contempt. For neither prince nor people appeared to
be curious in any part of knowledge, except mathematics and music, wherein I was far their inferior,
and upon that account very little regarded.

On the other side, after having seen all the curiosities of the island, I was very desirous to leave it,
being heartily weary of those people. They were
indeed excellent in two sciences for which I have
great esteem, and wherein I am not unversed; but
at the same time so abstracted and involved in
speculation that I never met with such disagreeable
companions. I conversed only with women, tradesmen, flappers, and court-pages, during two months

of my abode here; by which at last I rendered my-self extremely contemptible; yet these were the only people from whom I could ever receive a reasonable answer.

I had obtained, by hard study, a good degree of knowledge in their language; I was weary of being confined to an island where I received so little countenance, and resolved to leave it with the first opportunity.

There was a great lord at court, nearly related to the king, and for that reason alone used with respect. He was universally reckoned the most ignorant and stupid person among them. He had performed many eminent services for the crown, had great natural and acquired parts, adorned with integrity and honor; but so ill an ear for music that his detractors reported that he had been often known to beat time in the wrong place; neither could his tutors, without extreme difficulty, teach him to demonstrate the most easy proposition in the mathematics. He was pleased to show me many marks of favor, often did me the honor of a visit, desired to be informed in the affairs of Europe, the laws and customs, the manners and learning of the several countries where I had traveled. He listened to me with great attention, and made very wise observations on all I spoke. He had two flappers attending

him for state, but never made use of them, except at
court, and in visits of ceremony, and would always
command them to withdraw when we were alone
together.

I entreated this illustrious person to intercede in
my behalf with his majesty for leave to depart,
which he accordingly did, as he was pleased to tell
me, with regret; for, indeed, he had made me several
offers very advantageous, which, however, I refused,
with expressions of the highest acknowledgment.

On the 16th day of February I took leave of his
majesty and the court. The king made me a present
to the value of about two hundred pounds English,
and my protector, his kinsman, as much more, together with a letter of recommendation to a friend
of his in Lagado, the metropolis; the island being
then hovering over a mountain about two miles
from it, I was let down from the lowest gallery in
the same manner as I had been taken up.

The continent, as far as it is subject to the
monarch of Flying Island, passes under the general
name of *Balnibarbi;* and the metropolis, as I said
before, is called *Lagado.* I felt some little satisfaction in finding myself on firm ground. I walked to
the city without any concern, being clad like one of
the natives, and sufficiently instructed to converse
with them. I soon found out the person's house to

whom I was recommended, presented my letter from his friend, the grandee in the island, and was received with much kindness. This great lord, whose name was Munodi, ordered me an apartment in his own house, where I continued during my stay, and was entertained in a most hospitable manner.

The next morning after my arrival he took me in his chariot to see the town, which is about half the bigness of London; but the houses were very strangely built, and most of them out of repair. The people in the streets walked fast, looked wild, their eyes fixed, and were generally in rags. We passed through one of the town gates, and went about three miles into the country, where I saw many laborers working with several sorts of tools in the ground, but was not able to conjecture what they were about; neither did I observe any expectation either of corn or grass, although the soil appeared to be excellent. I could not forbear admiring* these odd appearances, both in town and country; and I made bold to desire my conductor that he would be pleased to explain to me what could be meant by so many busy heads, hands and faces, both in the streets and the fields, because I did not discover any

---

* Wondering: to "admire at" is still in common use in America.

good effects they produced; but, on the contrary, I never knew a soil so unhappily cultivated, houses so ill contrived and so ruinous, or a people whose countenances and habit expressed so much misery and want.

This lord Munodi was a person of the first rank, and had been some years governor of Lagado; but, by a cabal of ministers, was discharged for insuf-ciency. However, the king treated him with tenderness, as a well-meaning man, but of a low, contemptible understanding.

When I gave free censure* of the country and its inhabitants he made no further answer than by telling me that I had not been long enough among them to form a judgment; and that the different nations of the world had different customs; with other common topics to the same purpose. But when we returned to his palace he asked me how I liked the building, what absurdities I observed, and what quarrel I had with the dress and looks of his domestics? This he might safely do; because everything about him was magnificent, regular and polite. I answered that his excellency's prudence, quality, and fortune, had exempted him from those defects which folly and beggary had produced in others.

* Opinion or judgment.

He said if I would go with him to his country house, about twenty miles distant, where his estate lay, there would be more leisure for this kind of conversation. I told his excellency that I was entirely at his disposal; and accordingly we set out next morning.

During our journey, he made me observe the several methods used by farmers in managing their lands; which to me were wholly unaccountable; for, except in some very few places, I could not discover one ear of corn or blade of grass. But in three hours' traveling, the scene was wholly altered; we came into a most beautiful country; farmers' houses, at small distances, neatly built; the fields inclosed, containing vineyards, corn-grounds, and meadows. Neither do I remember to have seen a more delightful prospect. His excellency observed my countenance to clear up; he told me, with a sigh, that there his estate began, and would continue the same till we should come to his house. That his countrymen ridiculed and despised him for managing his affairs no better, and for setting so ill an example to the kingdom; which, however, was followed by very few, such as were old and wistful, and weak, like himself.

We came at length to the house, which was indeed a noble structure, built according to the best rules of ancient architecture. The fountains, gardens, walks, avenues, and groves, were all disposed with exact judgment and taste. I gave due praises to everything I saw, whereof his excellency took not the least notice till after supper ; when, there being no third companion, he told me, with a very melancholy air, that he doubted he must throw down his houses in town and country, to rebuild them after the present mode ; destroy all his plantations, and cast others into such a form as modern usage required, and give the same directions to all his tenants, unless he would submit to incur the censure of pride, singularity, affectation, ignorance, caprice, and perhaps increase his majesty's displeasure. That the admiration I appeared to be under would cease or diminish, when he had informed me of some particulars which, probably, I never heard of at court ; the people there being too much taken up in their own speculations to have regard to what passed here below.

The sum of his discourse was to this effect : That about forty years ago certain persons went up to Laputa, either upon business or diversion, and after five months' continuance, came back with a very little smattering in mathematics, but full of volatile spirits acquired in that airy region. That these persons, upon their return, began to dislike the management of everything below, and fell into schemes of putting all arts, sciences, languages, and mechanics, upon a new foot. To this end they procured a royal patent for erecting an academy of projectors in Lagado; and the humor prevailed so strongly among the people, that there is not a town of any consequence in the kingdom without such an academy. In these colleges the professors contrive new rules and methods of agriculture and building, and new iustruments and tools for all trades and manufactures; whereby, as they undertake, one man shall do the work of ten; a palace may be built in a week, of materials so durable as to last forever without repairing; all the fruits of the earth shall come to maturity at whatever season we think fit to choose, and increase an hundred-fold more than they do at present; with innumerable other happy proposals. The only inconvenience is, that none of these projects are yet brought to perfection : and, in the meantime, the whole country lies miserably waste, the houses in ruins, and the people without food or clothes. By all which, instead of being discouraged, they are fifty times more violently bent upon prosecuting their schemes, driven equally on by hope and despair : that, as for himself, being not of an enterprising spirit, he was content to go on in the old forms, to live in the houses his ancestors had built, and act as they did, in every part of life, without innovation. That some few other persons of quality and gentry* had done the same, but were looked on with an eye of contempt and ill-will, as enemies to art, ignorant, and ill commonwealth's men,† preferring their own ease and sloth before the general improvement of their country.

His lordship added, that he would not, by any further particulars, prevent the pleasure I should certainly take in viewing the grand academy, whither he was resolved I should go. He only desired me to observe a ruined building, upon the side of a mountain about three miles distant, of which he gave me this account : That he had a very convenient mill within half a mile of his house, turned by a current from a large river, and sufficient for his own family, as well as a great number of his tenants. That about seven years ago a club of those projectors came to him with proposals to destroy this mill, and build another on the side of that mountain, on the long ridge whereof a long canal must be cut, for a repository of water, to be conveyed up by pipes and engines to supply the mill ; because the wind and air upon a height

---

* Gentle birth. † Not men of public spirit.

agitated the water, and thereby made it fitter for motion ; and because the water, descending down a declivity, would turn the mill with half the current of a river whose course is more upon a level. He said that being then not very well with the court, and pressed by many of his friends, he complied with the proposal; and after employing an hundred men for two years the work miscarried, the projectors went off, laying the blame entirely upon him, railing at him ever since, and putting others upon the same experiment, with equal assurance of success, as well as equal disappointment.

In a few days we came back to town; and his excellency, considering the bad character he had in the academy, would not go with me himself, but recommended me to a friend of his, to bear me company thither. My lord was pleased to represent me as a great admirer of projects, and a person of much curiosity and easy belief; which, indeed, was not without truth; for I had myself been a sort of a projector in my younger days.

CHAPTER V.

The Author permitted to see the Grand Academy of Lagado—
The Academy largely described—The Arts wherein the
Professors employ themselves.

This academy is not an entire single building, but
a continuation of several houses on both sides of a
street, which, growing waste, was purchased and
applied to that use.

I was received very kindly by the warden, and
went for many days to the academy. Every room
hath in it one or more projectors; and, I believe, I
could not be in fewer than five hundred rooms.

The first man I saw was of a meager aspect, with
sooty hands and face, his hair and beard long,
ragged, and singed in several places. His clothes,
shirt, and skin were all of the same color. He had
been eight years upon a project for extracting sunbeams out of cucumbers, which were to be put into
vials hermetically sealed, and let out to warm the
air in raw, inclement summers. He told me he did
not doubt, in eight years more, he should be able
to supply the governor's gardens with sunshine at a

reasonable rate; but he complained that his stock was low, and entreated me to give him something as an encouragement to ingenuity, especially since this had been a very dear season for cucumbers. I made him a small present, for my lord had furnished me with money on purpose, because he knew their practice of begging from all who go to see them.

I saw another at work to calcine ice into gun-powder, who likewise showed me a treatise he had written concerning the malleability of fire, which he intended to publish.

There was a most ingenious architect, who had contrived a new method for building houses, by be-ginning at the roof, and working downward to the foundation; which he justified to me by the like practice of those two prudent insects, the bee and the spider.

There was a man born blind, who had several apprentices in his own condition; their employment was to mix colors for painters, which their master taught them to distinguish by feeling and smelling. It was indeed my misfortune to find them at that time not very perfect in their lessons, and the pro-fessor himself happened to be generally mistaken. This artist is much encouraged and esteemed by the whole fraternity.

In another apartment I was highly pleased with

a projector who had found a device of plowing the ground with hogs, to save the charges of plows, cattle, and labor. The method is this : In an acre of ground you bury, at six inches distance, and eight deep, a quantity of acorns, dates, chestnuts, and other mast or vegetables, whereof those animals are fondest; then you drive six hundred or more of them into the field, where in a few days, they will root up the whole ground in search of their food, and make it fit for sowing, at the same time manuring it with their dung; it is true, upon experiment, they found the charge and trouble very great, and they had little or no crop. However, it is not doubted that this invention may be capable of great improvement.

I went into another room where the walls and ceiling were all hung round with cobwebs, except a narrow passage for the artist to go in and out. At my entrance he called aloud to me not to disturb his webs. He lamented the fatal mistake the world had been so long in, of using silk-worms, while we had such plenty of domestic insects, who infinitely excelled the former, because they understood how to weave as well as spin. And he proposed further that, by employing spiders, the charge of dyeing silks should be wholly saved; whereof I was fully convinced when he showed me a vast number of flies, most beautifully colored, wherewith he fed his spiders, assuring us that the webs would take a tincture from them ; and as he had them of all hues, he hoped to fit everybody's fancy, as soon as he could find proper food for the flies, of certain gums, oils and other glutinous matter, to give a strength and consistence to the threads.*

There was an astronomer, who had undertaken to place a sun-dial upon the great weathercock on the town-house, by adjusting the annual and diurnal motions of the earth and sun, so as to answer and coincide with all accidental turnings by the wind.

I visited many other apartments, but shall not trouble my reader with all the curiosities I observed, being studious of brevity.

I had hitherto seen only one side of the academy, the other being appropriated to the advancers of speculative learning, of whom I shall say something, when I have mentioned one illustrious person more, who is called among them, "The universal artist." He told us he had been thirty years employing his

---

* Shortly before the time when GULLIVER'S TRAVELS were written a Frenchman of the name of Bon de Saint-Hilaire had succeeded in weaving stockings and gloves from spiders' threads. Other fabrics have been made from them at various times, but with no success commercially. For one thing, the material cannot be got in sufficient quantity.

thoughts for the improvement of human life. He had two large rooms full of wonderful curiosities, and fifty men at work. Some were condensing air* into a dry, tangible substance, by extracting the nitre, and letting the aqueous or fluid particles percolate; others softening marble for pillows and pincushions; others petrifying the hoofs of a living horse, to preserve them from foundering.† The artist himself was at that time busy upon two great designs; the first, to sow land with chaff, wherein he affirmed the true seminal virtue to be contained, as he demonstrated by several experiments, which I was not skillful enough to comprehend. The other was by a certain composition of gums, minerals, and vegetables, outwardly applied, to prevent the growth of wool upon two young lambs; and he hoped, in a reasonable time, to propagate the breed of naked sheep all over the kingdom.

We crossed a walk to the other part of the academy, where, as I have already said, the projectors in speculative learning resided.

The first professor I saw was in a very large room, with forty pupils about him. After salutation, observing me to look earnestly upon a frame, which

---

* The true nature of air was not known in Swift's time.

† Getting lame by inflammation.

took up the greatest part of both the length and breath of the room, he said, perhaps I might wonder to see him employed in a project for improving speculative knowledge, by practical and mechanical operations. But the world would soon be sensible of its usefulness; and he flattered himself, that a more noble, exalted thought never sprang in any other man's head. Every one knew how laborious the usual method is of attaining to arts and sciences; whereas, by his contrivance, the most ignorant person, at a reasonable charge, and with a little bodily labor, might write books in philosophy, poetry, politics, law, mathematics, and theology, without the least assistance from genius or study. He then led me to the frame, about the sides whereof all his pupils stood in ranks. It was twenty foot square, placed in the middle of the room. The superficies was composed of several bits of wood, about the bigness of a die, but some larger than others. They were all linked together by slender wires. These bits of wood were covered, on every square, with paper pasted on them; and on these papers were written all the words of their language, in their several moods, tenses, and declensions, but without any order. The professor then desired me to observe, for he was going to set his engine at work. The pupils, at his command, took each of them hold of an iron handle, whereof there were forty fixed round the edges of the frame, and giving them a sudden turn, the whole disposition of the words was entirely changed. He then commanded thirty-six of the lads to read the several lines softly, as they appeared upon the frame; and where they found three or four words together that might make part of a sentence, they dictated to the four remaining boys, who were scribes. This work was repeated three or four times, and, at every turn, the engine was so contrived that the words shifted into new places, as the square bits of wood moved upside down.

Six hours a day the young students were employed in this labor; and the professor showed me several volumes in large folio, already collected, of broken sentences, which he intended to piece together, and out of those rich materials, to give the world a complete body of all arts and sciences; which, however, might be still improved, and much expedited, if the public would raise a fund for making and employing five hundred such frames in Lagado, and oblige the managers to contribute in common their several collections.

He assured me that this invention had employed all his thoughts from his youth; that he had emptied the whole vocabulary into his frame, and made the strictest computation of the general proportion there is in books between the numbers of particles, nouns, and verbs, and other parts of speech.

I made my humblest acknowledgment to this illustrious person for his great communicativeness; and promised, if ever I had the good fortune to return to my native country, that I would do him justice, as the sole inventor of this wonderful machine;* the form and contrivance of which I desired leave to delineate upon paper. I told him, although it were the custom of our learned in Europe to steal inventions from each other, who had thereby at least this advantage, that it became a controversy which was the right owner; yet I would take such caution that he should have the honor entire, without a rival.

We next went to the school of language, where three professors sat in consultation upon improving that of their own country.

The first project was to shorten discourse, by cutting polysyllables into one, and leaving out verbs and participles, because, in reality, all things imaginable are but nouns.

The other was a scheme for entirely abolishing all

---

* The early editions give a figure intended to show the construction of this machine, but it is too rude and unintelligible to be worth reproduction.

words whatsoever, and this was urged as a great advantage in point of health as well as brevity. For it is plain that every word we speak is in some degree a diminution of our lungs by corrosion, and, consequently, contributes to the shortening of our lives. An expedient was therefore offered, that, since words are only names for things, it would be more convenient for all men to carry about them such things as were necessary to express the particular business they are to discourse on. And this invention would certainly have taken place, to the great ease as well as health of the subject, if the women, in conjunction with the vulgar and illiterate, had not threatened to raise a rebellion, unless they might be allowed the liberty to speak with their tongues, after the manner of their ancestors; such constant irreconcilable enemies to science are the common people. However, many of the most learned and wise adhere to the new scheme of expressing themselves by things, which hath only this inconvenience attending it, that if a man's business be very great and of various kinds, he must be obliged, in proportion, to carry a great bundle of things upon his back, unless he can afford one or two strong servants to attend him. I have often beheld two of those sages almost sinking under the weight of their packs, like pedlars among us; who, when they met in the street, would lay down their loads, open their sacks, and hold conversation for an hour together, then put up their implements, help each other to resume their burthens, and take their leave.

But for short conversations, a man may carry implements in his pockets, and under his arms, enough to supply him: and in his house he cannot be at a loss. Therefore the room where company meet who practice this art is full of all things, ready at hand, requisite to furnish matter for this kind of artificial converse.

Another great advantage proposed by this invention was that it would serve as a universal language, to be understood in all civilized nations, whose goods and utensils are generally of the same kind, or nearly resembling, so that their uses might easily be comprehended. And thus ambassadors would be qualified to treat with foreign princes, or ministers of state, to whose tongues they were utter strangers.

I was at the mathematical school, where the master taught his pupils after a method scarce imaginable to us in Europe. The proposition and demonstration were fairly written on a thin wafer, with ink composed of a cephalic* tincture. This the

---

* Affecting the head or the brain.

student was to swallow up on a fasting stomach, and
for three days following ate nothing but bread and
water.   As the wafer digested the tincture mounted
to his brain, bearing the proposition along with it.
But the success hath not hitherto been answerable,
partly by some error in the *quantum* or composition,
and partly by the perverseness of lads, to whom this
bolus is so nauseous that they generally steal aside
and discharge it upward before it can operate;
neither have they been yet persuaded to use so long
an abstinence as the prescription requires.

CHAPTER VI.

A further account of the Academy—The Author proposes
some Improvements, which are honorably received.

In the school of political projectors I was but ill
entertained, the professors appearing, in my judgment, wholly out of their senses; which is a scene
that never fails to make me melancholy. These
unhappy people were proposing schemes for per-
suading monarchs to choose favorites upon the score
of their wisdom, capacity, and virtue; of teaching
ministers to consult the public good; of rewarding
merit, great abilities, and eminent services; of
instructing princes to know their true interest, by
placing it on the same foundation with that of their
people; of choosing for employments persons qualified to exercise them; with many other wild,
impossible chimeras that never entered before into
the heart of man to conceive; and confirmed in me
the old observation, That there is nothing so
extravagant and irrational which some philosophers
have not maintained for truth.

But, however, I shall so far do justice to this part
of the academy as to acknowledge that all of them

were not so visionary. There was a most ingenious doctor, who seemed to be perfectly versed in the whole nature and system of government. This illustrious person had very usefully employed his studies in finding out effectual remedies for all diseases and corruptions to which the several kinds of public administration are subject, by the vices or infirmities of those who govern, as well as by the licentiousness of those who are to obey. For instance, whereas all writers and reasoners have agreed that there is a strict universal resemblance between the natural and the political body; can there be anything more evident than that the health of both must be preserved, and the diseases cured by the same prescriptions? It is allowed that senates and great councils are often troubled with redundant, ebullient,* and other peccant† humors; with many diseases of the head, and more of the heart; with strong convulsions, with grievous con tractions of the nerves and sinews in both hands, but especially the right; with spleen,‡ vertigoes,§ and deliriums; with scrofulous tumors, full of fetid, purulent matter; with sour, frothy ructations;¶ with canine appetites,‖ and crudeness of digestion, besides

---

* Overflowing.   † Unhealthy.   ‡ Melancholy.

§ Dizziness.   ¶ Belchings.

‖ Voracious, but diseased appetite.

many others needless to mention. This doctor therefore proposed, That, upon the meeting of the senate, certain physicians should attend at the three first days of their sitting, and at the close of each day's debate feel the pulses of every senator; after which, having maturely considered and consulted upon the nature of the several maladies and the method of cure, they should, on the fourth day, return to the senate house, attended by their apothecaries, stored with proper medicines; and, before the members sat, administer to each of them lenitives, aperitives, abstersives,* corrosives,† restringents,‡ palliatives, laxatives, cephalalgics,§ icterics,¶ apophlegmatics,‖ acoustics,** as their several cases required; and, according as these medicines should operate, repeat, alter, or omit them, at the next meeting.

This project could not be of any great expense to the public, and would, in my poor opinion, be of much use for the dispatch of business in those countries where senates have any share in the legislative power; beget unanimity, shorten debates, open a few mouths which are now closed, and close many more which are now open; curb the petulancy

---

* Cleansing medicines.　　† Dissolvents.　　‡ Astringents.
§ Remedies for headache.　¶ For jaundice.　‖ For phlegm.
** For hearing.

of the young, and correct the positiveness of the old; rouse the stupid, and damp the pert.

Again, because it is a general complaint that the favorites of princes are troubled with short and weak memories, the same doctor proposed, That whoever attended a first minister, after having told his business with the utmost brevity and in the plainest words, should, at his departure, give the said minister a tweak by the nose, or a kick on the belly, or tread on his corns, or lug him thrice by both ears, or run a pin into him, or pinch his arm black and blue, to prevent forgetfulness; and at every levee-day repeat the same operation, till the business were done, or absolutely refused.

He likewise directed that every senator in the great council of a nation, after he had delivered his opinion, and argued in the defense of it, should be obliged to give his vote directly contrary; because, if that were done, the result would infallibly terminate in the good of the public.

When parties in a state are violent, he offered a wonderful contrivance to reconcile them. The method is this: You take an hundred leaders of each party, you dispose of them into couples of such whose heads are nearest of a size, then let two nice operators saw off the occiput* of each couple

---

* Back part of the head.

at the same time, in such a manner that the brain may be equally divided. Let the occiputs thus cut off be interchanged, applying each to the head of his opposite party-man. It seems indeed to be a work that requires some exactness, but the professor assured us that if it were dexterously performed the cure would be infallible. For he argued thus : That the two half brains being left to debate the matter between themselves within the space of one skull, would soon come to a good understanding, and produce that moderation, as well as regularity of thinking, so much to be wished for in the heads of those who imagine they come into the world only to watch and govern its motion; and as to the difference of brains, in quantity or quality, among those who are directors in faction, the doctor assured us, from his own knowledge, that it was a perfect trifle.

I heard a very warm debate between two professors about the most commodious* and effectual ways and means of raising money, without grieving the subject. The first affirmed the justest method would be to lay a certain tax upon vices and folly ; and the sum fixed upon every man to be rated after the fairest manner by a jury of his neighbors. The

---

* Convenient or suitable.

second was of an opinion directly contrary: To tax
those qualities of body and mind, for which men
chiefly value themselves; the rate to be more or
less, according to the degrees of excelling; the decision whereof should be left entirely to their own
breast. The highest tax was upon men who are
the greatest favorites of the other sex, and the
assessments, according to the number and natures
of the favors they have received; for which they
are allowed to be their own vouchers. Wit, valor,
and politeness were likewise proposed to be largely
taxed, and collected in the same manner, by every
person's giving his own word for the quantum of
what he possessed. But as to honor, justice, wisdom, and learning, they should not be taxed at all,
because they are qualifications of so singular a kind
that no man will either allow them in his neighbor,
or value them in himself.

The women were proposed to be taxed according
to their beauty and skill in dressing, wherein they
had the same privilege with the men to be determined by their own judgment. But constancy,
chastity, good sense, and good nature were not
rated, because they would not bear the charge of
collecting.

To keep senators in the interest of the crown, it
was proposed that the members should raffle for

employments; every man first taking an oath, and giving security that he would vote for the court, whether he won or no; after which, the losers had, in their turn, the liberty of raffling upon the next vacancy. Thus, hope and expectation would be kept alive; none would complain of broken promises, but impute their disappointments wholly to Fortune, whose shoulders are broader and stronger than those of a ministry.

Another professor showed me a large paper of instructions for discovering plots and conspiracies against the governments. He advised great statesmen to examine into the diet of all suspected persons; their times of eating, upon which side they lay in bed, etc. The whole discourse was written with great acuteness, containing many observations, both curious and useful for politicians; but, as I conceived, not altogether complete This I ventured to tell the author, and offered, if he pleased, to supply him with some additions. He received my proposition with more compliance than is usual among writers, especially those of the projecting species, professing he would be glad to receive further information.

I told him that in the kingdom of Tribnia,* by

---

* That is, Britain : an anagram.

the natives called Langden,* where I had sojourned
some time in my travels, the bulk of the people
consist in a manner wholly of discoverers, witnesses,
informers, accusers, prosecutors, evidences,† swear-
ers, together with their several subservient and
subaltern‡ instrument, all under the color, the conduct, and the pay of ministers of state and their
deputies. The plots, in that kingdom, are usually
the workmanship of those persons who desire to
raise their own characters of profound politicians;
to restore new vigor to a crazy administration; to
stifle or divert general discontents; to fill their
coffers with forfeitures; and raise or sink the opinion of public credit as either shall best answer their
private advantage. It is first agreed and settled
among them what suspected persons shall be accused
of a plot; then effectual care is taken to secure all
their letters and papers, and put the owners in
chains. These papers are delivered to a set of
artists, very dexterous in finding out the mysterious
meanings of words, syllables, and letters; for instance, they can discover a flock of geese to signify
a senate; a lame dog, an invader; the plague, a
standing army; a buzzard, a prime minister; the

---

* England.

† Persons ready to give false or malicious evidence.

‡ Inferior or subordinate.

gout, a high-priest; a gibbet, a secretary of state; a sieve, a court lady; a broom, a revolution; a mouse-trap, an employment; a bottomless pit, a treasury; a sink, a court; a cap and bells, a favorite; a broken reed, a court of justice; an empty tun, a general; a running sore, the administration.

When this method fails, they have two others more effectual, which the learned among them call acrostics and anagrams. First, they can decipher all initial letters into political meanings. Thus, *N* shall signify a plot; *B*, a regiment of horse; *L*, a fleet at sea. Or, secondly, by transposing the letters of the alphabet in any suspected paper, they can lay open the deepest designs of a discontented party. So, for example, if I should say in a letter to a friend, "Our brother Tom has just got the piles," a skillful decipherer would discover that the same letters which compose that sentence may be analyzed into the following words, "Resist—a plot is brought home—the tour." And this is the anagrammatic method.*

---

* In the above Swift satirizes the kind of evidence that was brought against his friend Bishop Atterbury, who was accused of being engaged in a Jacobite plot, and deprived of his bishopric and banished. The evidence consisted largely of intercepted letters, papers written in secret writing, etc., and was by many considered quite insufficient to incriminate Atterbury.

The professor made me great acknowledgments for communicating these observations, and promised to make honorable mention of me in his treatise.

I saw nothing in this country that could invite me to a longer continuance, and began to think of returning home to England.

CHAPTER VII.

The Author leaves Lagado—Arrives at Maldonada—No ship ready—He takes a short voyage to Glubbdubdribb—His reception by the Governor.

THE continent, of which this kingdom is a part, extends itself, as I have reason to believe, eastward to that unknown tract of America westward of California and north to the Pacific Ocean, which is not above a hundred and fifty miles from Lagado; where there is a good port, and much commerce with the great island of Luggnagg, situated to the northwest, about 29 degrees north latitude, and 140 longitude. This island of Luggnagg stands southeastwards of Japan, about an hundred leagues distant. There is a strict alliance between the Japanese emperor and the king of Luggnagg, which affords frequent opportunities of sailing from one island to the other. I determined therefore to direct my course this way, in order to my return to Europe. I hired two mules, with a guide, to show me the way, and carry my small baggage. I took leave of my noble protector, who had shown me so much favor, and made me a generous present at my departure.

My journey was without any accident or adventure worth relating. When I arrived at the port of Maldonada (for so it is called), there was no ship in the harbor bound for Luggnagg, nor like to be in some time. The town is about as large as Portsmouth. I soon fell into some acquaintance, and was very hospitably received. A gentleman of distinction said to me, that since the ships bound for Luggnagg could not be ready in less than a month, it might be no disagreeable amusement for me to take a trip to the little island of Glubbdubdribb, about five leagues off to the southwest. He offered himself and a friend to accompany me, and that I should be provided with a small convenient bark for the voyage.

Glubbdubdribb, as nearly as I can interpret the word, signifies the island of sorcerers, or magicians.

It is about one-third as large as the Isle of Wight, and extremely fruitful; it is governed by the head of a certain tribe, who are all magicians. This tribe marries only among each other, and the eldest in succession is prince or governor. He has a noble palace, and a park of about three thousand acres, surrounded by a wall of hewn stone twenty foot high. In this park are several smaller enclosures for cattle, corn, and gardening.

The governor and his family are served and attended by domesties of a kind somewhat unusual. By his skill in necromancy, he has a power of calling whom he pleases from the dead, and commanding their services for twenty-four hours, but no longer; nor can he call the same persons up again in less than three months, except upon very extra ordinary occasions.

When we arrived at the island, which was about eleven in the morning, one of the gentlemen who accompanied me went to the governor, and desired admittance for a stranger, who came on purpose to have the honor of attending on his highness. This was immediately granted, and we all three entered the gate of the palace between two rows of guards, armed and dressed after a very antick* manner, and something in their countenances that made my flesh creep with a horror I cannot express. We passed through several apartments, between servants of the same sort, ranked on each side as before, till we came to the chamber of presence, where, after three profound obeisances and a few general questions, we were permitted to sit on three stools, near the lowest step of his highness' throne. He

---

* Odd or peculiar, or perhaps antique.

understood the language of Balnibarbi, although it were different from that of his island. He desired me to give him some account of my travels; and to let me see that I should be treated without ceremony, he dismissed all his attendants with a turn of his finger; at which to my great astonishment, they vanished in an instant, like visions in a dream when we awake on a sudden. I could not recover myself in some time, till the governor assured me that I should receive no hurt; and observing my two companions to be under no concern, who had been often entertained in the same manner, I began to take courage, and related to his highness a short history of my several adventures; yet not without some hesitation, and frequently looking behind me to the place where I had seen those domestic specters. I had the honor to dine with the governor, where a new set of ghosts served up the meat, and waited at table. I now observed myself to be less terrified than I had been in the morning. I stayed till sunset, but humbly desired his highness to excuse me for not accepting of his invitation of lodging in the palace. My two friends and I lay at a private house in the town adjoining, which is the capital of this little island; and the next morning we returned to pay our duty to the governor, as he was pleased to command us.

After this manner we continued in the island for ten days, most part of every day with the governor, and at night in our lodging. I soon grew so familarized to the sight of spirits, that, after the third or fourth time, they gave me no emotion at all; or, if I had any apprehensions left, my curiosity prevailed over them. For his highness the governor ordered me to call up whatever persons I would choose to name, and in whatever numbers, among all the dead from the beginning of the world to the present time, and command them to answer any questions I should think fit to ask; with this condition, that my questions must be confined within the compass of the times they lived in. And one thing I might depend upon, that they would certainly tell me truth, for lying was a talent of no use in the lower world.

I made my humble acknowledgments to his highness for so great a favor. We were in a chamber, from whence there was a fair prospect into the park. And because my first inclination was to be entertained with scenes of pomp and magnificence, I desired to see Alexander the Great at the head of his army, just after the battle of Arbela;* which, upon a motion of the governor's

---

* At which the Persian empire was overthrown in B.C. 331.

finger, immediately appeared in a large field, under the window where we stood.   Alexander was called up in the room; it was with great difficulty that I understood his Greek, and had but little of my own. He assured me upon his honor that he was not poisoned, but died of a fever by excessive drinking.*

Next, I saw Hannibal passing the Alps, who told me he had not a drop of vinegar in his camp.†

I saw Cæsar and Pompey at the head of their troops, just ready to engage.‡   I saw the former in his last great triumph.   I desired that the senate of Rome might appear before me in one large chamber, and a modern representative, in counterview, in another.   The first seemed to be an assembly of heroes and demi-gods; the other, a knot of pedlars, pickpockets, highwaymen, and bullies.

The governor, at my request, gave the sign for Cæsar and Brutus to advance toward us.   I was struck with a profound veneration at the sight of Brutus, and could easily discover the most con-

---

* Alexander died of a fever which seized him after a drinking bout.   There does not appear to have been any suspicion of poisoning.

† The story was that Hannibal used fire and vinegar to soften the rocks in making a path through the mountains.

‡ At the battle of Pharsalia, B.C. 48, in which Pompey was completely defeated.

summate virtue, the greatest intrepidity and firmness of mind, the truest love of his country, and general benevolence for mankind, in every lineament of his countenance. I observed with much pleasure that these two persons were in good intelligence with each other; and Cæsar freely confessed to me that the greatest actions of his own life were not equal, by many degrees, to the glory of taking it away. I had the honor to have much conversation with Brutus; and was told that his ancestor, Junius,* Socrates, Epaminondas,† Cato the younger,‡ Sir Thomas More, and himself, were perpetually together: a sextumvirate,§ to which all the ages of the world cannot add a seventh.

It would be tedious to trouble the reader with relating what vast numbers of illustrious persons were called up, to gratify that insatiable desire I had to see the world in every period of antiquity placed before me. I chiefly fed mine eyes with beholding the destroyers of tyrants and usurpers, and

---

* Who was the chief means of overthrowing the regal form of government in Rome.

† A famous Greek patriot and general, killed in battle 362 B.C.

‡ An eminent Roman, who took his own life in order that he might not live under Cæsar as supreme ruler of Rome.

§ Body of six men.

the restorers of liberty to oppressed and injured nations. But it is impossible to express the satisfaction I received in my own mind, after such a manner, as to make it a suitable entertainment to the reader.

CHAPTER VIII.

A further account of Glubbdubdribb—Ancient and Modern History corrected.

HAVING a desire to see those ancients who were most renowned for wit and learning, I set apart one day on purpose. I proposed that Homer and Aristotle might appear at the head of all their commentators; but these were so numerous that some hundreds were forced to attend in the court and outward rooms of the palace. I knew, and could distinguish those two heroes at first sight, not only from the crowd, but from each other. Homer was the taller and comelier person of the two, walked very erect for one of his age, and his eyes were the most quick and piercing I ever beheld.* Aristotle stooped much, and made use of a staff. His visage was meager, his hair lank and thin, and his voice hollow. I soon discovered that both of them were perfect strangers to the rest of the company, and had never seen or heard of them before. And I

---

* The common, but very improbable, tradition is that Homer was blind.

had a whisper from a ghost, who shall be nameless, that these commentators always kept in the most distant quarters from their principals, in the lower world, through a consciousness of shame and guilt, because they had so horribly misrepresented the meaning of those authors to posterity. I introduced Didymus and Eustathius* to Homer, and prevailed on him to treat them better than perhaps they deserved, for he soon found they wanted a genius to enter into the spirit of a poet. But Aristotle was out of all patience with the account I gave him of Scotus† and Ramus,‡ as I presented them to him; and he asked them whether the rest of the tribe were as great dunces as themselves?

I then desired the governor to call up Descartes §

---

* Didymus (1st century B.C.), and Eustathius (12th century A.D.), wrote esteemed commentaries on Homer.

† Duns Scotus, a famous philosopher of the middle ages (died 1308), wrote, among many other things, a commentary on Aristotle.

‡ Ramus was a distinguished French scholar of the 16th century who wrote in opposition to Aristotle's teaching. He perished in the massacre of St. Bartholomew.

§ Descartes (1596–1650), a French writer equally distinguish as a philosopher and a mathematician. His vortices mentioned below were certain whirling motions in the ethereal matter of space that he conjectured to exist, and by which he sought to explain the motions of the heavenly bodies.

and Gassendi, with whom I prevailed to explain their systems to Aristotle. This great philosopher freely acknowledged his own mistakes in natural philosophy, because he proceeded in many things upon conjecture, as all men must do; and he found that Gassendi,* who had made the doctrine of Epicurus as palatable as he could, and the vortices of Descartes were equally to be exploded. He predicted the same fate to attraction, whereof the present learned are such zealous assertors. He said that new systems of nature were but new fashions, which would vary in every age; and even those who pretend to demonstrate them from mathematical principles, would flourish but a short period of time, and be out of vogue when that was determined.

I spent five days in conversing with many others of the ancient learned. I saw most of the first Roman emperors. I prevailed on the governor to call up Eliogabalus'† cooks to dress us a dinner, but they could not show us much of their skill, for

---

* A French philosopher and mathematician, contemporary with Descartes. He attacked the doctrines of Aristotle as well as those of Descartes; and was a supporter of the philosophy of Epicurus.

† Heliogabalus, a Roman emperor infamous for debauchery and gluttony, killed A.D. 222.

want of materials. A helot of Agesilaus* made us a dish of Spartan broth, but I was not able to get down a second spoonful.

The two gentlemen who conducted me to the island, were pressed by their private affairs to return in three days, which I employed in seeing some of the modern dead, who had made the greatest figure, for two or three hundred years past, in our own and other countries of Europe; and having been always a great admirer of old illustrious families, I desired the governor would call up a dozen or two of kings, with their ancestors in order, for eight or nine generations. But my disappointment was grievous and unexpected; for, instead of a long train with royal diadems, I saw in one family two fiddlers, three spruce courtiers, and an Italian prelate. In another a barber, an abbot, and two cardinals. I have too great a veneration for crowned heads to dwell any longer on so nice a subject. But as to counts, marquises, dukes, earls, and the like, I was not so scrupulous. And I confess, it was not without some pleasure, that I found myself able to trace the particular features, by which certain families are distinguished, up to their originals. I could plainly

---

* A celebrated King of Sparta. The Spartan "black broth" was much spoken of in antiquity, but we do not know its composition. The Helots were the slaves of the Spartans.

discover from whence one family derives a long chin; why a second hath abounded with knaves for two generations, and fools for two more; why a third happened to be crack-brained, and a fourth to be sharpers; whence it came, what Polydore Virgil says of a certain great house, *Nec vir fortis, nec fœmina casta;** how cruelty, falsehood, and cowardice grew to be characteristics by which certain families are distingished, as much as by their coat of arms.

I was chiefly disgusted with modern history; for, having strictly examined all the persons of greatest name in the courts of princes for an hundred years past, I found how the world had been misled by prostitute writers, to ascribe the greatest exploits in war to cowards; the wisest counsel to fools; sincerity to flatterers; Roman virtue to betrayers of their country; piety to atheists; truth to informers; how many innocent and excellent persons have been condemned to death or banishment, by the practising of great ministers upon the corruption of judges and the malice of faction; how many villains have been exalted to the highest places of trust, power, dignity, and profit; how great a share in the motions and events of courts, counsels, and senates,

---

* No man brave nor woman chaste.

might be challenged by the vilest persons. How
low an opinion I had of human wisdom and integrity, when I was truly informed of the springs and
motives of great enterprises and revolutions in the
world, and of the contemptible accidents to which
they owed their success!

Here I discovered the roguery and ignorance of
those who pretend to write anecdotes, or secret
history; who send so many kings to their graves
with a cup of poison; will repeat the discourse
between a prince and chief minister, where no witness was by; unlock the thoughts and cabinets of
ambassadors and secretaries of state; and have the
perpetual misfortune to be mistaken. Here I discovered the true cause of many great events that
have surprised the world. A general confessed in
my presence, that he got a victory purely by the
force of cowardice and ill-conduct; and an admiral,
that for want of proper intelligence he beat the
enemy, to whom he intended to betray the fleet.
Three kings protested to me that in their whole
reigns they did never once prefer any person of
merit, unless by mistake, or treachery of some
minister in whom they confided; neither would they
do it if they were to live again; and they showed
with great strength of reason, that the royal throne
could not be supported without corruption, because

that positive, confident, restive temper, which virtue infused into a man, was a perpetual clog to public business.

I had the curiosity to inquire, in a particular manner, by what method great numbers had procured to themselves high titles of honor and prodigious estates; and I confined my inquiry to a very modern period; however, without grating upon present times, because I would be sure to give no offense even to foreigners (for I hope the reader need not be told that I do not in the least intend my own country in what I say upon this occasion). A great number of persons concerned were called up, and, upon a very slight examination, discovered such a scene of infamy, that I cannot reflect upon it without some seriousness. Perjury, oppression, subornation, fraud, and the like infirmities, were among the most excusable arts they had to mention, and for these I gave, as it was reasonable, great allowance. But when some confessed they owed their greatness and wealth to the betraying of their country or their prince; some to poisoning; more to the perverting of justice, in order to destroy the innocent; I hope I may be pardoned, if these discoveries inclined me a little to abate of that profound veneration which I am naturally apt to pay to persons of high rank, who ought to be treated with the utmost respect due to their sublime dignity by us their inferiors.

I had often read of some great services done to princes and states, and desired to see the persons by whom those services were performed. Upon inquiry I was told that their names were to be found on no record, except a few of them whom history hath represented as the vilest rogues and traitors. As to the rest I had never once heard of them. They all appeared with dejected looks and in the meanest habit; most of them telling me they died in poverty and disgrace, and the rest on a scaffold or a gibbet.

Among the rest there was one person whose case appeared a little singular. He had a youth about eighteen years old standing by his side. He told me he had for many years been commander of a ship; and in the sea-fight at Actium,* had the good fortune to break throught the enemy's great line of battle, sink three of their capital ships, and take a fourth, which was the sole cause of Antony's flight, and of the victory that ensued; that the youth standing by him, his only son, was killed in the

---

* B. C. 31, between Octavianus (afterward the Emperor Augustus) and Mark Antony. Historians explain Antony's flight differently : they tell us that he was so infatuated with Cleopatra as to follow her with some of his ships when she from timidity withdrew with the fleet that she had brought.

action. He added, that upon the confidence of some merit, this war being at an end, he went to Rome, and solicited at the court of Augustus to be preferred to a greater ship, whose commander had been killed; but, without any regard to his pretensions, it was given to a boy who had never seen the sea. Returning back to his own vessels, he was charged with neglect of duty, and the ship given to a favorite page of Publicola, the vice-admiral; whereupon he retired to a poor farm at a great distance from Rome, and there ended his life. I was so curious to know the truth of this story that I desired Agrippa might be called, who was admiral in that fight. He appeared and confirmed the whole account; but with much more advantage to the captain, whose modesty had extenuated or concealed a great part of his merit.

I was surprised to find corruption grown so high and so quick in that empire, by the force of luxury so lately introduced, which made me less wonder at many parallel cases in other countries, where vices of all kinds have reigned so much longer, and where the whole praise, as well as pillage, hath been engrossed by the chief commander, who, perhaps, had the least title to either.

As every person called up made exactly the same appearance he had done in the world, it gave me melancholy reflections to observe how much the race of human kind was degenerated among us, within these hundred years past.

I descended so low as to desire that some English yeomen of the old stamp might be summoned to appear, once so famous for the simplicity of their manners, diet, and dress; for justice in their dealings; for their true spirit of liberty; for their valor and love of their country. Neither could I be wholly unmoved, after comparing the living with the dead, when I considered how all these pure native virtues were prostituted for a piece of money by their grandchildren, who, in selling their votes, and managing at elections, have acquired every vice and corruption that can possibly be learned in a court.

CHAPTER IX.

The Author's return to Maldonada—Sails to the Kingdom of
Luggnagg—The Author confined—He is sent for to Court
—The manner of his Admittance—The King's great Lenity
to his Subjects.

THE day of our departure being come, I took
leave of his highness, the governor of Glubbdubdribb, and returned with my two companions to
Maldonada, where, after a fortnight's waiting, a
ship was ready to sail for Luggnagg. The two
gentlemen, and some others, were so generous and
kind as to furnish me with provisions, and see me
on board. I was a month in this voyage. We had
one violent storm, and were under a necessity of
steering westward to get into the trade wind, which
holds for above sixty leagues. On the 21st of April,
1708, we sailed into the river of Clumegnig, which
is a seaport town at the southeast point of Luggnagg. We cast anchor within a league of the town,
and made a signal for a pilot. Two of them came
on board in less than half an hour, by whom we
were guided between certain shoals and rocks,

which are very dangerous in the passage, to a large basin, where a fleet may ride in safety within a cable's length of the town wall.

Some of our sailors, whether out of treachery or inadvertence, had informed the pilots that I was a stranger and a great traveler; whereof these gave notice to a custom-house officer, by whom I was examined very strictly upon my landing. This officer spoke to me in the language of Balnibarbi, which, by the force of much commerce, is generally understood in that town, especially by seamen and those employed in the customs. I gave him a short account of some particulars, and made my story as plausible and consistent as I could; but I thought it necessary to disguise my country, and call myself an Hollander, because my intentions were for Japan, and I knew the Dutch were the only Europeans permitted to enter into that kingdom.* I therefore told the officer, that having been shipwrecked on the coast of Balnibarbi, and cast on a rock, I was received up into Laputa, or the Flying Island (of which he had often heard), and was now endeavoring to get to Japan, from whence I might find a convenience of returning to my own country. The

* This was the case at the date in the text, and for long after. See below, note 33 .

officer said I must be confined till he could receive orders from court; for which he would write immediately, and hoped to receive an answer in a fortnight. I was carried to a convenient lodging, with a sentry placed at the door; however, I had the liberty of a large garden, and was treated with humanity enough, being maintained all the time at the king's charge. I was invited by several persons, chiefly out of curiosity, because it was reported that I came from countries very remote, of which they had never heard.

I hired a young man, who came in the same ship, to be an interpreter; he was a native of Luggnagg, but had lived some years at Maldonada, and was a perfect master of both languages. By his assistance I was able to hold a conversation with those who came to visit me; but this consisted only of their questions, and my answers.

The dispatch came from court about the time we expected. It contained a warrant for conducting me and my retinue to *Traldragdubh*, or *Trildrogdrib*, for it is pronounced both ways, as near as I can remember, by a party of ten horse. All my retinue was that poor lad for an interpreter, whom I persuaded into my service, and, at my humble request, we had each of us a mule to ride on. A messenger was dispatched half a day's journey before us to give the king notice of my approach, and to desire that his majesty would please to appoint a day and hour when it would be his gracious pleasure that I might have the honor to lick the dust before his footstool. This is the court style, and I found it to be more than matter of form. For, upon my admittance, two days after my arrival, I was commanded to crawl on my belly, and lick the floor as I advanced; but, on account of my being a stranger, care was taken to have it swept so clean that the dust was not offensive. However, this was a peculiar grace, not allowed to any but persons of the highest rank, when they desire an admittance. Nay, sometimes the floor is strewed with dust on purpose, when the person to be admitted happens to have powerful enemies at court. And I have seen a great lord with his mouth so crammed that when he had crept to the proper distance from the throne he was not able to speak a word. Neither is there any remedy, because it is capital for those who receive an audience to spit or wipe their mouths in his majesty's presence. There is, indeed, another custom, which I cannot altogether approve of; when the king hath a mind to put any of his nobles to death in a gentle, indulgent manner, he commands the floor to be strewed with a certain brown powder of a deadly composition, which, being licked up, infallibly kills him in twenty-four hours. But in justice to this prince's great clemency, and the care he hath for his subjects' lives (wherein it were much to be wished that the monarchs of Europe would imitate him), it must be mentioned for his honor that strict orders are given to have the infected parts of the floor well washed after every such execution; which, if his domestics neglect, they are in danger of incurring his royal displeasure. I myself heard him give directions that one of his pages should be whipped, whose turn it was to give notice about washing the floor after an execution, but maliciously had omitted it; by which neglect a young lord of great hopes coming to an audience was unfortunately poisoned, although the king at that time had no design against his life. But this good prince was so gracious as to forgive the poor page his whipping, upon promise that he would do so no more, without special orders.

To return from this digression; when I had crept within four yards of the throne I raised myself gently upon my knees, and then, striking my forehead seven times against the ground, I pronounced the following words, as they had been taught me the night before: *Inckpling gloffthrobb squutserumm blhiop mlashnalt zwin tnodbalkguffh slhiophad gurdlubh asht.* This is the compliment, established by the laws of the land, for all persons admitted to the king's presence. It may be rendered into English thus: "May your celestial majesty outlive the sun eleven moons and a half!" To this the king returned some answer, which, although I could not understand, yet I replied as I had been directed: *Flute drin yalerick dwuldom prastrad mirpush,* which properly signifies, "My tongue is in the mouth of my friend;" and by this expression was meant that I desired leave to bring my interpreter; whereupon the young man already mentioned was accordingly introduced, by whose intervention I answered as many questions as his majesty could put in above an hour. I spoke in the Balnibarbian tongue, and my interpreter delivered my meaning in that of Luggnagg.

The king was much delighted with my company, and ordered his *bliffmarklub,* or high chamberlain, to appoint a lodging in the court for me and my interpreter, with a daily allowance for my table, and a large purse of gold for my common expenses.

I stayed three months in this country, out of perfect obedience to his majesty, who was pleased highly to favor me, and made me very honorable offers. But I thought it more consistent with prudence and justice to pass the remainder of my days with my wife and family.

CHAPTER X.

The Luggnaggians commended—A particular Description of
the Struldbrugs, with many Conversations between the
Author and some eminent Persons upon that subject.

THE Luggnaggians are a polite and generous people; and although they are not without some share
of that pride which is peculiar to all eastern countries, yet they show themselves courteous to strangers, especially such who are countenanced by the
court. I had many acquaintance among persons of
the best fashion, and being always attended by my
interpreter, the conversation we had was not disagreeable.

One day, in much good company, I was asked by
a person of quality whether I had seen any of their
struldbrugs, or immortals. I said I had not, and desired he would explain to me what he meant by
such an appellation, applied to a mortal creature.
He told me that sometimes, though very rarely, a
child happened to be born in a family with a red
circular spot in the forehead, directly over the left

eyebrow, which was an infallible mark that it should
never die. The spot, as he described it, was about
the compass of a silver threepence, but in the course
of time grew larger and changed its color; for at
twelve years old it became green, so continued till
twenty-five, then turned to a deep blue; at forty-
five it grew coal-black and as large as an English
shilling, but never admitted any further alteration.
He said these births were so rare that he did not
believe there could be above eleven hundred *struldbrugs*, of both sexes, in the whole kingdom, of which
he computed about fifty in the metropolis, and,
among the rest, a young girl born about three years
ago; that these productions were not peculiar to
any family, but a mere effect of chance, and the
children of the *struldbrugs* themselves were equally
mortal with the rest of the people.

I freely own myself to have been struck with in-
expressible delight upon hearing this account: and
the person who gave it me happening to understand
the Balnibarbian language, which I spoke very well,
I could not forbear breaking out into expressions,
perhaps a little too extravagant. I cried out, as in
a rapture: Happy nation, where every child has at
least a chance for being immortal! Happy people,
who enjoy so many living examples of ancient virtue, and have masters ready to instruct them in the

wisdom of all former ages! But happiest, beyond all comparison, are those excellent *struldbrugs*, who, born exempt from that universal calamity of human nature, have their minds free and disengaged, without the weight and depression of spirits caused by the continual apprehension of death! I discovered my admiration,* that I had not observed any of these illustrious persons at court; the black spot on the forehead being so remarkable a distinction, that I could not have easily overlooked it; and it was impossible that his majesty, a most judicious prince, should not provide himself with a good number of such wise and able counselors. Yet, perhaps the virtue of those reverend sages was too strict for the corrupt and libertine manners of a court. And we often find by experience that young men are too opinionative and volatile to be guided by the sober dictates of their seniors. However, since the king was pleased to allow me access to his royal person, I was resolved, upon the very first occasion, to deliver my opinion to him on this matter freely and at large, by the help of my interpreter; and whether he would please to take my advice or no, yet in one thing I was determined, that his majesty having frequently offered me an establishment in this coun-

---

* Showed my surprise.

try, I would with great thankfulness accept the
favor, and pass my life here in the conversation of
those superior beings, the *struldbrugs*, if they would
please to admit me.

The gentleman to whom I addressed my discourse,
because (as I have already observed) he spoke the
language of Balnibarbi, said to me, with a sort of
smile, which usually ariseth from pity to the ignorant, that he was glad of any occasion to keep me
among them, and desired my permission to explain
to the company what I had spoke. He did so, and
they talked together for some time in their own
language, whereof I understood not a syllable,
neither could I observe by their countenances what
impression my discourse had made on them. After
a short silence the same person told me that his
friends and mine (so he thought fit to express himself) were very much pleased with the judicious
remarks I had made on the great happiness and
advantages of immortal life, and they were desirous
to know, in a particular manner, what scheme of
living I should have formed to myself if it had fallen
to my lot to have been born a *struldbrug*.

I answered, it was easy to be eloquent on so
copious and delightful a subject, especially to me,
who had been often apt to amuse myself with visions of what I should do, if I were a king, a general,

or a great lord; and upon this very case, I had frequently run over the whole system how I should employ myself, and pass the time, if I were sure to live forever.

That, if it had been my good fortune to come into the world a *struldbrug*, as soon as I could discover my own happiness, by understanding the difference between life and death, I would first resolve, by all arts and methods whatsoever, to procure myself riches. In the pursuit of which, by thrift and management, I might reasonably expect, in about two hundred years, to be the wealthiest man in the kingdom. In the second place, I would, from my earliest youth, apply myself to the study of arts and sciences, by which I should arrive in time to excel all others in learning. Lastly, I would carefully record every action and event of consequence, that happened in the public, impartially draw the characters of the several successions of princes and great ministers of state, with my own observations on every point. I would exactly set down the several changes in customs, language, fashions of dress, diet, and diversions. By all which acquirements, I should be a living treasury of knowledge and wisdom, and certainly become the oracle of the nation.

I would never marry after threescore, but live in an hospitable manner, yet still on the saving side.

I would entertain myself in forming and directing
the minds of hopeful young men, by convincing
them, from my own remembrance, experience, and
observation, fortified by numerous examples, of the
usefulness of virtue in public and private life. But
my choice and constant companions should be a set
of my own immortal brotherhood ; among whom I
would elect a dozen from the most ancient, down to
my own contemporaries. Where any of these
wanted fortunes, I would provide them with convenient lodges round my own estate, and have some
of them always at my table; only mingling a few
of the most valuable among you mortals, whom
length of time would harden me to lose with little
or no reluctance, and treat your posterity after the
same manner; just as a man diverts himself with
the annual succession of pinks and tulips in his
garden, without regretting the loss of those which
withered the preceding year.

These *struldbrugs* and I would mutually com-
municate our observations and memorials* through
the course of time; remark the several gradations
by which corruption steals into the world, and
oppose it in every step, by giving perpetual warning and instruction to mankind ; which added to the

---

* Recollections.

strong influence of our own example, would probably prevent that continual degeneracy of human nature, so justly complained of in all ages.

Add to all this, the pleasure of seeing the various revolutions of states and empires; the changes in the lower and upper world; ancient cities in ruins, and obscure villages become the seats of kings; famous rivers lessening into shallow brooks; the ocean leaving one coast dry, and overwhelming another; the discovery of many countries yet unknown; barbarity overrunning the politest nations, and the most barbarous become civilized. I should then see the discovery of the longitude,* the perpetual motion, the universal medicine,† and many other great inventions brought to the utmost perfection.

What wonderful discoveries should we make in astronomy, by outliving and confirming our own predictions; by observing the progress and returns of comets, with the changes of motion in the sun, moon, and stars!

I enlarged upon many other topics, which the natural desire of endless life, and sublunary happi-

---

* A reward had been offered by government in 1714 for the best method of finding the longitude at sea.

† A medicine to cure all ailments. This was what the alchemists sought.

ness, could easily furnish me with. When I had ended, and the sum of my discourse had been interpreted, as before, to the rest of the company, there was a good deal of talk among them in the language of the country, not without some laughter at my expense. At last, the same gentleman who had been my interpreter said, he was desired by the rest to set me right in a few mistakes, which I had fallen into through the common imbecility of human nature, and upon that allowance* was less answerable for them. That this breed of *struldbrugs* was peculiar to their country, for there were no such people either in Balnibarbi or Japan, where he had the honor to be ambassador from his majesty, and found the natives in both those kingdoms very hard to believe that the fact was possible : and it appeared from my astonishment when he had first mentioned the matter to me, that I received it as a thing wholly new, and scarcely to be credited. That in two kingdoms above mentioned, where, during his residence, he had conversed very much, he observed long life to be the universal desire and wish of mankind. That whoever had one foot in the grave was sure to hold the other as strongly as he could. That the oldest had still hopes of living one day

---

* Excuse.

longer, and looked on death as the greatest evil, from which nature always prompted him to retreat. Only in this island of Luggnagg, the appetite for living was not so eager, from the continual example of the *struldbrugs* before their eyes.

That the system of living contrived by me was unreasonable and unjust, because it supposed a perpetuity of youth, health and vigor, which no man could be so foolish to hope, however extravagant he may be in his wishes. That the question therefore was not, whether a man would choose to be always in the prime of youth, attended with prosperity and health; but how he would pass a perpetual life under all the usual disadvantages which old age brings along with it. For although few men will avow their desires of being immortal, upon such hard conditions, yet in the two kingdoms before mentioned, of Balnibarbi and Japan, he observed that every man desired to put off death for some time longer, let it approach ever so late; and he rarely heard of any man who died willingly, except he were incited by the extremity of grief or torture. And he appealed to me, whether in those countries I had traveled, as well as my own, I had not observed the same general disposition.

After this preface he gave me a particular account of the *struldbrugs* among them. He said they commonly acted like mortals till about thirty years old ; after which, by degrees, they grew melancholy and dejected, increasing in both till they came to fourscore. This he learned from their own confession ; for otherwise, there not being above two or three of that species born in an age, they were too few to form a general observation by. When they came to fourscore years, which is reckoned the extremity of living in this country, they had not only all the follies and infirmities of other old men, but many more, which arose from the dreadful prospect of never dying. They were not only opinionative, peevish, covetous, morose, vain, talkative, but incapable of friendship, and dead to all natural affection, which never descended below their grandchildren. Envy and impotent desires are their prevailing passions. But those objects against which their envy seems principally directed, are the vices of the younger sort, and the deaths of the old. By reflecting on the former, they find themselves cut off from all possibility of pleasure ; and whenever they see a funeral, they lament and repine that others are gone to an harbor of rest to which they themselves never can hope to arrive. They have no remembrance of anything but what they learned and observed in their youth and middle age, and even that is very imperfect. And for the truth or particulars of any fact, it is safer to depend on common tradition than upon their best recollections. The least miserable among them appear to be those who turn to dotage, and entirely lose their memories; these meet with more pity and assistance, because they want many bad qualities which abound in others.

If a *struldbrug* happen to marry one of his own kind, the marriage is dissolved of course, by the courtesy of the kingdom, as soon as the younger of the two comes to be fourscore. For the law thinks it is a reasonable indulgence that those who are condemned, without any fault of their own, to a perpetual continuance in the world, should not have their misery doubled by the load of a wife.

As soon as they have completed the term of eighty years they are looked on as dead in law; their heirs immediately succeed to their estates, only a small pittance is reserved for their support; and the poor ones are maintained at the public charge. After that period they are held incapable of any employment of trust or profit; they cannot purchase lands, or take leases; neither are they allowed to be witnesses in any cause, either civil or criminal, not even for the decision of meers* and bounds.

---

* Boundary lines or landmarks.

At ninety they lose their teeth and hair; they have at that age no distinction of taste, but eat and drink whatever they can get, without relish or appetite. The diseases they were subject to still continue, without increasing or diminishing. In talking they forget the common appellation of things, and the names of persons, even of those who are their nearest friends and relations. For the same reason they never can amuse themselves with reading, because their memory will not serve to carry them from the beginning of a sentence to the end: and by this defect they are deprived of the only entertainment whereof they might otherwise be capable.

The language of this country being always upon the flux, the *struldbrugs* of one age do not understand those of another; neither are they able, after two hundred years, to hold any conversation (further than by a few general words) with their neighbors, the mortals; and thus they lie under the disadvantage of living like foreigners in their own country.

This was the account given me of the *struldbrugs*, as near as I can remember. I afterward saw five or six of different ages, the youngest not above two hundred years old, who were brought to me at several times by some of my friends; but although they were told that I was a great traveler, and had seen all the world, they had not the least curiosity to ask me a question; only desired I would give them *slumskudask*, or a token of remembrance; which is a modest way of begging, to avoid the law, that strictly forbids it, because they are provided for by the public, although, indeed, with a very scanty allowance.

They are despised and hated by all sorts of people. When one of them is born it is reckoned ominous, and their birth is recorded very particularly: so that you may know their age by consulting the register, which, however, hath not been kept above a thousand years past, or at least hath been destroyed by time, or public disturbances. But the usual way of computing how old they are is by asking them what kings or great persons they can remember, and then consulting history; for infallibly the last prince in their mind did not begin his reign after they were fourscore years old.

They were the most mortifying sight I ever beheld; and the women more horrible than the men. Besides the usual deformities in extreme old age, they acquired an additional ghastliness, in proportion to their number of years, which is not to be described; and among half a dozen I soon distinguished which was the eldest, although there was not above a century or two between them.

The reader will easily believe that, from what I

had heard and seen, my keen appetite for perpetuity of life was much abated. I grew heartily ashamed of the pleasing visions I had formed; and thought no tyrant could invent a death into which I would not run with pleasure from such a life. The king heard of all that had passed between me and my friends upon this occasion, and rallied me very pleasantly; wishing I could send a couple of *struldbrugs* to my own country, to arm our people against the fear of death; but this, it seems, is forbidden by the fundamental laws of the kingdom, or else I should have been well content with the trouble and expense of transporting them.

I could not but agree that the laws of this kingdom, relating to the *struldbrugs*, were founded upon the strongest reasons, and such as any other country would be under the necessity of enacting in the like circumstances. Otherwise, as avarice is the necessary consequence of old age, those immortals would in time become proprietors of the whole nation, and engross the civil power, which, for want of abilities to manage, must end in the ruin of the public.

CHAPTER XI.

The Author leaves Luggnagg, and sails to Japan—From thence he returns in a Dutch ship to Amsterdam, and from Amsterdam to England.

I THOUGHT this account of the *struldbrugs* might be some entertainment to the reader, because it seems to be a little out of the common way; at least I do not remember to have met the like in any book of travels that hath come to my hands; and if I am deceived, my excuse must be that it is necessary for travelers, who describe the same country, very often to agree in dwelling on the same particulars, without deserving the censure of having borrowed or transcribed from those who wrote before them.

There is, indeed, a perpetual commerce between this kingdom and the great empire of Japan; and it is very probable that the Japanese authors may have given some account of the *struldbrugs;* but my stay in Japan was so short, and I was so entirely a stranger to that language, that I was not qualified to make any inquiries. But I hope the Dutch, upon this notice, will be curious and able enough to supply my defects.

His majesty having often pressed me to accept some employment in his court, and finding me absolutely determined to return to my native country, was pleased to give me his license to depart; and honored me with a letter of recommendation, under his own hand, to the Emperor of Japan. He likewise presented me with four hundred and forty-four large pieces of gold (this nation delighting in even numbers), and a red diamond, which I sold in England for eleven hundred pounds.

On the 6th of May, 1709, I took a solemn leave of his majesty and all my friends. This prince was so gracious as to order a guard to conduct me to Glanguenstald, which is a royal port to the southwest part of the island. In six days I found a vessel ready to carry me to Japan, and spent fifteen days in the voyage. We landed at a small port town called Xamoschi, situated on the southeast part of Japan—the town lies on the western point, where there is a narrow strait leading northward into a long arm of the sea, upon the northwest part of which, Yedo, the metropolis, stands. At landing I showed the custom-house officers my letter from the King of Luggnagg to his imperial majesty. They knew the seal perfectly well; it was as broad as the palm of my hand. The impression was, a king lifting up a lame beggar from the earth. The magistrates of the town, hearing of my letter,

"They knew the seal perfectly well."

received me as a public minister: they provided me with carriages and servants, and bore my charges to Yedo; where I was admitted to an audience, and delivered my letter, which was opened with great ceremony, and explained to the emperor by an interpreter ; who then gave me notice, by his majesty's order, that I should signify my request, and whatever it were, it should be granted, for the sake of his royal brother of Luggnagg. This interpreter was a person employed to transact affairs with the Hollanders: he soon conjectured, by my countenance, that I was an European, and therefore repeated his majesty's commands in Low Dutch, which he spoke perfectly well. I answered, as I had before determined, that I was a Dutch merchant, shipwrecked in a very remote country, from whence I had traveled by sea and land to Luggnagg, and then took shipping for Japan; where I knew my countrymen often traded, and with some of these I hoped to get an opportunity of returning into Europe: I therefore most humbly entreated his royal favor, to give order that I should be conducted in safety to Nangasac.* To this I added another petition, that for the sake of my patron, the King of Luggnagg, his majesty would condescend to excuse my performing the ceremony imposed on my countrymen, of trampling upon the crucifix ;† be-

---

* Nangasaki or Nagasaki, a well-frequented seaport.

† The Dutch had no very good reputation in Europe at this time in connection with their dealings in Japan. And not without some justice, for they had been ready to aid the Japanese authorities in suppressing Christianity (in the form

cause I had been thrown into his kingdom by my misfortunes, without any intention of trading. When this latter petition was interpreted to the emperor, he seemed a little surprised; and said he believed I was the first of my countrymen who ever made any scruple in this point; and that he began to doubt whether I was a real Hollander or no; but rather suspected I must be a Christian. However, for the reasons I had offered, but chiefly to gratify the King of Luggnagg, by an uncommon mark of his favor, he would comply with the singularity of my humor; but the affair must be managed with dexterity, and his officers should be commanded to let me pass, as it were, by forgetfulness. For he assured me that if the secret should be discovered by my countrymen the Dutch, they would cut my

---

of Roman Catholicism) in the empire, and had tried to set the Japanese against other Europeans. Their reward was that they were the only foreigners admitted to trade with Japan, a state of matters that continued up to 1853. They were under the severest restrictions, however; they were confined to a small island near Nangasaki, from which they could not go on shore without leave; and they were prohibited from the observance of the Sabbath or from any outward manifestation of their faith. The trampling on the crucifix is a doubtful matter; but the Dutch, if the practice ever was in force, being Protestants, may have reconciled themselves to it from considering that the crucifix savored of Popery.

throat in the voyage. I returned my thanks, by
the interpreter, for so unusual a favor ; and some
troops being at that time on their march to Nangasac, the commanding officer had orders to convey
me safe thither, with particular instructions about
the business of the crucifix.

On the 9th day of June, 1709, I arrived
at Nangasac, after a very long and troublesome journey. I soon fell into the company of
some Dutch sailors belonging to the Amboyna, of
Amsterdam, a stout ship of four hundred and
fifty tons. I had lived long in Holland, pursuing my studies at Leyden, and I spoke Dutch
well. The seamen soon knew from whence I came
last : they were curious to inquire into my voyages
and course of life. I made up a story as short and
probable as I could, but concealed the greatest part.
I knew many persons in Holland ; I was able to invent names for my parents, whom I pretended to
be obscure people in the province of Gelderland. I
would have given the captain (one Theodorus Van-
grult) what he pleased to ask for my voyage to
Holland ; but understanding I was a surgeon, he
was contented to take half the usual rate, on condition that I would serve him in the way of my calling.
Before we took shipping I was often asked by some
of the crew whether I had performed the ceremony

above mentioned. I evaded the question by general answers; that I had satisfied the emperor and court in all particulars. However, a malicious rogue of a skipper went to an officer, and pointing to me, told him I had not yet trampled on the crucifix; but the other, who had received instructions to let me pass, gave the rascal twenty strokes on the shoulders with a bamboo; after which I was no more troubled with such questions.

Nothing happened worth mentioning in this voyage. We sailed with a fair wind to the Cape of Good Hope, where we stayed only to take in fresh water. On the 10th of April, 1710, we arrived safe at Amsterdam, having lost only three men by sickness in the voyage, and a fourth, who fell from the foremast into the sea, not far from the coast of Guinea. From Amsterdam I soon after set sail for England, in a small vessel belonging to that city.

On the 16th of April we put in at the Downs. I landed the next morning and saw, once more, my native country, after an absence of five years and six months complete. I went straight to Redriff, where I arrived the same day at two in the afternoon, and found my wife and family in good health.

PART IV.

A VOYAGE TO THE COUNTRY OF THE
HOUYHNHNMS.

PART IV.

A VOYAGE TO THE COUNTRY OF THE
HOUYHNHNMS

PART IV.

A VOYAGE TO THE COUNTRY OF THE HOUYHNHNMS.

CHAPTER I.

The Author sets out as Captain of a Ship—His Men conspire against him—Confine him a long time to his Cabin—Set him on shore in an Unknown Land—He travels up into the Country—The Yahoos, a strange sort of Animal, described—The Author meets two Houyhnhnms.

I CONTINUED at home with my wife and children about five months, in a very happy condition, if I could have learned the lesson of knowing when I was well. I left my poor wife, and accepted an advantageous offer made me to be captain of the Adventure, a stout merchantman of three hundred and fifty tons: for I understood navigation well, and being grown weary of a surgeon's employment at sea, which, however, I could exercise upon occasion, I took a skillful young man of that calling, one Robert Purefoy, into my ship. We set sail from Portsmouth upon the 7th day of September, 1710;

on the 14th we met with Captain Pocock of Bristol, at Teneriffe, who was going to the Bay of Campechy to cut logwood. On the 16th he was parted from us by a storm; I heard, since my return, that this ship foundered, and none escaped but one cabin-boy. He was an honest man, and a good sailor, but a little too positive in his own opinions, which was the cause of his destruction, as it hath been of several others. For, if he had followed my advice, he might have been safe at home with his family, at this time, as well as myself.

I had several men die in my ship of calentures,* so that I was forced to get recruits out of Barbadoes and the Leeward Islands, where I touched, by the direction of the merchants who employed me; which I had soon too much cause to repent; for I found afterward that most of them had been buccaneers.† I had fifty hands on board; and my orders were that I should trade with the Indians in the South Sea, and make what discoveries I could. These rogues, whom I had picked up, debauched

---

* A kind of fever said to attack seamen in hot climates.

† The buccaneers were little else than pirates. Their depredations, however, were chiefly confined to the Spaniards in America. The name was originally given to certain French refugees in the West Indies, from a Carib word meaning a place for smoking the meat of wild cattle.

my other men, and they all formed a conspiracy to seize the ship and secure me; which they did one morning, rushing into my cabin, and binding me hand and foot, threatening to throw me overboard if I offered to stir. I told them I was their prisoner, and would submit. This they made me swear to do, and then they unbound me, only fastening one of my legs with a chain, near my bed, and placed a sentry at my door with his piece charged, who was commanded to shoot me dead if I attempted my liberty. They sent me down victuals and drink, and took the government of the ship to themselves. Their design was to turn pirates, and plunder the Spaniards, which they could not do till they got more men. But first they resolved to sell the goods in the ship, and then go to Madagascar* for recruits, several among them having died since my confinement. They sailed many weeks, and traded with the Indians; but I knew not what course they took, being kept a close prisoner in my cabin, and expecting nothing less than to be murdered, as they often threatened me.

Upon the 9th day of May, 1711, one James Welch came down to my cabin, and said he had orders from the captain to set me ashore. I expostulated

---

* This island was a great haunt of pirates.

with him, but in vain; neither would he so much as tell me who their new captain was. They forced me into the long-boat, letting me put on my best suit of clothes, which were as good as new, and take a small bundle of linen, but no arms, except my hanger; and they were so civil as not to search my pockets, into which I conveyed what money I had, with some other little necessaries. They rowed about a league, and then set me down on a strand. I desired them to tell me what country it was. They all swore they knew no more than myself; but said that the captain (as they called him) was resolved, after they sold the lading, to get rid of me in the first place where they could discover land. They pushed off immediately, advising me to make haste, for fear of being overtaken by the tide, and so bade me farewell.

In this desolate condition I advanced forward, and soon got upon firm ground, where I sate down on a bank to rest myself, and consider what I had best to do. When I was a little refreshed I went up into the country, resolving to deliver myself to the first savages I should meet, and purchase my life from them by some bracelets, glass rings, and other toys, which sailors usually provide themselves with in those voyages, and whereof I had some about me. The land was divided by long rows of trees, not regularly planted, but naturally growing; there was great plenty of grass, and several fields of oats. I walked very circumspectly, for fear of being surprised or suddenly shot with an arrow from behind, or on either side. I fell into a beaten road, where I saw many tracks of human feet, and some of cows, but most of horses. At last I beheld several animals in a field, and one or two of the same kind sitting in trees. Their shape was very singular and deformed, which a little discomposed me, so that I lay down behind a thicket to observe them better. Some of them coming forward near the place where I lay, gave me an opportunity of distinctly marking their form. Their heads and breasts were covered with a thick hair, some frizzled, and others lank; they had beards like goats, and a long ridge of hair down their backs, and the foreparts of their legs and feet; but the rest of their bodies was bare, so that I might see their skins, which were of a brown buff color. They had no tails. They often sate on the ground, as well as lying down, and often stood on their hind feet. They climbed high trees as nimbly as a squirrel, for they had strong extended claws, before and behind, terminating in sharp points, and hooked. They would often spring, and bound and leap, with prodigious agility. The females were not so large as the males; they had long lank hair on their head, but none on their faces, nor anything more than a sort of down on the rest of their bodies. Their dugs hung between their forefeet, and often reached almost to the ground as they walked. The hair of both sexes was of several colors—brown, red, black, and yellow. Upon the whole, I never beheld, in all my travels, so disagreeable an animal, nor one against which I naturally conceived so strong an antipathy. So that, thinking I had seen enough, full of contempt and aversion, I got up, and pursued the beaten road, hoping it might direct me to the cabin of some Indian. I had not gone far when I met one of these creatures full in my way, and coming up directly to me. The ugly monster, when he saw me, distorted several ways every feature of his visage, and stared, as at an object he had never seen before; then approaching nearer, lifted up his forepaw, whether out of curiosity or mischief, I could not tell: but I drew my hanger, and gave him a good blow with the flat side of it; for I durst not strike him with the edge, fearing the inhabitants might be provoked against me, if they should come to know that I had killed or maimed any of their cattle. When the beast felt the smart, he drew back, and roared so loud that a herd of at least forty came flocking about me from the next field, howling, and making odious faces; but I ran to the body of a tree, and leaning my back against it, kept them off by waving my hanger.

In the midst of this distress I observed them all to run away on a sudden as fast as they could; at which I ventured to leave the tree, and pursue the road, wondering what it was that could put them into this fright. But, looking on my left hand, I saw a horse walking softly in the field, which my persecutors having sooner discovered was the cause of their flight. The horse started a little when he came near me, but, soon recovering himself, looked full in my face, with manifest tokens of wonder. He viewed my hands and feet, walking round me several times. I would have pursued my journey, but he placed himself directly in the way, yet, looking with a very mild aspect, never offering the least violence. We stood gazing at each other for some time; at last I took the boldness to reach my hand toward his neck, with a design to stroke it, using the common style and whistle of jockeys when they are going to handle a strange horse. But this animal seemed to receive my civilities with disdain, shook his head, and bent his brows, softly raising up his right forefoot to remove my hand. Then he neighed three or four times, but in so different a

cadence that I almost began to think he was speak‧
ing to himself in some language of his own.

While he and I were thus employed another horse
came up, who, applying himself to the first in a very
formal manner, they gently struck each other's right
hoof before, neighing several times by turns, and vary-
ing the sound, which seemed to be almost articulate.
They went some paces off, as if it were to confer
together, walking side by side, backward and forward, like persons deliberating upon some affair of
weight, but often turning their eyes toward me, as
it were to watch that I might not escape. I was
amazed to see such actions and behavior in brute
beasts, and concluded with myself that if the inhabitants of this country were endued with a proportionable degree of reason they must needs be the wisest
people upon earth. This thought gave me so much
comfort that I resolved to go forward until I could
discover some house or village, or meet with any of
the natives, leaving the two horses to discourse together as they pleased. But the first, who was a·
dapple gray, observing me to steal off, neighed after
me in so expressive a tone that I fancied myself to
understand what he meant; whereupon I turned
back, and came near to him, to expect his further
commands, but concealing my fear as much as I
could, for I began to be in some pain how this ad-

venture might terminate; and the reader will easily believe I did not much like my present situation.

The two horses came up close to me, looking with great earnestness upon my face and hands. The gray steed rubbed my hat all round with his right forehoof, and discomposed it so much that I was forced to adjust it better, by taking it off, and settling it again; whereat both he and his companion (who was a brown bay) appeared to be much surprised: the latter felt the lappet of my coat, and, finding it to hang loose about me, they both looked with new signs of wonder. He stroked my right hand, seeming to admire the softness and color, but he squeezed it so hard between his hoof and his pastern that I was forced to roar; after which they both touched me with all possible tenderness. They were under great perplexity about my shoes and stockings, which they felt very often, neighing to each other, and using various gestures, not unlike those of a philosopher when he would attempt to solve some new and difficult phenomenon.

Upon the whole the behavior of these animals was so orderly and rational, so acute and judicious, that I at last concluded they must needs be magicians, who had thus metamorphosed themselves upon some design, and, seeing a stranger in the way, were resolved to divert themselves with him, or perhaps were really amazed at the sight of a man so very different in habit, feature, and complexion, from those who might probably live in so remote a climate. Upon the strength of this reasoning I ventured to address them in the following manner: "Gentlemen, if you be conjurors, as I have good cause to believe, you can understand any language; therefore I make bold to let your worships know that I am a poor, distressed Englishman, driven by his misfortunes upon your coast; and I entreat one of you to let me ride upon his back, as if he were a real horse, to some house or village where I can be relieved. In return of which favor I will make you a present of this knife and bracelet" (taking them out of my pocket). The two creatures stood silent while I spoke, seeming to listen with great attention; and when I had ended they neighed frequently toward each other, as if they were engaged in serious conversation. I plainly observed that their language expressed the passions very well, and their words might, with little pains, be resolved into an alphabet more easily than the Chinese.

I could frequently distinguish the word *Yahoo*, which was repeated by each of them several times; and, although it was impossible for me to conjecture what it meant, yet, while the two horses were busy in conversation, I endeavored to practice this word upon my tongue; and as soon as they were silent I boldly pronounced *Yahoo* in a loud voice, imitating at the same time, as near as I could, the neighing of a horse, at which they were both visibly surprised; and the gray repeated the same word twice, as if he meant to teach me the right accent; wherein I spoke after him as well as I could, and found myself perceivably to improve every time, though very far from any degree of perfection. Then the bay tried me with a second word, much harder to be pronounced, but, reducing it to the English orthography, it may be spelt thus, *Houyhnhnm.* I did not succeed in this so well as in the former; but after two or three further trials I had better fortune, and they both appeared amazed at my capacity.

After some further discourse, which I then conjectured might relate to me, the two friends took their leaves, with the same compliment of striking each other's hoof, and the gray made me signs that I should walk before him; wherein I thought it prudent to comply, till I could find a better director. When I offered to slacken my pace, he would cry, *hhuun, hhuun.* I guessed his meaning, and gave him to understand, as well as I could, that I was weary, and not able to walk faster; upon which he would stand a while to let me rest.

CHAPTER II.

The Author conducted by a Houyhnhnm to his House—The
House described—The Author's reception—The Food of
the Houyhnhnms—The Author in distress for want of
Meat—Is at last relieved—His manner of feeding in this
Country.

HAVING traveled about three miles, we came to a
long kind of building, made of timber stuck in the
ground, and wattled across; the roof was low, and
covered with straw. I now began to be a little
comforted, and took out some toys, which travelers
usually carry for presents to the savage Indians of
America, and other parts, in hopes the people of the
house would be thereby encouraged to receive me
kindly. The horse made me a sign to go in first.
It was a large room, with a smooth clay floor, and
a rack and manger extending the whole length on
one side. There were three nags and two mares,
not eating, but some of them sitting down upon
their hams, which I very much wondered at, but
wondered more to see the rest employed in domestic

business : these seemed but ordinary cattle. However, this confirmed my first opinion, that a people who could so far civilize brute animals must needs excel in wisdom all the nations of the world. The gray came in just after, and thereby prevented any ill treatment which the others might have given me. He neighed to them several times in a style of authority, and received answers.

Beyond this room there were three others, reaching the length of the house, to which you passed through three doors, opposite to each other, in the manner of a vista : we went through the second room toward the third. Here the gray walked in first, beckoning me to attend ; I waited in the second room, and got ready my presents for the master and mistress of the house ; they were two knives, three bracelets of false pearls, a small looking-glass, and a bead necklace. The horse neighed three or four times, and I waited to hear some answers in a human voice, but I observed no other returns than in the same dialect, only one or two a little shriller than his. I began to think that this house must belong to some person of great note among them, because there appeared so much ceremony before I could gain admittance. But, that a man of quality should be served all by horses, was beyond my comprehension. I feared my brain was disturbed by my sufferings and misfortunes. I roused myself, and looked about me in the room where I was left alone; this was furnished like the first, only after a more elegant manner. I rubbed my eyes often, but the same objects still occurred. I pinched my arms and sides to awake myself, hoping I might be in a dream. I then absolutely concluded that all these appearances could be nothing else but necromancy and magic. But I had no time to pursue these reflections; for the gray horse came to the door, and made me a sign to follow him into the third room, where I saw a very comely mare, together with a colt and foal, sitting up on their haunches upon mats of straw, not unartfully made, and perfectly neat and clean.

The mare, soon after my entrance, rose from her mat, and coming up close, after having nicely observed my hands and face, gave me a most contemptuous look, then turning to the horse, I heard the word *Yahoo* often repeated betwixt them, the meaning of which word I could not then comprehend, although it was the first I had learned to pronounce. But I was soon better informed, to my everlasting mortification; for the horse, beckoning to me with his head and repeating the word *hhuun*, *hhuun*, as he did upon the road, which I understood was to attend him, led me out into a kind of court,

where was another building at some distance from
the house. Here we entered, and I saw three
of those detestable creatures which I first met
after my landing, feeding upon roots and the flesh
of some animals, which I afterward found to be that
of asses and dogs, and now and then a cow, dead
by accident or disease. They were all tied by the
neck with strong withes fastened to a beam; they
held their food between the claws of their forefeet,
and tore it with their teeth.

The master horse ordered a sorrel nag, one of his
servants, to untie the largest of these animals, and
take him into the yard. The beast and I were
brought close together, and our countenances diligently compared, both by master and servant,
who thereupon repeated several times the word
Yahoo. My horror and astonishment are not to be
described when I observed in this abominable animal a perfect human figure; the face of it indeed
was flat and broad, the nose depressed, the lips
large, and the mouth wide; but these differences are
common to all savage nations, where the lineaments
of the countenance are distorted by the natives
suffering their infants to lie groveling on the earth,
or by carrying them on their backs, nuzzling with
their face against the mother's shoulders. The forefeet of the Yahoo differed from my hands in noth-

ing else but the length of the nails, the coarseness
and brownness of the palms, and the hairiness on the
backs. There was the same resemblance between

"The beast and I were brought close together, and our countenances
diligently compared."

our feet, with the same differences which I knew
very well, though the horses did not, because of my
shoes and stockings; the same in every part of our
bodies, except as to hairiness and color, which I have
already described.

The great difficulty that seemed to stick with the

two horses was to see the rest of my body so very different from that of a Yahoo; for which I was obliged to my clothes, whereof they had no conception. The sorrel nag offered me a root, which he held (after their manner, as we shall describe in its proper place) between his hoof and pastern. I took it in my hand, and, having smelled it, returned it to him again as civilly as I could. He brought out of the Yahoo's kennel a piece of ass' flesh; but it smelled so offensively that I turned from it with loathing: he then threw it to the Yahoo, by whom it was greedily devoured. He afterward showed me a wisp of hay, and a fetlock* full of oats; but I shook my head, to signify that neither of these were food for me. And indeed I now apprehended that I must absolutely starve if I did not get to some of my own species; for, as to those filthy Yahoos, although there were few greater lovers of mankind at that time than myself, yet I confess I never saw any sensitive being so detestable on all accounts; and the more I came near them the more hateful they grew, while I stayed in that country. This the master horse observed by my behavior, and therefore sent the Yahoo back to his kennel. He

---

* What Swift means by this word is doubtful. Its proper signification is the tuft of long hair on a horse's pastern.

then put his forehoof to his mouth, at which I was
much surprised, although he did it with ease, and
with a motion that appeared perfectly natural; and
made other signs to know what I would eat; but I
could not return him such an answer as he was able
to apprehend; and if he had understood me, I did
not see how it was possible to contrive any way for
finding myself nourishment. While we were thus
engaged I observed a cow passing by, whereupon I
pointed to her, and expressed a desire to go and
milk her. This had its effect; for he led me back
into the house, and ordered a mare servant to open
a room, where a good store of milk lay in earthen
and wooden vessels, after a very orderly and cleanly
manner. She gave me a large bowlful, of which I
drank very heartily, and found myself well refreshed.

About noon I saw coming toward the house a
kind of vehicle drawn like a sledge by four Yahoos.
There was in it an old steed, who seemed to be of
quality; he alighted with his hind feet forward,
having by accident got a hurt in his left forefoot.
He came to dine with our horse, who received him
with great civility. They dined in the best room,
and had oats boiled in milk for the second course,
which the old horse eat warm, but the rest cold.
Their mangers were placed circular in the middle

of the room, and divided into several partitions, round which they sate on their haunches upon bosses of straw. In the middle was a large rack, with angles answering to every partition of the manger; so that each horse and mare ate their own hay, and their own mash of oats and milk, with much decency and regularity. The behavior of the young colt and foal appeared very modest, and that of the master and mistress extremely cheerful and complaisant to their guest. The gray ordered me to stand by him; and much discourse passed between him and his friend concerning me, as I found by the stranger's often looking on me, and the frequent repetition of the word Yahoo.

I happened to wear my gloves, which the master gray observing, seemed perplexed, discovering signs of wonder what I had done to my forefeet. He put his hoof three or four times to them, as if he would signify that I should reduce them to their former shape; which I presently did, pulling off both my gloves, and putting them into my pocket. This occasioned further talk: and I saw the company was pleased with my behavior, whereof I soon found the good effects. I was ordered to speak the few words I understood; and while they were at dinner, the master taught me the names for oats, milk, fire, water, and some others, which I could readily pronounce after him, having from my youth a great facility in learning languages.

When dinner was done, the master horse took me aside, and by signs and words made me understand the concern he was in that I had nothing to eat. Oats in their tongue are called *hlunnh*. This word I pronounced two or three times; for although I had refused them at first, yet, upon second thoughts, I considered that I could contrive to make of them a kind of bread, which might be sufficient, with milk, to keep me alive till I could make my escape to some other country, and to creatures of my own species. The horse immediately ordered a white mare-servant of his family to bring me a good quantity of oats in a sort of wooden tray. These I heated before the fire, as well as I could, and rubbed them till the husks came off, which I made a shift to winnow from the grain: I ground and beat them between two stones, then took water, and made them into a paste or cake, which I toasted at the fire, and eat warm with milk. It was at first a very insipid diet, though common enough in many parts of Europe, but grew tolerable by time; and having been often reduced to hard fare in my life, this was not the first experiment I had made, how easily nature is satisfied. And I cannot but observe that I never had one hour's sickness while I stayed in this island. 'Tis true, I sometimes made a shift to catch a rabbit, or bird, by springes made of Yahoos' hairs; and I often gathered wholesome herbs, which I boiled, or eat as salads with my bread; and now and then, for a rarity, I made a little butter, and drank the whey. I was at first at a great loss for salt, but custom soon reconciled me to the want of it : and I am confident that the frequent use of salt among us is an effect of luxury, and was first introduced only as a provocative to drink, except where it is necessary for preserving of flesh in long voyages, or in places remote from great markets : for we observe no animal to be fond of it but man :* and as to myself, when I left this country, it was a great while before I could endure the taste of it in anything that I eat.

This is enough to say upon the subject of my diet, wherewith other travelers fill their books, as if the readers were personally concerned whether we fare well or ill. However, it was necessary to mention this matter, lest the world should think it impossible that I could find sustenance for three years in such a country, and among such inhabitants.

When it grew toward evening, the **master horse**

---

*This is quite a mistake; cattle, sheep, horses, etc., **are very** fond of it.

ordered a place for me to lodge in: it was but six yards from the house, and separated from the stable of the Yahoos. Here I got some straw, and covering myself with my own clothes, slept very sound. But I was in a short time better accommodated, as the reader shall know hereafter, when I come to treat more particularly about my way of living.

CHAPTER III.

The Author studies to learn the Language—The Houyhnhnm, his Master, assists in teaching him—The Language described—Several Houyhnhnms of quality come out of curiosity to see the Author—He gives his Master a short account of his Voyage.

My principal endeavor was to learn the language, which my master (for so I shall henceforth call him) and his children, and every servant of his house, were desirious to teach me: for they looked upon it as a prodigy that a brute animal should discover such marks of a rational creature. I pointed to everything, and inquired the name of it, which I wrote down in my journal-book when I was alone: and corrected my bad accent by desiring those of the family to pronounce it often. In this employment a sorrel nag, one of the under-servants, was very ready to assist me.

In speaking, they pronounce through the nose and throat; and their language approaches nearest to the High Dutch, or German, of any I know in Europe; but is much more graceful and significant.

The Emperor Charles V. made almost the same observation when he said that if he were to speak to his horse it should be in High Dutch.

The curiosity and impatience of my master were so great that he spent many hours of his leisure to instruct me. He was convinced (as he afterward told me) that I must be a Yahoo; but my teachableness, civility, and cleanliness astonished him; which were qualities altogether opposite to those animals. He was most perplexed about my clothes, reasoning sometimes with himself, whether they were a part of my body; for I never pulled them off till the family were asleep, and got them on before they waked in the morning. My master was eager to learn from whence I came; how I acquired those appearances of reason which I discovered in all my actions; and to know my story from my own mouth; which he hoped he should soon do, by the great proficiency I made in learning and pronouncing their words and sentences. To help my memory, I formed all I learned into the English alphabet, and writ the words down, with the translations. This last, after some time, I ventured to do in my master's presence. It cost me much trouble to explain to him what I was doing; for the inhabitants have not the least idea of books and literature.

In about ten weeks' time I was able to understand most of his questions, and in three months could give him some tolerable answers. He was extremely curious to know from what part of the country I came, and how I was taught to imitate a rational creature; because the Yahoos (whom he saw I exactly resembled in my head, hands, and face, that were only visible), with some appearance of cunning, and the strongest disposition to mischief, were observed to be the most unteachable of all brutes. I answered that I came over the sea, from a far place, with many others of my own kind, in a great hollow vessel, made of the bodies of trees : that my companions forced me to land on this coast, and then left me to shift for myself. It was with some difficulty, and by the help of many signs, that I brought him to understand me. He replied that I must needs be mistaken, or that I said the thing which was not; for they have no word in their language to express lying or falsehood. He knew it was impossible that there could be a country beyond the sea, or that a parcel of brutes could move a wooden vessel whither they pleased upon water. He was sure no Houyhnhnm alive could make such a vessel, nor would trust Yahoos to manage it.

The word *Houyhnhnm*, in their tongue, signifies

a *horse*, and, in its etymology, *the perfection of nature.* I told my master that I was at a loss for expression, but would improve as fast as I could; and hoped in a short time I should be able to tell him wonders. He was pleased to direct his own mare, his colt and foal, and the servants of the family, to take all opportunities of instructing me; and every day, for two or three hours, he was at the same pains himself. Several horses and mares of quality in the neighborhood came often to our house, upon the report spread of a wonderful Yahoo that could speak like a Houyhnhnm, and seemed, in his words and actions, to discover some glimmerings of reason. These delighted to converse with me; they put many questions, and received such answers as I was able to return. By all these advantages I made so great a progress that in five months from my arrival I understood whatever was spoke, and could express myself tolerably well.

The Houyhnhnms, who came to visit my master out of a design of seeing and talking with me, could hardly believe me to be a right Yahoo, because my body had a different covering from others of my kind. They were astonished to observe me without the usual hair or skin, except on my head, face, and hands; but I discovered that secret to my master, upon an accident which happened about a fortnight before.

I have already told the reader that every night, when the family were gone to bed, it was my custom to strip, and cover myself with my clothes. It happened, one morning early, that my master sent for me by the sorrel nag, who was his valet. When he came I was fast asleep, my clothes fallen off on one side. I awaked at the noise he made, and observed him to deliver his message in some disorder; after which he went to my master, and in a great fright gave him a very confused account of what he had seen. This I presently discovered; for, going, as soon as I was dressed, to pay my attendance upon his honor, he asked me the meaning of what his servant had reported, that I was not the same thing when I slept as I appeared to be at other times.

I had hitherto concealed the secret of my dress, in order to distinguish myself, as much as I could, from the cursed race of Yahoos; but now I found it in vain to do so any longer. Besides, I considered that my clothes and shoes would soon wear out, which already were in a declining condition, and must be supplied by some contrivance, from the hides of Yahoos, or other brutes; whereby the whole secret would be known. I therefore told my

master that in the country from whence I came
those of my kind always covered their bodies with
the hairs of certain animals, prepared by art, as well
for decency as to avoid the inclemencies of air, both
hot and cold.

I expressed my uneasiness at his giving me so
often the appellation of Yahoo, an odious animal,
for which I had so utter an hatred and contempt: I
begged he would forbear applying that word to me,
and make the same order in his family and among
his friends whom he suffered to see me. I requested
likewise that the secret of my having a false covering to my body might be known to none but himself, at least as long as my present clothing should
last; for, as to what the sorrel nag, his valet, had
observed, his honor might command him to conceal it.

All this my master very graciously consented to;
and thus the secret was kept till my clothes began
to wear out, which I was forced to supply by several
contrivances that shall hereafter be mentioned. In
the meantime he desired I would go on with my
utmost diligence to learn their language, because he
was more astonished at my capacity for speech and
reason than at the figure of my body, whether it
were covered or no; adding that he waited with
some impatience to hear the wonders which I

promised to tell him. From thenceforward he doubled the pains he had been at to instruct me; he brought me into all company, and made them treat me with civility; because, as he told them privately, this would put me into good humor and make me more diverting.

Every day, when I waited on him, beside the trouble he was at in teaching, he would ask me several questions concerning myself, which I answered as well as I could; and by these means he had already received some general ideas, though very imperfect. It would be tedious to relate the several steps by which I advanced to a more regular conversation; but the first account I gave of myself in any order and length was to this purpose:

That I came from a very far country, as I had already attempted to tell him, with about fifty more of my own species; that we traveled upon the seas in a great, hollow vessel made of wood, and larger than his honor's house. I described the ship to him in the best terms I could, and explained, by the help of my handkerchief displayed, how it was driven forward by the wind. That, upon a quarrel among us, I was set on shore on this coast, where I walked forward, without knowing whither, till he delivered me from the persecution of those execrable Yahoos. He asked me who made the ship, and how it was possible that the Houyhnhnms of my country would leave it to the management of brutes? My answer was, that I durst proceed no further in my relation, unless he would give me his word and honor that he would not be offended, and then I would tell him the wonders I had so often promised. He agreed, and I went on by assuring him that the ship was made by creatures like myself; who, in all the countries I had traveled, as well as in my own, were the only governing rational animals: and that, upon my arrival hither, I was as much astonished to see the Houyhnhmns act like rational beings as he, or his friends, could be in finding some marks of reason in a creature he was pleased to call a Yahoo; to which I owned my resemblance in every part, but could not account for their degenerate and brutal nature. I said further that if good fortune ever restored me to my native country, to relate my travels hither, as I resolved to do, everybody would believe that I said the thing which was not, that I invented the story out of my own head; and (with all possible respect to himself, his family and friends, and under his promise of not being offended) our countrymen would hardly think it probable that a Houyhnhnm should be the presiding creature of a nation, and a Yahoo the brute.

CHAPTER IV.

The Houyhnhnms' notion of Truth and Falsehood—The
Author's discourse disapproved by his Master — The
Author gives a more particular account of himself, and
the Accidents of his Voyage.

MY master heard me with great appearances of
uneasiness in his countenance; because doubting, or
not believing, are so little known in this country
that the inhabitants cannot tell how to behave
themselves under such circumstances. And I remember, in frequent discourses with my master
concerning the nature of manhood in other parts of
the world, having occasion to talk of lying and false
representation, it was with much difficulty that he
comprehended what I meant, although he had otherwise a most acute judgment; for he argued thus:
That the use of speech was to make us understand
one another, and to receive information of facts;
now if any one said the thing which was not, those
ends were defeated, because I cannot properly be
said to understand him; and I am so far from re-

ceiving information that he leaves me worse than in ignorance; for I am led to believe a thing black when it is white, and short when it is long. And these were all the notions he had concerning that faculty of lying, so perfectly well understood, and so universally practiced among human creatures.

To return from this digression. When I asserted that the Yahoos were the only governing animals in my country, which my master said was altogether past his conception, he desired to know whether we had Houyhnhnms among us, and what was their employment? I told him we had great numbers; that in summer they grazed in the fields, and in winter were kept in houses with hay and oats, where Yahoo servants were employed to rub their skins smooth, comb their manes, pick their feet, serve them with food, and make their beds. "I understand you well," said my master; "it is now very plain, from all you have spoken, that whatever share of reason the Yahoos pretend to, the Houyhnhnms are your masters. I heartily wish our Yahoos would be so tractable." I begged his honor would please to excuse me from proceeding any further, because I was very certain that the account he expected from me would be highly displeasing. But he insisted in commanding me to let him know the best and the worst. I told him he should be obeyed. I owned that the Houyhnhnms among us, whom we called *horses*, were the most generous and comely animals we had; that they excelled in strength and swiftness; and, when they belonged to persons of quality, were employed in traveling, racing, or drawing chariots; they were treated with much kindness and care till they fell into diseases, or became foundered in the feet; and then they were sold, and used to all kind of drudgery till they died; after which their skins were stripped, and sold for what they were worth, and their bodies left to be devoured by dogs and birds of prey. But the common race of horses had not so good fortune, being kept by farmers and carriers, and other mean people, who put them to greater labor, and fed them worse. I described, as well as I could, our way of riding; the shape and use of a bridle, a saddle, a spur, and a whip; of harness and wheels. I added that we fastened plates of a certain hard substance, called iron, at the bottom of their feet, to preserve their hoofs from being broken by the stony ways on which we often traveled.

My master, after some expressions of great indignation, wondered how we dared to venture upon a Houyhnhnm's back; for he was sure that the weakest servant in his house would be able to shake off the strongest Yahoo, or, by lying down, and rolling on his back, squeeze the brute to death. I answered, that our horses were trained up, from three or four years old, to the several uses we intended them for; that if any of them proved intolerably vicious, they were employed for carriages;* that they were severely beaten, while they were young, for any mischievous tricks; that they were indeed sensible of rewards and punishments; but his honor would please to consider that they had not the least tincture of reason, any more than the Yahoos in this country.

It put me to the pains of many circumlocutions to give my master a right idea of what I spoke; for their language doth not abound in variety of words, because their wants and passions are fewer than among us. But it is impossible to express his noble resentment at our savage treatment of the Houyhnhnm race. He said, if it were possible there could be any country where Yahoos alone were endued with reason, they certainly must be the governing animal; because reason will, in time, always prevail against brutal strength. But, considering the frame of our bodies, and especially of mine, he thought no creature of equal bulk was so ill contrived for employing that reason in the

---

* Wagons or heavy vehicles must be meant here.

common offices of life; whereupon he desired to know whether those among whom I lived resembled me or the Yahoos of his country. I assured him that I was as well shaped as most of my age; but the younger, and the females, were much more soft and tender, and the skins of the latter generally as white as milk. He said I differed indeed from other Yahoos, being much more cleanly, and not altogether so deformed; but, in point of real advantage, he thought I differed for the worse. That my nails were of no use either to my fore or hinder foot. As to my forefeet, he could not properly call them by that name, for he never observed me to walk upon them; that they were too soft to bear the ground; that I generally went with them uncovered; neither was the covering I sometimes wore on them of the same shape, or so strong as that on my feet behind. That I could not walk with any security, for if either of my hinder feet slipped, I must inevitably fall. He then began to find fault with other parts of my body: the flatness of my face, the prominence of my nose, mine eyes placed directly in front, so that I could not look on either side without turning my head; that I was not able to feed myself without lifting one of my forefeet to my mouth; and therefore nature had placed those joints to answer that necessity. He knew not what could be the use of those several clefts and divisions in my feet behind; that these were too soft to bear the hardness and sharpness of stones, without a covering made from the skin of some other brute; that my whole body wanted a fence* against heat and cold, which I was forced to put on and off every day, with tediousness and trouble. And lastly, that he observed every animal in this country naturally to abhor the Yahoos, whom the weaker avoided, and the stronger drove from them. So that, supposing us to have the gift of reason, he could not see how it were possible to cure that natural antipathy which every creature discovered against us; nor, consequently, how we could tame and render them serviceable. However, he would, as he said, debate the matter no further, because he was more desirious to know my own story, the country where I was born, and the several actions and events of my life before I came hither.

I assured him how extremely desirous I was that he should be satisfied on every point; but I doubted much whether it would be possible for me to explain myself on several subjects, whereof his honor could have no conception, because I saw nothing in his country to which I could resemble them; that,

---

* Defense or protection.

however, I would do my best, and strive to express myself by similitudes, humbly desiring his assistance when I wanted proper words; which he was pleased to promise me.

I said my birth was of honest parents, in an island called England, which was remote from this country as many days' journey as the strongest of his honor's servants could travel in the annual course of the sun; that I was bred a surgeon, whose trade is to cure wounds and hurts in the body, gotten by accident or violence; that my country was governed by a female man, whom we called queen; that I left it to get riches, whereby I might maintain myself and family, when I should return; that in my last voyage I was commander of the ship, and had about fifty Yahoos under me, many of which died at sea, and I was forced to supply them by others picked out from several nations; that our ship was twice in danger of being sunk; the first time by a great storm, and the second by striking against a rock. Here my master interposed, by asking me how I could persuade strangers, out of different countries, to venture with me, after the losses I had sustained, and the hazards I had run? I said they were fellows of desperate fortunes, forced to fly from the places of their birth on account of their poverty or their crimes. Some

were undone by lawsuits; others spent all they had
in drinking, debauchery, and gaming; others fled
for treason; many for murder, theft, poisoning,
robbery, perjury, forgery, coining false money, for
flying from their colors,* or deserting to the enemy;
and most of them had broken prison: none of these
durst return to their native countries, for fear of
being hanged, or of starving in a jail; and therefore
they were under a necessity of seeking a livelihood
in other places.

During this discourse my master was pleased to
interrupt me several times. I had made use of
many circumlocutions in describing to him the
nature of the several crimes for which most of our
crew had been forced to fly their country. This
labor took up several days' conversation before he
was able to comprehend me. He was wholly at a
loss to know what could be the use or necessity of
practicing those vices: to clear up which I
endeavored to give him some ideas of the desire of
power and riches; of the terrible effects of lust, intemperance, malice, and envy. All this I was
forced to define and describe by putting of cases,
and making of suppositions. After which, like
one whose imagination was struck with something

---

* Deserting from their regiment.

never seen or heard of before, he would lift up his eyes with amazement and indignation. Power, government, war, law, punishment, and a thousand other things had no terms wherein that language could express them, which made the difficulty almost insuperable, to give my master any conception of what I meant. But being of an excellent understanding, much improved by contemplation and converse, he at last arrived at a competent knowledge of what human nature, in our parts of the world, is capable to perform, and desired I would give him some particular account of that land which we call Europe, but especially of my own country.

CHAPTER V.

The Author, at his Master's command, informs him of the
state of England—The causes of war among the Princes
of Europe—The Author begins to explain the English Constitution.

THE reader may please to observe that the following extract of many conversations I had with my
master contains a summary of the most material
points which were discoursed at several times for
above two years; his honor often desiring fuller
satisfaction, as I further improved in the Houyhnhnm tongue. I laid before him, as well as I could,
the whole state of Europe; I discoursed of trade
and manufactures, of arts and sciences; and the
answers I gave to all the questions he made, as they
arose upon several subjects, were a fund of conversation not to be exhausted. But I shall here only
set down the substance of what passed between us
concerning my own country, reducing it into order
as well as I can, without any regard to time or
other circumstances, while I strictly adhere to truth.
My only concern is, that I shall hardly be able to

do justice to my master's arguments and expressions, which must needs suffer by my want of capacity as well as by a translation into our barbarous English.

In obedience, therefore, to his honor's commands, I related to him the revolution under the Prince of Orange; the long war with France, entered into by the said prince, and renewed by his successor, the present queen, wherein the greatest powers of Christendom were engaged, and which still continued. I computed, at his request, that about a million of Yahoos might have been killed in the whole progress of it; and perhaps a hundred or more cities taken, and five times as many ships burned or sunk.

He asked me what were the usual causes or motives that made one country go to war with another? I answered they were innumerable, but I should only mention a few of the chief. Sometimes the ambition of princes, who never think they have land or people enough to govern; sometimes the corruption of ministers, who engage their master in a war in order to stifle or divert the clamor of the subjects against their evil administration. Difference in opinions hath cost many millions of lives; for instance, whether flesh be bread, or bread be flesh; whether the juice of a certain berry be blood or wine;* whether whistling be a vice or a virtue,† whether it be better to kiss a post, or throw it into the fire;‡ what is the best color for a coat, whether black, white, red, or gray;§ and whether it should be long or short, narrow or wide, dirty or clean, with many more. Neither are any wars so furious and bloody, or of so long continuance, as those occasioned by difference in opinion, especially if it be in things indifferent.

Sometimes the quarrel between two princes is to decide which of them shall dispossess a third of his dominions, where neither of them pretend to any right. Sometimes one prince quarreleth with another, for fear the other should quarrel with him. Sometimes a war is entered upon because the enemy is too strong, and sometimes because he is too weak. Sometimes our neighbors want the things which we have, or have the things which we want, and we both fight till they take ours, or give us theirs. It is a very justifiable cause of war to invade a country after the people have been wasted

---

* These are allusions to the doctrine of transubstantiation.

† Alluding to the use of music in churches.

‡ Alluding to the cross or crucifix.

§ Alluding to the use of vestments in churches.

by famine, destroyed by pestilence, or embroiled by factions among themselves. It is justifiable to enter into war against our nearest ally, when one of his towns lies convenient for us, or a territory of land that would render our dominions round and compact. If a prince sends forces into a nation where the people are poor and ignorant, he may lawfully put half of them to death, and make slaves of the rest, in order to civilize and reduce them from their barbarous way of living. It is a very kingly, honorable, and frequent practice, when one prince desires the assistance of another to secure him against an invasion, that the assistant, when he hath driven out the invader, should seize on the dominions himself, and kill, imprison, or banish the prince he came to relieve. Alliance by blood or marriage is a frequent cause of war between princes; and the nearer the kindred is, the greater is their disposition to quarrel. Poor nations are hungry, and rich nations are proud; and pride and hunger will ever be at variance. For those reasons the trade of a soldier is held the most honorable of all others; because the soldier is a Yahoo hired to kill, in cold blood, as many of his own species, who have never offended him, as possibly he can.

There is likewise a kind of beggarly princes in Europe, not able to make war by themselves, who hire out their troops to richer nations, for so much a day to each man ; of which they keep three-fourths to themselves, and it is the best part of their maintenance ; such are those in many northern parts of Europe.*

What you have told me, said my master, upon the subject of war, does, indeed, discover most admirably the effects of that reason you pretend to; however, it is happy that the shame is greater than the danger; and that nature hath left you utterly incapable of doing much mischief; for your mouths lying flat with your faces, you can hardly bite each other to any purpose, unless by consent. Then as to the claws upon your feet, before and behind, they are so short and tender that one of our Yahoos would drive a dozen of yours before him. And therefore, in recounting the numbers of those who have been killed in battle, I cannot but think that you have said the thing which is not.

I could not forbear shaking my head, and smiling a little at his ignorance. And being no stranger to the art of war, I gave him a description of cannons, culverins, muskets, carabines, pistols, bullets, powder, swords, bayonets, battles, sieges, retreats, attacks, undermines, countermines, bombardments,

---

* Some of the princes of the smaller German states did so.

sea-fights, ships sunk with a thousand men, twenty thousand killed on each side, dying groans, limbs flying in the air, smoke, noise, confusion, trampling to death under horses' feet, flight, pursuit, victory; fields strewed with carcasses, left for food to dogs, and wolves, and birds of prey; plundering, stripping, burning, and destroying. And to set forth the valor of my own dear countrymen, I assured him that I had seen them blow up a hundred enemies at once in a siege, and as many in a ship; and beheld the dead bodies drop down in pieces from the clouds, to the great diversion of the spectators.

I was going on to more particulars, when my master commanded me silence. He said whoever understood the nature of Yahoos might easily believe it possible for so vile an animal to be capable of every action I had named, if their strength and cunning equaled their malice. But as my discourse had increased his abhorrence of the whole species, so he found it gave him a disturbance in his mind, to which he was wholly a stranger before. He thought his ears, being used to such abominable words, might, by degrees, admit them with less detestation; that although he hated the Yahoos of this country, yet he no more blamed them for their odious qualities than he did a *gnnayh* (a bird of prey) for its cruelty, or a sharp stone for cutting his hoof. But when a creature pretending to reason could be capable of such enormities, he dreaded lest the corruption of that faculty might be worse than brutality itself. He seemed, therefore, confident, that, instead of reason, we were only possessed of some quality fitted to increase our natural vices : as the reflection from a troubled stream returns the image of an ill-shapen body, not only larger, but more distorted.

He added that he had heard too much upon the subject of war, both in this and some former discourses. There was another point which a little perplexed him at present. I had informed him that some of our crew left their country on account of being ruined by law ; that I had already explained the meaning of the word ; but he was at a loss how it should come to pass, that the law, which was intended for every man's preservation, should be any man's ruin. Therefore he desired to be further satisfied what I meant by law, and the dispensers thereof according to the present practice in my own country ; because he thought nature and reason were sufficient guides for a reasonable animal, as we pretended to be, in showing us what we ought to do, and what to avoid.

I assured his honor that law was a science in which I had not much conversed, further than by employing advocates, in vain, upon some injustices that had been done me; however, I would give him all the satisfaction I was able.

I said there was a society of men among us, bred up from their youth in the art of proving, by words multiplied for the purpose, that white is black, and black is white; according as they are paid. To this society all the rest of the people are slaves. For example, if my neighbor has a mind to my cow, he has a lawyer to prove that he ought to have my cow from me. I must then hire another to defend my right, it being against all rules of law that any man should be allowed to speak for himself. Now, in this case, I, who am the right owner, lie under two great disadvantages: first, my lawyer, being practiced almost from his cradle in defending false-hood, is quite out of his element when he would be an advocate for justice, which is an unnatural office he always attempts with great awkwardness, if not with ill-will. The second disadvantage is, that my lawyer must proceed with great caution, or else he will be reprimanded by the judges, and abhorred by his brethren, as one that would lessen the practice of the law. And therefore I have but two methods to preserve my cow. The first is, to gain over my adversary's lawyer with a double fee; who will then betray his client, by insinuating that he has justice on his side. The second way is, for my lawyer to make my cause appear as unjust as he can, by allowing the cow to belong to my adversary : and this, if it be skillfully done, will certainly bespeak the favor of the bench. Now your honor is to know that these judges are persons appointed to decide all controversies of property, as well as for the trial of criminals, and picked out from the most dexterous lawyers, who are grown old or lazy ; and having been biased all their lives against truth and equity, lie under such a fatal necessity of favoring fraud, perjury, and oppression, that I have known some of them refuse a large bribe from the side where justice lay, rather than injure the faculty, by doing anything unbecoming their nature or their office.

It is a maxim among these lawyers that whatever has been done before may legally be done again; and therefore they take special care to record all the decisions formerly made against common justice and the general reason of mankind. These, under the name of precedents, they produce as authorities to justify the most iniquitous opinions; and the judges never fail of directing accordingly.

In pleading they studiously avoid entering into the merits of the cause, but are loud, violent, and tedious in dwelling upon all circumstances which are not to the purpose. For instance, in the case already mentioned, they never desire to know what claim or title my adversary has to my cow; but whether the said cow were red or black; her horns long or short; whether the field I graze her in be round or square; whether she was milked at home or abroad; what diseases she is subject to, and the like; after which they consult precedents, adjourn the cause from time to time, and in ten, twenty, or thirty years come to an issue.

It is likewise to be observed that this society has a peculiar cant and jargon of their own that no other mortal can understand, and wherein all their laws are written, which they take special care to multiply; whereby they have wholly confounded the very essence of truth and falsehood, of right and wrong; so that it will take thirty years to decide whether the field left me by my ancestors for six generations belongs to me, or to a stranger three hundred miles off.

In the trial of persons accused for crime against the state, the method is much more short and commendable: the judge first sends to sound the disposition of those in power; after which she can easily hang or save a criminal, strictly preserving all due forms of law.

Here my master interposing, said it was a pity

that creatures endowed with such prodigious abilities of mind as these lawyers, by the description I
gave of them, must certainly be, were not rather
encouraged to be instructors of others in wisdom
and knowledge.   In answer to which I assured his
honor that in all points out of their own trade they
were usually the most ignorant and stupid gener-
ation among us, the most despicable in common conversation, avowed enemies to all knowledge and
learning, and equally disposed to pervert the general reason of mankind in every other subject of
discourse as in that of their own profession.

CHAPTER VI.

A continuation of the State of England under Queen Anne—
The Character of a First Minister of State in European
Courts.

My master was yet wholly at a loss to understand
what motives could incite this race of lawyers to
perplex, disquiet, and weary themselves, and engage
in a confederacy of injustice, merely for the sake of
injuring their fellow-animals; neither could he
comprehend what I meant in saying they did it for
hire: whereupon I was at much pains to describe to
him the use of money, the materials it was made of,
and the value of the metals; that when a Yahoo
had got a great store of this precious substance he
was able to purchase whatever he had a mind to;
the finest clothing, the noblest houses, great tracts
of land, the most costly meats and drinks. Therefore, since money alone was able to perform all
these feats, our Yahoos thought they could never
have enough of it to spend, or to save, as they found
themselves inclined, from their natural bent, either

to profusion or avarice; that the rich men enjoyed the fruit of the poor man's labor, and the latter were a thousand to one in proportion to the former; that the bulk of our people were forced to live miserably, by laboring every day for small· wages, to make a few live plentifully.

I enlarged myself much on these, and many other particulars, to the same purpose; but his honor was still to seek,* for he went upon a supposition that all animals had a title to their share in the productions of the earth, and especially those who presided over the rest. Therefore he desired I would let him know what these costly meats were, and how any of us happened to want them? Whereupon I enumerated as many sorts as came into my head, with the various methods of dressing them, which could not be done without sending vessels by sea to every part of the world, as well for liquors to drink as for sauces, and innumerable other conveniences. I assured him that this whole globe of earth must be at least three times gone round before one of our better female Yahoos could get her breakfast, or a cup to put it in. He said that must needs be a miserable country which cannot furnish food for its own inhabitants. But

---

* At a loss; puzzled.

what he chiefly wondered at was, how such vast tracts of ground as I described should be wholly without fresh water, and the people put to the necessity of sending over the sea for drink. I replied that England (the dear place of my nativity) was computed to produce three times the quantity of food more than its inhabitants are able to con-sume, as well as liquors extracted from grain, or pressed out of the fruit of certain trees, which made excellent drink, and the same proportion in every other convenience of life. But in order to feed the luxury and intemperance of the males, and the vanity of the females, we sent away the greatest part of our necessary things to other countries, from whence, in return, we brought the materials of diseases, folly, and vice, to spend among ourselves. Hence it follows, of necessity, that vast numbers of our people are compelled to seek their livelihood by begging, robbing, stealing, cheating, flattering, suborning, forswearing, forging, gaming, lying, fawning, hectoring, voting, scribbling, star-gazing, poisoning, canting, libeling, free-thinking, and the like occupations: every one of which terms I was at much pains to make him understand.

That wine was not imported among us from foreign countries to supply the want of water or other drinks, but because it was a sort of liquid

which made us merry, by putting us out of our
senses, diverted all melancholy thoughts, begat wild,
extravagant imaginations in the brain, raised our
hopes and banished our fears, suspended every
office of reason for a time, and deprived us of the
use of our limbs, till we fell into a profound sleep ;
although it must be confessed that we always
awaked sick and dispirited, and that the use of this
liquor filled us with diseases which made our lives
uncomfortable and short.

But, beside all this, the bulk of our people supported themselves by furnishing the necessities or
conveniences of life to the rich, and to each other.
For instance, when I am at home, and dressed as I
ought to be, I carry on my body the workmanship
of an hundred tradesmen, the building and furniture
of my house employ as many more, and five times
the number to adorn my wife.

I was going on to tell him of another sort of
people, who get their livelihood by attending the
sick, having upon some occasions informed his honor
that many of my crew had died of diseases. But
here it was with the utmost difficulty that I brought
him to apprehend what I meant. He could easily
conceive that a Houyhnhnm grew weak and heavy
a few days before his death, or by some accident
might hurt a limb ; but that nature, who works all

things to perfection, should suffer any pains to breed in our bodies he thought impossible, and desired to know the reason of so unaccountable an evil.

I told him we fed on a thousand things which operated contrary to each other; that we eat when we were not hungry, and drank without the provocation of thirst; that we sate whole nights drinking strong liquors, without eating a bit, which disposed us to sloth, inflamed our bodies, and precipitated or prevented digestion; that many diseases were propagated from father to son, so that great numbers come into the world with complicated maladies upon them: that it would be endless to give him a catalogue of all diseases incident to human bodies, for they could not be fewer than five or six hundred, spread over every limb and joint; in short, every part, external and intestine, having diseases appropriated to itself: to remedy which there was a sort of people bred up among us in the profession, or the pretense, of curing the sick.

But, besides real diseases, we are subject to many that were only imaginary, for which the physicians have invented imaginary cures; these have their several names, and so have the drugs that are proper for them; and with these our female Yahoos are always infested.

One great excellency in this tribe is their skill at

prognostics, wherein they seldom fail; their predictions in real diseases, when they rise to any degree of malignity, generally portending death, which is always in their power, when recovery is not; and, therefore, upon any unexpected signs of amendment, after they have pronounced their sentence, rather than be accused as false prophets, they know how to approve their sagacity to the world by a seasonable dose.

They are likewise of special use to husbands and wives who are grown weary of their mates, to eldest sons, to great ministers of state, and often to princes.

I had formerly, upon occasion, discoursed with my master upon the nature of government in general, and particularly of our own excellent constitution, deservedly the wonder and envy of the whole world. But, having here accidentally mentioned a minister of state, he commanded me, some time after, to inform him what species of Yahoo I had particularly meant by that appellation.

I told him that a first or chief minister of state, who was the person I intended to describe, was a creature wholly exempt from joy and grief, love and hatred, pity and anger; at least, makes use of no other passions but a violent desire of wealth, power, and titles; that he applies his words to all uses, except to the indication of his mind; that he never tells a truth, but with an intent that you should take it for a lie; nor a lie, but with a design that you should take it for a truth; that those he speaks worst of behind their backs are in the surest way to preferment; and whenever he begins to praise you to others, or to yourself, you are from that day forlorn. The worst mark you can receive is a promise, especially when it is confirmed with an oath; after which every wise man retires, and gives over all hopes.

There are various methods by which a man may rise to be chief minister; as by betraying or undermining his predecessor, or by a furious zeal in public assemblies against the corruptions of the court. But a wise prince would rather choose to employ those who practise the last of these methods; because such zealots prove always the most obsequious and subservient to the will and passions of their master. That these ministers, having all employments at their disposal, preserve themselves in power by bribing the majority of a senate or great council; and at last, by an expedient called an act of indemnity (whereof I described the nature to him), they secure themselves from after-reckonings, and retire from the public, laden with the spoils of the nation.

The palace of a chief minister is a seminary to breed up others in his own trade; the pages, lackeys, and porter, by imitating their master, become ministers of state in their several districts, and learn to excel in the three principal ingredients of insolence, lying, and bribery. Accordingly, they have a subaltern* court paid to them by persons of the first rank; and sometimes, by the force of dexterity and impudence, arrive, through several gradations, to be successors to their lord.

One day, in discourse, my master having heard me mention the nobility of my country, was pleased to make me a compliment which I could not pretend to deserve: That he was sure I must have been born of some noble family, because I far exceeded in shape, color, and cleanliness all the Yahoos of his nation, although I seemed to fail in strength and agility, which must be imputed to my different way of living from those other brutes; and, besides, I was not only endowed with the faculty of speech, but likewise with some rudiments of reason, to a degree that, with all his acquaintance, I passed for a prodigy.

He made me observe that among the Houyhnhnms the white, the sorrel, and the iron-gray were not

---

* Subordinate; of inferior degree.

so exactly shaped as the bay, the dapple-gray, and the black; nor born with equal talents of mind, or a capacity to improve them, and therefore continued always in the condition of servants, without ever aspiring to match out of their own race, which, in that country, would be reckoned monstrous and unnatural.

I made his honor my most humble acknowledgments for the good opinion he was pleased to conceive of me, but assured him, at the same time, that my birth was of the lower sort, having been born of plain, honest parents, who were just able to give me a tolerable education; that nobility among us was altogether a different thing from the idea he had of it; that our young noblemen are bred from their childhood in idleness and luxury; that when their fortunes are almost ruined they marry some woman of mean birth, disagreeable person, and unsound constitution (merely for the sake of money), whom they hate and despise; that a weak, diseased body, a meager countenance, and sallow complexion are the true marks of noble blood; and a healthy, robust appearance is disgraceful in a man of quality. The imperfections of his mind run parallel with those of his body, being a composition of spleen,* dullness, ignorance, caprice, sensuality, and pride.

---

* Ill temper, or peevishness.

Without the consent of this illustrious body, no law can be enacted, repealed, or altered ; and these nobles have likewise the decision of all our possessions, without appeal.

CHAPTER VII.

The Author's great Love of his native Country—His Master's
observations upon the Constitution and Administration
of England, as described by the Author, with Parallel
Cases and Comparisons—His Master's observations upon
Human Nature.

THE reader may be disposed to wonder how I
could prevail on myself to give so free a representation of my own species, among a race of mortals
who are already too apt to conceive the vilest
opinion of humankind, from that entire congruity
betwixt me and their Yahoos. But I must freely
confess, that the many virtues of those excellent
quadrupeds, placed in opposite view to human
corruptions, had so far opened my eyes, and enlarged
my understanding, that I began to view the actions
and passions of man in a very different light, and to
think the honor of my own kind not worth managing ;* which, besides, it was impossible for me to
do before a person of so acute a judgment as my
master, who daily convinced me of a thousand

---

* Dealing gently or sparingly with it.

faults in myself, whereof I had not the least per-
ception before, and which, with us, would never be
numbered even among human infirmities. I had
likewise learned, from his example, an utter detestation of all falsehood or disguise ; and truth appeared so amiable* to me that I determined upon
sacrificing everything to it.

Let me deal so candidly with the reader as to
confess that there was yet a much stronger motive
for the freedom I took in my representation of
things. I had not been a year in this country before I contracted such a love and veneration for the
inhabitants that I entered on a firm resolution
never to return to humankind, but to pass the rest
of my life among these admirable Houyhnhnms, in
the contemplation and practice of every virtue,
where I could have no example or incitement to
vice. But it was decreed by fortune, my perpetual
enemy, that so great a felicity should not fall to my
share. However, it is now some comfort to reflect
that in what I said of my countrymen I extenuated
their faults as much as I durst before so strict an
examiner, and upon every article gave as favorable
a turn as the matter would bear. For, indeed, who
is there alive that will not be swayed by his bias
and partiality to the place of his birth ?

---

* Deserving to be prized or loved.

I have related the substance of several conversations I had with my master during the greatest part of the time I had the honor to be in his service, but have, indeed, for brevity's sake, omitted much more than is here set down.

When I had answered all his questions, and his curiosity seemed to be fully satisfied, he sent for me one morning early, and commanded me to sit down at some distance (an honor which he had never before conferred upon me). He said he had been very seriously considering my whole story, as far as it related both to myself and my country ; that he looked upon us as a sort of animals, to whose share, by what accident he could not conjecture, some small pittance of reason had fallen, whereof we made no other use than, by its assistance, to aggravate our natural corruptions, and to acquire new ones which nature had not given us; that we disarmed ourselves of the few abilities she had bestowed, had been very successful in multiplying our original wants, and seemed to spend our whole lives in vain endeavors to supply them by our own inventions; that as to myself it was manifest I had neither the strength nor agility of a common Yahoo; that I walked infirmly on my hinder feet, had found out a contrivance to make my claws of no use or defense, and to remove the hair from my chin, which was intended as a shelter from the sun and the weather; lastly, that I could neither run with speed, nor climb trees like my brethren, as he called them, the Yahoos in his country.

That our institutions of government and law were plainly owing to our gross defects in reason, and by consequence in virtue; because reason alone is sufficient to govern a rational creature; which was, therefore, a character we had no pretense to challenge,* even from the account I had given of my own people; although he manifestly perceived that, in order to favor them, I had concealed many particulars, and often said the thing which was not.

He was the more confirmed in this opinion because he observed that, as I agreed in every feature of my body with other Yahoos, except where it was to my real disadvantage, in point of strength, speed, and activity, the shortness of my claws, and some other particulars, where nature had no part; so from the representation I had given him of our lives, our manners, and our actions, he found as near a resemblance in the disposition of our minds. He said the Yahoos were known to hate one another more than they did any different species of animals; and the reason usually assigned

---

* Claim.

was the odiousness of their own shapes, which all could see in the rest, but not in themselves. He had therefore begun to think it not unwise in us to cover our bodies, and by that invention conceal many of our own deformities from each other, which would else be hardly supportable. But he now found he had been mistaken, and that the dissensions of those brutes in his country were owing to the same cause with ours, as I had described them. For if, said he, you throw among five Yahoos as much food as would be sufficient for fifty, they will, instead of eating peaceably, fall together by the ears, each single one impatient to have all to itself; and therefore a servant was usually employed to stand by while they were feeding abroad, and those kept at home were tied at a distance from each other; that if a cow died of age or accident, before a Houyhnhnm could secure it for his own Yahoos, those in the neighborhood would come in herds to seize it, and then would ensue such a battle as I had described, with terrible wounds, made by their claws, on both sides, although they seldom were able to kill one another, for want of such convenient instruments of death as we had invented. At other times, the like battles have been fought between the Yahoos of several neighborhoods, without any visible cause; those of one district watching all opportunities to surprise the next, before they are prepared. But if they find their project hath miscarried, they return home, and for want of enemies engage in what I call a civil war among themselves.

That in some fields of his country there are certain shining stones of several colors, whereof the Yahoos are violently fond; and when part of these stones is fixed in the earth, as it sometimes happeneth, they will dig with their claws for whole days to get them out; then carry them away, and hide them by heaps in their kennels; but still looking round with great caution, for fear their comrades should find out their treasure. My master said he could never discover the reason of this unnatural appetite, or how these stones could be of any use to a Yahoo; but now he believed it might proceed from the same principle of avarice which I had ascribed to mankind: that he had once, by way of experiment, privately removed a heap of these stones from the place where one of his Yahoos had buried it; whereupon the sordid animal, missing his treasure, by his loud lamenting brought the whole herd to the place, there miserably howled, then fell to biting and tearing the rest, began to pine away, would neither eat, nor sleep, nor work, till he ordered a servant privately to convey the stones into the same hole, and hide them as before; which, when his Yahoo had found, he presently recovered his spirits and good-humor, but took care to remove them to a better hiding-place, and hath ever since been a very serviceable brute.

My master further assured me, which I also observed myself, that in the fields where the shining stones abound, the fiercest and most frequent battles are fought, occasioned by perpetual inroads of the neighboring Yahoos.

He said, it was common when two Yahoos discovered such a stone in a field, and were contending which of them should be the proprietor, a third would take the advantage, and carry it away from them both; which my master would needs contend to have some kind of resemblance with our suits at law; wherein I thought it for our credit not to undeceive him; since the decision he mentioned was much more equitable than many decrees among us; because the plaintiff and defendant there lost nothing besides the stone they contended for; whereas our courts of equity would never have dismissed the cause while either of them had anything left.

My master continuing his discourse, said there was nothing that rendered the Yahoos more odious than their undistinguishing appetite to devour everything that came in their way, whether herbs, roots, berries, the corrupted flesh of animals, or all mingled together: and it was peculiar in their temper that they were fonder of what they could get by rapine or stealth, at a greater distance, than much better food provided for them at home. If their prey held out, they would eat till they were ready to burst.

There was a kind of root, very juicy, but somewhat rare and difficult to be found, which the Yahoos sought for with much eagerness, and would suck it with great delight: it produced in them the same effects that wine hath upon us. It would make them sometimes hug, and sometimes tear one another: they would howl, and grin, and chatter, and reel, and tumble, and then fall asleep in the dirt.

I did indeed observe that the Yahoos were the only animals in this country subject to any diseases; which, however, were much fewer than horses have among us, and contracted, not by any ill treatment they meet with, but by the nastiness and greediness of that sordid brute. Neither has their language any more than a general appellation for those maladies which is borrowed from the name of the beast, and called *Hnea-yahoo*, or the Yahoo's-evil.

As to learning, government, arts, manufactures, and the like, my master confessed he could find little or no resemblance between the Yahoos of that country and those in ours; for he only meant to observe what parity there was in our natures. He had heard, indeed, some curious Houyhnhnms observe that in most herds there was a sort of ruling Yahoo (as among us there is generally some leading or principal stag in a park), who was always more deformed in body and mischievous in disposition than any of the rest; that this leader had usually a favorite as like himself as he could get. This favorite is hated by the whole herd, and, therefore, to protect himself, keeps always near the person of his leader. He usually continues in office till a worse can be found; but the very moment he is discarded, his successor, at the head of all the Yahoos in that district, young and old, male and female, come in a body and maltreat him. How far this might be applicable to our courts, and favorites, and ministers of state, my master said I could best determine.

I durst make no return to this malicious insinuation, which debased human understanding below the sagacity of a common hound, who has judgment enough to distinguish and follow the cry of the ablest dog in the pack, without being ever mistaken.

My master told me there were some qualities remarkable in the Yahoos, which he had not observed me to mention, or at least very slightly, in the accounts I had given him of humankind. One thing he wondered at in the Yahoos was their strange disposition to nastiness and dirt; whereas there appears to be a natural love of cleanliness in all other animals.

Another quality which his servants had discovered in several Yahoos to him was wholly unaccountable. He said a fancy would sometimes take a Yahoo to retire into a corner, to lie down, and howl and groan, and spurn away all that came near him, although he were young and fat, wanted neither food nor water; nor could the servants imagine what could possibly ail him. And the only remedy they found was to set him to hard work, after which he would infallibly come to himself. To this I was silent, out of partiality to my own kind; yet here I could plainly discover the true seeds of spleen,* which only seizes on the lazy, the luxurious, and the rich; who, if they were forced to undergo the same regimen, I would undertake for the cure.

At times if a female stranger came among them three or four of her own sex would get about her, and stare, and chatter, and grin, and smell her all

---

* Dullness or peevishness without any sufficient cause.

over, and then turn off, with gestures that seemed to express contempt and disdain.

Perhaps my master might refine a little in these speculations, which he had drawn from what he observed himself, or had been told him by others; however, I could not reflect, without some amazement and much sorrow, that the rudiments of coquetry, censure, and scandal should have place by instinct in womankind.

CHAPTER VIII.

The Author relates several Particulars of the Yahoos—The great Virtues of the Houyhnhnms—The Education and Exercise of their Youth—Their General Assembly.

As I ought to have understood human nature much better than I supposed it possible for my master to do, so it was easy to apply the character he gave of the Yahoos to myself and my country-men; and I believed I could yet make further dis-coveries from my own observation. I therefore often begged his honor to let me go among the herds of Yahoos in the neighborhood; to which he always very graciously consented, being perfectly convinced that the hatred I bore those brutes would never suffer me to be corrupted by them; and his honor ordered one of his servants, a strong sorrel nag, very honest and good-natured, to be my guard; without whose protection I durst not undertake such adventures; for I have already told the reader how much I was pestered by those odious animals upon my first arrival; and I afterwards failed very narrowly, three or four times, of falling into their clutches, when I happened to stray at any distance without my hanger. And I have reason to believe they had some imagination that I was of their own species; which I often assisted myself by stripping up my sleeves, and showing my naked arms and breast in their sight when my protector was with me. At which times they would approach as near as they durst, and imitate my actions, after the manner of monkeys, but ever with great signs of hatred; as a tame jackdaw, with cap and stockings, is always persecuted by the wild ones, when he happens to be got among them.

They are prodigiously nimble from their infancy. However, I once caught a young male of three years old, and endeavored, by all marks of tenderness, to make it quiet; but the little imp fell a squalling, and scratching, and biting with such violence that I was forced to let it go; and it was high time; for a whole troop of old ones came about us at the noise, but finding the cub was safe (for away it ran), and my sorrel nag being by, they durst not venture near us.

But what I could discover the Yahoos appear to be the most unteachable of all animals; their capacities never reaching higher than to draw or carry burdens. Yet I am of opinion this defect ariseth chiefly from a perverse, restive disposition; for they

are cunning, malicious, treacherous, and revengeful.
They are strong and hardy, but of a cowardly spirit,
and by consequence, insolent, abject, and cruel.

The Houyhnhnms keep the Yahoos for present
use in huts not far from the house; but the rest are
sent abroad to certain fields, where they dig up
roots, eat several kinds of herbs, and search about
for carrion, or sometimes catch weasels and *luhimuhs*
(a sort of wild rat), which they greedily devour.
Nature hath taught them to dig deep holes with
their nails on the side of a rising ground, wherein
they lie by themselves; only the kennels of the
females are larger, sufficient to hold two or three
cubs.

They swim from their infancy like frogs, and are
able to continue long under water, where they often
take fish, which the females carry home to their
young.

Having lived three years in this country, the
reader, I suppose, will expect that I should, like
other travelers, give him some account of the manners and customs of its inhabitants, which it was
indeed my principal study to learn.

As these noble Houyhnhnms are endowed by
nature with a general disposition to all virtues, and
have no conceptions or ideas of what is evil in a
rational creature, so their grand maxim is, to culti-

vate reason, and to be wholly governed by it. Neither is reason among them a point problematical, as with us, where men can argue with plausibility on both sides of a question, but strikes you with immediate conviction, as it must needs do, where it is not mingled, obscured, or discolored, by passion and interest. I remember it was with extreme difficulty that I could bring my master to understand the meaning of the word *opinion,* or how a point could be disputable; because reason taught us to affirm or deny only where we are certain; and beyond our knowledge we cannot do either; so that controversies, wranglings, disputes, and positiveness, in false or dubious propositions, are evils unknown among the Houyhnhnms. In like manner, when I used to explain to him our several systems of natural philosophy, he would laugh, that a creature pretending to reason should value itself upon the knowledge of other people's conjectures, and in things where that knowledge, if it were certain, could be of no use. Wherein he agreed entirely with the sentiments of Socrates, as Plato delivers them; which I mention as the highest honor I can do that prince of philosophers. I have often since reflected what destruction such a doctrine would make in the libraries of Europe, and how many

paths to fame would be then shut up in the learned
world.

Friendship and benevolence are the two principal
virtues among the Houyhnhnms, and these not confined to particular objects, but universal to the
whole race ; for a stranger from the remotest part
is equally treated with the nearest neighbor, and
wherever he goes, looks upon himself as at home.
They preserve decency and civility in the highest
degrees, but are altogether ignorant of ceremony.
They have no fondness for their colts or foals, but
the care they take in educating them proceeds entirely from the dictates of reason. And I observed
my master to show the same affection to his neighbor's issue that he had for his own. They will have
it that nature teaches them to love the whole
species, and it is reason only that maketh a distinction of persons where there is a superior degree
of virtue.

Courtship, love, presents, jointures, settlements,
have no place in their thoughts, or terms whereby
to express them in their language. The young
couple meet and are joined, merely because it is the
determination of their parents and friends ; it is
what they see done every day, and they look upon
it as one of the necessary actions of a rational being ;
and the married pair pass their lives with the same

friendship and mutual benevolence that they bear to all others of the same species who come in their way, without jealousy, fondness, quarreling, or discontent.

In educating the youth of both sexes their method is admirable, and highly deserves our imitation. These are not suffered to taste a grain of oats, except upon certain days, till eighteen years old; nor milk, but very rarely; and in summer they graze two hours in the morning, and as long in the evening, which their parents likewise observe; but the servants are not allowed above half that time, and a great part of their grass is brought home, which they eat at the most convenient hours, when they can be best spared from work.

Temperance, industry, exercise, and cleanliness are the lessons equally enjoined to the young ones of both sexes; and my master thought it monstrous in us to give the females a different kind of education from the males, except in some articles of domestic management; whereby, as he truly observed, one-half of our natives were good for nothing but bringing children into the world; and to trust the care of our children to such useless animals, he said, was yet a greater instance of brutality.

But the Houyhnhnms train up their youth to

strength, speed, and hardiness by exercising them
in running races up and down steep hills and over
hard and stony grounds; and when they are all in
a sweat they are ordered to leap over head and
ears into a pond or a river. Four times a year the
youth of a certain district meet to show their proficiency in running and leaping, and other feats of
strength and agility, where the victor is rewarded
with a song made in his or her praise. On this
festival the servants drive a herd of Yahoos into the
field, laden with hay and oats and milk, for a repast
to the Houyhnhnms; after which these brutes are
immediately driven back again, for fear of being
noisome to the assembly.

Every fourth year, at the vernal equinox, there is
a representative council of the whole nation, which
meets in a plain about twenty miles from our
house, and continues about five or six days. Here
they inquire into the state and condition of the
several districts; whether they abound or be deficient in hay or oats, or cows or Yahoos; and wherever there is any want (which is but seldom), it is
immediately supplied by unanimous consent and
contribution.

CHAPTER IX.

A grand debate at the General Assembly of the Houyhnhnms
—The Learning of the Houyhnhnms—Their Buildings—
Their Manner of Burials—The Defectiveness of their
Language.

ONE of these grand assemblies was held in my
time, about three months before my departure,
whither my master went, as the representative of
our district. In this council was resumed their old
debate, and indeed the only debate that ever happened in that country; whereof my master, after his
return, gave me a very particular account.

The question to be debated was, Whether the
Yahoos should be exterminated from the face of the
earth? One of the members for the affirmative
offered several arguments of great strength and
weight, alleging that as the Yahoos were the most
filthy, noisome, and deformed animal which nature
ever produced, so they were the most restive
and indocible, mischievous and malicious. They
would privately suck the teats of the Houyhnhnms'
cows, kill and devour their cats, trample down

their oats and grass, if they were not continually watched, and commit a thousand other extravagances. He took notice of a general tradition, that Yahoos had not been always in their country; but that, many ages ago, two of these brutes appeared together upon a mountain; whether produced by the heat of the sun upon corrupted mud and slime, or from the ooze or froth of the sea, was never known; that their brood in a short time grew so numerous as to overrun and infest the whole nation; that the Houyhnhnms, to get rid of this evil, made a general hunting, and at last enclosed the whole herd; and, destroying the old ones, every Houyhnhnm kept two young ones in a kennel, and brought them to such a degree of tameness as an animal so savage by nature can be capable of acquiring; using them for draught and carriage; that there seemed to be much truth in this tradition; and that those creatures could not be *ylnhniamshy* (or *aborigines** of the land), because of the violent hatred the Houyhnhnms, as well as all other animals, bore them; which, although their evil disposition sufficiently deserved, could never have arrived at so high a degree if they had been *aborigines;* or else they

---

* Earliest or original inhabitants.

would have long since been rooted out; that the inhabitants, taking a fancy to use the service of the Yahoos, had very imprudently neglected to cultivate the breed of asses, which are a comely animal, easily kept, more tame and orderly, without any offensive smell; strong enough for labor, although they yield to the other in agility of body; and if their braying be no agreeable sound, it is far preferable to the horrible howlings of the Yahoos.

My master approved of the tradition mentioned by the honorable member who spoke before, and affirmed that the two Yahoos said to be first seen among them had been driven thither over the sea; that, coming to land, and being forsaken by their companions, they retired to the mountains, and, degenerating by degrees, became in process of time much more savage than those of their own species in the country from whence these two originals came. The reason of this assertion was that he had now in his possession a certain wonderful Yahoo (meaning myself), which most of them had heard of, and many of them had seen. He then related to them how he first found me; that my body was all covered with an artificial composure of the skins and hairs of other animals; that I spoke in a language of my own, and had thoroughly learned theirs; that I had related to him the accidents which brought me thither; that when he saw me without my covering I was an exact Yahoo in every part, only of a whiter color, less hairy, and with shorter claws. He added how I had endeavored to persuade him that in my own and other countries the Yahoos acted as the governing, rational animal, and held the Houyhnhnms in servitude; that he observed in me all the qualities of a Yahoo, only a little more civilized by some tincture of reason; which, however, was in a degree as far inferior to the Houyhnhnm race as the Yahoos of their country were to me.

The Houyhnhnms have no letters, and consequently their knowledge is all traditional; but, there happening few events of any moment among a people so well united, naturally disposed to every virtue, wholly governed by reason, and cut off from all commerce with other nations, the historical part is easily preserved, without burdening their memory. I have already observed that they are subject to no diseases, and therefore can have no need of physicians. However, they have excellent medicines, composed of herbs, to cure accidental bruises, and cuts in the pastern, or frog of the foot, by sharp stones, as well as other maims and hurts in the several parts of the body.

They calculate the year by the revolution of the

sun and the moon, but use no subdivisions into weeks. They are well enough acquainted with the motions of those two luminaries, and understand the nature of eclipses; and this is the utmost progress of their astronomy.

In poetry they must be allowed to excel all other mortals, wherein the justness of their similes, and the minuteness, as well as exactness, of their descriptions, are indeed inimitable. Their verses abound very much in both of these, and usually contain either some exalted notions of friendship and benevolence, or the praises of those who were victors in races and other bodily exercises. Their buildings, although very rude and simple, are not inconvenient, but well contrived to defend them from all injuries of cold and heat. They have a kind of tree, which, at forty years old, loosens in the root, and falls with the first storm: it grows very straight, and being pointed like stakes with a sharp stone (for the Houy-hnhnms know not the use of iron), they stick them erect in the ground, about ten inches asunder, and then weave in oat straw, or sometimes wattles, betwixt them. The roof is made after the same manner, and so are the doors.

The Houyhnhnms use the hollow part between the pastern and the hoof of their forefeet as we do our hands, and this with greater dexterity than I could at first imagine. I have seen a white mare of our family thread a needle (which I lent her on purpose) with that joint. They milk their cows, reap their oats, and do all the work which requires hands in the same manner. They have a kind of hard flints, which, by grinding against other stones, they form into instruments that serve instead of wedges, axes, and hammers. With tools made of these flints they likewise cut their hay and reap their oats, which there grow naturally in several fields; the Yahoos draw home the sheaves in carriages, and the servants tread them in certain covered huts, to get out the grain, which is kept in stores. They make a rude kind of earthen and wooden vessels, and bake the former in the sun.

If they can avoid casualties they die only of old age, and are buried in the obscurest places that can be found · their friends and relations expressing neither joy nor grief at their departure; nor does the dying person discover the least regret that he is leaving the world, any more than if he were upon returning home from a visit to one of his neighbors. I remember my master having once made an appointment with a friend and his family to come to his house upon some affair of importance: on the day fixed the mistress and her two children came very late; she made two excuses; first for her husband, who, as she said, happened that very morning to *lhnuwnh*. The word is strongly expressive in their language, but not easily rendered into English: it signifies to retire to his first mother. Her excuse for not coming sooner was that her husband dying late in the morning, she was a good while consulting her servants about a convenient place where his body should be laid: and I observed she behaved herself at our house as cheerfully as the rest. She died about three months after.

They live generally to seventy or seventy-five years, very seldom to fourscore. Some weeks before their death they feel a gradual decay, but without pain. During this time they are much visited by their friends, because they cannot go abroad with their usual ease and satisfaction. However, about ten days before their death, which they seldom fail in computing, they return the visits that have been made them by those who are nearest in the neighborhood, being carried in a convenient sledge drawn by Yahoos; which vehicle they use, not only upon this occasion, but when they grow old, upon long journeys, or when they are lamed by any accident. And, therefore, when the dying Houyhnhnms return those visits they take a solemn leave of their friends, as if they were going to some remote part of the country, where they designed to pass the rest of their lives.

I know not whether it may be worth observing, that the Houyhnhnms have no word in their language to express anything that is evil, except what they borrow from the deformities or ill qualities of the Yahoos. Thus they denote the folly of a servant, an omission of a child, a stone that cuts their feet, a continuance of foul or unseasonable weather, and the like, by adding to each the epithet of *Yahoo.* For instance : *hhnm Yahoo, whnaholm Yahoo, ynlhmndwihlma Yahoo,* and an ill-contrived house, *ynholmhnmrohlnw Yahoo.*

I could, with great pleasure, enlarge further upon the manners and virtues of this excellent people ; but intending in a short time to publish a volume by itself expressly upon that subject, I refer the reader thither, and in the meantime proceed to relate my own sad catastrophe.

CHAPTER X.

The Author's Economy and happy Life among the Houy-
    hnhnms—His great improvement in Virtue by conversing
    with them—Their Conversations—The Author has notice
    given him by his master, that he must depart from the
    Country—He falls into a swoon for grief, but submits—
    He contrives and finishes a Canoe by the help of a
    fellow-servant, and puts to sea at a venture.

I HAD settled my little economy* to my own
heart's content. My master had ordered a room
to be made for me, after their manner, about six
yards from the house, the sides and floors of which
I plastered with clay, and covered with rush-mats
of my own contriving. I had beaten hemp, which
there grows wild, and made of it a sort of ticking;
this I filled with the feathers of several birds I had
taken with springes made of Yahoos' hairs, and
were excellent food.   I had worked two chairs with
my knife, the sorrel nag helping me in the grosser
and more laborious part.   When my clothes were

---

* Domestic concerns, or way of life.

worn to rags, I made myself others with the skins of rabbits, and of a certain beautiful animal about the same size, called *nnuhnoh*, the skin of which is covered with a fine down. Of these I made very tolerable stockings. I soled my shoes with wood, which I cut from a tree, and fitted to the upper-leather; and when this was worn out I supplied it with the skins of Yahoos dried in the sun. I often got honey out of hollow trees, which I mingled with water, or eat with my bread. No man could more verify the truth of these two maxims, That nature is very easily satisfied; and, That necessity is the mother of invention. I enjoyed perfect health of body and tranquillity of mind; I did not feel the treachery or inconstancy of a friend, nor the injuries of a secret or open enemy; I had no occasion of bribing or flattering to procure the favor of any great man, or of his minion; I wanted no fence against fraud or oppression: here was neither physician to destroy my body, nor lawyer to ruin my fortune; no informer to watch my words and actions, or forge accusations against me for hire; here were no gibers, censurers, backbiters, pickpockets, highwaymen, housebreakers, attorneys, buffoons, gamesters, politicians, wits, splenetics, tedious talkers, controvertists, murderers, robbers; no leaders or followers of party and faction; no encouragers to vice by seducements or examples; no dungeon, axes, gibbets, whipping-posts, or pillories ; no cheating shopkeepers or mechanics; no pride, vanity, or affectation; no fops, bullies, or drunkards; no ranting, expensive wives; no stupid, proud pedants; no importunate, overbearing, quarrelsome, noisy, roaring, empty, conceited, swearing companions; no scoundrels raised from the dust for the sake of their vices, or nobility thrown into it on account of their virtues; no lords, fiddlers, judges, or dancing-masters.

I had the favor of being admitted to several Houyhnhnms, who came to visit or dine with my master ; where his honor graciously suffered me to wait in the room and listen to their discourse. Both he and his company would often descend* to ask me questions and receive my answers. I had also sometimes the honor of attending my master in his visits to others. I never presumed to speak, except in answer to a question ; and then I did it with inward regret, because it was a loss of so much time for improving myself; but I was infinitely delighted with the station of an humble auditor in such conversations, where nothing passed but what was useful, expressed in the fewest and most significant

* That is, condescend.

words ; where, as I have already said, the greatest decency was observed, without the least degree of ceremony ; where no person spoke without being pleased himself, and pleasing his companions ; where there was no interruption, tediousness, heat, or difference of sentiments. They have a notion that when people are met together, a short silence doth much improve conversation : this I found to be true ; for during those little intermissions of talk, new ideas would arise in their minds, which very much enlivened their discourse. Their subjects are generally on friendship and benevolence, on order and economy ; sometimes upon the visible operations of nature, or ancient traditions ; upon the bounds and limits of virtue ; upon the unerring rules of reason ; or upon some determinations to be taken at the next great assembly ; and often upon the various excellences of poetry. I may add, without vanity, that my presence often gave them sufficient matter for discourse, because it afforded my master an occasion of letting his friends into the history of me and my country, upon which they were all pleased to descant, in a manner not very advantageous to humankind ; and for that reason I shall not repeat what they said : only I may be allowed to observe that his honor, to my great admiration, appeared to understand the nature of Yahoos in all countries much better than myself. He went through all our vices and follies, and discovered many which I had never mentioned to him, by only supposing what qualities a Yahoo of their country, with a small proportion of reason, might be capable of exerting; and concluded, with too much probability, how vile as well as miserable, such a creature must be.

I freely confess that all the little knowledge I have of any value was acquired by the lectures I received from my master, and from hearing the discourses of him and his friends; to which I should be prouder to listen than to dictate to the greatest and wisest assembly in Europe. I admired the strength, comeliness, and speed of the inhabitants; and such a constellation of virtues in such amiable persons produced in me the highest veneration. At first, indeed, I did not feel that natural awe which the Yahoos and all other animals bear toward them; but it grew upon me by degrees, much sooner than I imagined, and was mingled with a respectful love and gratitude, that they would condescend to distinguish me from the rest of my species.

When I thought of my family, my friends, and my countrymen, or the human race in general, I considered them, as they really were, Yahoos, in shape and disposition, only a little civilized, and qualified with the gift of speech; but making no other use of reason than to improve and multiply those vices whereof their brethren in this country had only the share that nature allotted them. When I happened to behold the reflection of my own form in a lake or a fountain I turned away my face in horror and detestation of myself, and could better endure the sight of a common Yahoo than of my own person.

By conversing with the Houyhnhnms, and looking upon them with delight, I fell to imitate their gait and gesture, which is now grown into a habit; and my friends often tell me in a blunt way that I trot like a horse; which, however, I take for a great compliment. Neither shall I disown that in speaking I am apt to fall into the voice and manner of the Houyhnhnms, and hear myself ridiculed on that account, without the least mortification.

In the midst of all this happiness, and when I looked upon myself to be fully settled for life, my master sent for me one morning a little earlier than his usual hour. I observed by his countenance that he was in some perplexity, and at a loss how to begin what he had to speak. After a short silence, he told me he did not know how I would take what he was going to say. That in the last general assembly, when the affair of the Yahoos was entered upon, the representatives had taken offense at his keeping a Yahoo (meaning myself) in his family, more like a Houyhnhnm than a brute animal; that he was known frequently to converse with me, as if he could receive some advantage or pleasure in my company; that such a practice was not agreeable to reason or nature, nor a thing ever heard of before among them. The assembly did therefore exhort him either to employ me like the rest of my species, or command me to swim back to the place from whence I came. That the first of these expedients was utterly rejected by all the Houyhnhnms who had ever seen me at his house or their own; for they alleged that because I had some rudiments of reason added to the natural pravity of those animals, it was to be feared I might be able to seduce them into the woody and mountainous parts of the country, and bring them in troops by night to destroy the Houyhnhnm's cattle as being naturally of the ravenous kind, and averse from labor.

My master added that he was daily pressed by the Houyhnhnms of the neigborhood to have the assembly's exhortation executed, which he could not put off much longer. He doubted it would be impossible for me to swim to another country, and therefore wished I would contrive some sort of vehicle, resembling those I had described to him, that might carry me on the sea, in which work I should have the assistance of his own servants, as well as those of his neighbors. He concluded that, for his own part, he could have been content to keep me in his service as long as I lived, because he found I had cured myself of some bad habits and dispositions, by endeavoring, as far as my inferior nature was capable, to imitate the Houyhnhnms.

I should here observe to the reader that a decree of the general assembly in this country is expressed by the word *hnhloayn*, which signifies an exhortation, as near as I can render it; for they have no conception how a rational creature can be compelled, but only advised or exhorted; because no person can disobey reason without giving up his claim to be a rational creature.

I was struck with the utmost grief and despair at my master's discourse; and being unable to support the agonies I was under, I fell into a swoon at his feet. When I came to myself he told me that he concluded I had been dead (for these people are subject to no such imbecilities of nature). I answered in a faint voice that death would have been too great a happiness; that although I could not blame the assembly's exhortation, or the urgency of his friends, yet, in my weak and corrupt judgment, I thought it might consist with reason to have been less rigorous; that I could not swim a league, and probably the nearest land to theirs might be distant above an hundred; that many materials necessary for making a small vessel to carry me off were wholly wanting in this country; which, however, I would attempt, in obedience and gratitude to his honor, although I concluded the thing to be impossible, and therefore looked on myself as already devoted to destruction; that the certain prospect of an unnatural death was the least of my evils; for supposing I should escape with life, by some strange adventure, how could I think with temper of passing my days among Yahoos, and relapsing into my old corruptions, for want of examples to lead and keep me within the paths of virtue? that I knew too well upon what solid reasons all the determinations of the wise Houyhnhnms were founded, not to be shaken by arguments of mine, a miserable Yahoo; and therefore, after presenting him with my humble thanks for the offer of his servants' assistance in making a vessel, and desiring a reasonable time for so difficult a work, I told him I would endeavor to preserve a wretched being; and if ever I returned to England was not without hopes of being useful to my own species by celebrating the praises of the renowned Houyhnhnms, and proposing their virtues to the imitation of mankind.

My master, in a few words, made me a very gracious reply; allowed me the space of two months to finish my boat; and ordered the sorrel nag, my fellow-servant (for so, at this distance, I may presume to call him), to follow my instructions; because I told my master that his help would be sufficient, and I knew he had a tenderness for me.

In his company my first business was to go to that part of the coast where my rebellious crew had ordered me to be set on shore. I got upon a height, and looking on every side into the sea, fancied I saw a small island toward the northeast. I took out my pocket-glass, and could then clearly distinguish it about five leagues off, as I computed; but it appeared to the sorrel nag to be only a blue cloud; for as he had no conception of any country beside his own, so he could not be as expert in distinguishing remote objects at sea as we who so much converse* in that element.

After I had discovered this island I considered no further, but resolved it should, if possible, be the first place of my banishment, leaving the consequence to fortune.

I returned home, and consulting with the sorrel nag, we went into a copse at some distance, where I

---

* Occupy ourselves; carry on business.

with my knife, and he with a sharp flint, fastened very artificially, after their manner, to a wooden handle, cut down several oak wattles, about the thickness of a walking-staff, and some larger pieces. But I shall not trouble the reader with a particular description of my own mechanics; let it suffice to say, that in six weeks' time, with the help of the sorrel nag, who performed the parts that required most labor, I finished a sort of Indian canoe, but much larger, covering it with the skins of Yahoos, well stitched together with hempen threads of my own making. My sail was likewise composed of the skins of the same animal; but I made use of the youngest I could get, the older being too tough and thick; and I likewise provided myself with four paddles. I laid in a stock of boiled flesh, of rabbits and fowls, and took with me two vessels, one filled with milk, and the other with water.

I tried my canoe in a large pond near my master's house, and then corrected in it what was amiss, stopping all the chinks with Yahoo's tallow, till I found it stanch, and able to bear me and my freight; and when it was as complete as I could possibly make it, I had it drawn on a carriage very gently by Yahoos to the seaside, under the conduct* of the sorrel nag and another servant.

---

* Guidance or leadership.

When all was ready, and the day came for my departure, I took leave of my master and lady, and the whole family, mine eyes flowing with tears, and my heart quite sunk with grief. But his honor, out of curiosity, and perhaps (if I may speak it without vanity) partly out of kindness, was determined to see me in my canoe, and got several of his neighboring friends to accompany him. I was forced to wait above an hour for the tide; and then observing the wind very fortunately bearing toward the island to which I intended to steer my course, I took a second leave of my master; but as I was going to prostrate myself to kiss his hoof, he did me the honor to raise it gently to my mouth. I am not ignorant how much I have been censured for mentioning this last particular. For my detractors are pleased to think it improbable that so illustrious a person should descend to give so great a mark of distinction to a creature so inferior as I. Neither have I forgot how apt some travelers are to boast of extraordinary favors they have received. But if these censurers were better acquainted with the noble and courteous disposition of the Houyhnhnms, they would soon change their opinion.

I paid my respects to the rest of the Houyhnhnms in his honor's company, then getting into my canoe I pushed off from shore.

CHAPTER XI.

The Author's dangerous Voyage—He arrives at New Holland, hoping to settle there—Is wounded with an arrow by one of the Natives—Is seized, and carried by force into a Portuguese ship—The great civilities of the Captain—The Author arrives in England.

I BEGAN this desperate voyage on February 15, 1714–15,* at nine o'clock in the morning. The wind was very favorable; however, I made use at first only of my paddles; but considering I should soon be weary, and that the wind might chop about, I ventured to set up my little sail, and thus, with the help of the tide, I went at the rate of a league and a half an hour, as near as I could guess. My master and his friends continued on the shore till I was almost out of sight; and I often heard the

---

* That is 1714 Old Style, 1715 New Style. Before the introduction of the new or reformed way of reckoning, the year began on the 25th of March; hence the portion from January 1 up to this date may be considered as belonging to the end of one year and the beginning of another—the latter being the proper year according to modern reckoning.

sorrel nag (who always loved me) crying out, *Hnuy illa nyha majah Yahoo;* Take care of thyself, gentle Yahoo.

My design was, if possible, to discover some small island uninhabited, yet sufficient, by my labor, to furnish me with the necessaries of life, which I would have thought a greater happiness than to be first minister in the politest court of Europe; so horrible was the idea I conceived of returning to live in the society, and under the government of Yahoos. For in such a solitude as I desired, I could at least enjoy my own thoughts, and reflect with delight on the virtues of those inimitable Houyhnhnms, without any opportunity of degenerating into the vices and corruptions of my own species.

The reader may remember what I related when my crew conspired against me, and confined me to my cabin; how I continued there several weeks, without knowing what course we took; and when I was put ashore in the long-boat, how the sailors told me, with oaths, whether true or false, that they knew not in what part of the world we were. However, I did then believe us to be about 10 degrees southward of the Cape of Good Hope, or about 45 degrees southern latitude, as I gathered from some general words I overheard among them, being, I supposed, to the southeast in their intended voyage to Madagascar. And although this were but little better than conjecture, yet I resolved to steer my course eastward, hoping to reach the southwest coast of New Holland, and perhaps some such island as I desired, lying westward of it. The wind was full west; and by six in the evening I computed I had gone eastward at least eighteen leagues, when I spied a very small island about half a league off, which I soon reached. It was nothing but a rock with one creek naturally arched by the force of tempests. Here I put in my canoe, and climbing a part of the rock, I could plainly discover land to the east, extending from south to north. I lay all night in my canoe, and repeating my voyage early in the morning, I arrived in seven hours to the southeast point of New Holland. This confirmed me in the opinion I have long entertained that the maps and charts place this country at least three degrees more to the east than it really is,* which thought I communicated many years ago to my worthy friend, Mr. Herman Moll,† and gave him my

---

* Gulliver here shows a greater knowledge of the position and dimensions of Australia than he displays in telling of the whereabouts of Lilliput, etc.

† This person published in 1723 a work entitled "Compleat Geographer, or the Chorography and Topography of al' the known parts of the Earth."

reasons for it, although he hath rather chosen to follow other authors.

I saw no inhabitants in the place where I landed,

"They discharged an arrow, which wounded me deeply on the knee."

and being unarmed I was afraid of venturing far into the country. I found some shellfish on the shore, and eat them raw, not daring to kindle a fire for fear of being discovered by the natives. I continued three days feeding on oysters and limpets to save my own provisions; and I fortunately found a brook of excellent water, which gave me great relief.

On the fourth day, venturing out early, a little too far, I saw twenty or thirty natives upon a height, not above five hundred yards from me. They were stark naked, men, women, and children, round a fire, as I could discover by the smoke. One of them spied me, and gave notice to the rest; five of them advanced toward me, leaving the women and children at the fire. I made what haste I could to the shore, and getting into my canoe, shoved off; the savages observing me retreat, ran after me, and before I could get far enough into the sea, discharged an arrow, which wounded me deeply on the inside of my left knee; I shall carry the mark to my grave. I apprehended the arrow might be poisoned; and paddling out of the reach of their darts (being a calm day), I made a shift to suck the wound, and dress it as well as I could.

I was at a loss what to do; for I durst not return to the same landing-place, but stood to the north, and was forced to paddle; for the wind, though very gentle, was against me, blowing northwest. As I was looking about for a secure landing-place, I saw a sail to the north-northeast, which appearing

every minute more visible, I was in some doubt
whether I should wait for them or no; but at last
my detestation of the Yahoo race prevailed, and,
turning my canoe, I sailed and paddled together to
the south, and got into the same creek from whence
I set out in the morning, choosing rather to trust
myself among these barbarians than live with
European Yahoos. I drew up my canoe as close as
I could to the shore, and hid myself behind a stone
by the little brook, which, as I have already said,
was excellent water.

The ship came within half a league of this creek,
and sent out her long-boat with vessels to take in
fresh water (for the place, it seems, was very well
known); but I did not observe it till the boat was
almost on shore, and it was too late to seek another
hiding-place. The seamen, at their landing, observed my canoe, and, rummaging it all over, easily
conjectured that the owner could not be far off.
Four of them, well armed, searched every cranny
and lurking-hole, till at last they found me, flat on
my face, behind the stone. They gazed awhile in
admiration* at my strange, uncouth dress: my coat
made of skins, my wooden-soled shoes, and my furred
stockings; from whence, however, they concluded I

---

* Wonder.

was not a native of the place, who all go naked.
One of the seamen, in Portuguese, bid me rise, and
asked who I was. I understood that language very
well, and, getting upon my feet, said I was a poor
Yahoo, banished from the Houyhnhnms, and desired they would please to let me depart. They
admired* to hear me answer them in their own
tongue and saw by my complexion I must be an
European; but were at a loss to know what I meant
by Yahoos and Houyhnhnms; and at the same time
fell a-laughing at my strange tone in speaking,
which resembled the neighing of a horse. I
trembled all the while betwixt fear and hatred. I
again desired leave to depart, and was gently
moving to my canoe; but they laid hold of me, desiring to know what country I was of? whence I
came? with many other questions. I told them I
was born in England, from whence I came about
five years ago, and then their country and ours were
at peace. I therefore hoped they would not treat
me as an enemy, since I meant them no harm, but
was a poor Yahoo, seeking some desolate place
where to pass the remainder of his unfortunate life.

When they began to talk I thought I never heard
or saw anything so unnatural; for it appeared to

---

* Wondered.

me as monstrous as if a dog or a cow should speak
in England, or a Yahoo in Houyhnhnm-land. The
honest Portuguese were equally amazed at my
strange dress, and the odd manner of delivering my
words, which, however, they understood very well.
They spoke to me with great humanity, and said
they were sure their captain would carry me *gratis*
to Lisbon, from whence I might return to my own
country; that two of the seamen would go back to
the ship, inform the captain of what they had seen,
and receive his orders: in the meantime, unless I
would give my solemn oath not to fly, they would
secure me by force. I thought it best to comply
with their proposal. They were very curious to
know my story, but I gave them very little satisfaction, and they all conjectured that my misfortunes
had impaired my reason. In two hours the boat,
which went laden with vessels of water, returned
with the captain's command to fetch me on board.
I fell on my knees to preserve my liberty, but all
was in vain; and the men, having tied me with
cords, heaved me into the boat, from whence I was
taken into the ship, and from thence into the captain's cabin.

His name was Pedro de Mendez; he was a very
courteous and generous person. He entreated me
to give some account of myself, and desired to know

what I would eat or drink; said I should be used as well as himself; and spoke so many obliging things that I wondered to find such civilities from a Yahoo. However, I remained silent and sullen; I was ready to faint at the very smell of him and his men. At last I desired something to eat out of my own canoe; but he ordered me a chicken, and some excellent wine, and then directed that I should be put to bed in a very clean cabin. I would not undress myself, but lay on the bedclothes, and in half an hour stole out, when I thought the crew was at dinner, and, getting to the side of the ship, was going to leap into the sea, and swim for my life rather than continue among Yahoos. But one of the seamen prevented me, and, having informed the captain, I was chained to my cabin.

After dinner Don Pedro came to me, and desired to know my reason for so desperate an attempt; assured me he only meant to do me all the service he was able; and spoke so very movingly that at last I descended to treat him like an animal that had some little portion of reason. I gave him a very short relation of my voyage; of the conspiracy against me by my own men; of the country where they set me on shore, and of my five years' residence there. All which he looked upon as if it were a dream or a vision; whereat I took great offense:

for I had quite forgot the faculty of lying, so peculiar to Yahoos in all countries where they preside, and consequently the disposition of suspecting truth in others of their own species. I asked him whether it were the custom in his country to say the thing that was not? I assured him that I had almost forgot what he meant by falsehood, and if I had lived a thousand years in Houyhnhnm-land I should never have heard a lie from the meanest servant; that I was altogether indifferent whether he believed me or no; but, however, in return for his favors, I would give so much allowance to the corruption of his nature as to answer any objection he would please to make, and then he might easily discover the truth.

The captain, a wise man, after many endeavors to catch me tripping in some part of my story, at last began to have a better opinion of my veracity. But he added, that since I professed so inviolable an attachment to truth, I must give him my word of honor to bear him company in this voyage, without attempting anything against my life; or else he would continue me a prisoner till we arrived at Lisbon. I gave him the promise he required; but at the same time protested that I would suffer the greatest hardships rather than return to live among Yahoos.

Our voyage passed without any considerable accident. In gratitude to the captain, I sometimes sat with him at his earnest request, and strove to conceal my antipathy to humankind, although it often broke out ; which he suffered to pass without observation. But the greatest part of the day I confined myself to my cabin, to avoid seeing any of the crew. The captain had often entreated me to strip myself of my savage dress, and offered to lend me the best suit of clothes he had. This I would not be prevailed on to accept, abhorring to cover myself with anything that had been on the back of a Yahoo. I only desired he would lend me two clean shirts, which, having been washed since he wore them, I believed would not so much defile me. These I changed every second day, and washed them myself.

We arrived at Lisbon, November 5, 1715. At our landing the captain forced me to cover myself with his cloak, to prevent the rabble from crowding about me. I was conveyed to his own house; and at my earnest request he led me up to the highest room backward. I conjured him to conceal from all persons what I had told him of the Houyhnhnms ; because the least hint of such a story would not only draw numbers of people to see me, but probably put me in danger of being imprisoned, or burned by the Inquisition. The captain persuaded me to accept a suit of clothes newly made; but I would not suffer the tailor to take my measure: however, Don Pedro being almost of my size, they fitted me well enough. He accoutered me with other necessaries, all new, which I aired for twenty-four hours, before I would use them.

The captain had no wife, nor above three servants, none of which were suffered to attend at meals ; and his whole deportment was so obliging, added to a very good human understanding, that I really began to tolerate his company. He gained so far upon me that I ventured to look out of the back window. By degrees I was brought into another room, from whence I peeped into the street, but drew my head back in a fright. In a week's time he seduced me down to the door. I found my terror gradually lessened, but my hatred and contempt seemed to increase. I was at last bold enough to· walk the street in his company, but kept my nose well stopped with rue, or sometimes with tobacco.

In ten days Don Pedro, to whom I had given some account of my domestic affairs, put it upon me, as a matter of honor and conscience, that I ought to return to my native country, and live at home with my wife and children. He told me there was an English ship in the port just ready to sail, and he would furnish me with all things necessary. It would be tedious to repeat his arguments, and my contradictions. He said it was altogether impossible to find such a solitary island as I had desired to live in; but I might command in my own house, and pass my time in a manner as recluse as I pleased.

I complied at last, finding I could not do better. I left Lisbon the 24th day of November, in an English merchantman, but who was the master I never inquired. Don Pedro accompanied me to the ship, and lent me twenty pounds. He took kind leave of me, and embraced me at parting, which I bore as well as I could. During this last voyage I had no commerce* with the master or any of his men; but, pretending I was sick, kept close in my cabin. On the 5th of December, 1715, we cast anchor in the Downs about nine in the morning, and at three in the afternoon I got safe to my house at Redriff.

My wife and family received me with great surprise and joy, because they concluded me certainly dead; but I must freely confess the sight of them filled me only with hatred, disgust, and contempt; and the more, by reflecting on the near alliance I had to them. For although, since my

---

*Intercourse; conversation.

unfortunate exile from the Houyhnhnm country, I had compelled myself to tolerate the sight of Yahoos, and to converse with Don Pedro de Mendez, yet my memory and imagination were perpetually filled with the virtues and ideas of those exalted Houyhnhnms.

As soon as I entered the house my wife took me in her arms and kissed me; at which, having not been used to the touch of that odious animal for so many years, I fell into a swoon for almost an hour. At the time I am writing, it is five years since my last return to England; during the first year I could not endure my wife or children in my presence; the very smell of them was intolerable; much less could I suffer them to eat in the same room. To this hour they dare not presume to touch my bread, or drink out of the same cup; neither was I ever able to let one of them take me by the hand. The first money I laid out was to buy two young horses, which I kept in a good stable; and, next to them, the groom is my greatest favorite; for I feel my spirits revived by the smell he contracts in the stable. My horses understand me tolerably well; I converse with them at least four hours every day. They are strangers to bridle or saddle; they live in great amity with me, and friendship to each other.

CHAPTER XII.

The Author's Veracity—His design in publishing this Work—
His Censure of those Travelers who swerve from the
Truth—The Author clears himself from any sinister ends
in writing—An objection aswered—The method of planting Colonies—His native Country commended—The right
of the Crown to those Countries described by the Author
is justified—The Difficulty of conquering them—The
Author takes his last leave of the Reader—Proposeth his
Manner of Living for the future—Gives good Advice, and
concludes.

Thus, gentle reader, I have given thee a faithful
history of my travels for sixteen years and above
seven months; wherein I have not been so studious
of ornament as of truth. I could, perhaps, like
others, have astonished thee with strange, improbable tales; but I rather chose to relate plain matter
of fact in the simplest manner and style; because
my principal design was to inform, and not to
amuse thee.

It is easy for us who travel into remote countries,

which are seldom visited by Englishmen or other Europeans, to form descriptions of wonderful animals both at sea and land. Whereas a traveler's chief aim should be to make men wiser and better, and to improve their minds by the bad, as well as good example, of what they deliver concerning foreign places.

I could heartily wish a law was enacted that every traveler, before he were permitted to publish his voyages, should be obliged to make oath before the Lord High Chancellor, that all he intended to print was absolutely true to the best of his knowledge; for then the world would no longer be deceived, as it usually is, while some writers, to make their works pass the better upon the public, impose the grossest falsities on the unwary reader. I have perused several books of travels with great delight in my younger days; but having since gone over most parts of the globe, and been able to contradict many fabulous accounts from my own observation, it hath given me a great disgust against this part of reading, and some indignation to see the credulity of mankind so impudently abused. Therefore, since my acquaintance were pleased to think my poor endeavors might not be unacceptable to my country, I imposed on myself, as a maxim never to be swerved from, that I would strictly adhere to truth; neither indeed can I be ever under the least temptation to vary from it, while I retain in my mind the lectures and example of my noble master and the other illustrious Houyhnhnms, of whom I had so long the honor to be an humble hearer.

I know very well how little reputation is to be got by writings, which require neither genius nor learning, nor indeed any other talent, except a good memory, or an exact journal. I know likewise that writers of travels, like dictionary makers, are sunk into oblivion by the weight and bulk of those who come last, and therefore lie uppermost. And it is highly probable that such travelers, who shall hereafter visit the countries described in this work of mine, may, by detecting my errors (if there be any), and adding many new discoveries of their own, jostle me out of vogue, and stand in my place, making the world forget that ever I was an author. This indeed would be too great a mortification if I wrote for fame; but as my sole intention was the public good, I cannot be altogether disappointed. For who can read of the virtues I have mentioned in the glorious Houyhnhnms, without being ashamed of his own vices, when he considers himself as the reasoning, governing animal of his country? I shall say nothing of those remote nations where Yahoos preside; among which the least corrupted are the

Brobdingnagians, whose wise maxims in morality and government it would be our happiness to observe. But I forbear descanting further, and rather leave the judicious reader to his own remarks and applications.

I am not a little pleased that this work of mine can possibly meet with no censurers; for what objections can be made against a writer who relates only plain facts that happened in such distant countries, where we have not the least interest with respect either to trade or negotiations? I have carefully avoided every fault with which common writers of travels are often too justly charged. Besides, I meddle not with any party, but write without passion, prejudice, or ill-will against any man, or number of men, whatsoever. I write for the noblest end, to inform and instruct mankind; over whom I may, without breach of modesty, pretend to some superiority, from the advantages I received by conversing so long among the most accomplished Houyhnhnms. I write without any view toward profit or praise. I never suffer a word to pass that may look like reflection, or possibly give the least offense, even to those who are most ready to take it. So that I hope I may with justice pronounce myself an author perfectly blameless; against whom the tribes of Answerers, Considerers,

Observers, Reflectors, Detectors, Remarkers,* will never be able to find matter for exercising their talents.

I confess it was whispered to me that I was bound in duty, as a subject of England, to have given in a memorial to a secretary of state at my first coming over; because whatever lands are discovered by a subject belong to the crown. But I doubt whether our conquests in the countries I treat of would be as easy as those of Ferdinando Cortez over the naked Americans. The Lilliputians, I think, are hardly worth the charge of a fleet and army to reduce them; and I question whether it might be prudent or safe to attempt the Brobdingnagians; or whether an English army would be much at their ease with the Flying Island over their heads. The Houyhnhnms indeed appear not to be so well prepared for war, a science to which they are perfect strangers, and especially against missive weapons. However, supposing myself to be a minister of state, I could never give my advice for invading them. Their prudence, unanimity, unacquaintedness with fear, and their love of their

---

* Alluding to writers who bring out books or pamphlets dealing with other books, and giving their productions such titles as Answers to, Considerations on, Observations on, etc., such or such a work.

country, would amply supply all defects in the military art. Imagine twenty thousand of them breaking into the midst of an European army, confounding the ranks, overturning the carriages, battering the warriors' faces into mummy by terrible yerks from their hinder hoofs; for they would well deserve the character given to Augustus, *Recalcitrat undique tutus.** But, instead of proposals for conquering that magnanimous nation, I rather wish they were in a capacity, or disposition, to send a sufficient number of their inhabitants for civilizing Europe, by teaching us the first principles of honor, justice, truth, temperance, public spirit, fortitude, chastity, friendship, benevolence, and fidelity, the names of all which virtues are still retained among us in most languages, and are to be met with in some modern as well as ancient authors; which I am able to assert from my own small reading.

But I had another reason, which made me less forward to enlarge his majesty's dominions by my discoveries. To say the truth I had conceived a few scruples with relation to the distributive justice of princes upon those occasions. For instance a crew of pirates are driven by a storm they know not whither; at length a boy discovers land from the

---

* He kicks out behind, safe on every side.

topmast; they go on shore to rob and plunder; they see a harmless people; are entertained with kindness; they give the country a new name; they take formal possession of it for their king; they set up a rotten plank, or a stone, for a memorial; they murder two or three dozen of the natives, bring away a couple more by force, for a sample; return home and get their pardon. Here commences a new dominion acquired with a title by divine right. Ships are sent with the first opportunity; the natives driven out or destroyed; their princes tortured to discover their gold; a free license given to all acts of inhumanity and lust, the earth reeking with the blood of its inhabitants; and this execrable crew of butchers, employed in so pious an expedition, is a modern colony, sent to convert and civilize an idolatrous and barbarous people !*

But this description, I confess, doth by no means affect the British nation, who may be an example to the whole world for their wisdom, care, and justice in planting colonies; their liberal endowments for the advancement of religion and learning; their choice of devout and able pastors to propagate Christianity; their caution in stocking their prov-

---

* This, unfortunately, is too true a picture of the manner in which some European colonies have been founded, as, for instance, those of the Spanish in America.

inces with people of sober lives and conversations, from this the mother kingdom; their strict regard to the distribution of justice, in supplying the civil administration through all their colonies with officers of the greatest abilities, utter strangers to corruption; and, to crown all, by sending the most vigilant and virtuous governors, who have no other views than the happiness of the people over whom they preside, and the honor of the king their master.*

But as those countries, which I have described, do not appear to have a desire of being conquered and enslaved, murdered or driven out by colonies; nor abound either in gold, silver, sugar, or tobacco, I did humbly conceive they were by no means proper objects of our zeal, our valor, or our interest. However, if those whom it more concerns think fit to be of another opinion, I am ready to depose, when I shall be lawfully called, that no European did ever visit those countries before me. I mean, if the inhabitants ought to be believed, unless a dispute may arise concerning the two Yahoos, said to have been seen many ages ago upon a mountain in Houyhnhnm-land.

But, as to the formality of taking possession in

---

* These statements are, of course, ironical on Swift's part.

my sovereign's name, it never came once into my thoughts; and if it had, yet, as my affairs then stood, I should perhaps, in point of prudence and self-preservation, have put it off to a better opportunity.

Having thus answered the only objection that can ever be raised against me as a traveler, I here take a final leave of all my courteous readers, and return to enjoy my own speculations in my little garden at Redriff; to apply those excellent lessons of virtue which I learned among the Houyhnhnms; to instruct the Yahoos of my own family, as far as I shall find them docible animals; to behold my figure often in a glass, and thus, if possible, habituate myself by time to tolerate the sight of a human creature; to lament the brutality of Houyhnhnms in my own country, but always treat their persons with respect, for the sake of my noble master, his family, his friends, and the whole Houyhnhnm race, whom these of ours have the honor to resemble in all their lineaments, however their intellectuals came to degenerate.

I began last week to permit my wife to sit at dinner with me, at the furthest end of a long table; and to answer (but with the utmost brevity) the few questions I asked her. Yet the smell of a Yahoo continuing very offensive, I always keep my nose well stopped with rue, lavender, or tobacco leaves. And although it be hard for a man late in life to remove old habits, I am not altogether out of hopes, in some time, to suffer a neighbor Yahoo in my company without the apprehensions I am yet under of his teeth or his claws.

My reconcilement to the Yahoo kind in general might not be so difficult if they would be content with those vices and follies only which nature hath entitled them to. I am not in the least provoked at the sight of a lawyer, a pickpocket, a colonel, a fool, a lord, a gamester, a politician, a physician, an evidence,* a suborner, an attorney, a traitor, or the like; this is all according to the due course of things; but when I behold a lump of deformity and diseases, both in body and mind, smitten with pride, it immediately breaks all the measures of my patience; neither shall I be ever able to comprehend how such an animal and such a vice could tally together. The wise and virtuous Houyhnhnms, who abound in all excellences that can adorn a rational creature, have no name for this vice in their language; which hath no terms to express anything that is evil, except those whereby they describe the detestable qualities of their

---

* One who brings false accusations.

Yahoos; among which they were not able to distinguish this of pride, for want of thoroughly understanding human nature, as it showeth itself in other countries where that animal presides. But I, who had more experience, could plainly observe some rudiments of it among the wild Yahoos.

But the Houyhnhnms, who live under the government of reason, are no more proud of the good qualities they possess than I should be for not wanting a leg or an arm; which no man in his wits would boast of, although he must be miserable without them. I dwell the longer upon this subject from the desire I have to make the society of an English Yahoo by any means not insupportable; and therefore I here entreat those who have any tincture of this absurd vice that they will not presume to come in my sight.

THE END.

A. L. Burt's Catalogue of Books for Young People by Popular Writers, 52-58 Duane Street, New York ❧ ❧ ❧

BOOKS FOR BOYS.

Joe's Luck: A Boy's Adventures in California. By

HORATIO ALGER, JR. 12mo, cloth, illustrated, price $1.00.

The story is chock full of stirring incidents, while the amusing situations are furnished by Joshua Bickford, from Pumpkin Hollow, and the fellow who modestly styles himself the "Rip-tail Roarer, from Pike Co., Missouri." Mr. Alger never writes a poor book, and "Joe's Luck" is certainly one of his best.

Tom the Bootblack; or, The Road to Success. By

HORATIO ALGER, JR. 12mo, cloth, illustrated, price $1.00.

A bright, enterprising lad was Tom the Bootblack. He was not at all ashamed of his humble calling, though always on the lookout to better himself. The lad started for Cincinnati to look up his heritage. Mr. Grey, the uncle, did not hesitate to employ a ruffian to kill the lad. The plan failed, and Gilbert Grey, once Tom the bootblack, came into a comfortable fortune. This is one of Mr. Alger's best stories.

Dan the Newsboy. By HORATIO ALGER, JR. 12mo,

cloth, illustrated, price $1.00.

Dan Mordaunt and his mother live in a poor tenement, and the lad is pluckily trying to make ends meet by selling papers in the streets of New York. A little heiress of six years is confided to the care of the Mordaunts. The child is kidnapped and Dan tracks the child to the house where she is hidden, and rescues her. The wealthy aunt of the little heiress is so delighted with Dan's courage and many good qualities that she adopts him as her heir.

Tony the Hero: A Brave Boy's Adventure with a

Tramp. By HORATIO ALGER, JR. 12mo, cloth, illustrated, price $1.00.

Tony, a sturdy bright-eyed boy of fourteen, is under the control of Rudolph Rugg, a thorough rascal. After much abuse Tony runs away and gets a job as stable boy in a country hotel. Tony is heir to a large estate. Rudolph for a consideration hunts up Tony and throws him down a deep well. Of course Tony escapes from the fate provided for him, and by a brave act, a rich friend secures his rights and Tony is prosperous. A very entertaining book.

The Errand Boy; or, How Phil Brent Won Success.

By HORATIO ALGER, JR. 12mo, cloth illustrated, price $1.00.

The career of "The Errand Boy" embraces the city adventures of a smart country lad. Philip was brought up by a kind-hearted innkeeper named Brent. The death of Mrs. Brent paved the way for the hero's subsequent troubles. A retired merchant in New York secures him the situation of errand boy, and thereafter stands as his friend.

Tom Temple's Career. By HORATIO ALGER, JR. 12mo,

cloth, illustrated, price $1.00.

Tom Temple is a bright, self-reliant lad. He leaves Plympton village to seek work in New York, whence he undertakes an important mission to California. Some of his adventures in the far west are so startling that the reader will scarcely close the book until the last page shall have been reached. The tale is written in Mr. Alger's most fascinating style.

For sale by all booksellers, or sent postpaid on receipt of price by the publisher, A. L. BURT, 52-58 Duane Street, New York.

BOOKS FOR BOYS.

Frank Fowler, the Cash Boy. By HORATIO ALGER, JR.

12mo, cloth, illustrated, price $1.00.

Frank Fowler, a poor boy, bravely determines to make a living for himself and his foster-sister Grace. Going to New York he obtains a situation as cash boy in a dry goods store. He renders a service to a wealthy old gentleman who takes a fancy to the lad, and thereafter helps the lad to gain success and fortune.

Tom Thatcher's Fortune. By HORATIO ALGER, JR.

12mo, cloth, illustrated, price $1.00.

Tom Thatcher is a brave, ambitious, unselfish boy. He supports his mother and sister on meagre wages earned as a shoe-pegger in John Simpson's factory. Tom is discharged from the factory and starts overland for California. He meets with many adventures. The story is told in a way which has made Mr. Alger's name a household word in so many homes.

The Train Boy. By HORATIO ALGER, JR. 12mo,

cloth, illustrated, price $1.00.

Paul Palmer was a wide-awake boy of sixteen who supported his mother and sister by selling books and papers on the Chicago and Milwaukee Railroad. He detects a young man in the act of picking the pocket of a young lady. In a railway accident many passengers are killed, but Paul is fortunate enough to assist a Chicago merchant, who out of gratitude takes him into his employ. Paul succeeds with tact and judgment and is well started on the road to business prominence.

Mark Mason's Victory. The Trials and Triumphs of

a Telegraph Boy. By HORATIO ALGER, JR. 12mo, cloth, illustrated, price $1.00.

Mark Mason, the telegraph boy, was a sturdy, honest lad, who pluckily won his way to success by his honest manly efforts under many difficulties. This story will please the very large class of boys who regard Mr. Alger as a favorite author.

A Debt of Honor. The Story of Gerald Lane's Success

in the Far West. By HORATIO ALGER, JR. 12mo, cloth, illustrated, price $1.00.

The story of Gerald Lane and the account of the many trials and disappointments which he passed through befoi he attained success, will interest all boys who have read the previous stories of this delightful author.

Ben Bruce. Scenes in the Life of a Bowery Newsboy.

By HORATIO ALGER, JR. 12mo, cloth, illustrated, price $1.00.

Ben Bruce was a brave, manly, generous boy. The story of his efforts, and many seeming failures and disappointments, and his final success, are most interesting to all readers. The tale is written in Mr. Alger's most fascinating style.

The Castaways; or, On the Florida Reefs. By JAMES

OTIS. 12mo, cloth, illustrated, price $1.00.

This tale smacks of the salt sea. From the moment that the Sea Queen leaves lower New York bay till the breeze leaves her becalmed off the coast of Florida, one can almost hear the whistle of the wind through her rigging, the creak of her straining cordage as she heels to the leeward. The adventures of Ben Clark, the hero of the story and Jake the cook, cannot fail to charm the reader. As a writer for young people Mr. Otis is a prime favorite.

For sale by all booksellers, or sent postpaid on receipt of price by the publisher, A. L. BURT, 52-58 Duane Street, New York.

BOOKS FOR BOYS.

Wrecked on Spider Island; or, How Ned Rogers Found

the Treasure. By JAMES OTIS. 12mo, cloth, illustrated, price $1.00.

Ned Rogers, a "down-east" plucky lad ships as cabin boy to earn a livelihood. Ned is marooned on Spider Island, and while there discovers a wreck submerged in the sand, and finds a considerable amount of treasure. The capture of the treasure and the incidents of the voyage serve to make as entertaining a story of sea-life as the most captious boy could desire.

The Search for the Silver City: A Tale of Adventure in

Yucatan. By JAMES OTIS. 12mo, cloth, illustrated, price $1.00.

Two lads, Teddy Wright and Neal Emery, embark on the steam yacht Day Dream for a cruise to the tropics. The yacht is destroyed by fire, and then the boat is cast upon the coast of Yucatan. They hear of the wonderful Silver City, of the Chan Santa Cruz Indians, and with the help of a faithful Indian ally carry off a number of the golden images from the temples. Pursued with relentless vigor at last their escape is effected in an astonishing manner. The story is so full of exciting incidents that the reader is quite carried away with the novelty and realism of the narrative.

A Runaway Brig; or, An Accidental Cruise. By

JAMES OTIS. 12mo, cloth, illustrated, price $1.00.

This is a sea tale, and the reader can look out upon the wide shimmering sea as it flashes back the sunlight, and imagine himself afloat with Harry Vandyne, Walter Morse, Jim Libby and that old shell-back, Bob Brace, on the brig Bonita. The boys discover a mysterious document which enables them to find a buried treasure. They are stranded on an island and at last are rescued with the treasure. The boys are sure to be fascinated with this entertaining story.

The Treasure Finders: A Boy's Adventures in

Nicaragua. By JAMES OTIS. 12mo, cloth, illustrated, price $1.00.

Roy and Dean Coloney, with their guide Tongla, leave their father's indigo plantation to visit the wonderful ruins of an ancient city. The boys eagerly explore the temples of an extinct race and discover three golden images cunningly hidden away. They escape with the greatest difficulty. Eventually they reach safety with their golden prizes. We doubt if there ever was written a more entertaining story than "The Treasure Finders."

Jack, the Hunchback. A Story of the Coast of Maine.

By JAMES OTIS. Price $1.00.

This is the story of a little hunchback who lived on Cape Elizabeth, on the coast of Maine. His trials and successes are most interesting. From first to last nothing stays the interest of the narrative. It bears us along as on a stream whose current varies in direction, but never loses its force.

With Washington at Monmouth: A Story of Three

Philadelphia Boys. By JAMES OTIS. 12mo, ornamental cloth, olivine edges, illustrated, price $1.50.

Three Philadelphia lads assist the American spies and make regular and frequent visits to Valley Forge in the Winter while the British occupied the city. The story abounds with pictures of Colonial life skillfully drawn, and the glimpses of Washington's soldiers which are given shown that the work has not been hastily done, or without considerable study. The story is wholesome and patriotic in tone, as are all of Mr. Otis' works.

BOOKS FOR BOYS.

With Lafayette at Yorktown: A Story of How Two

Boys Joined the Continental Army. By JAMES OTIS. 12mo, ornamental
cloth, olivine edges, illustrated, price $1.50.

Two lads from Portmouth, N. H., attempt to enlist in the Colonial
Army, and are given employment as spies. There is no lack of exciting
incidents which the youthful reader craves, but it is healthful excite-
ment brimming with facts which every boy should be familiar with,
and while the reader is following the adventures of Ben Jaffrays and
Ned Allen he is acquiring a fund of historical lore which will remain
in his memory long after that which he has memorized from text-
books has been forgotten.

At the Siege of Havana. Being the Experiences of

Three Boys Serving under Israel Putnam in 1762. By JAMES OTIS. 12mo,
ornamental cloth, olivine edges, illustrated, price $1.50.

"At the Siege of Havana" deals with that portion of the island's
history when the English king captured the capital, thanks to the
assistance given by the troops from New England, led in part by Col.
Israel Putnam.

The principal characters are Darius Lunt, the lad who, represented as
telling the story, and his comrades, Robert Clement and Nicholas
Vallet. Colonel Putnam also figures to considerable extent, necessarily,
in the tale, and the whole forms one of the most readable stories founded on
historical facts.

The Defense of Fort Henry. A Story of Wheeling

Creek in 1777. By JAMES OTIS. 12mo, ornamental cloth, olivine edges,
illustrated, price $1.50.

Nowhere in the history of our country can be found more heroic or
thrilling incidents than in the story of those brave men and women
who founded the settlement of Wheeling in the Colony of Virginia. The
recital of what Elizabeth Zane did is in itself as heroic a story as can
be imagined. The wondrous bravery displayed by Major McCulloch
and his gallant comrades, the sufferings of the colonists and their sacrifice
of blood and life, stir the blood of old as well as young readers.

The Capture of the Laughing Mary. A Story of Three

New York Boys in 1776. By JAMES OTIS. 12mo, ornamental cloth, olivine
edges, price $1.50.

"During the British occupancy of New York, at the outbreak of the
Revolution, a Yankee lad hears of the plot to take General Washington's
person, and calls in two companions to assist the patriot cause. They
do some astonishing things, and, incidentally, lay the way for an
American navy later, by the exploit which gives its name to the
work. Mr. Otis' books are too well known to require any particular
commendation to the young."—Evening Post.

With Warren at Bunker Hill. A Story of the Siege of

Boston. By JAMES OTIS. 12mo, ornametnal cloth, olivine edges, illus
trated, price $1.50.

"This is a tale of the siege of Boston, which opens on the day after
the doings at Lexington and Concord, with a description of home life
in Boston, introduces the reader to the British camp at Charlestown,
shows Gen. Warren at home, describes what a boy thought of the
battle of Bunker Hill, and closes with the raising of the siege. The
three heroes, George Wentworth, Ben Scarlett and an old ropemaker,
incur the enmity of a young Tory, who causes them many adventures
the boys will like to read."—Detroit Free Press.

For sale by all booksellers, or sent postpaid on receipt of price by the
publisher, A. L. BURT, 52-58 Duane Street, New York.